THE VEIL RIDERS

A Tale By Guardbro

Columbus, Ohio

This book is a work of fiction. The names, characters and events in this book are the products of the author's imagination or are used fictitiously. Any similarity to real persons living or dead is coincidental and not intended by the author.

The views and opinions expressed in this book are solely those of the author and do not reflect the views or opinions of Gatekeeper Press. Gatekeeper Press is not to be held responsible for and expressly disclaims responsibility of the content herein.

The Veil Riders: A Tale By Guardbro

Published by Gatekeeper Press
2167 Stringtown Rd, Suite 109
Columbus, OH 43123-2989
www.GatekeeperPress.com

Copyright © 2021 by Guardbro

All rights reserved. Neither this book, nor any parts within it may be sold or reproduced in any form or by any electronic or mechanical means, including information storage and retrieval systems, without permission in writing from the author. The only exception is by a reviewer, who may quote short excerpts in a review.

The cover design and editorial work for this book are entirely the product of the author. Gatekeeper Press did not participate in and is not responsible for any aspect of these elements.

ISBN (paperback): 9781662911163
eISBN: 9781662911170

To my wife Jamie, thank you for
Supporting me and being by my side through all these days.

To my Mother and Father, good job, but
It's a miracle I survived this long.

To my Grandfather Ron, thank you for
Fostering my love of reading.

To James and Megan,
You are the ones who got me here.

And to my many Fans and Readers,
Let's climb to glory.

Catch me online on youtube/guardbeardia_beardio

CONTENTS

Chapter 1	1
Chapter 2	11
Chapter 3	25
Chapter 4	35
Chapter 5	47
Chapter 6	57
Chapter 7	67
Chapter 8	75
Chapter 9	89
Chapter 10	109
Chapter 11	121
Chapter 12	143
Chapter 13	163
Chapter 14	181
Chapter 15	193
Chapter 16	205
Chapter 17	235
Chapter 18	263
Chapter 19	285
After Action Report	301

CHAPTER 1

"Auf die Heide blüht ein an kleines blu-umele-"
"Shut the hell up, Dregs."
The raucous rattle of laughter echoed up and down the cave tunnel as the formation of militia members marched through. The sound of their voices bounced off the walls and wrapped around the cavern as if the mountain itself was laughing with them. At the head of the formation was Tom Yule, a large man at six-foot even and heavy-haired, a braided beard running down his chin with shaggy, curly hair falling outside of his field green patrol cap. The man he was speaking to was Dakota Dregs, a wiry man that grinned at Yule cheekily. Dregs was from New York, Yule from Oklahoma, and almost all the States of America were represented as the seventy five men and women walked into the darkness, their flash lights casting shadows on the damp, rocky walls.

The hills of the Appalachian Mountains were always steeped in rumor and mysticism; folk tales and hearsay often speaking of people going missing, miners that mined so deep they were never seen again, weird shadows that stalked the depths of the forests, and noises unknown to human ears calling out from within. Children spoke of whispers amongst the bushes, and glittering lights deep in the woods that tried to lure those out, within. It was rare that a child was actually dumb enough to chase the sparkles in to the dark green boughs of the trees, until one was.

Little Emellie McCaline was the one child to throw the modern world into chaos and bridge the gap between fantasy and reality, dragging the whole of humanity in with her to the realm in between. With her small, size five shoes she would leave an imprint on the lives of millions. It started out with a simple missing persons report from her Mother, as little Emellie failed to show up for dinner at the time they agreed on. The trail was quickly tracked by a pair of search dogs (Rosko and Rosie, both very good canines who deserve many treats for their hard work), leading their handlers up to a wide-mouthed cave. The history of the cave was brief, and much of the writings from past miners, inspectors, and the odd spelunker all came to the same conclusion: "Do. Not. Enter."

A pair of rescue personnel were hooked to drag lines and slowly entered the cave, their head lamps fighting to illuminate the fathomless darkness before them. They called out for little Emellie as they walked along the winding pathway that had been carved out from the rock by miners decades before. After getting half way in, they noticed that the path changed, going from roughly hewed rock to smooth walls, as if carved away by impossibly hot beams of energy, or large circular blades that cut deep and straight, forming out this artery in the mountain. When reporting this information, a quick search showed no evidence of such devices ever being used in the in the shaft's history. This irregularity was a part of the cave's legacy, and also a part of its warning. After the rescuers had spent an hour in the depths of the cave, the surface crew witnessed the drag lines suddenly tighten around their spools, only to go slack in a single inhale of breath. The team truly began to panic after they wound back the drag lines, working the mechanisms as fast as their fear fueled muscles could manage. They found the lines severed in a way so clean and devoid of shredding, that it was as if a giant scissor had come down and chopped the line clean in half.

The rescuer's radios remained silent as those outside called out for those in the tunnel to respond to their calls. The only thing that answered back was the static on the other end and the whispering hollows that called out from the inner walls of the cave mouth.

A few of the team ran into the cave, going in as far as they dared, and stopped right where the footprints of those before terminated. Their hair stood on end, rippling up and down their bodies as they stared into the impossible black, a darkness so deep and intense that not even their LED flash lights could pierce the murk that ran along the walls. By the time they emerged from the cave opening, they were drenched in sweat and covered in small wounds from colliding with the walls during their rapid escape. No matter who they sent in during the following days, whether it was human, animal, or robot, nothing ever came back from the 'The Veil' as some began to call it. The disappearance of the rescue crew, the missing child, and the mysticism about the cave caused many in the scientific and cryptozoology communities to take an interest. After just a few days of studying and running tests, the findings spurred on even more communities to compile their own experiments on The Veil. Eventually, a breakthrough was made when a pair of college scientists were able to somehow receive and understand a signal from the Veil itself. The signal was the very essence of chaos, as the budding scientists found it to collide and scatter across every spectrum of sound and light known to mankind. To capture and make sense of the tangled signals, they began to attack it with every piece of equipment they could manage to get their hands on. In their words, they 'threw as much shit at the walls as they could', and the things that stuck were worked into their system of translating whatever it was that was coming through. After many late nights staring at glowing screens and rubbing tired eyes, a recognizable pattern appeared. What they got out of this pattern . . . was a language they could not understand. Anyone who studied languages and alien dialects creamed their shorts after learning the news, and began to tear apart the message to try and understand it. It turned out to be a combination of ancient Celt, Icelandic, and some version of Welsh, which made a lot of different people's ears perk up, and the entire world waited to see what the team would put out.

    Hours of blood and tears went into the work of translating the alien dialects, but the words came one night on a screen surrounded by huddled linguists: "*Break the Veil* (there was much smugness from the people who coined the name first) *and enter where your ancients walked. Take with you the mountain glass, bind yourself, and come see the world of dreams.*"

    The smarty boys who translated the scrabbled signals realized what the other bit of extra signal was, and working with the linguists, figured out what this '*bind yourself*' talk was. It was a return code of sorts, which they assumed would need to be etched onto obsidian, a fragile volcanic glass that would cut the shit out of you with little issue. The government, who had jumped in mid way and was paying for all of this, was suddenly in the business of rock collecting and paying top dollar for any chunk of obsidian they could get their hands on. The other nations of the world were almost ready to invade it seemed like, all of them jockeying to try and hem the United States into letting their own assets join in, but the President, a very... prideful man, at the time, wasn't going to let them on American soil.

"This cave, our cave, is a very nice cave, and I only want Americans going inside that cave. You could say it's, 'Ca-ve-se Closed' on letting others in. Okay? Okay."

There were small tests done using the obsidian markers, sending in scouts to search the other side within a short distance of the opening. The reports on what they found on the other side, and its... possibilities, made the United States suddenly very protective of its new little nest egg. Any reports and news on what they found were stopped within minutes, and no longer were journalists or news agencies allowed near the cave. This did not sit well with the other countries in the slightest, and suddenly the American borders were bristling with military hardware around every single edge the United States had. For the first time in history, America was pointing her guns in every direction at once. This did, however, lead to a man power problem. A problem of who would delve inside the Veil, be disposable at the same time, and could be easily replaced with larger quantities if the notion came. The American government and its military advisers pleaded their cases, stating that the country needed its military personnel for possible conflicts from the other nations, and that they had invested money and training into their more professional soldiers. Ideas were thrown around until a bright idea came from the branches of the Army and the Marines, both of the advisors having been leaning towards each other and talking the entire time. These two had their own assets on the inside during the main cave exploration, and acquired nuggets of critical information. This information that had been fed to the Army and Marine advisors had their brains working over time. The scouting parties sent ahead did not venture too far past the Veil opening, taking rock samples from just a few feet within. The more adventurous of the scouting party poked their heads outside the mouth of the cave on the other side and scooped up soil samples, even digging down to take core samples on the untouched interior. What they found was promising, and the elements discovered just within the rock of the cave were as alluring as the wide open spanse of land and timber that sat in the distance.

A light bulb had gone off in their heads, and they brought forth their combined efforts to the other members of the cabinet to deal with this dilemma of manpower.

"What about a volunteer militia?" The Marine adviser asked, poising the question to those around him.

The Army advisor followed up behind the Marine adviser without missing a beat. "There are more veterans and militarily inclined citizens in the general population than there are actual active military from all the branches combined. A lot of them already have the training, and some of them even have their own gear and weapons. A little bit of funny money thrown their direction and perhaps they could be the well armed guinea pigs to establish a foothold on this 'new world'."

While a few of those in charge were not keen on throwing American civilians into the meat grinder purely in the interest of saving money, others were leaning towards saving their professional soldiers for whatever may happen when they announce what they find on the other side. If they found large deposits of gold or platinum, larger and more militarized nations may try and make a gambit for supremacy, something they simply could never allow to happen. This special little cave could be the final piece of puzzle when it came to absolute domination of Earth's markets, allowing the United States to control every piece on the chess board. In the end, those in power agreed that a few dead volunteers was worth the risk of controlling the entire planet.

Word spread from around the internet that they were looking for a few good citizens who were willing to go into the Veil and explore a realm known to none. Most of the professional mercenary companies were looking more to capitalize on the soon-to-come war they could all smell stinking on the wind, and others were too afraid to risk getting gored open by some mythical beast, or 'risk leaving the light of God and never going to heaven' if they died. There were, however, those who dreamed of seeing a land of the fantastical . . . and killing whatever lived there if it was hostile.

Yes, those brave volunteers of the Militia were down for a little cave diving, and the pay was good enough to boot as well. It was money so good that it was almost irresistible when linked with the promise of actually being able to do the things read about in fantasy novels and sci-fi adventures. It would be worth noting that, indeed, a lot of the volunteers for this expedition were more or less garnered from the far corners of the internet, and more than a fair share would not be missed if something went awry. After all, what is more disposable than a bunch of veterans and militia members that wanted a crack at shooting a Dragon with a machine gun, or blowing a Gryphon out of the sky with a Carl Gustav anti-tank weapon. The American government signed off on the equipment, cut the checks, and sent the merry men and women on their way, their unit patch being a gun toting unicorn wearing aviators. Their gear was a scattered collection of many different countries and military surplus, some even going as far as to only take the Improved Outer Tactical Vest (IOTV), offered by the U.S Military just to have a set of armor plates. To say the American volunteers were a walking military surplus store . . . would be an understatement.

When it came to weapons, the U.S Military offered their 'best' for the volunteers, which were mostly sand filled Gulf War leftovers and a bunch of rattly M9 pistols. Yule took one of those M9s, calling it an old friend he could always travel with, and managed to find a stack of magazines with a functional follower spring. A lot of the poorer volunteers took the M4's, M16's and such quite readily, while others used their preferred weapon from their own armory.

One of the volunteers, another veteran that went by 'Savage', spoke up in the darkness. "Anyone else wondering why they gave us all the old ACU pattern shit? You'd think they'd at least give us some Marpat to wear . . ."

"Why would they waste Marpat on a bunch of dead men?" Quipped the unit's other co-commander, an army veteran that went by Koko.

The cave once again filled with laughter, while Yule chewed idly on a large corn-cob pipe in his mouth and panned his flash light from side to side, looking for the Veil to pop up. His Daewoo K2 rattled slightly as he stopped, and Koko held up his fist. The formation of volunteer militia came to a halt as the two Commanders peered ahead into the void, the resolute darkness behaving like a possessed misty fog.

"They weren't kidding," Murmured Yule, pushing his pipe to the other side of his mouth with a slight knock of his teeth, "Damn thing chews up all the light. We're supposed to just walk into this fuckin' thing?"

"Yeah, sounded like bullshit to me too, but it's what we signed up for." Koko replied, eagerly hooking his thumbs into his chest rig.

"I'm glad we dressed for the occasion." Chuckled Yule, and the two men looked at each other's tropical themed button ups.

"That's a big cave . . ." Koko murmured.

Yule held his hand cupped in front of his mouth, so his voice sounded hollow. "For you."

There was more tittering behind them, as jokes were traded back and forth amongst the other troopers.

"Marker check!" Yule barked out suddenly, the report echoing down the cave as everyone held aloft their fragile obsidian recall markers. Yule saw that everyone had theirs held aloft, and he nodded, turning back towards the inky unknown of the Veil.

"One for the money . . ." Yule whispered, stepping forward towards the otherworldly portal with his rifle gripped in his hands.

Koko breathed out harshly, matching step with Yule "Two for the show . . ."

"Three to make ready." Yule answered back as his arm entered the whirling void, his flesh suddenly going numb as if he was getting instant frostbite.

"Here we fucking go!" Roared Dregs, and one by one the militia volunteers entered the unknown.

* * *

The shocking and brutal cold of the transition was harsh enough to suck the air from the lungs of all who dared pass through it, and both Yule and Koko came out the other side of the Veil heaving for air and clutching themselves, frost giving every exposed piece of their body and clothes a light sprinkling of ice and verglas.

"H-h-holy sh-sh-shit!" Roared Yule, shaking his arms and legs to get the feeling back in them. Koko crashed into his back from behind and sent him flying forwards, scrabbling at the walls of the cave as his legs fought to remain jelly-like and unyielding to his commands.

Koko's feelings on the matter were similar as he rolled onto his back, having crumpled to the ground in a heap. "What in the *hell* man! They didn't say anything about nothing being able to breathe!"

His voice echoed up and down with Yule's as he clamped at his ears with his palms, rubbing them painfully as his feet stamped at the ground.

The same reaction was shared with all of the volunteers as they exited the Veil, some of them falling temporarily unconscious as they hit the warm air, their system not knowing how to handle the shock of the transitioning from the warmth of the cave to the sudden arctic blast of the Veil. After the chorus of screams was finally over, Yule and Koko checked over all of their troopers, and then moved back towards the Veil entrance. There was a pause, and then four crates appeared, barely poking out from the black and the surfaces riddled with ice.

At least they keep their word I suppose . . . Yule thought, and they began yanking the crates all the way through the Veil. These were to be their rations and survival gear, enough to keep them fed, watered, and warm until they were due to rendezvous back with the team on the other side. Everything was split up among the troopers as well as extra ammo distributed to those who desired it, just in case. The call to move out was ordered, and the volunteers began their walk through the cave towards the entrance.

"It smells different here." A voice echoed from the rear, and indeed, many of those who sniffed at the air found it to smell different. Older . . . yet somehow cleaner.

Koko pointed the barrel of his FAL down at the dirt of the cave path, gesturing towards a lone line of boot and foot prints. "Tracks."

"Heads on a swivel people." Yule called out to those behind him, and he squatted down, eyeing the prints curiously.

What he found was a set of small ones, and multiple other sets of larger ones. Yule sniffed a little and ground his teeth onto the stem of his pipe. He had told himself he would try and find that little girl's body if he could, but how the hell could he even promise that there would be a body to find in the first place. There was no telling what was near the outside of this tunnel, and even less of an idea what was beyond even that. As quietly as they could, and rifles at the low ready, the volunteers stepped along the path until they turned a corner, and dusky sun light drifted down the sides of the jagged rock.

"Daylight." Yule murmured, and he gripped his K2 firmly.

"Boys we're near the exit, I want those weapons on fire, and if you got a giggle switch, get it chuckling." Koko called out, and began clicking the settings of his optical sight to deal with the incoming light

Near the center of the formation, two male volunteers were crouched low to the ground, one holding a K98 rifle while the other held an Enfield tightly, the bayonet already attached. "Gon' get me an Elf babe, just you wait Toby."

Toby shook his head silently, and slapped the other volunteer on the chest to get him to pay attention. There was a chorus of clicks as all the weapons went hot, word of the command making its way down the formation. A heavy weapons team racked their crew served machine guns, locking into place the bolts of multiple M249's, 240B's, and a single M2 that they all had agreed should be nicknamed 'Black Betty, Bamalam'. They had her and her tripod ready to deploy, being carried by a pair of female volunteers that looked as if they had just come in from a speed metal concert. The U.S Army almost didn't part with the M2, but the question of "What if theres a fucking Dragon?" was enough to let the volunteers borrow an older model. Black Betty's date and number marked her as an ancient Korean War model that was a warehouse queen, and after dusting her off, spraying her down with enough Whale sperm (a coined term for the lubricant used by the U.S Army) to drown a small child, and giving her a good wipe up, she was good enough for mowing down Elves and Dragons if anyone could guess.

The formation crept forward right to the mouth of the cave, and the soft warm air of an unknown morning sun caressed the faces of Koko and Yule.

"As planned?" Yule said, poking the edge of his patrol cap bill around the edge of the cave lip.

"Yeah, as planned." Koko affirmed, his trigger finger trembling just as hard as Yule's was.

"Go!" Koko roared as Yule raised up his K2 and launched forward, the two of them rushing out of the cave in split directions.

The rest of the unit poured out of the cave entrance like a horde of ants that got wind of a cherry lollipop, running the number of steps they were told to. Each member of the unit bounded forward to set up a quick cascading line of fire to cover every direction, forming a giant U-shape from the mouth of the cave. The crew served machine guns ran out and set up on whatever high ground they could find, mostly being the edges of the cave and it's connected hill.

The air was clean and crisp, warm and inviting, as if it was an old friend welcoming them back from a long journey. The sun rising from the horizon was so vividly colored that many of the volunteers had trouble yanking their eyes from it. A few camera clicks from cell phones were heard . . . and someone was going to get a smack for it.

A few minutes passed as everyone stared out around them. The area was free of buildings or any unnatural structures, with only a few clusters of trees nearby and other larger hills in the distance. A rather long tree line could be seen almost seven hundred yards away, and a volunteer who took care of hummingbirds back home took note of the specimens of avians that hung in the air. Ones that flew around them overhead and in the distance were very similar to the ones that he had seen through his years of bird care, and the volunteer found that to be somewhat comforting. Eyes peered through sights, gun barrels swung back and forth slowly, and everyone searched for targets that may lay in the distance.

After a solid five minutes of silence, Yule and Koko waved at each other, signaling they saw nothing, and got the lads in order. A female volunteer on one of the 240B's cursed angrily and picked at a wedgie, growling to her female compatriot that the two of them wearing combat thongs as a joke was a stupid idea. As everyone stood up and looked around more intricately, a call went up from a sniper named Domino.

Domino hopped from one foot to the other, his hands drumming on his M24 excitedly. "Hey! I think I found those fuckin' rescue guys!"

Koko and Yule shared a look before running over to see what he was on about.

He had indeed found the lost Rescue team . . . or what was left of them, anyway.

CHAPTER 2

A VOLUNTEER RIFLEMAN LOOMED over his battle brother, looking over his shoulder at the ripped up Human carcass in front of both of them. "What do you think, Kole?"

"I . . . am not quite sure." Kole opened his large hand and lightly traced his fingers above the huge rake marks that were left in the meat and bone of the corpse. The creature that had attacked must have had claws so immense that they cleaved right through the ribs of the rescue team member and dug into the flesh below. "A bear? Bears aren't even close to being this big, not even polar bears . . ."

"Spoopy." Murmured the trooper that was leaning over his shoulder, and he began to walk back to the main encampment, leaving the small group huddled around the ripped up bodies. He found Yule yawning and mixing up a pouch of dehydrated coffee, a small group of riflemen huddled around the small jet stove waiting for their own water to heat.

"Sir." The trooper said, placing his fist against his chest in a mocking Jaeger salute.

Yule continued his yawn, groaning out softly before looking at the trooper with his eyes half lidded, the exhaustion plain on his face. Preparing for the journey in had left him with very little sleep, and finding nothing on the other side willing to attack him, his body was now more than ready to catch a few winks. "You'll find no 'sir' here, just a Yule."

The trooper grinned and instead did a normal military salute. "Right. Sir Yule, sir!"

All the riflemen gathered around the quietly roaring jet stove chuckled appreciatively of the well timed humor, while Yule shook his head and dumped a white packet of sugar into his coffee, the small piece of the packet's paper top still in his teeth. "Report'."

"Well, as far as Kole can tell, it was some kind of bear. But bigger than a polar bear."

"Sounds like a problem for Betty to fix." Yule said, spitting the piece of paper off of his lip while the rest of the riflemen murmured their agreement, taking the rumbling pot off the jet burner and pouring the hot water into their own retort pouches. Yule sent the trooper off to grab Kole, then turned slightly and took stock of their little fortification set up. They quickly realized that they had a pretty good firing position with the little bit of elevation on the hill and the sprawling grasslands before them. Without any real construction tools and with the trees up on top of the rocky little boulder hills behind them being too thin, they decided to go full Bulge on this one and dig fox holes and trench lines throughout the base, as well as digging emplacements up on the hill itself. These hill emplacements were where Betty and the rest of the crew served machine guns sat, the volunteers behind them staring down at the locations below like curious birds of prey. There was also a new addition to the weapon teams after Koko sent the smallest of the troopers back through the Veil to not only test the obsidian marker stones, but to also send requests for more supplies. The trooper came back squalling about the deep bitter cold of the Veil, and some days after him came around six to seven crates. In these crates were more food, water, stoves, fuel, ammunition for Betty and the other crew serves . . . and a very special treat for anything that gets within three thousand yards of the camp.

Koko's request for an 81mm Mortar had apparently been approved. The tube itself had seen better days and the ground plate looked like it had been run over, but the militia volunteers were more than happy to take these army sloppy seconds and put it into an advantaged position. There were plenty of spare spaces up on the top side of the cave's mountain that could play home to the beat up mortar. After all the shovel work they had done so far, digging the nice little hole for their new favorite toy to sit in was but another day on the other side of the Veil. With the mortar came a few boxes of HE and illumination rounds, just in case they needed to see something coming at night where the flash lights couldn't reach.

All around the cave entrance the company of troopers had dug trenches and fox holes, using rotations of volunteers who occupied them and kept watch over the entryway to their encampment. Yule also noted, as he touched the reconstituted coffee to his lips, that the volunteers were already making this place into a home. Someone had made a sign reading: "Welcome to Fort Kick Ass, No Elves Allowed", near the front of the little camp, and others had set up lean-toos or hooches where they slept or relaxed. He also noticed with much annoyance that someone had actually dragged a body pillow here.

Good thing Megumin could pull sentry duty, he supposed.

"C'mon mate, what kind of place would this be without a waifu in tha' mix."

Yule looked over his shoulder at the Australian sitting sprawled out in the grass behind him, having seen Yule stare daggers at the body pillow which wore a helmet and had an M4 strapped to it.

"Shattap, Cockram."

Jovial Australian flavored laughter bounced off Yule's back as he began to walk away to inspect the fortification lines. It was honestly a miracle that the kangaroo kicker even made it into the outfit, having sold everything he owned and burned every favor he had to get a ticket to the states with a fake vacation visa, or whatever it was they did in order to get into the United States for a while. As Yule was helping stack sacks of earth to create a small pillbox, his coffee pouch steaming happily nearby, Kole finally arrived and made his report. Yule stood up, dusted the dirt off of his pants and hands, and walked up the rough earthen entry way into the pillbox, picking up his retort pouch on the way out.

"Ah, Mr. Kole," Yule drawled out in a friendly manner, "I hear you think a giant bear got a snack in before we arrived."

Kole rubbed his palms together as he thought, formulating the words in his head. "Not just before we arrived, but certainly some time before. The bodies were heavily decomposed, and not as much as they should have been for how long they've been missing for."

Yule raised a brow as he took a sip from the retort pouch of coffee. The time from when the rescue team was cut off to the time they arrived had been relatively short for government work, the bodies shouldn't be so decomposed in such mild weather. Yule knew there were other factors that could be in play, none of which he particularly liked. "Mr. Kole, are you implying we're dealing with a big ball of wibbly-wobbly timey wimey stuff?"

Kole shrugged. "To some degree."

Yule *hmm'd* and tapped the corner of his retort pouch to his chin. This did explain how that 81mm mortar was approved so fast, or how they got all their supplies together so quickly, despite the Terran side of the cave being out in the sticks of Coal Country.

"Thank you Mr. Kole, that's all I needed."

Kole gave Yule a Lazy salute but Yule didn't return it. This was a militia after all and Yule didn't even hold a rank besides 'Co-Commander' with Koko. That was only because he was one of the few older guys in the outfit, and he'd be damned if others were going to call him 'Sir'. That night, all those who were not on watch, or sleeping, gathered up near the middle of the camp. Those who had not yet eaten took that moment to rip open MREs and sneak in a late supper, having been too busy digging in the ground like demented moles earlier in the day. In front of them was one of the tech-geeks, or as most of them in the camp called her, "The */G/remlin"*

Gremlin was a very slight woman, mostly muscle and sinew at 5'1, but she knew her tech and also owned a stockpile of personal drones that she had brought with her through The Veil. During the day she had thrown up a pair of the monster quad-copters, which had been circling in an ever growing radius around the camp and feeding information to her little set up of toughbooks and gaming laptops. Piece by piece, she was building a map of the area with actual pictures taken from her drones, and it was all coming together in the murky gloom of the night. Due to the many reasons of 'don't want to be seen', Fort Kick Ass No Elves Allowed had a policy where no campfires were to be lit during the day or night, the camp relying instead on chemical heaters and jet stoves to heat things up or cook. Due to this, the lights from the six laptops threw eery shades of green and blue onto the small group behind Gremlin, of which Yule and Koko were a part of. This time both Yule and Koko had retorts of coffee, and somehow Koko had found a silly straw which he used to slurp his field-mocha with.

"Lots of trees so far, plenty of open plains, more hills behind us." Yule muttered to Koko, his thick mustache almost perched on the top of his retort pouch

Koko's silly straw gurgled as he stopped drinking, gesturing with the pouch at the map slowly filling up the screens. "And there's a village right there to consider. Looks to be rustic, I don't see any metal roofs or anything, and those are clearly some kind of animals pulling carts."

Yule nodded slightly, now chewing worriedly on the lip of the pouch. "Thinkin'... Iron Age? Middle Age? Those buildings look like somethin' you would have found in a French village during Charlemagne."

Koko chucked his teeth a few times. "Definitely Middle Ages, which means we can keep fire superiority."

"Yeah until one of those sonsa' bitches throws a fireball at us or some shit." Yule growled.

Gremlin, Koko, and everyone else around the laptops laughed quietly, and after a few more minutes, Gremlin had the maps printed out and in the co-commanders' hands. It was thanks to Gremlin they could even get some kind of electrical power going, as she knew how to work the little wind generator that happily spun and whizzed twenty feet above them on a pole. Yule was curious as to how the No Weenies Allowed and Gadsden flags also got up there under the generator, but no one wanted to own up to it, and he just didn't have the fucks to spare when it came to taking it down. Besides, if anything living saw the flags and tried to make contact, they would be facing the bristling guns of Fort Kickass.

After conversing with Koko a bit more about the village, they both agreed that they should at least put it under some kind of observation, just to see what is going on there and what kind of people inhabit the place. It was within enough of a distance that some form of overlap is inevitable, and if they ever let loose the entire firing line worth of rifles into a target, there is no way the village will not hear the crack and pop of ordnance turning some Goblin into jelly.

When the maps were all in hand and all the fun over, the small gaggle of troopers dispersed with Yule slowly walking in the dark towards his own hooch he had dug into the ground. Yule groaned as he kicked back onto his sleeping system, bundling his wool camping blanket behind his shoulders and head to prop him up. He had a small light attached to the roof of his little camping hooch and clicked it on the red setting, casting Yule in a grim dull crimson light as he looked at the maps.

"Mystery village to the West..." He sighed, draining the last of his coffee pouch, "Empty mysterious forest to the North and East... and us." He tapped a finger where the camp lay to the South, on its little range of hills. The night crept on as sentries changed rotations, men and women chatted as they gathered together around the softly glowing lights of stoves, and Human eyes peered out into the dim of the distance of the unknown lands

* * *

"Alllrighty. So. Your job is to take a looky-loo at the town or whatever it is, let us know whats going on, and then boogy on home. Any questions?"

Yule stood before the gaggle of eight men and women before him, one hand in his pocket as another held a protein bar, his fingers fiddling with the wrapper. He didn't mind the first strike bars that cropped up in the MREs, but they really did a number on his teeth just trying to chew through them. The group was hand picked from the volunteers who had the best cardio and optics, three of which were men, and five were women. The women were avid runners and joggers and had the legs to prove it judging from the contours of their uniform trousers. Two of the men were fun-runners, their rifles sporting long distance optics that could peer down into the town from an advantaged position. One of the men was Domino, he was not a fun runner, but was just super eager to get a scope on something breathing in this realm. Yule could understand; they had expected to be besieged by Goblins and slathering beasts as soon as they came out of the Veil, but so far it had been mostly a group camping trip while trying to lure in strange birds with pieces of MRE crackers.

A bubbly blonde held up her rifle and her camera phone at the same time. "Are we allowed to take pictures?"

"Yes." Yule said flatly, feeling that there were even more dumb questions to follow.

"Are we allowed to kill them if they become hostile?" Asked one of the men, who idly rubbed a finger along the eyepiece rim of his scope.

"I'd prefer if you didn't, just try to wing them or something and make a quick get away. Remember, the key here is to *not* get seen and to just report." Yule eyed them, slightly peeved with his patience running short almost immediately. He'd failed to realize just how bad his back was and sleeping on the ground was no longer suited to him. It was starting to make him crankier in the mornings, and warping away his patience to boot.

After ironing out some other small details of the mission, he sent them off, and they went happily jogging away from Fort Kick Ass. There was some mild jeering as well from those on sentry duty, half of whom had their comic books or mangas out to take advantage of the morning sunlight to read. As the sounds of boots hitting the ground faded away, Yule heard the chunks of actions being worked from up on the hill, and saw the crew serves were taking the time to do daily maintenance. He had to yell at them yesterday because they were doing it all at once, but today they were thankfully doing it one at a time, so that way only one weapon was down compared to all of them at once.

He blinked blearly into the sky and sniffed, bringing the protein bar to his mouth as he thought to himself. It was probably good that he sent the group off with two sets of maps, the last thing he needed was a bunch of trigger-happy kommandos walking around fantasyland, looking for a reason to split some poor creatures' faces apart or something.

"Well good morning sunshine." Koko crooned with a smile, and Yule rolled his eyes in response. Koko continued on, shaking a retort pouch of rehydrating coffee. "Did you send out that group of runners already?"

* * *

The team jogged happily across the plush grasslands of the field, and didn't even break much of a sweat thanks to the cool, fresh morning air that they gulped down in thankful lungs. The travel was silent, with nothing more than the jangle of canteens or rattle of magazines to break the silence. Using the maps, they were able to recognize some terrain features and use them on the move, not needing to stop to take out the compass and had an easy time dead reckoning their way to the village. When they finally arrived 300 yards away, they broke line of sight and crawled through the brush the rest of the way, finding a nice clear spot to peek out of. Ahead of them on the edge of the village, humanoids were going about their morning dailys, heeding or paying no mind to those who watched them, hidden in the undergrowth of the tree line.

"Farmers eh?" Whispered Domino as he looked down the optic of his rifle, trailing the Mildot sight along behind a man who was carrying a bundle of wood.

"Very curious, look at their ears." Murmured another volunteer, a raven haired female who everyone called Kentucky, due to her father owning a chain of fried chicken restaurants and her constantly bringing it up in conversation. "They're really low, elves maybe?"

Gabriel, who was from Georgia, flicked back and forth between his optic's settings. "Definitely elves, but I expected... Fancier elves. Y'know, Lord of the Rings and all that."

The group quietly chatted to each other, while the bubbly blonde, who went by 'Chicks', busily snapped pictures with her phone, holding the camera near the eye piece of her scope.

They sat and watched the Elves for hours, and those down in the sprawling buildings went about their village routines. The place was definitely more elvish up close, with many of the houses sporting long spiraling carvings, the windows seeming to be more for show than actual use, and even the animals they used seemed more lithe than what anything on earth would be. What was truly strange was how normal they looked compared to the expectations of the Humans who watched them from afar. There wasn't much spell casting or great feats of magic, but regular people going about their lives. Children giggled and played in the streets or yards of the homes, dogs barked and chased after them, and the parents watched from time to time while working. Every home had its own little plot of land, each had their own little gardens and every Elf seemed to have made it their own in one way or another. A house would be sporting a fish theme, another a bird theme, each one attempting to convey the thoughts and feelings of those who lived within. They reckoned the village must have around two hundred or so elves in it, and must have been exporting some kind of grain judging by the amount of fields that surrounded the little cluster of homes.

The group spotted a decently wooded area nearer to the village and low-crawled to it, keeping their heads low just to make sure they weren't spotted. Chicks had been chewing bubble gum the entire time, which caused a few pucker factor moments when she forgot she couldn't blow bubbles, but the team made it to the wooded area with no alarm being raised. Chicks went back to taking pictures while everyone else scoped it on the bigger buildings near the center of the village, the largest of which had to be assumed as the Inn judging by the amount of Elves around it. The closer the buildings got to the center of the village, the more elaborate the carvings and themes became, many of which sported wooden carvings of animals that grazed or frolicked in the small, tidy front yards.

"Betcha Yule would sell one of our souls for a bed in that." Kentucky said with a chuckle, and focused her own reticle at a pair of Elves sitting outside of the Inn on a bench table. The two Elves were smiling happily as they drank from artistically made mugs as they talked to each other, and Kentucky found herself unable to follow the language as she read their lips.

Domino giggled to himself quietly as his own eye was glued to his optic, he himself watched an Elven woman hang up her laundry, the long flowing sheets having attacked her and swallowed her. The Elf seemed to be having a bit of trouble getting out of it, and ended up ripping it off the line with a grimace.. "He would certainly growl less. Man bear pig at its finest."

From this close they got an actual good look at the elves. They were pretty, for certain, but many of them had rugged features that compared nicely to their lines of work and the general feel of the village. Their ears were lower on their heads and went more sideways than up at a high angle, their hair seemed to always be braided, and the men actually sported small rugged beards that were adorned with some kind of bead.

Gabriel spotted one such man sitting on a small chair outside of his home and the Elf seemed to be whittling himself a new pipe of some kind, while next to him, a large jug sat nearby, out of which the Elf would refill a cup he drank from. "They look a lot like Finns, but friendlier."

The team all guffawed at each other silently but kept taking down notes in field books. Besides whatever it was they farmed here, they also seemed to be breeding horses. They hadn't seen them yet personally, but on the other side of the village were what looked like racks and racks of stables, and further out could be seen big herds of multicolored forms that ran around on occasion. They were sleek looking creatures that looked well tended after, as far as the volunteer group of Humans could tell from this distance anyway. Hell, even the damn chickens looked elvish, their feathers way too sleek and clean when compared to anything they had back at home on Earth.

Kentucky silently whistled to herself as she panned her reticle over a pair of brightly colored fowl, the birds pecking at the ground while strutting about. "Wonder how they taste in secret herbs and spices . . . "

Again quiet laughter was shared amongst the team, but was cut short when a distant rumble and boom was heard.

"Ya'll hear that?" Gabriel snapped, twisting his head to look behind him. The sound was constant now, a chorus of booms and thuds that sent chills running up and down their flesh in goosebumps. Gunfire, echoes of gunfire and battle was reverberating in the distance, and it could only be comin from one place.

"Movement. Lots of movement!" Chicks said in a slightly higher tone than what she usually used to, and was looking down the scope of her rifle. She saw the people in the village perking up to the noise and they seemed to be worried, some of them running to their homes and fetching what looked like long, elegant spears. The entire village had heard the noises as well and Chicks could only assume that they had no idea what it was, but knew it couldn't be anything good. Children ran and ducked into homes, women bundled up babies into their arms and went for cover, while the men and able bodied began gathering weapons from wherever they had them stored.

"Time to go!" Domino cheered, and picked up his M24 as he stood. Element of surprise now gone, they stood up and immediately began to sprint back to Fort Kick Ass at full speed, paying no mind to the cries of the villagers behind them.

* * *

"Mortars! Get that fucken' mortar going!" Roared Yule as he waved his arms at the team up on the hill. The .50cal was barking its challenge along with the spitting M249s and 240Bs arranged around it, and together they whipped a stream of leaden death down below at the Dire Wolves charging Camp Kick Ass. The hulking things had come up so fast and suddenly that the camp defenders barely had time to register what was even coming at them, costing them precious seconds to lay down their fields of fire. AR15s, AK47s, and WWII bolt action rifles roared in defiance to the bays of the Dire Wolves charging at them from below.

"I'll give you that," Koko yelled, slamming a fresh magazine into his FAL as Kole ripped the pin out of a grenade, holding it tight to his chest as he fired his rifle with one hand, resting the forward grip on a sandbag, "They're bigger than polar bears!"

The .50 caliber rounds from Betty slammed home into the charging pack of Dire Wolves, ripping chunks of meat and fur away in great gouts of crimson that spilled down onto the grass and rushing paws below, but it took a lot of concentrated fire to bring down even one. Yule saw one volunteer fire a Mosin at a Dire Wolf that was over a hundred and fifty yards away, and then watched the 7,62x54r round loudly ricochet off the skull of its target. Yule grimaced at the thought that this thing had a skull tough enough to bounce such a powerful round, but thankfully the mortar team had figured itself out and finally belched out its first round fired in anger.

The high explosive round took awhile to come down due to its arc, but with luck they managed to bring it down a hundred yards in front of the trench network and right beside two charging Dire Wolves. Dire wolves were tough, but they weren't 81mm high explosive round tough. The mortar rent the ground apart and the two Dire Wolves were nearly blown into giblets of meat by the shockwave of the round, the shrapnel from it screeching through the air and doing the rest of the job with ease. The military veterans didn't even flinch when the round came down, while others dived for cover, their weapons clattering down beside them. When the Dire Wolves were almost on top of them, Kole threw his grenade, as did many others, and the fragmentation did it's intended purpose on the Dire Wolves, tearing muscle and meat away from bone and body. Ripples of concussive air played a tune of death and destruction on the ears of the living as the grenades cooked off, sounding almost as if a giant was tap dancing on the graves of the beasts that were so folly to charge the lines. Their charge staggered and the Dire Wolves gave a deadly pause, allowing Betty to rake across the last remaining Dire Wolves that still drew breath into their huge lungs. The crews focused their fire while the mortar let fly another round and after it landed, there was no more threat to the camp to be seen. The mortar crews had decided to risk the biscuit and had angled the mortar down into an unnatural position so the round would land faster. Not the greatest or most logical idea, but such things came from the minds of the irregular.

Yule decocked the hammer on his M9 and looked around, checking for wounded but thankfully found none. A lot of people were scared out of their fucking minds, but they were alive and thats what counted.

"If they're alive, put 'em down." Koko shouted, and a few of the volunteers with larger calibers walked out and began emptying entire magazines directly into the skulls of any Dire Wolf that even twitched when they approached. Kole was squatting down beside one that lay dead further away, staring at it in fascination as he ran his hand along its bloody neck fur. This one had gone down by a lucky .50cal to the top of its skull, and was mostly intact.

"Jesus Christ . . ." He whispered, when he managed to actually get his hand around one of its paws and admire the claws of it. It was with little doubt that these were the things that tore that rescue team a part when they came through the Veil in search of the lost kid. They wouldn't have even had a chance with how fast these giant wolves were, and as soon as the massive paws had gotten onto their target, there was no coming back from a swipe like that.

When the sniper team finally arrived, Fort Kick Ass was attempting to haul the more torn apart Dire Wolves off and away while the machine guns looked on, other volunteers having gone into the process of trying to skin the ones that were mostly intact and having a hell of a time of it. The Dire Wolves were so large that some of the volunteers had shucked their clothes, and now looked like blood covered Gremlins as they scrambled over the carcasses to cut and saw away the hides.

Yule saw the sniper team loitering near the most forward trench and waved them over, once again finding him with a pouch of coffee in hand.

"Any good news, I hope?" Yule murmured over the din of more digging and the occasional volunteer lumbering around with ammo cans.

"Yeah!" Chicks panted softly, her face bright and happy, "We found Elves!"

Yule raised his eyebrows, teeth gripping the top of a sugar packet mid tear. Koko had arrived as well, wiping what looked like bloody water away from his face. Both of them said the word 'Elves' at the same time, the inflections of their responses standing apart from each other. While Koko seemed excited, Yule seemed hesitant. The sniper team gave their report while Chicks showed them the many... many pictures she had taken on her phone, giving the two commanders more or less a general overview of the village. Neither of them were particularly happy to hear that the village had over heard the gunfire of them battling the Dire wolves.

Koko nudged Yule with his elbow, causing Yule almost fumbling the open sugar packet. "It's only a matter of time until they come over here. Humans are curious enough as it is."

Yule stared down angrily at the coffee pouch in his hand as he slowly tipped the sugar packet down into it, tapping the small packet on the rim of the pouch. To be quite frank, he was terrified of meeting Elves. The thought alone had plagued him for days as he prepared to head into the Veil; If every myth was to be true, they're heading into the lair of apex predators a few notches above a normal Human. If things went south, they would no longer hold the advantage, and god forbid if a volunteer died and somehow the Elves got a hold of their weapon. Yule could appreciate Koko's enthusiasm, but he'd be damned if the idea didn't make him pucker so hard, he could pass as a submarine when he closed his mouth.

The two co-commanders talked it over for quite some time, both of them explaining their reservations or objections when it came to the Elves that the sniper team had found. In the end, Koko won the bout, with much groaning about it from Yule. Yule picked up his rifle, put on his entire combat kit, and tugged his olive drab green patrol cap on snuggly. When he walked out, Koko and the squad of volunteers he had put together were almost vibrating from the excitement coursing through their bodies, twenty pairs of eyes wide open and waiting for the order to move out.

Yule narrowed his eyes, and pointed at a rifleman in the rear who was carrying something that would be of no help on this particular mission. "That fuckin' body pillow stays *here*, Brady."

CHAPTER 3

THE FORMATION OF Humans walked in a staggered infantry column down a well cut dirt road, their wide variety of boots crunching on the gravel as they moved. They had decided while en route to the village to perhaps not spook them by walking up and out of the forest all of a sudden, and take a more direct and open approach down a road they knew existed thanks to the labors of Gremlin. While one Human had their suspicion of germs and possible fantasy diseases, Yule and Koko didn't really have a worry in that regard, as it was more than likely these people, or the people of this land, had many ways to cure the ill and any kind of sickness. After all, these were Elves; they weren't walking into a Goblin stronghold or something of that sort or getting shot with shit covered arrows.

As far as Yule was concerned, it was actually quite nice going for a walk after being coop'd up in Fort Kick Ass for all these weeks, and to hear the wind rustling through the leaves of trees was bringing back memories of his birth state of Oklahoma. While Yule and some of the other Humans walked with rifles low and enjoying the overall ambiance, others walked at the low ready, as if expecting a Dire Wolf to lunge out of the woods that surrounded them on each side and drag their body into the brush for a snack. Yule told the volunteers while on the way out that they needed to be as calm as possible and walk as if there wasn't a threat. The last thing he wanted was for the Elves to perceive that they were stalking along the road and not actually walking out to greet them and make contact.

Hours passed on in relative serenity before Yule began to notice a severe lack of traffic on the road. A lot of the wagon ruts and runs were extremely old, with very little new tread or marks on the surface at all. He pocketed that information in the back of his head, as ahead of them were a few scattered outer buildings that seemed to be just beyond the edge of the trees.

Yule sniffed, flicking his rifle over his shoulder, still keeping his M9 well at hand and off safe. "Smiles engaged people, lets not cause a ruckus and spook the locals."

The Humans walked out into the sun, the bugs buzzing around them with brightly colored grasshoppers buzzed about and flew away from their approach onto the open road to the village. It took a matter of minutes for the Elves of the village to become highly aware of their presence, Yule thinking it more a town in scope now that he was closer. Well, that's not entirely true, since it was mostly just one Elf that really became highly aware of their presence. The second building they passed had a little girl sitting outside near a very ornate wooden gate and a large golden colored dog was in front of her. She was cooing at it in her language and the dog seemed to be soaking up the attention, its tail wagging and tongue lolling out happily. When she looked up, she locked eyes with Yule who had walked within ten yards of her, and the five Humans who had slinked up around him for a better look.

For the first time in who knows how long, Terran and Fantastical looked at each other eye to eye with no Veil between them. The little Elf girl tilted her head and Yule took his hat off, giving a slight bow to the girl, loose strands of his curly hair coming down across his forehead. Yule usually kept his hair tied back with a string of leather so the curly mass wouldn't blind him every time he bent over to grab something. The dog growled at the strange smelling men and women, but the little Elf girl quickly smooshed the dogs cheeks with her palms and talked to it in a stern manner. When she was sure the dog wasn't going to rip off the strange man's leg, she hopped up and bowed slightly back to Yule. Yule smiled, and the little Elf girl smiled back.

Yule couldn't help but chuckle a little. It was so odd seeing an actual honest to god Elf in real life. Their flesh looked just like his, she had little freckles on her face and her eyes just had the slightest almond shape to them. The calm was broken by the sound of breaking pottery, and the formation's eyes snapped up to see Mama Elf standing in the doorway, the floor of which looked to be covered in some kind of pinkish water and a shattered vessel. There was a long pause, the little Elf girl looking from Yule to her mama, while the dog, sensing the tension, loudly lapped at its genitals; After all, what better time for a self lick than the tension of death and destruction. The two Elves shared the same amber honey eye color and flaxen yellow hair, their cheeks also sporting the same sprinkling of sun kissed freckles that rippled down from their cheeks to the tops of their shoulders, disappearing under the necklines of well made and expertly cut summer wear. Their clothes spoke of hard earned function, sparing very little for grandeur and sophistication, and only the barest forms of decoration poked out here and there. Flowers of bright thread danced here and there along the bottom hem of the mother's trousers, while the same flowers adorned the little girls field dress. Both wore a kind of soft leather vest that protected their upper torsos. It was not battle worthy in any way, but really brought the entire outfit together.

Chicks popped her head around the gate, and gave her best cheery smile and wave. "Hiiii!"

Everyone's eyes snapped to Chicks, who gave a nervous chuckle and slowly bent her fingers down, shrinking slightly from the number of gazes being pointed her way. The little Elf girl waved back and mimicked Chicks's 'Hi' with her own, showing a lot of teeth as she did. All the female volunteers coo'd and aww'd at her, while the rest of the male volunteers were wondering where Papa bear was in all this. The Mother Elf made no moves, but glared at the Humans and kept motioning for her daughter to come inside.

Yule saw that they didn't attack on first contact, but could tell from the worry lines on the female Elf's face that they were stressing her out from being so near her kid. "Lets move on, before the Elf-Mama decides to cast a spell on us."

The Humans gave a short chorus of laughs before the formation began moving onwards down the road, and one of the volunteers near the rear set down a small pack of dehydrated coffee and a protein bar near the gate of the home. When the last volunteer was well away, the Mama Elf ran out and snatched her daughter up like a hawk and dragged her inside, leaving the dog to sniff curiously at the small packages the foreigners left behind.

"I don't want to worry you guys," Yule began, looking over his shoulder at the home behind them. "But this may have been a stupid idea."

Any Elf within eye shot of the formation of Humans stopped what they were doing and watched them. While some took off at a sprint to their homes, others walked up in curiosity to get a better look.

After all, these strange beings were not being outwardly aggressive and were waving at them in a friendly manner. After passing the first house-filled area, the Humans became surrounded by Elves who stood back a distance in groups, talking in their language to each other and pointing. When a Human would wave, they would wave back and smile, then go back to talking to their friends excitedly. The formation strode right into the middle of the town, coming to a halt where a small fountain and park resided. The Humans behind Yule and Koko were quietly thinking of ways to get back at Yule in case something went wrong and they happened to survive getting mobbed by a bunch of fantasy creatures. The villagers of this Elf town had made a large ring around them and were talking very busily amongst themselves. Koko had made sure to get as many Terran language speakers as possible in this group in case there was a shared language, but none of them were picking up on what these Elves were speaking.

"Alright, try to avoid looking scary. Be like the penguins boys, smile and wave." Yule murmured, raising his hand and waving at a small group of men who were clutching spears in their hands, the points looking wicked and glinting in the sun light. The Humans who got the reference glanced at Yule, almost annoyed, but still did their best to smile and wave at anyone they could. The female volunteers were awestruck by the amount of pretty men in the crowd, while the males were quite pleased to see the mythos about Elven maidens and their beauty was indeed true. Yule told the group to take a knee and rest, while he and Koko remained standing.

Yule looked over at Koko. "How long till the chief or mayor shows up you think?"

"Probably as soon as he puts on his favorite necktie." Koko said with a bright smile, and stood on his tip toes, trying to peer around for a split in the crowd, but found none.

"Hey hey hey, quit given' away your shit, we don't know if we'll need that here soon." Yule barked at a Human trying to hand away an entire MRE, and threw his hat at him to get his attention. "This is an Elf village, not a mountain hamlet in Afghanistan, 'aight?"

For the most part . . . the interaction was going okay. The Elves were doing a lot of pointing and behind the hand talking, while the Humans were openly winking and flirting with just about everything that had a bodice or their clavicles showing. It was around the time Chicks was taking selfies with a group of male Elves that the apparent governor finally arrived, surrounded by what looked like a guard retinue. Koko nudged Yule, and Yule squinted slightly at the sight.

The honor guard was wearing a strange form of intricate lamellar armor that looked very silvery instead of the usual tint of steel, and deep maroon gambesons underneath that armor. Curiously, they wore simple soft hats that were cocked to the side in a rakish fashion, and a skirt of plates with trousers underneath. They carried simple spears and a triangle shaped shield that seemed to be more for fashion than a workhorse, but with Elven craftsmanship there's no telling what kind of stuff they shoved inside that wood to make it stronger.

"These mother fuckers got some style." Yule laughed, tipping his cap back, while Koko whistled and clapped at the guards.

"Real shame they're knife-ears though." Koko retorted, and ran his fingers along his ears while grinning wolfishly at them. The Elven guards smirked at the clapping and gestures, and their eyes crinkled with humor. Some things just translate seamlessly between soldiers, no matter where they are from. The governor opened his arms in welcome to Yule and Koko, speaking to them in his native Elven language. The two commanders held their hands over their ears and shook their heads slightly. The Governor seemed crestfallen for a minute, before putting back on his smile and waving them over to a slightly smaller building near the Inn. The troop of volunteers walked behind their co-commanders, who walked beside the Governor, whose own guard walked behind him. The governor was pointing out things to Yule and Koko, who politely looked and made appreciative noises when he pointed out something particularly pretty, or some kind of architecture.

Yule looked over his shoulder when he had a chance, and saw Domino and a few other troopers offering the Elves the candy sides from their MREs. Chicks was also taking more selfies with a rather handsome guard, who stared in fascination at his own face.

"Hey, *hey*, stop it! Pss! Stop!." Yule whispered furiously, waving his hand as discreetly as he could. "Knock that shit off!"

The Humans snapped back into place, but as soon as Yule had turned around, one of the Elven guards held out his hand, and Domino plopped more brightly colored spheres into it. The walk to the governor's building was short and the crowd of Elves slowly followed the entire time, chattering to themselves. The interior of the building was lavish and spartan at the same time. There were no silken curtains or velvet cushions, but a lot of carpenter made furniture and simple chairs or seats. What made it lavish was the amount of work that went into the design and carvings of almost everything in the room. From the large desk that lay scattered with papers, to the little side table in the corner, everything had what seemed like hours upon hours of finely detailed and intricate carving done into every surface, except the areas that were supposed to be the seat or table top.

Only Yule and Koko walked inside, while the rest of the Humans waited outside and schmoozed with the crowd. If their goal was to build a good rapport with the locals, they were certainly making a solid crack at it. The governor sighed happily and clapped his hands together, raising his eyebrows at both of the Human commanders. The governor himself was a very slight man, but still had a bit of a pudgy appearance around the middle despite his Elvish nature. Yule noted that with a smile, seeing as to how no matter what race you seem to be, people in high places seem to fall victim to the spare tire of authority.

Yule held his hand out to the Elf, while pointing with his other hand at himself. "Yule. Im Yule."

The Elf took his hand and gave it a little shake, while chuckling happily that Yule had introduced himself without too much prompting. Yule then pointed at Koko.

"Im Koko." Koko said with a smile he put every ounce of charm he had into, and held out his hand. As soon as the Elf took his hand, the boyish delight of shaking hands with a mythical creature became like a mask on his face.

The elven governor placed both hands upon his chest, his ruffled cuffs shaking slightly as he did. "Respen! Al Alorey Respen!"

Yule and Koko pointed at the Elf, both saying "Respen." At the same time.

The Elf gestured at them. "Yool, Koko!"

Koko and Yule bowed slightly to him, and the Elf bowed back. After that, the group began to try and communicate via drawings while also showing the Governor the maps that they had brought with. The Governor began to slowly draw out the village's name, a script neither of the commanders could read, and also what they seemed to grow. The Elf governor drew out what looked like wheat, potatoes, a long looking carrot, and a few other kinds of produce that they couldn't draw a parallel to. The Elf then drew horses and furniture, which they both assumed was some kind of manufacturing clue to what they made here as well. The Elf then handed them the quill and the two of them did their best to scrawl their story: The cave, their world, who they were, what they were here for, etc. Their penmanship looked like a newborn writing with its mouth in comparison, but the Elven governor seemed to have gotten the general idea of who they were. They were at this for almost an hour when Yule peeked outside through the window, saw his troopers lounging around and playing with the local Elves, but the one thing he did see going on made him jerk open the window and bellow down below.

"Get that weapon out of her hands before I come down there and kick in your skull!"

Down below, a male Human had let a female Elf hold his rifle, showing her how it worked and what the ammunition looked like, something that Yule simply could not abide. There was some laughter behind Yule, and as he pulled his head away from the window and closed it, he turned to see Koko offering the Governor some retort coffee.

Yule sighed in exasperation. "Oh c'mon man we have no idea how they'll handle caffeine . . ."

Daylight began to just dip over the horizon when the formation of Humans began to walk back down the road on the way to Camp Kick Ass, a lot of them laden with the fruits of their visit. While Yule was furious with them for doing it, the volunteers had managed to somehow trade with the locals, and now their pockets or day packs were stuffed with bread, baked goods, and bottles of wine. Yule also had to double check and make sure all of them still had their weapons, as they had been showing the locals what they were and even let some of them hold the damn things even after Yule had yelled at them. They learned a lot from the Governor during their visit, as he had taken the time, between sips of coffee, to show Yule and Koko his own maps, which outlined all the other towns and cities that they were not aware of. Thankfully they were dropped off in a rather sparsely populated area, but it seemed the further North they went, the more races and cities that cropped up. So far, after the Elf drew them to the best of his ability, there were more elven varieties, some kind of beast people, something that had horns, and what appeared to be Orkish like races all over the place and were scattered around in some semblance of territories. What raised even more questions was that there didn't seem to be any humans at all, or at least the Elf didn't know of any.

Later on, when the troop were walking up the little dug out path to the first trench network, they were joined by one of the collection details Yule had set up before they had gone out to see the Elves.

"Got all your wormies and leafies?" Yule asked, taking off his cap and slapping it on his hand.

A male volunteer held up a jar and gave it a little wiggle, showing off a peeved looking insect inside of it. "Yes Mr.Yule! It's quite startling how similar yet different everything is around here."

The rest of the volunteers held up their own containers that had been sent through the Veil earlier with the mortar. Inside were tubes of soil samples, leaves taken from trees, earthworms, insects, and even a live mouse they had managed to capture. The mouse had some kind of rock ballad mohawk, but other than that looked like a regular mouse to Yule.

Yule thumped his pack down near his hooch while the others began sharing their goods with the other volunteers, regaling them with stories about the town and the Elves that lived there. Chicks was showing off her pictures as well, and had quite the crowd gathered around her. Gremlin walked up to Yule, patting him on the shoulder to get his attention. He turned and she handed him a stack of papers.

"Went as high as I could today. Seems this place is almost twice the size of our Earth if the numbers are correct." She said shortly, tapping the papers with her slender finger.

"Yay." Yule groaned, and slapped the papers down onto his little earth and wood field desk. He plopped down onto his hole home, leaned back onto his bundled wool blanket, and dug into the pile of folders next to him. He picked out one and flipped through it, running his finger down a timeline.

"Eggheads should be showing up here in about a month, but something tells me this schedule is worth only its weight as ass tissue."

The next morning, the next wave of volunteers arrived, a complement of sixty more men and women who brought more supplies in with them as well. These troopers arrived a full three weeks early, which did confirm the findings that Kole had pushed forward, and the new arrivals were shocked to hear that they were in fact early. They also brought with them a pair of U.S government scientists, who raged and threatened Yule with jail time for daring to come into contact with anything local.

"Think of the damage you could have done! You could have

inadvertently given them all kinds of infectious diseases from our planet! What if you caught some kind of rare Elf cold?!" The oak stalk of a man in front of Yule was fuming, while Yule bemusedly sucked on a cigar and blew smoke out of his nose. He took the scientist by the shoulders and slowly spun him until he was looking at the gigantic Dire Wolf pelt that adorned the makeshift roof over Gremlin's computing station, someone having stuck a stick in its giant maw so it stayed open, exposing the huge fangs for all to see.

"A cold is by far the least of this world's worries, Eggy."

After that, they tried to speak only to Koko, and would refuse to talk to Yule due to how he treated them. They collected their samples and sent them back through the Veil on an almost daily basis, and would constantly bemoan the living conditions of Fort Kick Ass. They were ignored by the volunteers, but the news told by the fresh volunteers from the other side of the Veil was not. According to them, the rest of the countries were putting an inordinate amount of pressure on the United States, which was causing the entire country to become jittery. It was also coming under harassment from the UN as well, which was making the internet fly with conspiracy theories so lavish, that it almost seemed like the Cold War had come back to haunt the minds of Americans. Due to this, the U.S military was bolstering every strategic location they could, and this was causing a major drain on manpower that they were wanting to send over to replace the volunteer Veil militia.

A few days later Veil time, news came that the samples taken from the new world were indicators of it being resource laden and would be a major power component for the U.S, which caused every country with a magical background to jump around and try to find their own hidden door to the Veil. All it took was some rock samples being mineral rich, and now every country had a target firmly painted on coal country. Hoping to keep their nest egg safe, the U.S military was giving the volunteers in the Veil even more toys to play with and fortify. A few more Veil days after the news came, the portal inside the cave became a flurry of activity as more weapons, supplies, and then a complement of ATVs and Dirt bikes arrived, the fuel to feed them strapped onto every surface a ratchet and bungee cord could hook.

'Living the Mad Max life' was a term used a lot over the next week and metal became the new standard of music that blared out of phones and digital stereos, right alongside the usuals. Things were going quite swimmingly, everything considered, as the Elves came to visit a few times, and were shown around the base, the scientists raving the entire while about how the volunteers were going to get them killed with Human bacteria. Despite Yule's protests, a few were even given demonstrations of the weapons, which perked up a lot of Elven ears to the power of these strange beings in even stranger clothing. Fuel and supplies came steadily, slowly allowing them to build a stockpile in their hill fort, until one day, the scientists that had come across the Veil decided to check back in person with their own command structure on the other side. They said they would be back within a day, and the Veil militia walked them in, made sure they went through safely, then waited.

The days passed . . . with no signs of the scientists. Even more days passed with no signs of the scientists and no more supplies, either. Yule was getting suspicious, as why would they suddenly halt sending them things they clearly needed, such as fuel, and ammo? A week went by, and finally there was activity from the Veil, the one guard inside running out to alert Yule to the coming arrivals. Yule, finally relieved the Eggs were going to come back with supplies, began walking towards the cave entrance with a few riflemen in tow to help unload whatever came through. It was however, with shock, that Yule stopped and gripped his pistol with his right hand. Walking out from the cave were ten men, all of which were wearing long coats and a blue helmet. On the front of which were two letters: U.N.

CHAPTER 4

THE OVERALL MOOD of the camp changed as if someone was watching hentai without their earbuds in at a funeral. All eyes were on the blue helmets that strode out from the mouth of the cave, all of them walking in a triangle like formation with the leader at the point. There was a kind of arrogance in their footfalls as they walked out into the main parade of the camp, and they looked around as if trying to find somebody in charge, despite Yule standing in the open in front of them flanked by ten riflemen himself. The one that appeared to be in command spoke aloud in Belgian accented English, casting his eyes around at all the Americans who stood watching, deathly silent with their weapons in their hands.

"Vich one of you is Yoole?"

Yule's hairs all stood on end as he took in the situation. There was absolutely no way that the U.S would allow U.N forces on its home soil. He was told as much, not only in person, but also in the files that he had been given before going on the other side of the Veil. What the hell was going down on the other side? He took the scuttlebutt of invasion just as it was, scuttlebutt, but now there was a group of U.N blue helmets looking at him right in the face. He idled forward, his boots crunching on the loose rock, and he rested his hand on his M9 in a false-relaxed manner as if that was where his hand had always found itself.

"Im Yule, co-commander of the United States Veil Militia. State your business." All the volunteer militia looked over at Yule, as he rarely ever spoke to his rank, and it was even rarer when he called himself co-commander. The command, however, was registered in the tone of his voice, and very quietly behind where he stood, a lot of rifles' safeties clicked and snapped to their firing positions.

"Ah, Mr.Yoole. I have been sent here by eh, your President and his commandants to relieve you of your duty. We have all come to an agreement and your services are no longer needed. We are all going to share this world for the betterment of all! We will need you to all surrender your weapons . . . of course, and proceed through the Veil, back home to America. Everyone is waiting for you."

The man smiled smugly the entire time as he said this, as if relishing the elevation he had above these rustics in command.

"Oh, is that right?" Yule slid his left foot out ever so slightly, taking a modified isosceles stance and cocked his right foot just enough so his balance was right. He could hear the hands of the riflemen beside him tightening on their weapons, the creaking strain of their slings on their shoulders, the subtle 'tick' of fingers laying across triggers.

Yule tilted his head down slightly, resting the sight man's head just under the rim of his patrol cap. "I was not under the impression . . . we were working with the U.N."

Yule's own grip tightened further with the ever so soft sound of flesh gripping metal. The riflemen beside him became rigid, unblinking, winding up their muscles as if they were a readied spring. On the hill above the cave entrance, in the heavy weapons positions that had been dug into it, he saw the cews lift up their weapons as silently as they could, and the barrels of multiple machine guns begin to slowly traverse onto the bundle of blue helmets below, the sun peaking and gleaming on the barrel brakes as they swung.

"Ah, like I have said, we came to an agreement, I have it all down on these documents here." The man held out a small bundle of papers. "Please set down your weapons, we are friends now. There is nothing to worry about."

Yule stepped forward to reach for the papers, holding out his left hand to take them. As soon as his hand gripped the papers, many things happened at once. First, something caught his eye from inside the cave to the Veil, movement and the dancing of a few shadows within the darkness, illuminated by the light that struggled to pierce the gloom. This sent the very nervous ambush squirrel inside his brain chittering and running around like mad, but what came next was something he could not miss. The wind seemed to blow hard for just a moment, and the long fronts of these blue helmets' coats were blown open just enough to see within. Inside the coat, he saw that the U.N soldiers wore fatigues, full battle rattle . . .

And had drum fed shotguns hanging at their sides.

Yule locked eyes with the commander of these troopers and stopped dead in his tracks, left hand gripping the papers. There was barely any space between them, just the stack of papers that each commander gripped. The blue helmet commander's eyes twitched down at Yule's right hand white knuckling his M9, and Yule's eyes flicked to the other man's hand cocking to reach into his own coat. When the wind died down as suddenly as it came, there was a breaths pause, before Yule jerked his arm right as the blue helmets swirled their coats open. There was a whirl of fabric, the crisp click of the M9 leaving its holster, and dozens of lungs sucking in breath all at once. Time churned to a crawl as blue helmets and militia roared to life, bringing their weapons up to bear on the enemy before them.

In a smooth motion, Yule drew his M9 level with the face of the man in front of him while never letting go of the papers with his left, the pistol's dingy white sights aligned right on his nose, and belched out a singular 9mm ball round. The full metal jacket round splacked wetly as it blew spatters of brain matter and bone onto the man standing behind the U.N. commander, blood and tissue littering their eyes, blinding them. The bullet kept going, being thrown off course by the amount of bone and meat and jerked in the air, colliding with the collar bone of the blinded blue helmet. The sudden death caught the blue helmets off guard, but not the Veil militia, who were all waiting for the first move. A sudden burst of automatic and rifle fire tore into the blue helmets, ripping their coats apart in a flurry of crimson and broken flesh, scattering their blood across the main formation area of the camp. Rounds snapped and cracked past Yule's face as the riflemen behind him saw the movement in the cave as well, and began pumping fire into the opening. Return fire was immediate, but brief, taking down just three militia during the exchange. Yule, Koko, and a small group of riflemen rushed the cave, firing at anything that moved and executing anything that was still breathing. Laying wait inside were a group of almost thirty blue helmets, Koko and Yule presuming their goal being to ambush the militia when they were disarmed, or attack anyone who didn't surrender their weapons.

Yule strode forward into the hazy darkness of the cave, blood spattered all over the walls and filling the interior with the coppery tang of death. He stepped over the cooling bodies of the blue helmets, gunshots ringing out behind him as militia found a few playing possum, and he kept walking until he came to the front of the Veil. The darkness pooled and ebbed in front of him. He had a mind to blow it, destroy it so no one could come through, but that would also mean none of the volunteers could ever go back home. If his assumptions were right, things were not as they were when they left and it was possible that they were being... invaded? Strong armed? He stood before the glooming portal for some time, his hand still holding his M9 as he stared into the pitched black of the Veil.

* * *

"Pack it up! All of it! We're moving out! Get those ATVs loaded with as much as they can haul and carry!" Yule bellowed, throwing his hastily repacked rucksack over his shoulders.

After the fallen militia were buried to the side of the camp, and their I.D. cards taken by Yule, he and Koko came to a hasty decision. They were going to split their forces, and in a mutual joke between them, called it Order 66. Sixty six riflemen for Yule, sixty six riflemen for Koko. They would do an even split on the crew serves, with Yule taking Betty and Koko taking his 81mm mortar, with a complement of 240bs and M249s between them. Same went for ammo, fuel, food, and vehicles. In the spanse of an hour, the entire camp was torn down and two Companies of militia moved out with a quickness. Koko's Zerg Company was going North West. Yule's Cosmoline Company was heading North East. Gremlin was going with Yule as well, but had taught someone else her guru ways with technology and sent them with Zerg Company, so the two companies had some way to keep in touch.

Koko and Yule stood in front of each other as the militia volunteers buzzed around them, and Yule looked down at the dead blue helmet commander. Koko looked down at him too, and gave the dead man's boot a light prod with his own.

"These guys would never be allowed to do this, right? Never in a million years would the states allow U.N forces to just set up shop." Koko murmured.

Yule twitched his lips and squatted down, the skeleton of his rucksack groaning as he did, and he picked up the small packet of papers still clutched in the dead man's hands. When he opened it past the cover page, he found the page to be blank. He furrowed his brows, and thumbed another page into view . . . and it was also blank. "Koko . . . look at this."

Koko leaned over Yule's shoulder, then leaned past it, shuffling through dozens of pages at once. Each and every page was blank, not even a single mark on them. The only page to have any ink on it at all was the cover page bearing the official looking markings of a government document and then nothing else at all.

Koko screwed up his face. "This reeks."

"Extremely. We need to get the fuck out of here." Yule said quickly, and tossed the papers on the ground before returning his rifle to his hands. Koko and Yule stood before each other as behind them, their companies were forming up and doing head counts, double checking that everyone was accounted for.

Yule nodded once, his eyes barely visible from under his patrol cap. "Good luck. I'll get in contact when I can."

Koko nodded back and held out his hand, his face never losing its confident smile. "We'll figure this out and be back home before you know it. Ride the Veil, Yule."

Yule blinked, then smiled back, reaching out and taking Koko's hand firmly. "Make 'em wail, Koko."

Those nearby looked to each other and within seconds, the same sentiments were being shared among every volunteer that would not be traveling in the same company. The Humans had come onto the Veil as a militia group, but they would be leaving it and heading out into the Veil world something else entirely. They would be leaving, and living, as Veil Riders. The two Companies left with speed, running and roaring into the night, while Fort Kick Ass was left behind, the bodies of the blue helmets left where they had fallen. The papers of the fallen commander scattered and fluttered across the now empty camp, tumbling and soaking into the bloodied mud that now stained the ground. The blue helmet commander's empty eyes stared up into the sky, the neat hole between his brows marking the first shot fired in anger at a humanoid by the militia group, which, ironically, was at another Human from their own realm. Whether or not they were correct, or righteous in this shot remained to be seen, but now only one thing was for certain in the mind of every man and woman in the Veil Riders; They may never be able to go back home after this, after the decision made at the mouth of the cave. For now, they would have to remain here on this side of the Veil.

Cosmoline Company began their march in standard infantry columns while the motorized vehicles trundled down the middle, hauling trailers filled with supplies. Dirt bikes raced ahead and scouted, then waited for the column to catch up before racing off again. The column took the direct path through the town, dirt bikes being as quiet as they could while rolling through and the townsfolk came out to see what the noise was, despite the time of night. The governor, still wearing his sleeping clothes, came out of his home and waved Yule over. While he spoke to Yule in his language and the Human had no hope of understanding it, Yule could tell he was asking what was wrong by the inflection and look on his face. Yule pulled out his notepad and drew a U.N helmet, then drew an X through it and pointed the way towards the cave. He drew a skull next to the helmet as well, and a rough drawing that implied the Elves should stab the blue helmets with their spears. After which he gave the governor one of the fallen Veil Rider's patches, still speckled in blood, and patted him on the shoulder before moving on with his troops. They burned out of the city as fast as they could without being too rude, and Yule used the pictures he took of the Elf's maps to direct their path, following a main roadway to the next village. If he remembered right, these should be Elves as well, according to what the governor had drawn before. He had to admit, having some kind of cell signal here would've been nice, but all they had were short distance radios. It wouldn't be long before they would leave comm range and no longer be in contact with Zerg Company.

Cosmoline Company humped along the road all the way through the night and well into the morning, before finally stopping to rest and let everyone take a breather. Chicks was groaning about not being able to ride on the ATVs, having to lug her heavy rifle by herself for miles, while Domino happily chewed on a first strike bar and just admired the scenery around them with little complaint. The company broke down into watches and pickets while the main body rested and checked on their vehicles. Yule poured over the had drawn notes on his phone and the maps Gremlin had printed out all that time before, and quickly came to the conclusion that the other village was almost a six-day walk. He sighed, thumping his head against his phone as he thought. They needed something to barter with in order to get food and water, maybe some horses, but they needed almost every damn thing on the trailers and ATVs. He supposed that, when the blue helmets finally take over the Camp and start trying to push their influence, they could start taking what they needed from whom they killed, but who knew how long that would be, or if that would even come to pass.

Yule looked up at his troopers sprawled out across the grass, napping or curled up on their rucksacks like heavily armed cats. He hoped this city ahead had some kind of magic users in it or a college of some sorts, just for the vain hope that someone could read his mind and know what he wanted. He let Cosmoline Company rest for several hours before calling them back onto their feet to continue marching. They continued this pattern for two more days, halting inside a heavily forested area that the road cut through due to slamming rains that came down in fat drops from the clouds above. With the trees, they were able to cast up tarps and tie them to the trunks and limbs for cover, and everyone hunkered down together to wait out the storm. Yule looked out into the misty trees and sulked; This was perfect coffee weather, but without that constant supply line coming in, he was having to ration his dehydrated coffee as much as he was able, but the urge to down a steaming retort came at every waking moment of the day. As he stared out into the trees and slowly wound a piece of grass around his finger, he heard Gremlin nearby arguing with another Rider.

"It doesn't make sense. If the planet is larger than earth, we should be squished. Like, trees and plants falling down and crushed"

"Maybe the core is made out of fairy dust, Gremlin"

"Fairy dust?! Fairy dust doesn't make tectonic plates move, create mountains, or even keep the atmosphere from floating away!"

The two continued to bicker at each other over the patter of the rain, Yule grinning to himself as he listened. He thought that there was no point in getting mad over something like this when walking through alien lands, as it was best to come to terms with what they had dealt with so far. Yule heard a rustle in the bushes a few feet from him, and rested his hand on his M9 while sighing. He waited, and after a few minutes a fox poked his head out from a nearby bush, its eyes looking at Yule curiously. The fox looked no different than a normal fox back home, and the only speakable difference was that its eyes had a slight luminescent glow to them. Yule leaned forward, rubbing his fingers together with a rasp of dry skin to try and beckon the fox closer.

"Hey buddy, but we all smell weird, huh?"

The fox jerked its head back inside the bush and Yule heard it run deeper in the woods. He laughed airily to no one in particular and leaned back against the ATV he was sitting next to. The rain continued to play a rhythmic beat on the tarps, and Yule stared out into the forest, his mind still mulling over the events that happened in front of the cave mouth. He hoped his instincts were correct, because if they weren't, there would be no way for him to go back to Earth without sitting in a cell for the rest of his life. That would be if there were actual words on the orders, something that still made his skin crawl every time he thought about it.

On the fourth day, they finally came into contact with something on the road. A small train of wagons was heading down the road towards the known Elf village, and all the Veil Riders pulled off the road to let them pass. The wagons however, stopped, and the language barrier made itself painfully apparent once again as the Elves tried to identify just who these strange people with short ears were. Yule was able to show them the pictures of the maps from the other village, and the Elves confirmed the Veil Riders were heading to the bigger city, tapping on the little marker and pointing down the road. Pantomiming became a sudden skillset that Yule had to master, as he tried to figure out just how to convey 'how fucking long till Im there' via hand signals and hand puppeting. Painfully, and awkwardly, he finally got his answer of 'a day or two', and they waved the wagons goodbye as they continued on their way. A lot of the Veil Riders were annoyed, as these Elves only had produce and raw materials, no booze or anything fun to trade, and it left them all in a dark mood as they trundled down the road.

As a matter of fact, none of the Veil Riders were in a good mood; a week of humping gear through the woods, getting rained on, having no way to bathe and water rationing had everyone in a sour mood. There was also the looming cloud of fuel running out, as the ATVs and dirt bikes chewed through gasoline far worse than they had thought, and they had but a few days of gasoline left to power the guzzling machines. The good news was that, the fuel getting burned up made a lot of the weight go away. Good news and bad news, all in the same knot. Time moved at a crawl, but he at least had a time frame now and he trudged on with his Company, plowing ahead into the unknown.

* * *

Yule slapped his filthy patrol cap on his knee and sighed ruefully. He wanted a bath. He didn't want to admit it, being an adamant shower man, but a good soak in warm water called to him like a seductive siren cooing across a coral filled shore. He was stirred from his soap-bubble daydream by another Elven child tugging on his pants, and he playfully slapped at their hand with his hat and blew a raspberry at them. The traffic was thicker here, and the Veil Riders moved completely off the road to give the locals their right of way. Naturally all traffic stopped when the Riders walked into the outskirts of the city, but they just trudged on towards the walls and the massive gate house. It seemed the main keep and inner city were protected by the walls, while the rest of the homes and other districts lay outside of the city. It all seemed very nice, actually, and must have been just what the middle ages looked like in Europe.

The Egg's would have loved this, Yule thought to himself, and thought back on the Eggs and how they never came back through the Veil to link back up. He hoped they were okay, but knew they were probably snatched up by whatever was waiting for them on the other side.

Yule looked up and saw that Kentucky was slowly trundling around in first gear with her ATV covered in Elven children. "Keep it tight guys, also don't let those kids on the ATVs, I don't want one accidently gettin' hurt on the damn things . . ."

The Veil Rider's moods picked up sharply with all these giggling children running around, who in turn jumped on and played with every single damn part of Yule's convoy. This brought it to a screeching halt a hundred yards from the gate house, having pulled off into a clearing nearby that was usually used for storing wagons. Veil Riders gave piggy back rides while in full combat kit, gave away their hoarded snacks, or let them play with their phones and take pictures of themselves while all parties laughed, enjoying the break in the gloom. Yule should have been mad, but he just couldn't muster it. He smiled, still annoyed, but smiling, while sitting on an ATV seat sideways and leaning forward on his knees. He cast his eyes along his men and women, then onto the district to his right.

It was a large city, so large that the living and working districts spilled out of the walls and onto the plains surrounding it, sprawling out in chaotic lanes and roads like the arteries of a heart. They had arrived the morning of, marching through the night just to finally get here and get it over with. Yule darkly hoped that maybe they would be slaughtered and their time here ended, but It seemed that was not the case. When they arrived, walking along the road in a column, the district they were approaching came out in force to greet them. They brought water and food to the ragged Veil Riders and their hospitality was suspiciously generous. Yule was on edge for the first hours of the morning... but didn't have the energy anymore after the women brought out jars of honey, jams, bread, and fruits for them to gnaw on. Yule himself drained half a jar of honey with a loaf of bread, leaving the rest of the better food to his troopers as well as the watered down wine.

Yule kept staring at the district, the Elves walking back and forth in their business and going about their routines. The normality of it all was almost culture shocking. They were just... normal folk, with long ears. They had their urges for food, wine, beer, entertainment, work, money... they were just like his Veil Riders in most ways.

Except the guns, the guns were a bit different.

He twisted in his seat and looked behind at the rear of the scattering of Veil Riders. He had told the crew serves to set up a rear firing screen, covering the tree line in case they were being followed. Instead of seeing a group of hardened killers watching their six, he saw a little girl sitting on the receiver of Betty, as a female Veil Rider teeter tottered her up and down.

"Christ alive..." Yule muttered, laughing dryly and plopped his cap on the little boy who kept bugging him. The boy sniffed it and made a horrified face, which made Yule bark out a genuine laugh instead.

It was okay, for now, to let his troopers relax for the moment. Yule took his hat back and plopped it back on his own head, while the little Elf boy rustled his hair to try and get the smell out of it. There was a sudden burst of chatter from near the district, and all the Veil Riders turned their heads to the noise. Yule hopped off the ATV and brought his K-2 around off his back and at the low ready, while all the other Veil Riders tucked children behind them and a chorus of weapon bolts slammed forward as everyone prepared for... whatever it was heading towards them from the nearby district. The Elves parted around a pack of figures walking through the crowd and Yule lowered his rifle, waving at the rest of the Veil Riders to lower theirs as well. He didn't see anything particularly scary, not even weapons, and instead sat back down on the ATV, pulling one of his few last cigars from his side pouch. As he fished out his MRE matches and struck one, his eyes followed the figure in the lead. This one didn't look like a governor or mayor, or king for that matter. It looked like . . . a hobo, to be frank, but everyone parted for her as she walked towards the Veil Riders.

"Make a lane." Yule muttered out, shaking the match to put it out and taking a drag from his cigar, puffing tiredly as he rubbed at his eyelid with his thumb. Yule finally saw her as she broke out from the crowd, and she smiled at the Veil Riders around her. She was barefoot and wearing a myriad of different colored articles of clothing. It was almost as if she picked out random ends and cut offs and sewed them together, creating an article of clothing from a pile of castaways. Tying it all together was a thick leather belt that held an armament of pouches, which held in place a kind of leather skirt that went down to her ankles. Yule then noticed she held a pair of leather sandals in her hand, and surmised that she must be enjoying the feeling of the grass on her feet. She was pretty slight in build, with a fresh and young looking face, the eyes of which sparkled with intelligence and excitement. Yule rolled his eyes as he puffed his cigar. These people appeared to not believe in bras, seeming to be proud of their cleavage if they had any, and this Elf was no different than the rest. He did his best to keep his view on her face, watching the eyes that bore into him from around their laugh lines.

The Elf woman placed her hands on her waist and looked at Yule with a big toothy smile, while he tipped up the bill of his hat and said 'Hello' with a gesture of his cigar. She pulled out an ornate looking necklace and held it to her forehead and tapped her foot patiently. The necklace seemed to be filled with some kind of amber and crimson liquid that refused to emulsify together for whatever reason, reminding him of a salad dressing.

Yule furrowed his brows and smiled awkwardly after a few minutes of silence passed, feeling a need to break the impasse. "Going to tell my fortune, long ear?"

The Elf closed her eyes, then opened them seconds later, a triumphant smile etched across her thin lips. "Only if you give me this 'coffee' I have heard about." Her voice was light and playful, and the known words flowing out of it was a welcomed thing to Yule's ears.

He closed his eyes, cocked his head ever so slightly, then opened them again, before he thrust up his arms, clenching his cigar in his teeth and shouting to the sky in true joy. "A magician! Thank you so much! I am so tired of pantomiming, I'm so bad at it . . ."

The Elf just giggled and waved at the Elves behind her to come forth.

CHAPTER 5

T**HE DELUGE OF** questions that came rushing at Yule from the Elf woman that day was enough to make his head spin, but it spun a little less with sleep at one of the local Inns and a belly full of food that didn't come dehydrated or out of a pouch. Yule had a pang go through his chest during breakfast when he thought of the Eggs, and how they would probably begin to rant and rave about him eating fantasy bacon and oatmeal. Whether they were okay or not, he did not know, and that lack of information really bugged him. He looked up while chewing on a particularly meaty egg white and surveyed the dining area of the Inn and the Veil Riders scattered within. The Sparkling Unicorn was going above and beyond the call of hospitality when the sorceress announced they were all guests of the city, and was hosting them for free.

Yule had an idea that it had something to do with their Unit patch, but was more than happy to accept the bed and free chow. What he did not like was the lack of plumbing, something that every Veil Rider was coming to grips with. Pooing in a hole in the woods is one thing, having a special pot for your deposits was another. Then knowing you had to carry your own special soup down to a special hole to dump it was a true otherworldly experience. Yule drummed up some NCOs for his Veil Riders and told them to 'Mind the Inn' while he waited outside for the sorceress. She was going to take him in for questioning again in a more formal setting, this time about the perceived threats coming through the Veil and about his own purpose here.

He stood by the front of the Inn, nodding and waving to the Elves around him. Here and there, he saw some of the other races going about their day on the street or working nearby. There were 'free folk' here, a mixed melody of Orcs, Dwarves, Giant-types, Folks with strange horns on their heads, and even a few Harpies clicked their way here and there along the road, busily speaking to their friends in their short, chirpy language.

"I wonder how smug that Monmusu guy will be when he learns he was right about Harpies." Yule said aloud to himself, idly chewing on a piece of what tasted a lot like rye bread.

"Who is Monmusu?" The sorceress asked, having stalked her way behind him from a hidden alleyway beside the Inn. She leaned forward and poked her head around the corner, spooking the absolute hell out of Yule, who swatted at the hair around her with his hands, sending his bread spiraling into the street.

The mohawked rat that grabbed it squeaked, quite pleased with itself.

"Fucks sakes don't do that! The last thing I want to do is draw on accident and send people scatterin'!"

The sorceress just giggled and bid Yule good morning. The two made their way through the busy street towards a larger manor on the inside of the city walls. They had requested Yule come alone to ask questions, and in return his Company was going to stay on the city's dime. This was, naturally, sketchy, and Yule had multiple knives in his boots and his M9 in his holster, while leaving his K2 behind with an NCO for safe keeping. The Elf woman kept insisting on holding his hand to make sure he didn't get lost, reaching over for it or trying to sneakily get a hold of his fingers. Yule wasn't for it in case she tried to take over his mind or something and always yoinked his hand away, until he finally just shoved his hands in his pockets. Not wanting to be out maneuvered and admit defeat, she hooked a finger in one of his belt loops, both of them satisfied with the silent negotiation. The walk to the meeting location went smoothly, except for the gawking, and Yule was ushered inside to a larger group of Elves along with a few other races mixed in.

He expected this, but a few of the races the governor had described were not present. The fancier, moodier Elves that, as he learned, resided to the south of the Veil did not have any representatives here in the city. There were however Valley Elves, Dwarves, and a few of the horned people there. Yule stood in front of them, staring at the little collection of fantastical creatures in the room. There was a kind of . . . agreed pause, as they let Yule just gaze at them, his eyes falling on one, then the other, in a polite progression of recognition.

Yule turned to the wizardess with an awkward smile on his face. "Never thought I'd see something like this. You guys are the beings . . . of our stories. Things that were told to us as children, subjects of our fantasy books . . . Yet here you are. Right in front of me. Can I shake the Dwarf's hand? Im curious how strong their grip is."

The sorceress snorted with laughter, and he audibly heard her switch into the Dwarven language, which sounded a lot like Norwegian or Icelandic, but he didn't really hear any words he understood. The Dwarf listened to her curiously, then barked out in his own laughter, slapping his knees happily before holding out his huge vice grip of a hand to Yule. Yule took it and quickly learned that Dwarves could probably weld metal together with just a pinch of their pointer and forefinger.

After this, Yule took a moment to just indulge himself, and the Elven woman was able to convince the other race ambassadors to let him do so. He was allowed to lightly touch the tip of the horned races head spikes in trade for letting one of the women play with his fingers, checking out Yule's nails and finger pads. The other horned race ambassador was a male and wanted to look at Yule's boots and uniform, rubbing the cloth between his fingers and running his nail lightly on the scuffed black leather of Yule's boots. One of the horned races were called Onii, a tall and muscular race that appeared to be craftsfolk and weavers. The others were called Brimtouched, which to Yule, looked more like regular Humans, but just had slightly different shades of skin and long horns that came out from their skulls, and with no horns, seemed to be the same. The Dwarf wanted to, naturally, look at Yule's pistol. Yule cleared it, handed it to the Dwarf, and then the ejected round of 9mm. The Dwarf was busily taking the M9 apart and looking at the various pieces when Yule looked over at the Elven sorceress.

"Why am I here? You didn't bring me here to play with my fingers and house my troopers for free without something in return."

The Elf nodded once and began to walk behind the row of ambassadors, of which the Dwarf was admiring the spring of the pistol, holding it up to the light. "This is true. You and your people are the first to ever come through the Queen's Gate in any real number."

Yule furrowed his brows. "First in any real number?"

"Some of you come through, every once in a while. I don't think they mean to. Their clothes are always different, different skin colors, different eye colors, different languages spoken by them. It appears the Queen's Gate has gotten bored of its lack of use, in all these years since its creation, and has been going about its own business." The Elf pulled out an old tome and opened it, the spine cracking from age. All the ambassadors looked up to her and watched her flip through the pages.

"You have been tracked, all this time, the little instances of when your people have survived the first few minutes from the Gate. Very precious few have made it to Sanrion or another village. The only instance before you being a group of men who said they got lost, hiking. They said they were 'Deutsche', and served under a 'Maximillian'."

Yule blanched. How on Earth could landsknechts be the most recent example of Humans arriving? Have there been more but just died too quickly to the elements? He cleared his throat and folded his arms. "How . . . long ago was this?"

The Elf looked down at the book in her hands. "Mmm . . . appears this was recorded roughly one hundred and ten or so years ago, if my math is correct."

Yule reeled, reacting bodily to the news and taking a few steps backwards, his arms unfolding and coming out before him. Yules' mind raced; That was over 600 or so years ago when the Landsknechts worked under Maximilian, what kind of worm hole madness is going on over here?

Yule turned back to the Elf, placing his hands together and pointing them at her. "They were soldiers. They functioned roughly 600 years ago, from our time. What the hell is going on with this place?"

The Elf looked to the other ambassadors and translated what Yule said, and one of the horned folk, a female Onii, spoke up. Her voice was almost a seductive purr as she moved her hands in different directions of each other, as if she were holding a ball that was split down the middle, and both sides rotated in opposite directions. The two spoke back and forth for a few minutes and the Elf turned back to Yule.

However, when she spoke to Yule, he just heard the same language. Yule furrowed his brows and tapped his ear a few times to show he couldn't hear what she was saying. The Elf sighed, like her remote control stopped working during channel surfing, and pulled out a knife from the insides of her robes. It was then that Yule remembered the Dwarf was still playing with the pieces of his pistol, and suddenly he was worrying about two things rather than just one.

She pulled a bottle from one of her pouches and poured a few drops into the little necklace she held near her head when she spoke, but then made a slice on her finger with the knife, squeezing the digit so a steady stream of blood flowed into the necklace. Yule stared, one eyebrow raised while the other furrowed wildly at what she was doing. However, from how she acted with such a nonchalant attitude, Yule assumed that she must do this all the time. The Elf licked her finger then stuck it in her mouth while shaking the necklace in her other hand, and when she was satisfied the mixture was shaken enough, she held it back near her forehead and continued talking to Yule. He however held up his hand. She looked surprised and raised her eyebrows in response.

Yule bobbed his head forward slightly, then turned up his hands in a questioning motion. "Are you gonna tell me what the fuck all that was about?"

"What, the bloody finger?"

"Yes I am referring to you cutting your finger with a *knife*."

"I have to keep the Translation Amulet fueled for it to work."

"With blood!?" Yule said, incredulous, and looked from the Elf, to the other beings, and held out his hands in a universal sign of 'is she for real with this shit?'

The Dwarf had broken down every part of his M9 by this time and was studying the trigger mechanism, ignoring everything else in the room, while the other Elves and the horned folk just shrugged, not knowing what Yule just said.

The Elf however just giggled, and patted Yule on the shoulder. "This is how magic works here. You either need Dwarven Agni Umingi," The Dwarf held up his fist in a cheers type motion while squinting at the extractor of the M9, "Or you need good quality blood to power magical artifacts or cast spells of power."

Yule was dumbfounded, eyes held wide at her as she continued.

"Anyway, Miss Yui here said her people, the Onii, have been working with the Brimtouched, and have a theory that our worlds work on different planes, like two wheels side by side. Yours spins faster than ours, causing time to stretch between the two sides of the gate. When the two sides of the gate are extremely close, time is even on each side. But as your side begins to move past, time stretches, yours going forward and leaving ours behind until it aligns again. Those who wander through the Veil during the big stretches are wandering in from different times unrelated to our own, your own time speeding past us and leaving us behind. For the longest time, we were ahead of you in technologye, when your people were..."

She flipped through the pages, clicking her tongue as he did.

"... But simple creatures wrapped in furs and wielding sharpened sticks. But your world, your time... you are outpacing us. Extremely quickly. And for the first time, the Veil has been big enough that a whole village of your kind has come through at once. And now, you're telling us that more of you, with bad intentions, will be coming through?"

Yule tightened his lips, deep in thought. All of their eyes were on him as his mind whirled and roared with the gears of his brain gnashing together. Time is going to race by on their side of the world compared to this one. People are going to age faster over there, and the longer they stay here, the faster their world is going to pull away and stretch time like a fresh mozzarella stick. He and Koko had split their forces and fled away from the Veil to get space. But now... now that means they ran from the only way to get back into their world and get back to their families before they aged to the point of no return. Yule knew that none of his Veil Riders had husbands or wives, but they still had families. Then there was the issue of the Blue Helmets being on American soil, and what they may do next.

Yule ran his hand from his mustache down to the end of his beard, staring at the ground. He needed to get back to his Veil Riders and break the news. They still had their markers, and those who wanted to would be able to get back home, maybe. Yule looked up from his thoughts, and locked eyes with those before him.

"Let me tell you why you need to be careful about my people. My Veil Riders and I did not come here in the beginning with good intentions. My world... is a hungry place, and you guys are more or less an all-you-can-eat buffet. Let me tell you, why Im going to stay, and why some of my people may need to go back home. Let me tell you... about what may come."

* * *

Some hours later, Yule opened the door to the Sparkling Unicorn and skulked in, closing the door behind him to keep the deafening cacophony inside from stunning those outside. Inside, the Veil Riders were roaring and shaking their mugs at some bard that was singing and dancing about on a small stage, and Yule spied one of those translation amulets strapped on . . . her forehead? Yule assumed she was one of the Brimtouched judging from the rear anchored horns on her head, and her slitted pupils were sparked with the delight that all entertainers had as they got high from the crowd's reaction. She danced and sang on the stage, the amulet changing her words to American English, spinning a yarn about a dragon who fell in love with a blind Dwarf, and his Veil Riders were drunk enough to cheer at anything at this point. Yule waved his NCOs over, taking his K2 back and slinging it over his shoulder, before pulling them in close.

"Company Meeting in the morning. I have bad news and weird news, and we need to get word to Zerg Company in the morning. Ask Gremlin if she knows a way. Make sure the lads don't get taken to bed by that prancing demon on stage. Good night."

Yule clapped them on the shoulders, then turned away, thumping up the stairs to the room he was given by the Inn. He closed the door behind him, kicked the door stopper in to jam it shut, and began to get ready for bed. It was funny how the things one learns playing dungeons and dragons can come in handy, when not on Earth. He was mentally fried, and rubbed his palms under his eyes as he sighed heavily.

"We were so gung ho and just ran into the unknown . . . what have I gotten us into, I wonder." Yule said with a sigh, and stared out the window into the dancing lights of the city, quietly ringing his hands as his thoughts buzzed and sparked in his brain.

The next morning, as all the Veil Riders gathered groggily into the main room of the Sparkling Unicorn to hear what Yule had to say, the Elven barmaids were making sure to pass around mugs of water and oatmeal to help with their throbbing heads. There was also an issue of one of the female Veil Riders coming down later than the rest, having the collar of her shirt folded up and desperately trying to pat her hair down. Yule looked from her, then to his NCOs.

The NCO that caught Yule's eye pulled the spoon from his mouth, and said one word around his full cheek of oatmeal. "Bard."

"You did only say lads y'know." Piped up another, who then pointed to the NCO who the female Veil Rider was under.

Yule stared at him, and the NCO at least had the decency to cough into his fist and try to look somewhere else besides Yule or the female Veil Rider with the bite marks all over her neck and collarbones. Yule had to take a few minutes to suppress his frustrated anger, but began to finally talk about his concerns a little time after. He explained their situation, and the room sobered quickly when the implications of the time movements became apparent. When Yule got to the part about the world being separate and being two different time lengths, you could hear a pin drop from the next building over. Yule explained all that he could, and sat down tiredly in a chair before his men and women.

"I won't demand you stay. For all I know, our homes are in danger, and we are launching forward in time by years... If you want to go, you have your markers. I'll personally make sure you get back to the Veil and on the other side myself. I know my decision, as it is," Yule pulled off his obsidian marker stone, and held it aloft before him, "My wife is dead, my daughter is grown up and living in Montana on the farm. She's safe. She also knows what I told her about me leaving. She knows the deal. I'll be here till whatever end comes, to lead you folk, and make sure you get what you need. Even If it costs me my soul. I have a bad feeling about what is going to come next. You all saw those papers... they were blank. They were going to hand me blank orders, and for what?"

Yule looked at the marker stone, then set it down on the table in front of him.

"Something is coming from the other side of the Veil, and it reeks. I'm going to stay and see just what that might be, but you don't have to stay with me. Raise your hand if you want to ride the Veil back stateside. There's nothing wrong with saying you want to."

A creak from Yule's chair filled the quiet room as he leaned forward and interlocked his fingers, resting them on top of the marker that lay on the table. Seconds ticked by as the Veil Riders of Cosmoline Company became lost in thought, many of them sliding their hands into their armor or battle jackets to pull out their own obsidian marker, the only way home. Their eyes fell on many things: The markers, the floor, their own boots, some had small pictures in their wallets or tucked away in a pocket, but all of them had their minds working around one thought; the chance of a lifetime. Every Veil Rider here, including Yule, had signed an insurance policy. If they died, whomever they put down on the paperwork would get a lot of money, more than enough money to set them up for life. Naturally none of them wanted to die, and they were there when the blank orders were discovered. This was not

THE VEIL RIDERS

going to be some quick in and out twenty minute adventure... and something did in fact, reek. Now, Yule had laid out the heavy shit, that time was not playing by the rules they knew on Earth. But this new information, that time was not only playing by its own rules, but also putting the gas pedal down and slinging their families into the future, was something they did not count on.

Seconds... Minutes... Time ticked on in silence as sixty six Veil Riders, and Yule, sat in the Sparkling Unicorn. The Elven barmaids were looking at each other worriedly, as even though they didn't know the language, the vibe seeping from those in the dining area was like a cloud that hung over the place. After ten minutes, Chicks was the first to stand, and her boots thudded softly as she stepped towards Yule, her marker held to her chest with both hands.

Yule looked up at her, smiling sadly with his whole face as she came to a stop in front of him. "I can get some Riders together and get you back within a fe-" Yule started, but his voice slowly drawled away as Chicks set down her marker next to his. Yule looked down at her marker laying near his own, then back up sharply at Chicks face. She smiled back, and he could see a kind of guilty sadness welling up in her eyes.

Her voice broke a bit as she began to speak, but she pulled herself up in a determined posture and cleared her throat. "Pretty Elf boys and Fairies, what's a girl not to like?"

Yule watched her walk away back towards her chair, and he looked down at the two markers, his fingers reaching over and touching Chick's. He heard multiple chairs skirt on the wooden floor boards as they were pushed back and away from the tables, and more thuds of boots echoed their way towards Yule. One by one, every Veil Rider dropped their marker stone onto the pile where Chicks had first laid hers. When everyone had dropped their marker and went back to their seat, he looked up and swept his gaze slowly from one side of the room to the other, etching every face into his memory, and the name to go along with it. All of his Veil Riders were standing with their feet together at attention in front of Yule, who slowly rose from his chair, the clink of the markers tinkling as he gathered them all in his left fist.

"All of you called the bet. Now we're all in." Yule pulled out a roll of 500mph tape and wrapped the olive drab green strips around and around the markers, until just the very bottoms of them poked out. There was a hook on the roof for a lantern, and he tied the tangled of neck bands around the hook after getting on top of a table. The markers hung there like a bundle of herbs made of stone, and Yule jumped down onto the wooden boards with a loud romp of rubber boot soles.

He turned and looked at his Veil Riders, and pulled out a little scroll of paper. "Our new friends needed someone to solve a little problem. I told them I knew just the people for the job."

The roar from the Veil Riders shook the windows of the Sparkling Unicorn.

CHAPTER 6

Yule blinked the rain out of his eyes as beads of water defied the laws of common sense, tracing down the bottom of his bill to drip onto his face. Cosmoline Company's 1st Dragoons were stretched out in a complex ambush, watching over a road that led to the city of Imlnoris, roughly three days ride away. The rain tinked off of a rifle here, an M249 there, but the deafening roar of falling water drowned out whatever noise was out beyond the trees that lined the road. Yule lifted his head ever so slightly to check his Veil Riders and heard Yethis beside him shift, looking up at him with questioning eyes. He placed his finger on his lips as the sound of rumbling engines grew in the distance.

1 month prior

Cosmoline Company had been dispatched by the city council of Imlnoris, under the directive of the King that ran the joint, to clear out a Goblin infestation in a system of caves, which went quickly due to the miracle of fragmentation grenades. When they had gotten back to the city, Yule was granted the prize of not only a place that welcomes his troopers with open arms, but also a Translation Amulet, which needed blood in order to work. A rather eager female Valley Elf named Yethis had inserted herself into the Company happily, and was to be Yule's blood supply. She was a chipper sort, her face soft, kind, and framed nicely by her straw-bale colored hair, which she usually wore in a long braid. With her lightly freckled face, happy amber eyes and full hips, she was naturally adopted quite readily into the Company. Those in the Company doted on her as if she were a new family member, going out of their way to make her feel welcomed... except for Yule and Gremlin. Gremlin believed her to be annoying, finding herself furious on multiple mornings when she would wake up to find Yethis had braided her hair as she slept. Yule thought her unwarranted affection draining, and found himself having to fight her to get his own food or do his own laundry. When it came to the Amulet, he was warned not to use his own blood, as it could break the enchantment that was placed upon it, so Yule had to rely on this younger looking Elf girl to cut herself open and drain her own original recipe into the little bottle. He didn't gel with the idea, to be frank, but he took their warning to heart. This brought his troop count to sixty seven, the ladies of Cosmoline Company having a lovely time rigging out the Elf in their spare uniforms and found her a side arm to use as well. Yethis could also make use of healing magic, which caused a lot of the Veil Riders to breathe easy for a change in case of booboo's and bangbang holes. Additionally, Gremlin managed to get in touch with Zerg Company, but not in the way she thought she would.

Gremlin had run out of ways to power her drones reliably, since the batteries took so long to charge on the solar charger, and there was no fuel to spare for the generators. To get around this, Gremlin came into negotiations with the Harpies that lived in the city of Imlnoris. With a bit of coin, she managed to work out a deal with them to carry messages between Zerg Company and Cosmoline Company. For the first time in a long time, Koko and Yule had to write reports to each other by hand. A Harpy would then take the letter and fly off with it, being dubbed the Pump-a-Rum Delivery Service by the Veil Riders. The Harpies, for one reason or another, took to the name with pride, and would eagerly cry out 'Pump-a-Rum!' when they swooped down to land nearby and deliver their packages or letters.

Zerg Company had made their way to Artry, a mixed town much like Imlnoris; however they had chosen to make a small encampment on the outside of the city, while Cosmoline company had made their base more or less inside the Sparkling Unicorn. Koko convinced a few druids to help him move earth around after seeing them practicing the craft one morning, in which the Veil Riders of Zerg Company made a Star Fort, ringed with pointed timbers, and had dubbed it 'Fort Kick Ass: Return of the Zerg'. The locals of Artry adored both Koko and his Riders due to their naturally charismatic nature and the Terrans had taken to teaching the locals how to make soap.

While reading the report on the day it arrived, Yule had read the bit about the soap and blinked to himself a few times. "That's . . . actually a pretty good idea. Hey Kole! Do you know how to make soap?!"

The slice of life enjoyment changed sharply when a Harpy that had been sent on a special mission returned to Yule directly, blood streaming down his shoulder from what looked like bird shot. Cosmoline Company bristled at the knowledge that someone had tried to shoot down their little spy Harpy, but it didn't take a huge leap of brain power to figure out who it was.

Their little spy was a Sparrow Harpy who introduced himself as 'Chikily', answering the call when Yule requested a flyer with a bit of a daredevil in their heart. Chikily was tasked with watching over the Veil and keeping track of what was spewed out of it, and had been coming back and forth with reports of personnel movements, resources being brought in or taken out and anything else of note. What had gotten Chikily shot was his attempts to get close enough and talk to some of the local Valley Elves that were taken from the town just outside the Veil. A small contingent of them had been marched up to the small base the blue helmets had built up around the Veil, and were quickly put to work building look out towers, buildings and doing other general labor. Chikily then had seen the Southern Elves strutting around the compound and hurling abuse at the Valley Elves, which is what finally drove him to dive down and try to speak to them.

"Chikily see many Valley Elf digging, building, carving wood. Valley Elfs all look sad, while High Elfs preen and sometimes smack other Elfs with sticks. Blue hats also building things. They put together wagons with big wheels that growl like monsters. Little Veil village much big now, stretching out and swallowing land around cave. Many people now, and Elves."

Chikily grimaced as Jakob, or Gruesome as the rest called him, dug out the pellets from his shoulder. Gruesome was a former Navy Corpsman with a scarred face from an IED that retired him. When Gruesome would pluck a little ball of steel out, Yethis would touch the wound and heal it.

"Chikily try to talk to Valley Elfs. They sad, scared, told to come or bad things happen. They sleep outside of the fort, on grass. Blue hats see Chikily, shout at Chiklily, then shoot when Chikily fly away"

Yule patted Chikily's head, and then gave his cheek a soft pinch. "You done good Chikily, thank you. Pump-a-Rum should be proud of such a brave Sparrow-Harpy like you."

Chikily's chest swelled with pride and fire as he grinned up at Yule, and Yule grinned back before looking over at his NCOs. Domino, who had been promoted to such a Veil Rider rank, flicked a coin off his thumb with a crisp cling while grinning from ear to ear. Yule clapped his hands together, and Domino caught his coin, the rest of the NCOs sitting up and rolling their shoulders.

"No stick wielding goblinoids this time. There's something going on at the Veil and there are apparently Southern Elves already acting chummy with the Humans coming through. I told you this whole thing reeks. Get some men together, we're going to go take a look."

Cosmoline company whirled into motion as everyone loaded themselves out to the gills with the ammunition they could spare; there were shortages, but there was some help from the special magics that whirled around this realm. The Dwarves in particular had a special kind of sack that could duplicate certain things inside of it, which once discovered, was immediately put to work. Sack was a generous term, though, as it was more like a small coin purse. Getting back ammo was a slow and tedious process as it took almost a week for the complex chemistry of the bullet to be reproduced. They had however pioneered the science of lubricants, which was fantastic news for the health of Cosmoline Company's weapons.

A message was sent to Zerg Company, carried defiantly by Chikily, while Yule hired a female Hawk-Harpy named Airis to stick with them to carry messages. When every Rider had their gear in order and the throng was mustered, all of the Company elements moved out of the city. This time they had proper wagons and horses, something a lot of the Veil Riders highly enjoyed, including Yule. Like Yule, a lot of the men and women of Cosmoline Company were from the South or Midwest, and grew up learning how to ride horses. Thirty of the Veil Riders were on horseback, the rest driving or riding in wagons, allowing them to have a wing of Dragoons with Yule heading them. Saddles were modified for the carrying of Betty and the other machine guns, but other than that, they were a force that could ride out, deploy, and ambush in quick succession.

That same wing of Dragoons lay out in the sopping wet grass now, watching down the road that ran from Sanrion to Imlnoris. Yethis looked to Yule, and very slowly raised her head from the ground cover he and her lay behind.

"What is it?" She asked timidly, her voice tight with excitement and fear.

"Vehicles, keep your head down." Yule grabbed her shirt collar with a finger and jerked her head down. They had been on the way to the Veil when Airis had seen 'little boxes' moving down the road, causing Yule to deploy his men and women in a hasty ambush position, unsure of what could be coming at them. He nodded to Domino across the road in the other ambush position and held up his hand in front of his face, then pointing to Domino.

"Do you see?"

Domino gripped his hat brim.

"I See."

Yule made a fist and moved it from side to side, then pointed to his eye.

"Vehicles, you see?"

Domino gave him a thumbs up, held up his three middle fingers, then made an L shape with his hand.

"I see. Six trucks."

Yule made a trigger pull action with his hand, then pointed to his eye again.

"You see infantry?"

Domino again gave him a thumbs up, held up an 'O' shape with his fist, then another one next to it. He thin made an L shape with his pointer finger and thumb, and held it as high as he dared.

"I see infantry. Twenty Rifles."

Yule held up an 'okay' hand gesture at him, then pointed at his ear, and then at himself.

"Listen for me."

Domino nodded, hunkered down in his cover,and looked down his scope. Chicks was next to him, and she slowly chewed a local gum replacement as she stared down her optics.

Yule turned to Yethis, speaking in a hushed voice as the trucks drew closer, placing his chest against her head so the amulet would activate. "Stay low, don't scream. It's going to get very loud, and a lot of people are going to die."

Yethis looked at him wide eyed before he threw the netting over her to conceal her, then he began to low crawl along the side of the road's brush line to the main battery of 240b's and Betty, which stared straight down the road from the curve they lay on.

The gunners stared hawkishly down their sights or optics at the oncoming tan Humvees that had come into view, an overly large blue U.N spray painted on the hoods. Yule thought that odd, and creepy, that they were using U.S military hardware and putting such blatant symbols on the hood, but shook the idea from his mind as he crawled up next to his heavy hitters. "Turn that first truck into swiss cheese with Betty, ding anyone running for it with the 240s."

They nodded, and Yule crawled on to the rest of the Veil Riders hiding in shallow fighting holes and obscured from sight along the brush line. "Bettys going to take the first truck. Shoot to kill, any prisoners are just a bonus." Yule clapped Kole on the shoulder as he stepped over him at a low hunch, his boots thudding soppily on the standing water that lay about, and knelt against a wide tree, making sure that he could see Domino on the other side.

His K2's buttstock was in his shoulder at a low ready as he slowly leaned his head around the edge of the tree trunk, his hat covered with netting and leaves. He could see the lead Humvee was about fifty yards away, the diesel engine growling as it trundled along at low speeds due to the road being so worn and potholed. Yule looked at Domino, told him to hold fire. He pointed at a smaller male Veil Rider and gave him a thumbs up. Yule had planned for a trooper to run across the road in order to gauge what the reaction would be from the enemy. If they stopped, there may be a time for talking. If they opened fire, there would be no talking at all. At the signal, the trooper stood and ran across the road, his boots splashing loudly in the standing water. The oncoming vehicles did not stop, and instead of such, the lead vehicle's gunner let loose a spray of bullets that kicked up water and chased the Veil Rider across the road. The trooper dove into the safety of the brush, and Yule then looked at Betty's gunners, making a chopping motion with his hand.

There was a pause, a click, then Betty thumped into action, sending .50 caliber rounds shredding down the road and into the front of the lead truck. The concussion from her muzzle sent water flying when a round left the barrel, and steam began to slowly rise from her receiver as water made contact with the heated metal. Tracers from her barrel hissed and danced through the air, steel sparking harshly as the burning round burrowed its way inside the vehicle. The lead truck's pristine front window suddenly had a cluster of holes in it as her aim traversed from high left to low right, the driver being turned into a blood covered sponge as soon as three rounds made contact with him. His window was cracked to let a bit of air in, and crimson spray flew out of it and down onto the road thickly.

Yule noticed with curiosity, as he lifted his K2 and shot the gunner in the chest from near point blank range, that there were an awful lot of people in the Humvee. He could tell this from the amount of blood that came pouring out from the bottoms of the light doors that they had on it, there being gaps here and there, and it spilled out onto the road as if it were a can of cherry juice being shot with BB guns. The gunner screamed from the round bursting out the back of his chest, and lurched forward to grab the 240b mounted to the gunner ring and get it back to firing. Domino stood up sharply and shot once, the entire top skull of the man spattering onto the back of the rear hatch cover, and he thudded lifelessly on top of the machine gun. Chicks fired as well, and another gunner in a middle truck screamed out in horror as his heart was turned to mush and blown out of his own shoulder blade.

Betty chunked out a few more rounds and went quiet and soldiers from the other Humvees began to spill out, a scattering of accents flying to the air as they all tried to fall out into the ruts off the side of the road for cover. It was when they were all in the open that the Veil Rider's own 240b's thundered in challenge of their big sister, joined by the rhythmic staccato of the rifles cutting men and women down left and right.

WWII, Korean, Vietnam, and Gulf War rifles barked to life and shed blood once again, after being at rest for so long. Extractors sang as brass flew through the air, their payloads expended into the bodies or doors of the enemy before them. Angry lead shot buzzed and hissed through the air before thudding into flesh and bone, the cries of the stricken and dying echoing off the trees along with the reports of gunfire. Bodies crumpled onto the rain soaked road as they were hit mid step, splashing down onto the wells of water and puddles. The lead truck, never being put into park or the brake applied, continued to roll forward, turning slightly as it began to rumble towards the ambush lines. Yule stepped forward and signaled for the rest of the rifles to move up, waving his hand side to side to tell the machine guns to cease fire. As the Veil Riders mopped up anyone who kept fighting, Yule opened the door to the lead truck, walking along with it as he reached over to turn the engine selector off. He looked at the driver, who was missing large chunks of meat from his torso, and wrinkled his nose slightly.

"Gross."

Yule leaned in further as the crack and pop of a rifle here and there echoed outside and saw that there were the remains of an officer sitting in the passenger seat, along with a roll of papers in the Valley Elf language still clutched in his blood stained hands. The Humvee was also completely packed, Yule seeing that some bodies actually lay dead in the rear compartment or slumped over the middle divider where the dead gunner's feet dangled. He snatched the scrolls up, spat on the ventilated corpse of the officer and leaned out of the riddled vehicle.

Yethis ran up beside him, sputtering in her language, and Yule dragged out the amulet, touching it to his temple.

"Hurt?! Are you hurt?!" She cried, checking his clothing as if she expected him to be full of holes.

Yule chuckled. "Im fine Yethis, go check on the others."

Yethis sped off, yelling and waving her hands at the other Veil Riders. Gremlin and Domino came trotting up to him, and the three walked down the road towards the other body covered Humvees.

"One survivor, German female. She took a 5.56 to the leg and went down, then hid behind the wheels of her truck." Domino pointed her out, currently pinned to the ground with a knee in her back and getting her hands tied with rope.

"Lots of fuel in these heaps." Gremlin piped up, patting an almost pristine Humvee that just had a hole or two where the gunner was mowed down. "Should keep my 'gennys running for a while."

"And ammo and food." Yule murmured, looking in the rear of the truck and seeing stacks of ammo cans. Over all, twenty nine blue helmets were gunned down in the road with no losses to the Veil Rider's 1st Dragoons. While the lead truck was a mess, the other trucks were in usable condition, toting a lot of hardware and supplies to boot. For one reason or another, these trucks were loaded down with almost two weeks worth of food and ammo, as well as explosives and detonators. This made no sense to him. They knew he was out here and was using Harpies to scout, why would they send packed vehicles driving down a well used road? Moreover, why did they have so much supplies with them? And why were those inside of the vehicles European?

Yule held the Amulet to his temple, and yelled up into the sky. "Airis ma'am, I need you."

Airis flitted down from a tree nearby, having watched the show, and landed neatly on the back of a dead blue helmet before Yule. She lifted her chin to him, her claws digging into the bleeding flesh of the cooling corpse.

"Could you please go tell Koko that the ambush was a success? We have vehicles and more ammo if he needs them."

"Airis hears." She purred, and then opened her wings wide, beating them until she was clear into the sky and heading east.

Yule watched her go, making sure no one was going to try and shoot her down from some unknown location, before he moved on down the road. The rain still hammered down, and red trails of crimson spidered like little miniature rivers from the bodies that lay on the rough gravel and dirt of the road. Judging from their shocked and surprised faces, they never expected the Veil Riders to be here.

"Ooga Booga.." Murmured Yule, as he kicked one of their blue helmets into the brush. The Veil Riders were stripping bodies of ammo and anything else of use and tossing them into the Humvees, while a growing stack of weapons was in the rear trunk of another. Little ceremony was given to the bodies, just being chucked off the side of the road to clear it. Those who knew how were already moving the Humvees and driving them back towards where their horses were staked, and they rumbled by as Yule knelt down in front of their only captive.

Gruesome had already yanked out the slug, and Yethis had healed the wound. She was definitely German, her jaw was strong, with chestnut brown hair and brown eyes that glimmered with little sparks of honey here and there. Her face was contorted in both fury and fear as she craned her neck to and fro, the rain spattering off of her face and off of those around her. Veil Riders stood near and about her, squatting down while smoking local vices or cleaning the blood from their knives on the bodies of the dead. The one thing they all shared was the resentful look that was cast down upon her, and panic began to crawl up her neck in a red flush.

Yule knelt down in front of her, the buttstock of his K2 splashing onto the ground as he used it for support. He took a moment to take out his well worn and chewed corn cob pipe and tucked it into his mouth, clenching it in his teeth as he gave her the grin that all predators have when the hunt has gone well.

"Hallo liebling, Willkommen auf der Schleier."

CHAPTER 7

THE RAIN NEVER stopped thundering down the entire way back to the city of Imlnoris, soaking those who were on horseback and deafening those who rode inside the trucks. To ease the burden of the horses, the wagons were hitched to the Humvees and dragged behind them. The curious thing about these Elven horses was their innate intelligence, and were more than happy to trot behind the towed wagons without any handlers or ropes to guide them. Yule and ten of his Dragoons arrived before the rest, having ridden ahead with their captive strapped to the saddle of one of their horses, while the rest of the Dragoons escorted the trucks back to the city. If it weren't for the fact she was female, they would have dragged her behind the horses the entire way, but while Yule was angry, he was not a monster.

Chikily landed soon after Yule arrived, fresh from visiting Zerg Company, and was almost beside himself when he laid eyes on the captive blue helmet. Chikily was more than happy to maul and eat the woman after her compatriots shot him and had to be physically restrained by the Dragoons and dragged away before he got his way. Indeed, the blue helmet prisoner was not being looked upon favorably, as news of Chikily's findings had gotten around the City quickly, and it was a fair assumption that many inhabitants of the city wouldn't mind getting a piece of her, one way or another.

As the rain poured on, tenders from the Sparkling Unicorn ran out to assist the Veil Riders and their horses, letting the Veil Riders retrieve their water-logged gear after they dismounted and then taking their mounts back to the stables that were attached to the Inn. The prisoner was unhooked as well and shoved harshly forward towards the door of the Inn. Chicks found herself lacking the patience to let her look around; as the German woman craned her neck to look up and gape at the rain slicked buildings, Chick's boot checked her in the small of the back and sent her flying forward into the mud and run-off of the street.

Chicks clicked her tongue as the prisoner splashed down and made a show of unshouldering her long rifle. "Move it, Hun."

The woman sputtered, shaking the water from her face and hair as she looked back at the forward element of the Dragoons, all of whom glowered down at her while fingering their weapons. Chikily was there as well, and grinned his massive fangs at her while rumbling in his throat. She winced up at them, wiping the mud and grime from her face as her uniform became soaked with the same muck she tried to brush off.

"That's enough of that, she already has a rough time ahead of her..." Yule's said, his boots splashing softly on the street as he stepped towards the group, having given his horse an affectionate pat on the rump while the tender led it away. He had coaxed his pipe back to life, and it glowed red from under the bill of his hat, casting his face in eery scarlet. "Take this one inside, she has information we need. Give her water, don't want her dying before I get what I want out of her."

Yule puffed on his stem as Chicks and Domino leaned down to grab an arm each, dragging her roughly through the mud. Her knees and boot toes dragged, leaving grooves in the soft earthen road before thumping onto the stone sidewalk and then the front door of the inn.

"Mr.Chikily, do you have a letter for me?"

Chikily ground his teeth for a minute, eyeing the prisoner hotly as she was dragged away, but snapped out of it and quickly stepped his way over to Yule.

"Chikily has letter from Koko!"

Yule took the letter from Chikily's hand with an appreciative smile, and splashed through the street from the rain to read it, Chikily plodding along behind him. The letter was already fairly soaked due to the rain, but he still made way for the cover of the Inn porch roof before he opened it. The Dragoons that didn't go inside crowded around him to read as well.

Kole gave a snort. "Dakota got himself a girlfriend eh?"

"Seems like it." Yule observed with a laugh, and continued

reading. Koko stated that he could use the trucks they picked up and the ammo, as well as any other extra things they could spare since they didn't have the Dwarves in town like Yule did. Yule hummed to himself as he tapped the back of the wet letter with his fingers, then looked over to Chikily, who was rocking back and forth on his long clawed avian feet.

"Chikily?"

He perked up his head and looked up to Yule expectantly.

"Do me a favor, would you? Could you grab some of the Harpies that can carry heavier loads and have them meet me here tomorrow? I would like them to maybe run ammo and food for us."

"Chikily Hears!" He chirruped proudly, and instead of flying, took off at a run down the street, his nails clicking softly on the road. Seems he had enough of flying through the rain for the day.

Yule watched him go with a smile, his pipe stem clicking in his teeth as he did, before turning back to his Veil Rider Dragoons who stood about, thumbs hooked in their riggings or picking at their nails with their knives. Yule's face turned from amused to serious with a smooth transition, and he puffed hotly on his pipe, blowing the heavy, greenish tinted smoke from his nostrils. He had run out of tobacco from Terra long ago, and had switched to the local varieties.

"The Kraut blue helmet, what are we doing with her?" Kole asked, crossing his arms and tipping back his soaked stetson.

Yule bared his teeth, and as he spoke, air funneled down the stem to heat the coals in the bowl of his pipe, casting red flecks of rage in his blue eyes. "Break her. I want the truth of whats going on."

And break her, they did.

There was a little room in the rear of the Sparkling Unicorn that was normally used for meetings. For today, it was an interrogation room. Yethis was still with the vehicle convoy that was slowly making their way here, so instead they had Ylyndar, the Inn's resident healer on duty. Those who joined Yule for the interrogation, a mixture of male and female Veil Riders, dropped their wet gear and uniform tops onto the table and chairs nearby. Dusky light filled the room as a few lamps were lit and the window curtains swished shut. Panic once again swam in the eyes of the blue helmet as she was tied to the chair, her uniform top still covered with the mud of the road and the blood of her dead fellows. There were no questions or reverence to begin with. No speeches or admonishing to be found. The Veil Riders just worked the blue helmet over for a few minutes a piece ace until their knuckles smarted from the impacts. Her face would have been a ruin if it wasn't for Ylyndar, who clicked his tongue and healed her face back to perfection every time it was needed, just for the next Veil Rider to ruin it. The cycle continued until she finally sputtered out in accented English "Vat?! Vat do you vant!?"

The Veil Riders looked back at Yule, who sat in a chair a few feet away facing the prisoner and watched quietly. His Riders looked something akin to tavern brawlers as they panted or rubbed their knuckles angrily, some drinking from large flagons or smoking the local cigars made from mugroot.

"Did you think of somen' interestin' to tell me?" He asked, puffing out a little cloud of smoke while raising his tankard to his mouth.

She sputtered and looked about in a panic. "B-but I!"

Yule Flicked his fingers at the female Veil Rider that was currently on tenderizing duty, watching the German woman over the rim of his tankard as the Veil Rider backhanded her knuckles across the prisoners jaw so hard that a tooth rattled off the wall nearby. They continued to beat her for another ten minutes, Ylyndar putting her back together each time with a bemused look on his face, until Yule finally cleared his throat. The woman was panting and crying out, her boots scrabbling on the wooden floor boards as she writhed. She was completely intact, but the mental trauma was definitely doing its job. The pain stayed fresh in her brain, as it was only the physical damage that was being whisked away.

Smoke obscured Yule's face as he spoke, his voice a threatening rumble. "Why are you here. How did you come to be on American Soil?"

"I...I...Vas...I..." She moaned as she struggled to keep her eyes open, her entire body squirming in anguish. A Veil Rider stepped up, cocking back an elbow, but Yule held up his hand.

"That's enough. Why are you traveling through American soil, Rheinling? Answer me. There is no way a European combat force would ever be allowed to borrow American military hardware and travel freely like you all have in the Midwest."

She panted once...twice. Then mewled out an answer. "Deals. They say deals on the inside."

The rumble of engines outside alerted Yule to the arrival of the trucks, but his attention was squarely on the woman in front of him.

Smoke hung in the air like stringy wisps of ghosts, and Yule clenched his tankard, the flesh groaning on the metal as he did.

"What deals."

"There vas a change of power in Amerikan government, your President vas impeached and the other party quickly gained control. The Veil vas changed to a world effort, and ve vere invited to go through and hunt down American defectors." She panted, squinting her eye out of reflex, the body believing that it should be blackened despite having no damage to it. "You have all been labeled terrorists for killing the first team that came in."

"Horseshit." Murmured Kole.

"That cant be true." Whispered another.

Yule glared at them, then back to the woman tied to the chair.

"Democrats are in control of the White House now? There's no way that shit would have passed with the Republican majority in the house."

The woman lurched forward, tears streaking down her face, her voice almost lamenting. "I dont know! I dont know I svear! All I know ist deals vere made, bribery may have happened I dont know! Its all rumors! Your midvest is almost in rebellion as it is and now Russia is pressuring the other European nations for a bigger cut. Ve're here to control the roads and make a pipeline for getting resources back to the other side."

She panted, looking around for any kind or merciful eye . . . but she found none in the room, not even from Ylyndar.

"And the folk who live here?" Yule demanded, pulling his pipe from his mouth.

The woman panted in pain again, and then shrugged helplessly, before sagging in her restraints. "We vere told . . . zey vere just another resource. Ve are only working vith the Elves to the South."

Wulf, a Rider from Missouri, growled in his throat and gripped his Peacemaker with a rattle from his gun belt. "Fuckin' scum . . ."

Yule smacked him on the leg with the back of his hand and raised an angry eyebrow at him. There was no need to act so high and mighty. Yule knew full well that there was no telling what the U.S was going to do with the locals, they only held the high ground now because someone else was currently the bad guy.

"Not very kind of you to treat the locals like slave labor." Yule stood and exhaled, plucking his pipe from his teeth and dumping the coals into a little dish the Inn had provided before the interrogation had begun.

"Take her to a room, ask the Inn if they have a room with no windows. If they do, toss her in there and lock it. If she knew what was good for her," Yule looked down at the continually wincing woman, her eyes filled with constantly welling tears, "She'd stay in there and not make a fuss. Elves may use her for a couch liner if they get ahold of her."

She was untied from the chair, but her legs couldn't even bear to hold her weight, buckling as she tried to stand. She fell to the floor in a crumpled heap, and had to be once again lifted up by a pair of Veil Riders who dragged her up the stairs while calling for the Innkeeper. Yule watched them drag her away as he took off his patrol cap and ran his fingers through his hair. If the government was working with the UN just to try and wrestle power in a party struggle, it was going to make a mess of home. The news of the Midwestern states almost being in rebellion wasn't exactly a shock to him, there's always been hushed bar talk of balkanization and succession if the government did something backwards or in opposition to the middle of America. But the Democrats bending the knee? Had to be money changing hands, there was no way... just no way... That woman held more information in her head. He'd let her rest... then play good cop here soon.

Yethis came splashing into the front door of the Inn with everyone else and shook her head to rid her hair of the excess rainwater that clung to it. When his NCOs came to report, Yule told them of all he was told by the prisoner, and told them to make sure the rest of the Veil Riders knew of it. Yule thought to himself as he took off Yethis's hat and gave it a shake, scattering water all over Gremlin who was happily hugging a full fuel can to her chest. Perhaps... perhaps he had been too hasty in not taking more prisoners. Next time, he'll tell his Veil Riders to try and keep maybe one or two alive on purpose, instead of lucking out and just winging one. The trucks brought in from the ambush were just parked along the road and left there, as no one in the city knew how to turn them on, let alone drive and operate one. The Dwarves that walked by in their traveling cloaks showed an immense interest in the trucks, playing with the wheels and doors, and were able to wrestle a Veil Rider out of the Inn to show them the engine. After a few minutes, it was like an entire clan of the stout fellows had popped out of the ground, and were scouring the trucks and taking notes in their little note pads, or taking measurements of certain spaces in the engine. Yule just watched from the door with a hot cup of tea in his hand, smiling at them as the steam filtered up through the air.

The night passed with little else of note, besides the Veil Riders drinking and cheering themselves into a stupor while telling the locals how the ambush went. Some Veil Riders took the initiative to actually start learning the local language, so bits and pieces were very slowly translated to those who drank around and or with the Veil Riders, while other times a lot of pantomiming was used instead. If the Veil Riders ever went back home and got involved in a game of charades, they would be unbeatable by even the most seasoned of players.

The next morning, Chikily arrived with a cluster of Harpies that were whole heads taller than him, a mixture of males and females that all had a kind of primal grimness to their faces. Unlike Chikily's smaller and more lithe sparrow body type, these Harpies looked as if someone had taken condors, or great eagles, and spliced them together with a Human. Their arms were thicker, their chests broader, and their eyes burning with an intelligence that made Yule a bit nervous

"Chikily ask Himalayas to help! They agree in exchange for goods."

Yule looked down at Chikily, then to the stalwart leader of this little band, a female with multi-colored hair that was speckled with spots of browns, whites, and reds that reminded him a lot of flecktarn.

"Whaddya' mean 'Goods'?"

The leader of the Harpies stepped forward, her long black talons clacking on the ground as she did. Chikily bowed his head slightly and stepped back, standing beside Yule now. She was far, far bigger than Chikily, but still shorter than Yule, her nose coming up to around the middle of his ribcage.

"Yes . . . We wish to exchange services for Veil Rider wares. You have fine clothes, light weight, won't weigh us down in flight. You also have fancy tools we could use."

Yule noticed that unlike Chikily, these Harpies had a few more toes than the other ones he had seen, and even their wing claws had an extra digit, to which long rending claws were attached. "Tools, you say?"

"Yes . . . those little thunder sticks you sometimes use. We believe they could be . . . of use to us. If you trade us a thunder stick for us to play with, and maybe make us some clothes... we will happily help you and your squires."

Yule looked down at this little Harpy warrioress with a mixture of curiosity and... acknowledgment. He gingerly handed his tin cup of tea to Chikily and dusted his hands off on his pants, before holding out his hand. "Well. Tell me your name so I know what to call you, and I think we can work out a deal here."

The Harpy stalked forward smoothly, bending her head down to brush her face against Yule's hand and pin it against her cheek with her wing. She smiled softly as she leaned back up, her large pointed fangs glinting in the morning sun as her eyes studied him, her color speckled hair falling prettily over her face.

"Saverisss." She whispered, and she fixed Yule with another kind of predatory stare.

With the light on her eyes, Yule saw that they were not the brown color he thought they were at first, but a deep, murky merlot, and the color reminded him of old blood and rotting meat. Chikily made a nervous sound next to Yule, and hunched his shoulders a little in fear, tea spilling over the rim of the cup and spattering onto the ground below.

The meeting ended quickly after a few more things were hashed out. When they were done, and Yule safely getting his hand back in one piece, the Himalayas flapped off to grab some gear they needed from their 'roost'. When the coast was clear, Yule spun around, scooped up Chikily while flinging the contents of his tin up into a bush nearby, and stepped off at a run to get as far away from that Harpy woman as possible.

"Did you see her fucking teeth?!" Yule panted at Chikily, looking over his shoulder to see she was in fact watching him while hanging in the air in a kind of backward flying hover.

"She makes Chikily seem like hatchling! Her claws like tiny swords!" Chikily craned his neck to look over Yule's shoulder and his eyes widened as he too saw that she was watching them run.

Yule skittered around a corner and saw the trucks in the distance down the road, and waved his hand to the Veil Riders that were loitering outside and smoking. "Chikily, lemme tell you, next time you find some Harpies to help us, could you find less scary ones?!"

"Chikily Agrees!"

CHAPTER 8

Saveriss looked up at Domino with her merlot red eyes glowing with fury and rage. When she came back with her clan and their flying rigging, she expected to see Yule there and wanted to have another crack at him. Instead, she was looking up at some other Terran who looked as done as he sounded when it came to the bird woman. Around the two, Harpies walked to and fro or were given satchels by Veil Riders who were more versed in the common tongue of the land, or were assisted by donated lesser boons of communication that didn't require, or didn't use, as much blood as the true translation amulets.

"What do you mean he's busy? I can smell him here . . ." Saveriss leaned to the left of Domino, and squinted her eyes as she peered at the windows of the Sparkling Unicorn, eyebrows furrowed in frustration.

Domino slid to the left to block her view of the window and cleared his throat. "Sorry Miss Saveriss, but I'm afraid Yule is busy with official Veil Rider business. However, I have told you all I was given when it came to the request and where to go."

Saveriss tilted her head back up to Domino and investigated his eyes for lies, while her feathers fluffed with open annoyance. "Yes yes yes I know."

She narrowed her gaze, and said in a more grim and dangerous tone, "I *know*."

Domino fixed his face in a professional blank look, then raised his eyebrows at her. To be fair, he was fighting down the urge to smile as she began to slowly simmer and fume, her feathers getting more splayed out and her face getting redder as Domino refused to budge on where Yule was.

She finally broke, spinning on her clawed feet and screeching at her Harpies in their mother tongue. She must have been saying some rather creative expletives, as the Harpies all scrambled in a panic to take off with their parcels, and those with the more simple translators looked at each other in confusion, mouthing the alien words as puzzlement played across their faces.

Domino watched them all flap away, some of the smaller mail Harpies soaring in to flap alongside and pepper them with questions. There was a good amount of food, coffee, ammo, and oil heading to Artry, which was good news for Zerg Company. Domino stepped towards the Sparkling Unicorns front door and jerked it open, lurching inside with a hop step and whirling to the right. His suspicions were accurate; Yule had been watching just past the crack of the curtains the entire time, Chickily riding on his shoulders and doing the same. Even now they both peeped through the bright slit of sunshine that lit up both of their eyes.

"She gone, Domino?" Yule murmured, one of his hands draped over Chikily's feet to keep him from falling off and the other holding his tin up, out of which steam rose and curled in the air.

Domino rolled his eyes. "Yes, the big bad bird lady is gone."

Chikily Piped up, his winged arms resting on top of Yule's crumpled hat. "She wore hunting markings here when she had them not this morning."

Chikily looked down at Yule. "She's probably hunting you, Mr.Yule."

"Super." Yule muttered, and lifted his cup to his lips.

"Why do you not like her so much? For a Harpy she's awfully well filled out in all the right places." Domino moved his hands as if they were shaping an hour glass and looked at Yule as if he was a lunatic.

Yule took a pull from his cup and swallowed. "She reminds me of a rather large hawk, eagle, condor, whatever bird of prey she may be. I never liked them. Give me the heeby jeebies."

Chikily nodded up and down a few times in agreement and drummed his wings on Yule's head for a beat or two. "Heeby jeebies!"

The drumming on Yule's head caused the Amulet to almost fall out of his hat, Yule having just given up and wrapped it around the innards of his patrol cap so he was more or less always wearing it.

"You going to get that bear of a tailor to make their clothes like you did Chik's?" Domino asked, waving at a bar-woman and pointing at Yules cup, wanting one for himself.

Yule had found the roughly hewn clothes worn by Chikily and the other mail Harpies to be unsightly, and hired an absolute unit of a man to make them fresh clothes based on the myriad of uniforms the Veil Riders wore. A pair of ACU bottoms was offered as tribute, and were quickly deconstructed. The person in question was just a quiet man that liked sewing and making clothes. Never mind the fact he was almost seven feet tall and weighed as much as multiple Terrans due to his muscle mass. He was also distinctly bald, with a thick, black handlebar mustache that was always worked into fine points with wax. The Veil Riders called him Armstrong once they figured out his Veil name was Urmstronj, and he seemed to just shrug it off and take it as some kind of weird nickname or butchering of his real name. There were bets being taken that either his daddy liked him some giant muscle girls, or his mama was a size queen, either way, their offspring was a monster of an man, and may be part Giant. Urmstronj was able to quickly rack out light and breathable military style pants for the Harpies in a fine quality, and afterwards a lot of Veil Riders went to him for repairs or their own personal items made. Urmstronj was also pioneering the new cloth types the Veil Riders brought with them, determined to recreate it and have a tidy monopoly on the material.

"Yeah, Urmstronj is the only guy who could do it in the right way. Probably have to funnel a little money his way." Yule gave Chikily's pant leg a little tug to get his attention, and then lifted him up and off his shoulders, planting him on the ground with a soft click of avian nails. The Veil Riders had been making a tidy profit themselves, selling ideas of engineering and production to those who had the mind and resources to use them.

Domino hummed contentedly when a lovely Valley Elf barmaid swooped in with his mug, and he took it with a happy smile. "What about the Kraut?"

Yule frowned a bit at the mention of her. He hadn't slept well over it, and ruefully thought that technically he did the evil mercenary thing that he always made fun of movies for. He had let spite rule his actions that day after the ambush, and the aftermath left that woman in ruins and Yule second guessing himself every minute the morning after. Then came that dreadful bird woman . . .

"I jumped the gun on that one. Gonna have to unfuck the situation, kiss and make up. "

"Mmm, yes, kiss and make up after you almost blew her soul out of her asshole with blunt force trauma." Domino chided Yule, clicking his tongue like a disparaging parent.

Yule exhaled out of his nose while making his lips a thin line. "Never said I was a smart man, mama did have a tendency to drop me."

Domino just chuckled darkly and walked off into the inn, leaving Yule to stew in his own self spite. Chikily tugged on the hem of Yule's shirt, and he looked down at the Sparrow Harpy with eyebrows raised.

"Chikily don't mind you beating her up."

Yule's eyelids dropped slightly, and he smiled sadly, ruffling the Harpy's hair half heartedly. "Thanks bud, but I did an oopsy because I wasn't thinking."

Yule looked over his shoulder at the staircase, while outside Veil Riders chatted to each other and cleaned their weapons in the warming sunshine. "Now I gotta go apologize and try to make this situation proper."

Yule ruffled Chikily's hair one more time before ordering him some breakfast, as the Harpy was a prolific dumpster diver, and Yule was trying to break him of the habit. When Yule had Chikily all sorted out, he thumped his way up the stairs and down the hallway where the prisoner's quarters were. On guard this particular morning was Alphonse, another Army Veteran who was drinking tea and reading a comic book.

When Alphonse saw Yule walking down the hallway, he raised his mug in a salute and unlocked the door, not even bothering to get up out of his chair.

Yule didn't mind; He opened the door and stepped in, only to be greeted by a war screech and the German woman slamming into him.

Yule grunted in confusion, but splayed out his arms and legs to jam the doorway with his body, popping his chest and jutting the woman back into her room a couple of feet. Her boots tangled each other as she tried to regain her footing, and she slammed down onto her back, knocking the air out of her lungs.

Alphonse turned the page of his comic book and looked over his shoulder, taking a sip from his mug before leaning forward in his chair. It creaked, and he yelled down the hallway for a healer.

A hot pain was radiating from Yule's stomach, and he looked down to see a rough wooden shiv the size of a femur bone had been plunged into his belly. His body was still trying to figure out what exact flavor of pain this was, so the roar from the wound was still dulled as Yule dusted off his chest, blood beginning to pour down his uniform top and onto his pant legs. He looked down at the woman who was gasping in lungfuls of air and trying to get onto her feet.

"Y'know what? That's fair." He said through gritted teeth, and leaned down despite the shiv digging into his guts, offering her a hand to help her up.

Yethis came skittering down the hallway and almost slid past the door as she put on the brakes, and Yule saw she had already sliced open her hand with a ragged cut.

"Boss's been shanked." Alphonse stated flatly, and gestured with his mug at Yule, who had helped up the still heaving German woman, and was now doing his best to apologize as Human fruit punch soaked down onto his pants and boots. Yethis, seeing Yule bleeding out for the first time in her stint as his personal blood bank and dedicated medical bodyguard ... fainted. Her body thudded to the ground, causing the knife to clatter off the wooden floor boards and cartwheel down the hallway a few feet, her hand continuing to bleed from its ragged cut.

It could be called a stroke of luck that Ylyndar was professional enough to come running as well despite Yethis haven taken off at a sprint at the first call for a healer, and now saw both Yule bleeding from the stomach and Yethis passed out on the ground, bleeding all over the floor from her hand.

Ylyndar, never one to pass up the chance for a quick spot of ill-timed humor, looked down at Alphonse as he brought up his translator to his forehead.

"What chapter are you on then?"

"Bismarck called Montana a burger eating monstrosity." Alphonse answered dryly, and flipped another page of his comic.

It took him a few minutes, but since Yethis was already bleeding, he used her blood to heal both her and Yule, yanking out the shank matter of factually so it wouldn't fuse into Yule's skin. After Yethis's hand was healed, Yule being healed enough so he wasn't going to bleed out all over the floor, and the German woman checked over for damage, Ylyndar hefted up Yethis and dragged her away to lay her down somewhere so she could nap off her little fainting spell.

While she could not quite hear Yule through the sound of her body trying to force air into her lungs and the sounds of her head buzzing from the back of her head hitting the ground, she was now a little more attentive after Yule hadn't killed her for shoving what was basically a giant wooden splinter into his guts. Yule picked up the spare chair in the room and placed it a foot or two away from her bed, of which she sat upon, and sat down on the chair while taking off his blood soaked uniform top.

"Yeah. Like I said, this is fair. Can't be too upset when the prisoner you tortured decides to introduce your large intestine to a piece of their bed frame. By the way, Erlan is not going to be very happy that you sawed off part of the bed frame leg." Yule draped his uniform top over the back of his chair and sighed, as there was still blood drying in his boots and all over his pants.

"Sorry... Vas going to try and escape." She shrugged matter of factly and played with her fingers on her lap. "Honestly I'm surprised you haven't shot me yet."

"Oh don't worry about that, the day is still young. But, to be honest, I don't really have the ammunition to spare." Yule flashed a charming, yet painful, grin at her as he leaned back in his chair, the legs of which groaned under his non-Elf weight. "What's your name."

"Britta."

Yule took off his patrol cap and plopped it on his less bloody knee, fixing Britta's eyes with his own. "Im sorry, Britta. I jumped the gun having my lads work you over like a steak. Post battle brain, you guys walking through American territory... kind of made me throw intelligence out the window."

He sighed and scratched at his chin. "Yeah... I kind of did the evil bad guy thing, didn't I?"

"You vere a bit of a Schwackkopf. Kind of rubbing it in, torturing me after killing some of my friends, isn't it?" She spoke dryly, lookin at Yule as if he were an idiot.

Yule blinked, not knowing what a Schwackkopf was, and looked at her with his eyes open and eyebrows raised for a few breaths. He opened his hands and made a wry, agreeful face. "If the blood filled boot fits I guess. Were you telling the truth about the questions we asked you?"

Britta's eyes hardened, as did her mouth. "No. I told you what I believed you wanted to hear."

Yule's mouth twitched as a healing pang went through his stomach, the magic still knitting his flesh back together. He followed the twitch with a stroke of his beard and a sigh. "Aye I could see why you would want to do that. Only so many times you can grow your own teeth back before you'd say anything to end it."

Britta remembered the feeling of how it felt when her teeth *did* begin to grow back after the Elf would do his magics on her, and she clicked her tongue against those new teeth. "Arschgeige."

Yule, again, was not really aware of this word, and waited a few pauses before he spoke again. "Fair."

Alphonse gave a snort from outside the door. He knew the German word for *ass violin,* and it was always a treat to hear it.

Yule ran his hand through his hair, and looked back at Britta after staring at the wall for a few minutes. He wasn't sure how to proceed with all of this. His plan to play good cop got a little askew when she decided to try and shank him, and he didn't know what the correct option was.

". . . Want to see the city and chat for a bit?"

After getting her answer, he left Britta's guarded room and put on some fresh clothes, sending his holed top off to Urmstronj with Chikily, and then spoke to his NCOs. They all had a good laugh over the knowledge that Yule got a stabbing from Britta and chided him like Domino did.

"Lack of awareness I see, mmm, not a good showing from our mighty commander." They all rubbed the top of their fingers in the 'shame shame' display, and Yule fixed his face in a contemptuous smile as they continued to make fun of him. When they had finished their fun, he let them know what he was up to. His NCOs were puzzled at why he was letting her out of the room only a day after her interrogation, but after he explained himself, they could understand why he may be feeling a little guilty.

"Be sure to take her by the market square with all the weapons, it should be a fun time hearing what she sticks you with next."

Yule had to endure a few more minutes of his NCOs taking bets on what she was going to stab him with before Alphonse showed up with Britta, her hands tied with rope behind her back. Britta smiled happily when the warm sunshine lit up her face and she took in the blue sky above her. She didn't think she'd see it again after surviving the ambush, being tortured, then stabbing Yule. Yule grabbed her shoulder, and led her away towards the inner districts of the city and the trading markets.

While they walked, and Britta took in the buildings and people, she talked to Yule. While the parts about the Midwestern states being up in arms was true, the rest of it had been a bit embellished to get the Veil Riders to stop their beating. Britta did not know the deep intricacies of it all, but began to outline the timeline between when he left, to when she crossed the Veil herself. When news of the world beyond the Veil was released, every nation on Earth wanted to be in on this cash cow of resources and land. America, naturally, wanted it all for themselves, and made to stiff-arm the planet in order to keep it all for the red, white, and blue. Even under threats from other super powers, the United States would not bend, but there were those on the inside who saw this as a way to make a lot of money and hedge in their power very quickly. To ease the tensions of all out war and the threat of nuclear weapons being aimed at each other, Congress began to take certain nations to the negotiation tables to try and hash out some form of deal. The current President saw this as a sign of weakness, as well as many of the American states, and slammed the actions as "Un-American and cowardly".

The already strained relations between states rose to a fever pitch, as did those in the government, and the cracks were easily spotted by the European nations as well as the other countries that believed they should have a stake in the Veil. Under the table, bids were being made, and suddenly each Senator had a price tag on them to try and shift the balance in someone's favor. Russia, China, and Europe began a shadow war to see who could woo the most senators to their side. It was never a doubt that Senators could be bought ... they were bought all the time, but these countries needed someone more agreeable, someone more ... pliable, leading the United States and leaning more towards their favor. In the end, the war was won by the greater nations of Europe, and not even the Republicans were safe from the gentle plying of money offered with an open hand and a smile. The President was quickly swept out when there was no longer a stone wall of Republican Senators keeping him in, and the Vice President was sworn into Office ... with a pocket full of European money and influence. Wishing to hold this office for as long as possible, talks began almost overnight with the European leaders.

In the end, The United States of America teamed up with Europe to tackle the Veil, hands were shaken, and for the first time since the 1800's, the boots of European military personnel touched down on American soil in mass. The deal, as Britta was told, was that they would fly into an airport near the Veil and then truck over directly, enter the Veil, and follow their orders. When Britta and her comrades of many nations arrived, the middle states of America were incensed and began drafting letters of succession as soon as it was confirmed that these people were, in fact, armed Europeans.

"Our plane even had bullet holes in it, from some of your people shooting at us vith hunting rifles as ve came in to land." Britta mused, as she leaned over a stall that was selling apples so golden in color they almost looked metallic.

Russia, China . . . and frankly anyone else that was not in on the deal, became soured by it, and were now putting pressure on both Europe at large and the United States for a slice of the pie, even going as far as leveraging debts or stolen national secrets for blackmail. While the East Coast could calm down a little with its military posturing, the West Coast bristled further, Alaska not having the amount of military hardware on it in these numbers since World War II.

"It's all a mess . . . really." Britta sighed, and squatted down on her heels to try pet a cat that was curled up nearby. Yule saw this, and pulled out his knife. Britta stood up in alarm, but Yule just cut away her hand bindings. If she ran, she would not get far. He looked up to see a few Harpies watching from the rooftops, and they had been shadowing them the entire time. He gave Airis a little wave before putting his knife away.

"What about that thing with the Elves and such being another resource, and us being terrorists?" Yule questioned, handing her some kind of meat that was grilled on a stick.

Britta took the stick, and eyed the meat thoughtfully. "That . . . is some vhat true, actually. A lot of us are not alright with the notion of enslaving mythical creatures, and ve only learned this vhen we came across the Veil. These . . . Broody elves from the South have allied themselves vith us, and promised us so much land and magics as ve need if ve bring them the other elves. Their blood is better for magic, so they say."

She took a bite of the meat and chewed softly, while idly petting the cat with her fingers. "Chosen of Ulthary . . . or something, thats vhat they call themselves. Have kommand vrapped around their finger since showing them they could make stuff vith the blood of the other Elves."

Yule thought back to that nice little village, and grimaced as he imagined them all being bled dry to make gold or whatever it was those creepy Ulthary elves were doing. "And you're okay with this?"

". . . No." Britta bit out, her fingertips now resting on the happily purring cat. "Ve didn't know before ve came over. Germany offered almost half of the troops that flew in. Do you think ve would have hopped on the plane if ve knew this vas going on? Ve don't even have markers to go back after ve found out and vanted to report it."

Yule spat in shock, sending a little nugget of meat flying onto the street. "You don't have markers?!"

"No! It vas implied ve vould be given them if ve *needed* them, they're all kept in the kommand building." Britta looked up at Yule with a kind of indignant anger. "The French and Belgians are headlining ze whole thing, dragging in us Germans, some Polish, a sprinkling of Czechs and such, but the majority of command is French or Belgian. They've also been getting very . . . buddy buddy with the Elves."

"Are you aware of the Time Stretch then?"

Britta looked away from the cat to Yule again, her face questioning. "Time Stretch?"

"Yes, the time stretch. How time is much faster on our side than their side? . . . Didn't the Chosen of . . . Ulawhatevers tell you that?"

Britta stared at Yule for a long time, then down to the cat, then back to Yule, turning her head to look down the street as she thought.

"Time . . . is moving faster, on Earth?"

Yule's flesh prickled. From what Chikily last reported, minus those killed in the ambush, there were still hundreds of personnel running around the base they have set up at the Veil. Did all of them have no idea they were being left behind? "Britta . . . They have records here. I was told that there were Landsknechts from Maximilian here only *a hundred* years ago."

Sweat began to slowly bead on Britta's forehead and neck, she smiled nervously and puffed air out from her teeth. "N-no. Theres no vay. They said it vas like a door, ve can valk back and forth vithout trouble . . . ve could go home on leave and come back no problem . . . Right? Thats vat you vere doing, right?"

The cat mewed and rubbed its head against the hand of Britta, who had stopped petting it and its tail flicked back and forth in annoyance.

Yule swallowed, the meat in his mouth dulled by his mind buzzing in alarm. Why wouldn't they tell them about the time stretch? Surely they noticed by now that things were not on a schedule . . . They were Germans for fucks sakes, they are experts on keeping schedules.

Yule knelt down and placed a hand on Britta's shoulder. "Britta . . . how many of you have husbands, wives, children, all that stuff."

Britta shook her head a little and shrugged. "None of us, this vas only offered to unmarried soldiers and volunteers. I mean some of us have gotten a little friendly on this side with each other but that's mostly out of boredom . . ."

"You didn't think that odd? That they only took single folk and didn't even bother to give you markers so you can get back home? Let's forget about you using U.S Army vehicles and all that shit, what else do you remember from your briefing?"

"It vas . . . just like any other mission or deployment. Just with a chance of unicorns and Goblins . . ." Britta began to look more worried. "Ve vere told there vere radical American militiamen on the other side that vere killing anyone not American, that they vere very dangerous, heavily armed, mentally unhinged, all of that, and that they vere kill on sight. They also said you vere abusing the locals and using them to your own gains, living amongst them under threat of death, and anyone who you allied vith vere to be treated the same. In this case, you vere the uh . . . Terrorists in Afghanistan. It ist only natural that the UN got involved as well to try and placate everyone. I'm still shocked to learn that the whole thing actually started in San Francisco . . ."

Yule sighed and stood back up. "To be fair, they were right about a few of those. I did have your jaw broken several times."

"I did not enjoy that bit, no. I still think you're a bit of a . . ." Britta grasped for the words, closing her eyes as she thought. When she had the terms she wanted to use, she opened her eyes and looked back up to Yule. "Fucking cock-face."

Yule shrugged. "Fair. But none of this smells right. I can get a lot of it. But a lot of it also is highly sketch. Out of curiosity . . . How many of your fellows would want to uh . . . defect? After learning a little bit more of what's going on there."

A sardonic grin played upon her lips as she began to let the cat nibble on the meat, slowly turning the stick in her hand. "The Chosen of Ulthary remind us too much of our past histories. Proud, self confident, believing themselves above others . . . they also bled a man dry to feed their magic, just slit his throat and poured him into a bowl. Vhen ve asked to leave, ve vere told no, then admonished for 'lacking the spine to follow through on our vord'. I don't know how many more of those Elves they've killed, or vhatever else . . . But I know a lot of us and the Polish are disgruntled. I'm not happy about you butchering my friends, but the majority of the convoy vas not German. Maybe only five or six."

The cat purred as it chewed, its tail flicking back and forth happily. Britta knitted her brows together. "Things are not like I thought. Not what ve agreed to, anyvay. The Ulthary are enslaving other Elves and using the military backbone of our forces to do it. Kommand is letting them. They're also not giving us the freedom to travel back and forth. Its all so. suspicious. Plus how kommand acts like the Ulthary are like old friends . . ."

"Do you think they'll be open to suggestions? Those fellows of yours"

Britta kept turning the stick in her hand so the cat could feed. "If you think you can refrain from beating them nearly to death, they might be. But vhy should we help you? Vhy shouldn't I just make a run for it and tell them vere your little company of murder-hobos are hiding?"

Yule sat down on the ground near Britta and the cat, who was now chewing on the stick and trying to figure out where all the meat went. "You shouldn't trust us. No sane person would after what we did. I'm not exactly proud of it, and I'm making a mess of this whole commander thing because i'm acting too impulsively. Hell, bringing you out here unguarded was impulsive, you've only been a prisoner for a day now. I don't know . . . I just get weird thoughts here." Yule whirled his fingers in front of his face. "Judgments are all funny and I'm afraid of getting my Rider's killed. I don't even know what happens to our souls on this part of the Veil. What I am going to do though, is ask you; Do you think things are weird with how your command is acting?"

". . . Yes."

"Does it worry you, or make you feel doubt."

Britta puffed out a bit of air. "Things are not as 'ritten, that's for sure."

Yule looked over at her, and pointed a finger loosely at the Valley

Elves and other races that walked about, talked, or laughed with their families. "Do you want to see them suffer like you did at the base?"

Britta stayed quiet for a long time, picking up the cat and placing it in her lap. She rubbed its cheeks with her fingers as she looked out into the crowd of races that mingled back and forth. She hated Yule, or at least thought she did, and didn't enjoy what happened yesterday, or that a few of her friends were slaughtered like animals in the ambush. Yule was putting her in a weird position and she pondered for a moment if it was some kind of trick. He'd already brutalized her once, now he was being all nice . . . was he trying to Stockholm her or something? "Even if some of us defected, vhat vould you do, anyway?"

"Figure out which of them really wanted to go home, then give them our own markers for atonement. I think that's fair." Yule slid his hands together as he thought, the sound raspy and dry. "Whoever wanted to stay . . . I dunno. Make them Veil Riders, or poke them over to Zerg Company. Or just make them their own company, who knows. I'm just taking this place day by day and trying not to fuck it up too badly for tomorrow"

CHAPTER 9

Yule brought Britta back to the Sparkling Unicorn a few hours later and dropped her off in her room, telling the guard outside to let her go back and forth, but with someone accompanying her. It was evening, and Yule hadn't eaten much except for stall snacks and needed something more filling. Down in the Sparkling Unicorn's main dining area, it was hopping and popping as normal, with a solid amount of the Veil Riders gearing up to hike it to the pleasure district. Yule didn't approve of it, but the money made from selling blueprints for advancements in the city was spread evenly, as it should be, and they were able to spend it as they saw fit. Why they chose to spend it on flesh, Yule would never know. He sat down at one of the long tables near Gremlin and a few other Veil Riders who ate and chatted, while Chikily snored drunkenly from a chair in the corner, curled up and drooling on himself.

"Howdy Gremlin, how goes it?"

Her eyes had their usual sleepy bags under them, but she seemed to be in a chipper mood. "Got all my drones recharged, besides that, been mostly trying to figure out how the time thing works, magic in general, why there's not enough gravity here for the size of the planet, that kind of stuff."

"Trying to solve all the world's mysteries are you?" Yule waved at a barmaid, who whirled through the many chairs and tables to see what he wanted. He asked for tea and whatever they were serving for dinner, and she rushed off to the kitchen to put it in.

Yule then went on to tell Gremlin what he was told by Britta.

"Acting buddy buddy? Buddy buddy how? We talking drinking

buddies or old frat brothers buddy buddy?" Gremlin was multitasking, trying to eat around her laptop and talk to Yule, while simultaneously playing a match of Towns and Castles III. The Elves of the Inn were worried she wasn't eating enough, and were constantly plying her with food. This seemed to have jump started something in her, and now she was constantly in a state of either eating or teching, while sleep seemed to always be on the back burner.

"Don't know, all she said was 'buddy buddy' and didn't really elaborate... You don't think they're in on it right? In the role playing games there was always stuff like Changelings running around, Doppelgangers, Fae who lived for centuries... That couldn't happen right?" Yule turned to Gremlin and saw that the entire table had gone quiet, and Gremlin's mouth was in an odd, appreciative grin, her teeth showing brightly blue and green in the glow of her laptop.

"Yule... you aren't going conspiracy on us, are you?"

Veil Riders exchanged glances and smiled at each other, while leaning in to listen further.

"Well, c'mon now, I'm not talkin' like, illuminati or somethin', but what if somethin' passed through and has been guiding Humans back to the Veil?" Yule felt stupid as soon as the words left his mouth.

"Oh.. you mean like secret societies that are based solely on conspiracy theories?" Gremlin asked wryly, and folded her hands under her chin while the other Veil Riders at the table began pulling out their notebooks. "Oh Yule, I knew you would fall to the dark side with us."

All Yule could do is lean back in his seat with a look of dawning defeat as the table suddenly erupted in a chorus of chatter, with Gremlin shouting "I told you! I fucking told you!" over the lot of them. It appeared that under Yule's nose, a lot of Veil Riders had been weaving their own web of theories about what was going on all this time and how it may tie in to the mythos of home, including such things as Stonehenge, the Pyramids, Nostradamus actually being a really tall Dwarf, Davinci being a Valley Elf, and of course the secret societies that worked in the shadows.

The barmaid walked back over and began setting down Yule's food and drink in front of him, being sure to brush her chest on his shoulder as she did. She looked down to see if he was paying attention, but instead of seeing lust for her flesh in his eyes, he was instead staring with soulless dread at his Veil Riders, who were now gesturing wildly and yelling at each other while holding up their notebooks. The barmaid glared with him and furrowed her brows at the Veil Riders as they ranted, still holding onto his mug.

They're ruining my chances every damn day... She thought to herself, and huffed, releasing Yule's mug and sauntering away back towards the kitchen. The Veil Riders and Gremlin were now almost yelling at each other and pointing at Yule, who just tried to pretend the butter was saying nice things to him as he spread it on his bread.

"Even Yule thinks there's something going on! You heard him say it!" Gremlin spun around her laptop and began tapping the screen. "Look! It all makes sense if you plot the major events along with the supposed intervals that the two sides of the Veil align in time! For all we know, the grassy knoll shooter could have been a Fairy!"

This comment made the entire table uproar, and other Veil Riders overheard, walking over to throw in their two cents. While they argued around him, Yule sat in the middle, doing his best to just eat his food and not feed into what he started. As a ball of paper bounced off his head and two Veil Riders began a loud argument over whether or not Franz Ferdinand could have been killed by a rogue Kobold, Yule quietly wished he had just kept his mouth shut.

From the main bar, a few of the Valley Elf barmaids were watching the event unfold with amusement. None of them knew what was being said, but it certainly seemed like a heated discussion.

One of the barmaids leaned towards the other barmaid coming back from Yule, a smug grin playing along her teeth. "Mmm, looks miserable don't he? Any luck with woo'ing the pure and noble Yule, Kali?"

"Fuck off Syllia."

Kali strode past them with a face rife with indignation and shoved open the door to the kitchens with fire. The rest of the girls laughed at her expense, before one turned to Syllia.

"Pure and noble? What are you on about? I've seen him eyeball a leg or two during breakfast."

Syllia shrugged while cleaning some of the tankards with a wet rag. "He's one of the few that don't travel the pleasure districts or hit on anything with a hole between its legs. Chikily there," She nodded her auburn haired head towards the still snoozing Harpy, "Says that Yule has even been fighting off that Himalayan Matriarch. Yethis says that he even rebuked the head sorceress that first met him . . . and herself.

She tried offering to help him bathe and he locked her in a closet. Guy is a strange one for sure."

"Strange, no, sad . . . Perhaps."

All the girls looked at Alavara, the second in command when it came to the Inn. She was an older Valley Elf, and she watched Yule slowly drink from his mug as Gremlin desperately tried to get him to look at her screen and tell the rest of the Veil Riders she was right. Alavara's hair was a rarer crimson color, and her eyes followed the same touch of red, being called one of the Blood Touched. She also had the ability to grift the thoughts of others and steal ideas. She could not mind read per say, but could surf on the waves that people who don't mind themselves send out as they think, or remember. It helped her pick up on people who didn't pay their tabs, or were sneaking away with the cutlery.

Alavara stared at Yule with her arms crossed under her ample chest, as she did on many nights, and felt the same waves of self doubt, and loss. "I think . . . Yule had a wife at one time. When he catches himself staring at a rump or thigh, he gives off huge waves of shame and sorrow before closing himself off. From how he acts, and how he feels . . . he may have lost her violently, or in a way he was not okay with."

Alavara slapped Syllia on the shoulder with the back of her hand and pointed at Yule. "Get him more tea, and be nice about it. Don't go pressing your tits against him like that tart Kali."

Syllia grumbled and rubbed her shoulder before going into the kitchen to grab another mug for him. Alavara looked back to Yule, and leaned down onto the counter to rest on her elbows, her chin perched on her hands. Her scarlet tinged eyes bore holes into Yule as he tried to make his Veil Riders calm down and talk in a lower tone of voice. She was able to worm her way in and pick out a single thought, as Syllia distracted him by putting down a fresh mug of tea and picking up his empty one. Of course, he was already distracted by his men at arms, all of them trying to get him to agree with whatever it was they had written down on their pads of paper.

Alavara murmured under her breath as she snatched up his thought, his memory, and ferreted it away inside her own mind. "Not like she used to make it, eh? Good to know . . . I'll see you at breakfast, then."

Despite the energy pulsing through the dining room, the Veil Riders eventually made their way to their rooms, including Yule, who had more than enough of conspiracy theories for one day. The next morning, everyone was still in bed when the sun came up and the cock crowed, except for two of the Company. Chikily was still passed out asleep in the chair he fell in, and someone had draped a wooby over him before they had gone to bed, in which he was curled up and snoring softly. Down stairs with him, Yule was already busily scribbling away at paperwork and writing his reports to Koko so he could stay in the loop. Beside him, Airis was having breakfast and sipping tea, waiting for Yule to finish up with his letter so she could take it to Zerg Company.

Airis kind of liked this morning ritual she had fallen into, but was worried because it always seemed like Yule never slept, always waiting for her when she arrived just as the sun was rising. As he wrote, he would always buy her food and make sure she had the energy for what the Harpies called 'The Zerg Run', ferreting mail and correspondence between the two companies of Humans. Yule always made sure she drank her tea for some reason, and wouldn't let her set off until the bowl of whatever they gave her was empty. Airis didn't like the stuff they put in the mugs, but Yule seemed to think it was important, so she put up with it. It was the most stable time of her life, as far as she could remember, and this weird little ritual was like the cornerstone of her day.

Airis leaned over to peer at the letters Yule had spread around the table top as she held her mug in her wing digits; She could recognize the language of the Valley Elves and the runes of the Dwarves, and could pick up on a little of what Yule was doing: It seemed that he was trading information to the Dwarves on something called a 'blast furnace', and a kind of bell that helps make steel. To the Valley Elves he kept mentioning some kind of special mold on bread, which they were equally keen to learn more of. Airis raised her eyebrows over the rim of her mug as she saw the number of zeros after the negotiation prices... and quietly pondered if any of the Veil Riders under Yule were into bird women. She would have tried with Yule, but he never seemed interested, and she wasn't going to push the issue. That and, she thought with a shiver of fear, Saveriss was trying to get her claws into him, and the Butcher would probably turn her into fillings for a pillow if she got in her way.

Airis turned her head as she slurped, and saw that one of the night workers was here this morning, the one with the red hair and eyes like that of a coal fire. Her large eyes swiveled back and forth from Yule beside her to the woman walking over. Alavara had another mug in her hand, a bit larger than Airis's and not made for Harpies to hold. She had spent the better part of her morning trying to figure out the concoction that Yule's wife used to make for him during his breakfast, and believed she had done it. She wore something a bit prettier than what she usually would, adorning her ears with winding silver dragon jewelry and a dress that gave her hips a little more sway than they really needed.

Yule stopped scribbling for a moment to flex his hand, grumbling, annoyed at his aching wrist. Airis gave him a quick pop in the ribs with her elbow and when he looked over at her, she nodded forward towards Alavara while still hiding behind the rim of her mug. Yule gave his head a wiggle to make sure the amulet was touching his head under his patrol cap.

"Alavara?" Yule mused, still flexing his writing hand while rubbing his wrist with the other. "You're here awfully early, I thought you didn't like working the mornings."

"I don't." Alavara said with a kind smile, and placed the mug softly down in front of him with a slight thump of the wooden table top. "I had an idea and wanted you to try it for me. This one isn't poisoned, promise."

Alavara looked at Yule as she rested her pointer finger on the rim of the mug, out of which steamed curled and drifted through the air. Yule looked down at the mug and saw it looked a lot darker and milkier than what they usually gave him, and smelled some familiar elements to it that he would have had back at home.

"Huh. I didn't think you guys had cinnamon here." Yule set down his pen and reached over for the mug, Alavara's nail making a slight 'tink' sound as the mug was lifted away from her finger.

"It's called Kirri bark here, and we mostly use it to keep away bugs. From what I've seen of what you people eat, I'm not shocked you think a poison for insects as a tasty treat." Alavara's steady smile stayed trained on Yule as she watched him sniff the rim of the mug.

Airis knew about Kirri bark as well, and dropped the mug slightly so her mouth was no longer behind it and unmuffled. "We use Kirri Bark for our nests too, keeps away Egg Beetles."

"We also used a lot of things called 'peppers' in our food." Yule murmured over the steam of the mug, and blew on it a little to cool it.

"There's some spices so hot that they can actually blind you or make your lungs become inflamed."

Alavara gave a chuckle and rested her head on the back of her left hand. "Sounds like something a Human would enjoy. I still get complaints that our sauces aren't spicy enough all the time."

The fruits of her labors came to ripen as Yule took a deep pull from the mug, and she could almost feel the wave of homesickness that wafted away from him, as if he were the tide and she were the beach. She opened the hooks of her mind and grappled anything that came away, the tendrils poised and ready. Something about this drink, the spices . . . whatever it was, made Yule let his guard completely down, and she was awash in his memories. She saw his wife, their home, their lives, the small things she would do for him, and the small things he would do for her.

Alavara's eyes softened as she took in this deluge of information and digested it. Yule lowered the mug and stared down into it, holding the liquid in his mouth as if afraid to swallow . . . but eventually did. She saw his chest breath in and out deeply, as his thoughts traced among themselves. Even Airis could sense something was up, and thought the Elf had casted some kind of spell on Yule. She furrowed her brows at Alavara and bared a fang as she prepared to get messy.

Yule tilted his head to the side slightly and set the mug down next to his report going to Koko, murmuring to the two women near him."This is very similar to something I used to have back at my home. My wife used to make it for me in the mornings before I would start work."

Yule looked at Alavara with eyes wreathed in sorrow. ". . . I'm not sure how you came up with this, but thank you."

"How long ago did you lose her?" Alavara inquired, not in a rude way, but in the tone of voice that most women are born with, and master, in order to coax the answers from naughty children, or stubborn husbands.

Yule's mouth twitched as he picked up his pen, and his lips came back to form a thin line. His other hand stroked his beard, once, before coming back down to settle the paper as he continued to write.

Airis and Alavara were left in silence for several seconds, the scribble of pen tip to paper the only thing answering them, until Yule broke the silence.

"It's been three years, Earth time."

He continued to write as Alavara caught another wave of thoughts radiating from Yule, and heard terse words and shouting.

She spoke up again, and poked the mug towards Yule ever so lightly, the tea inside sloshing a little bit as she did. "Old Age? Sickness?"

Yule kept writing, formulating his answer in his head as he remembered the entire scene from start to finish, the same scene that has plagued his dreams for three years. Airis set her mug down on the table and leaned forward to get a look at Yule's face.

"Accident."

Alavara's mind picked up the sounds of screeching metal which caused her to startle slightly, the sound reminding her of the nightmares that men at arms get when the two lines of armored warriors clash into one another. She saw a kind of carriage . . . but mangled beyond repair, torn and ripped nt as if a dragon had laid its claws into it.

"A-Accident?" She stuttered, the feelings and thoughts of sadness quickly churning into self loathing and rage. She could see the pen digging into the parchment, cutting deep grooves unlike his other, lighter hand writing.

Yule closed his eyes and breathed in deep, filling his nose with the scent of cinnamon, milk, and chamomile that wafted up from the cup. He opened his sad blue eyes and set down his pen, leaning back and sitting up straight. His hands smoothed out his pant legs and then folded around the mug of tea, soaking up the warmth.

"We got into a fight. We had been married for over a decade, were a team, hell our marriage survived things that would have ruined others. One day we got into a stupid . . . argument. Over paint, of all things. She wanted the room purple." Yule looked at Alavara with a bitter, forlorn look. "I wanted it grey. I told her she always got her way with everything else, I just wanted my office area grey. She said purple would make me feel better."

Yule picked up the mug and took another drink from it, before exhaling out his mouth and setting the mug back down. "I'm a bitter man at times. I know this. My experiences in the military, private security sector, just dealing with people . . . made me so bitter, and I always tried to scrub it away when I was around her. For some reason . . . I don't know. I was having a bad day, stress of work, and I snapped at her, yelled at her like I would have a naughty soldier. 'Can you just fucking let me have a damn thing my way for once?' I said, 'Isn't it enough you get everything else?'."

He shook his head slowly from side to side, ruefully. "Being an asshole . . . over paint. She got mad at me, poured the tea she made me into the sink and left, saying she was going to go get me my 'stupid boring grey paint'. I think she just wanted her space. She left the house . . . and got into an accident. There was another uh . . . Carriage, and the person driving it wasn't paying attention. Was using one of these things."

Yule held up his beat to hell smartphone and wiggled it, mostly using it to look at pictures and do calculations. "He ran into her and hit her directly in the side of the tr-, carriage, and killed her instantly, broke her body, and they couldn't bring her back."

Yule began to slowly roll up his report to Koko, the parchment rasping against his hands as he rolled it up. "Last thing I ever said to her was 'Take your time, your opinion won't be missed.' I was mad about her bugging me about paint, and instead of saying 'I love you, come home safe', I sent her off in dejection and her believing she didn't matter to me. I waited all day for her to come home . . ."

Alavara saw him from his point of view, sitting on a porch step and wringing his hands as he stared down the road way, then saw him check his phone, put it up to his ear, hear some kind of voice, and then turn off his phone. He did this what seems like thirty times or so. He wound the scrolled up paper in its bindings, and began heating wax on a little candle nearby. Yule's eyes were heavy with emotion but he wrinkled his nose and grimaced, the deep frown scoring his face.

"Police came by, or guards, if you will, and told me what happened. I had to go identify her body and fill out the paperwork." He swirled the rolled up paper in front of his eyes as the wax was melting. "I still see her bruised and cut up face when I sleep, and knowing that in that head of hers were my last words, imprinted on her soul. I said I was sorry, and bawled like a baby over her corpse as it lay there on the rack . . . but it was too late for apologies."

Yule sniffed angrily and poured a little bit of wax on the scrolled letter, and stamped it with the signet of the Veil Riders to seal it. Yule's fingers fiddled with the scroll of paper, rolling it around as he thought. He looked up to Alavara, and smiled with melancholy as he handed the scroll to Airis. "I purified her body and scattered the ashes in the mountains of her birthplace. Then I painted my office purple, and never forgave myself for being the asshole that I am."

Airis reached up and took the scroll gently, her eyes wide with the sudden revelations of the Human man beside her. Yule looked over at her and gave her a little pat on the shoulder. "You're free to go Airis. Be safe."

Airis nodded and stood up awkwardly, stuffing the scroll into her leg harness while looking back and forth between Yule and Alavara, the Elf looking a little stricken and a bit remorseful herself. Airis . . . wasn't sure what to do or how to leave, having never been sent off by Yule in such a fashion. She hopped on the balls of her clawed feet a few times, trying to make up her mind, before hugging Yule from behind as best as she could. She thumped her wings on him a few times, and Yule just chuckled sadly, patting his hands on the joints of her wings where her grip claws were. "Im okay, Airis."

Airis disengaged her hug and cleared her throat, before she spun on her avian heel and trotted out of the Sparkling Unicorn, stumbling around the door and closing it behind her.

* * *

After Airis had departed from Yule's company, Alavara also left to gather herself and mull over what she had learned. She made the excuse of needing to talk to the cooks about some matters with the meat freshness, and boogied out of the dining area to leave Yule alone. She expected perhaps an old fling, or a partner departed on some what more amicable means, but this just added a whole new level of intricacy to the mysterious plot of Yule.

After a few more hours had passed, the rest of the Veil Riders were finally able to drag themselves down from their beds, and Chikily rousted from his chair nest to take a parcel of letters to some of the nobles staying in the city of Imlnoris. As his Veil Riders breakfasted around him, bickering still about the topics of last night, Alavara would poke her head out from around the corners of the staff area to peek at Yule. He still sat there, writing out more letters and correspondence while chatting to his troopers and asking them how they slept, or if they needed anything.

When she felt comfortable enough to go behind the bar, she busied herself with cleaning glasses and tankards left over from the night before. Something was bugging Alavara though: How the hell can a man still be mourning after three years? She understood the reasons behind it all, but to never even give yourself the liberty of at least enjoying the comforting touch of another person? To share a bed and stay warm against each other, flesh to flesh? The thought of suffering for so many years, alone, filled her with enough mixed emotions that it threw off her Inn hustle that she usually did with easy stride. What she gleaned from this morning . . . she kept to herself. Even the recipe of the tea stayed secret to her, and she didn't tell the other bar workers what she had learned. She was not folly either, as she knew she never cared for marriage. Four failures at the shtick left her fed up with the whole affair, and simply took pleasure in the partners she accompanied to her chambers every once in a while when the fancy took her . . . but three years? Three years wrapped up in the blanket of grief was too much, even for the most stubborn of people. Unhealthy even . . . it was no wonder that the man never got any sleep, and was constantly sucking down anything with a drop of caffeine in it.

Alavara steeled herself, slapping a wet rag onto the bar top as she once again studied Yule, who was getting up to leave. She pried harder, gripping and ripping at any thought that came her way, tucking them into her mind as if she were a pick pocket in the market square.

"I'll bed you for your own health, if not for my own liking." She murmured, and pulled out another glass from under the storage area.

Outside, Yule stretched in the sun, his spine crackling like someone wringing a bundle of spaghetti noodles. It was really nice that Alavara had him taste test that tea she brought earlier. Bringing back old memories was not really as nice, nor was unloading that heavy shit onto her. He thwacked his hat on his thigh to get some dust off of it, and quietly wished he'd just keep his mouth shut sometimes. As he wacked his hat, the amulet jingled inside of the rim and he checked it while the thought was on his mind. As he held it up to the sun, he saw the magical fluid inside was running low, and he again sighed in frustration.

Having to go and bug that poor woman for blood really weighed on Yule. He didn't like it, no matter how readily she was to do so. It was an evil, that while necessary, he could live without. He figured he would give Yethis time to relax; He knew a little bit of the Valley Elf 'Tunkah', and was doing his damnedest to learn more just to ease the burden off of Yethis. Yule checked in with the NCOs idling outside the Inn, who were working on retrofitting some kind of weird dwarvish pole-arm to the front of a Humvee, and went for a little walk to get some fresh hair, see the market, and think.

He liked to walk and think, it was something he did all the time on

Terra when he was stumped about something, or had a worry on his mind. Yule was getting reports from Zerg Company that more Valley Elves were fleeing from the smaller villages east from the Veil, flooding North and North East. Thankfully, those Kingdoms were on good, if not friendly, terms with the Valley Elves, and were taking the refugees in with a stride. Yule waved to Urmstronj as he passed his shop, and talked to a group of school kids walking down the road in a gaggle around their teacher, asking them how their morning was as he passed, and they all yelled out their answers to him while giggling.

Yule's friendly smile faded like a ghost from his face as he returned to his mind and the reports from Koko. Koko's Veil Riders were having to employ hit and run guerrilla tactics to buy time for the Valley Elves, and had accomplished the goal of seizing multiple vehicles from the blue helmets as well, including a M1117, fully armed with its MK19 automatic grenade launcher and the M2 beside it. They used it mostly for hauling around the mortars, as fuel was short on hand. Zerg Company had minor losses here and there, taking up the majority of the combat actions from the Veil Riders as a whole, and were slowly folding Valley Elves into their ranks and arming them with the spare weapons they had on hand.

He rounded the street corner and came out onto the market square, which was bustling with traders and stalls harking their vegetables or other wares. Yule breathed in the deep scents of sweat, charcoal smoke, and leather that hung around the place. It was as close as he could get to a military surplus store, and it anchored him as close to reality as he could manage. As he browsed a rack of weird rings and jars, he thought about the Veil. If the forces coming from the Veil were able to transport and put together an armored vehicle, of all things, he was going to have to push his time table forward by months in order to combat the leaps and bounds of materials the Opfor were getting from Earth. He gave a sigh, and knew he needed more Intel on the site for both he and Koko, and that would mean either hiring more Harpies on private order . . .

Or talking to Saveriss, the thought of which brought goosebumps to his flesh.

Yule decided to tackle the first thing, and that was hiring more scouts. He patted the money pouch he kept in his battle-vest pocket, which jangled heavily with coin. Selling technological advances was keeping his Veil Riders well paid, but he kept the lion's share just for occurrences like these. Hanging proudly from a low, long building was a sign reading "Pump-a-Rum Package Service", out of which the chittering of Harpy speak echoed. Yule put his hat on tight to his head, and opened the door to the rather unenthusiastic mug of Roland, the Elf who ran the place and did most of the book keeping. Beside him was a wide eyed Horned Owl Harpy, named Norea, that helped him manage the packing ledgers, as they had a few extra digits on their wings that allowed them to hold a pen with some accuracy. They both greeted him in their own fashions, Norea being chipper while Roland sounded as if he could just give up on life at any moment.

Yule put in an order for six of their sneakiest Harpies they had in the place, and Norea stepped away to go fetch them. As she did, she twisted her neck 180 degrees to the rear and peered at him with her bright yellow eyes.

"Are you fine with any Harpy, Mr.Yuuule?"

"Yep, thank you." Yule's stomach turned as she smiled and twisted her head back around. He understood why she could do it, but damn it to hell if it wasn't the freakiest thing in the world to see.

Roland busied himself with doing paperwork, leaving Yule to rock back and forth on his boot heels until Norea arrived with a little gang of Harpies behind her. Most of these were male, with only one of the five being female. These were a curious bunch, and reminded him a lot of Nighthawks from back home. Their hair and feathers were stippled and camouflaged to the point they could probably fall into a pile of leaves and never be found, which was helped by their sun kissed skin and dark, almost black eyes. Even more curious were their facial markings, which looked a lot like freckles but ranged in size and shape, probably camouflage as well if Yule had to make a guess.

They introduced themselves as the Brush Feathered, and were keen to be paid for their work first and foremost. They didn't even ask what the work was, just how much coin would be jingling in their pockets. This caught Yule off guard, but he rallied quickly and told them to follow him. The Brush Feathered followed him outside, down the street, and finally into the Sparkling Unicorn, in which Yule then began to explain his plan. For a hefty sum of gold, they were to collect intelligence as close to the camp as possible, even getting as close to hear people talking or even read things left out in the open. The Brush Feathered told him this would be no problem.

"We've been paid to sneak before, this will be no different. Brush

Feathers know how to not be seen." One spoke up, an older male who grinned at Yule with pearly white fangs.

Yule could understand their aptitude for subterfuge; these Harpies lacked any real claws, digits, or even long fangs for combat. Yule confirmed the deal with them, gave them some spare BDU and flecktarn shorts, as well as a few ghillie suits that they could use if they believed they could come in handy. The Brush Feathered snatched them up almost immediately, and were talking excitedly in their mother tongue about the strange suits for some time. After leaving to retrieve their own specially made satchels and pack-sacks, Yule went up to talk to Britta. She was reading inside her room, having been given her rucksack after she identified it from the loot, and looked up to Yule as he opened the door.

"Going to stick another splinter in me?" Yule asked, raising his eyebrows as the guard outside her door also leaned to the side to peek in at her.

"No, vould be a shame to ruin your nice uniform again."

"Ha ha." Yule mused in a low tone, and crossed his arms. "I'm sending out some tourists to the Veil Base you have set up. I want you to write me a few let-"

"Already have" Britta interrupted, her face set as she pulled out ten sheets of parchment with names written on them, and the other sides littered with paragraphs of German in tight, orderly script.

Yule couldn't help but smile as he reached over and took the papers in a cool manner. "Peak German efficiency."

Britta snorted, and opened her book back up. Yule closed the door behind him, then pressed his patrol cap to his scalp . . . but the letters didn't change as they usually did. Yule growled out a 'Hecken Heck' to the ceiling of the Inn before rumbling down the stairs and looking for Yethis. She was thankfully bugging Gremlin, sitting next to her and brushing her hair as she played Dorf Fortress on her laptop. Yule made his way to her and tapped her on the shoulder.

"Sorry lovely, no blood." He said in Tunkah to her, and Yethis spun around on her rump to face him. In the blink of an eye she had her special little dagger out and had sliced open her finger while rummaging in her side pouch for the other ingredient, something that they called 'True Earth Ink'. Yule watched her slice open her flesh with gathered eyebrows, glaring down at the little wound as he pulled out his Amulet. He hated this part, he really did. She pulled the stopper out with her teeth, the sharp 'pop!' of it causing her to smile around the cork in her mouth. The dark inky liquid flowed into the Amulet Yule held in his fingers, which she re-corked and then placed her finger over the lip of the well, letting her blood drain slowly into the amulet.

She smiled up at him and wrinkled her nose while wiggling back and forth on her rump. Unknown to Yule, Yethis took this as a great honor, that her blood was the one to fuel the Amulet that he would use, as well as being his personal healer. She felt a bit silly for fainting when he needed her earlier, but still counted the healing as her own doing, since it was her blood that was used after all. Yethis was known as a 'Clean Blood', an Elf whose blood was rich and flowing with the necessities that were needed for strong, formidable magic. She took a lot of pride in this, and to be serving a commander of the Veil Riders was an honor all in itself.

When the amulet well was full, she licked her finger clean by poking it in her mouth and tapped the amulet to get it back to working again. Yule tucked it up into his hat, then placed it on his head before speaking to her.

"I don't like this, you know."

Yethis smiled up at him from around her finger before pulling it from her mouth and wiping the saliva on her pant leg. "I know that, you've told me enough. But it has to be done."

"Not the only thing..." They both just barely heard, and they turned to see Alavara walking away with a tray loaded with empty mugs. Yethis glared at her, standing up and brushing past Yule to stalk after her. Yule went to speak up but the front door of the Sparkling Unicorn thudded open, and the Brush Feathered were back with their equipment, calling after Yule while other Veil Riders stood behind them and tucked random goodies into their sacks. Yule quickly read through the letters as he made his way towards the chittering Harpies, who were pumped up for the mission given to them and buzzing with anticipation. He didn't see anything negative in the letters as he read, and began folding them up into squares.

Besides the random things tucked into their sacks, the Harpies were given some rations, water, and a few knives just in case they needed to saw or cut away at anything. Yule then gave them the letters, and gave them examples of the unit flags they should look out for, them being the German, Polish, and Czech flags respectively. After everything was double checked, the Brush Feathered set off on foot out into the grasslands to move on the ground during the day, then fly during the night to avoid detection.

Yule turned back into the Inn while rubbing his temples, and called out for Domino and the other NCOs. When they were gathered, he sent them off to do supply checks on their troopers, everything from ammunition to the amount of money they still had on them. There was a small issue of Veil Riders blowing all their money on stupid stuff and not giving the Inn a small portion of it, whether that was in tips or paying for their food. While the city was paying for a lot of the supplies and space the Veil Riders took up, that didn't mean he wanted he and his troopers to look like bums.

Hours were buzzing by as Yule went to and fro, doing housekeeping on his unit, when for the second time that day, the door was kicked open. Yule turned to see who it was, just having set off to see how many mechanics he had total for Humvee check ups. "Ah for fucks sakes..."

A Dwarf called out, pulling a traveling hood from his head. "Oi! Veil-ling!"

Yule's previous gentle temple rubbing turned into vigorous massaging as Fokhet Alewrench shouldered past the door, two of his engineers following behind him. Chicks rolled her eyes, shutting the door for them with the side of her boot while clicking her teeth in annoyance.

"Fokhet, how are you? I thought you were still back in your hold, I just sent a letter tod-"

"Takes too long, So I came here." He interrupted, and pointed to a table in the corner while walking over to it. Chicks's blonde eyebrows shot up, and she smirked mockingly at Yule while jutting out her lips.

"Shattap, you're lucky you don't have to deal with this shit..." Yule hissed, and walked over to the Dwarves while Chicks chuckled and brought her ale tankard to her lips. Yule, for one, was getting tired of being interrupted, and waved over at the bar area for some drinks. Alavara wasn't there anymore, and neither was Yethis, but a barwoman saw him and began pouring for the Dwarves. He sat down at the table, and looked into the face of Fokhet.

Fokhet was an Engineer Prince, son of Snorri Alewrench, who was Thane of the Engineering Hold called Kirbadir. Snorri, as it turns out, was the first Dwarf he met in the city, the same one that almost crushed his hand, and had sent his son Fokhet to try and garner some designs from the Veil Riders. These Dwarves of Kirbadir were all in on the Icelandic look, and for all Yule knew, probably invented it themselves; Hair short cropped on the sides while long on top, braided hair and beards adorned with strategically placed gold beads and spiraling dragons that curled through the rough strands, and all of them had long walking axes that really reminded Yule of a certain Dwarf that was famous for sprinting short distances. He could see from the crossed pistols on the chest of the female engineer that they were already headlining a Dwarven semi-automatic pistol of sorts, which looked oddly like a Sig P226 . . . except chunkier and covered in runes.

Yule nodded towards them. "How many of those are there?"

The Dwarf female chuckled and gave her bountiful chest a jiggle. "Just two, love."

Yule cast his eyes heavenward as all the Dwarves at the table hooted and slapped the table top, roaring with laughter at his expense. *I fucking swear . . .* Yule thought to himself, as the barmaid made her way over and began setting down tankards that were peaked with foam. Now that she had made them jiggle, Yule had to fight to keep his eyes up and off of her, and the she-Dwarf was certainly taking notice, hooding her eyes and folding her arms under her breasts so they looked even more prominent.

"You know what I mean, Ma'am. Snorri only had a quick hand on my pistol for but a few minutes, and you have already managed to make something that looks like a proper semi-automatic pistol."

The She-Dwarf smirked at Yule, and he felt her boot heel rest on top of his own boot's toe. "Dwarves don't need long to make an idea reality. We just need to get our *hands* on it for awhile and it all comes naturally."

Yule quietly wished that Fokhet had chosen a bigger table, and had to keep moving his foot to keep the Dwarf from trying to pin it down with her own.

"For Fridd's sakes Gilla leave 'em be." Spoke up the other Engineer, before motioning to Fokhet and then taking a drink from his tankard.

"Right." Began Fokhet. "Im sure yeh' heard from down south those old Ultharian bastards are getting a big head of themselves and snatching up folk, as well as using your people's resources to seek their own gains. Ain't good, not at all. We need to increase war production and begin pumping out weapons that can contend with yours. My sister went over to see your friend Koko and is already taking plans for those things they called 'danger toobs' back to the hold. I ain't 'gonna yank you around on this. We want one of your rifles to take back, and one you would recommend. We've been working hard on the quick to get up to date on those manufacturing techniques for the cartridges. Which by the way!" "Fokhet parted the drapes of the window and gestured. "We have a nice little present for you."

Yule leaned to the side and peeped out to see there were crates sitting on the road by the Humvees, in which Veil Riders were crowding around and plucking handfuls of brand new, gleaming ammunition, and sprinkling them on each other. The Dwarves around them laughed and helped sprinkle the new ammunition on a female Rider who was making a brass angel. Yule had to admit, these Dwarves were slicker than goose shit when it came to getting jobs down quick.

"And now . . ." Yule said, leaning back into his seat as Gilla winked and kissed her lips at him.

"Now, we want a present too. And no Gilla, we stick to the plan, quit being weird." Fokhet slapped Gilla on the shoulder with the back of his hand and she laughed rakishly, as she was pointing at Yule and was about to lean over and say something to Fokhet. Yule ignored her, and moved his jaw around as he thought, mulling over the fact that he really did owe Fokhet for bringing this much ammunition and getting the jobs done within days when he had set aside entire months in time frames. He looked up to the Dwarves.

"Pick a caliber."

This single statement made all three dwarves turn on their serious faces, and they leaned in while gripping their tankards.

"That 5.56 round can fly forever it seems like, passed from mountain to mountain without much issue." Stated the other male engineer.

"Aye but that 7.62 has a lot of . . . power behind it." Purred Gilla, and once again Yule felt her boot start touching his.

Both Yule and Fokhet thought the same phrase at her tone of voice, and both of them glared at her as 'Please Stop' filtered through their thoughts.

Fokhet flicked his eyes back to Yule. "We were curious. After finding the materials, working on the alchemy behind the propellant, figuring out the right flash powder for the caps, we made some rough barrels and shot a few dummies just to see what they could do. We were a bit embarrassed that this kind of design hadn't come to us sooner, as it is quite simple in principle once the kinks were worked out."

"You worked out the kinks in only a few days while it took us... well, more time. Anyway... I favor the 5.56, it holds up better at longer ranges and has less recoil. That being said, I also prefer the 7.62×51 when it comes to stopping power. Then there's the weapon issue, I suppose..."

Yule wasn't sure this was the right idea, but he stood up. "I'll be right back."

He left, and returned with his K2 and a spare FAL after a few minutes, setting them on the table. "Of all the rifles I have used, this one has never failed me, and has performed better than any of my other rifles. Then this is a very iconic rifle that uses the 7.62 round, and is a favorite of my other co-commander, Koko. Here are a few magazines from the other rifles we use." He set the metal magazines next to the K2 and FAL, having borrowed some from the Veil Riders who were using FALs and M14s, and his own stanag magazine. "If I were to hedge my bets, these rifle designs would serve you well in either caliber, I don't doubt you guys can figure out the simple Human science behind it. We could also use more magazines if you can find a way to get them out to us."

Fokhet clapped his hands together cheerfully. "Excellent! Are you sure you don't mind? This is your personal rifle, after all."

Yule looked down at the K2 laying on the table, and nodded. "It's fine. Just treat her nice and bring her back when you're done."

Fokhet and the other male engineer grinned toothily and began to get up, draining their tankards as they did, and grabbing the K2 as well as the FAL.

Gilla stood up after gathering the magazines together, and when Yule had gotten up from his seat, she bumped him with her hip. "Need anything else taken care of while I'm here?" Her eyes crinkled with humor as she grinned up at Yule, who looked down at her while trying to keep his eyes away from her deep cleavage.

"You really are horrible."

Gilla cackled and slapped Yule on the seat of his pants as she walked behind him and strode towards the door, where her fellow dwarves were exiting out into the late day sun. She stood at the door, and gave him another sultry wink.

"I know." She breathed, and closed the door behind her when she left.

Chicks had an eyebrow raised, looking from the door over to Yule from where she leaned against the wall. "Man, men probably go into her as salami and come out a slim jim from muscles that strong."

"Chicks, please, dont, I would like to enjoy my dinner here in a bit." Yule sulked, and wiped a bit of sweat from his brow. Where the hell was the bit in the stories about Dwarf women being man-eaters?

Chicks just chuckled to herself, more at her joke than anything, then nodded and spoke in Tunkah. "Hey Yethis."

Yule turned, and behind him Yethis stood, beaming her bright smile and holding a mug in both of her hands. Out of the mug came the spiraling scent of cinnamon, and the sweet smell of comfort.

Yethis held out the mug to him. "Alavara said you might need this after that mean Dwarf woman, what's in it anyways? It smells kind of like bug repellent."

CHAPTER 10

YULE WOKE UP with a start, lurching up off his pillow and gripping the M9 that sat on the bedside table to his right. Sweat coursed down his body and glinted with the morning sunlight that shined through the window as he looked around, his chest heaving.

"Ugh, fuck..." Yule groaned, and flopped backwards onto his sweat soaked sheets. He looked to his left as his hair stuck wildly to his face, and saw the empty mug that Alavara had left the night before. She had been bringing him that tea every night now to help with his sleep, but Yule was starting to believe that not even that could calm his hay wired nerves.

Four days had passed since he had paid the Brush Feathered to go and gather intelligence data on the Veil Camp, and they were way overdue for a check in of any kind. The fact there was neither hide or feather to be seen of the Harpies had left Yule in a slowly growing state of apprehension, and again wondering if he had sent a group of innocent Veil dwellers off to their doom. Yule had even gone as far as to have Gremlin send out a drone to see if she could spot one of the Brush Feathered alive, but their camouflage was so accurate to ground foliage that she had no idea where they were, and lacked any other sensors to find them, unless she found a FLIR system in a captured convoy sometime in the future.

He was afraid to move out his Veil Riders to take the fight to the enemy unless he had accurate information on where they were, and what they had, but nothing of that like was coming his way in spades. Koko was ramping up his own side of the offensive, and the weeks were filled with constant skirmishes and contacts where the men and women of Zerg Company would do battle with those from their home world. There was however a solid breakthrough on Yule's side of things, as he had been struggling to find something to do when it came to his own research and information gathering, and found some pay dirt in the library and records building within the city of Imlnoris, a few days after the Brush Feathered had left.

The sorceress whom he had first met outside the city walls was more than happy to show him around the place when he was finally able to track her down, and the two spent many an hour together among the dusty tomes and ledgers of the library. The library was a mixture of grand and destitute, and it seemed like half of the library was simply a pile of books and scrolls with something akin to a general idea to them, while the other half looked more like a proper library system, with rows of shelves and tall ladders that swung on guided rails.

With her help, Yule was able to dig deep into the old legends and lore of the land, with the sorceress plugging in the things he couldn't understand. The two usually sat shoulder to shoulder while they rummaged through books, having meals together as they prowled on for hours at a time for three solid days of reading. She was always kind and patient with Yule, meeting his frustrations with a smile and encouraging words. Yule would go to get angry, or clench his fists in frustration when a lead would dead end, just to have her pat his hands.

"It's okay, there is always another book to read."

One particular record, when unearthed from the bottom of a pile of books labeled 'Other Visitors', was the gold nugget Yule was looking for, and he ended up dragging Gremlin and five of the other more conspiracy inclined Veil Riders to the library with him on the fourth day. The sorceress, who Yule finally learned was named Imra Ira Olora, was a bit annoyed when he showed up with his little motley crew, but she put on a brave face and began helping them set up their Crazy Wall. As Yule poured over a page detailing an old war in the early bronze age of the realm, he looked up to see Gremlin and Imra trailing red yarn from one book to another, Imra laughing as Gremlin happily danced among the many strings.

He took a moment and watched Gremlin, his finger rasping to a pause on the page. It was rare to see her smile, as she was usually glowering at the screens of her laptops, or fussing over the internals of her over used drones. It was strange how similar, yet alien the two were to each other: Gremlin was wiry and short, her hair black, but not as

Raven-esque as Kentucky's, her eyes usually tired looking and seemed to always look strained from staring at screens. Domino had said she had a 'Tomoko vibe' going, and there were times when Yule had to agree with the statement. On the other hand, Imra was tall, sleek, well muscled and regal in her appearance, with her ears long and eyes sharp with wit and intelligence. Her chestnut hair seemed to have never been cut, the long braid probably able to tickle her heels if she didn't wrap it on itself with ribbon. The eyes were the only thing that their people seemed to share with the Terrans, while the rest was incompatible with each other on almost every level.

Yule puffed a bit of air from his nose and looked back down to his book, following a line of script before he paused and stood up with the book in his hand. The book was so old that his finger actually made a dust line along the page as he followed the Elvish script, his Amulet working over time as it tried to cobble the letters together into something Yule could read. Everyone turned to look at Yule as he began to speak, walking towards them with lingering steps. Yule was wrong . . . this wasn't a book, but a journal, and the person who was writing in it seemed to be writing something he had seen or witnessed.

"To the world of gray, and iron legs, we flee, with the power of the rust blood we shall return and begin our revenge." Yule looked up to Imra, his eyes dark with curiosity. "What is this guy talking about?"

Imra shrugged. "Probably something from the old Fae Wars. Fairies are not what they seem after all, and a grand struggle happened between almost everyone else, and those who aligned themselves with the courts, such the Chosen Children. The Fae believed they were the true rulers and inheritors of this realm, and launched their master plan to control those on this plane and bend them to their will. No one was really happy with the idea of being ruled by the very embodiment of madness, so the Fae were pushed into a corner during the Great Fae Wars thousands of years ago. I mean, for instance, the Dwarves have records that mention they were still using stone weapons in that time to bludgeon things to death, and the Elves were still a single jewel compared to the many shards we are now."

Gremlin, who was tying the end of a string to a book, turned her head, her eyes wide with interest. "Grand plan, you say?"

Imra nodded, and sat down on a nearby chair, taking off her shoes and giving her toes a spread in order to stretch the sore muscles. "They wanted complete control over all. They were the true Fae, those beings that held the glory of having blood that was pink and flecked with gold. In their stories, the core of this planet has the same blood, and made them true offspring of this place. Well, turns out they may be more magical, but they still die when whacked over the head with a heavy stick. They and the Chosen Children of Ulthary were pushed all the way down into the Southern portion of the continent. Queen Ulthary, from which they get their name, was as old and powerful as they come, but not even she could stop the unified might of the many races."

Imra reached around the side of the chair and plucked up a bottle of wine and drank a few glugs from it, after popping off the cork and tossing it aimlessly into the library, sloshing the last drink around her mouth a bit before continuing to speak.

"The next bit of the legend is a bit murky, as the Chosen Children see fit to keep their so called 'Prophecy' a secret, but from what we have been able to gather, she swore revenge and just . . . vanished. Took all the Fae with her, even the few good ones. Some say she's the one who created the Veil, tearing a hole in both worlds and dragging her court to the other to rest, rebuild, and scheme.

The Veil Riders were watching Imra, who sighed happily and rested her feet on a pile of nearby books, while her head nestled into the plush wing of the reading chair. She had been helping them tirelessly and she was starting to feel the exhaustion setting in after days of reading books and scrolls.

Gremlin roamed the lines, tapping her hands on the thighs of her pants as Yule read on. After that little bit, it continued on about the writer's other smaller findings in some kind of old ruined stronghold way north where the war began, but nothing else of much note except his journey home and being hounded by a debt collector when he failed to bring back any treasure. Yule shut the book carefully and set it on a low nearby shelf, before looking back at Imra.

"What kind of Fae?" Yule asked, who rubbed at his aching eyes.

"Oh, you know." Imra murmured, her eyes still closed as she took another drink from the bottle. She shifted a bit and breathed out air tinged with honey wine. "Fae folk. They look alot like us Elves but they have all black eyes that are larger than ours. A lot of them have wings, or can shape-shift, and they rely heavily on magic and manipulation to get their way. They can also live on indefinitely, never to know the blight of a wrinkle." Imra sniffed and Yule saw her poke a little at the side of her eyes where women are known to develop crows feet. "A lot of the greater Fae followed her through the Veil I suppose, since we only really have Pixies and Brownies left here. Everything with an ounce of real power skipped over to the next world, yours I suppose."

Yule's mind had frozen after the word *shape-shift*, but was polite enough to wait till Imra finished. "What does rust blood mean?"

Imra again shrugged her shoulders and held out her hands, one of which still clasped the bottle. "I don't know, maybe your folk? We don't experiment with magic on your people. It can act funny, which is why I assigned Yethis to you."

"What about those German fellows that came through?" Yule asked, looking over at Gremlin who was talking with the other Veil Riders and scribbling things on their Crazy Wall

"Oh. I read up on them after our first meeting. They partied with the Dwarves till they died a few years later. They and a Dwarven adventuring party drunkenly thought it would be a swell idea to go hunting trolls one night naked. You can figure out how that went." Imra drew her finger across her neck while making a ripping noise in the back of her throat.

"Right." Yule murmured, and patted Imra on her knee. "Thanks for the help with all this."

Imra raised her wine bottle in a salute, and then pressed it to her lips to drink from it again as Yule moved on to his Veil Riders.

"A lot of writing going on over here."

Gremlin spun around, her eyes fever bright with some kind of understanding.

"Yule, what if our legends are real? What if the whole Seelie courts thing is real, and the Unseelie court has been farming us for thousands of years?"

Yule blinked a few times. "What?"

Gremlin groaned angrily and pushed Yule towards the board, at which two Veil Riders were writing down major dates of conflicts and casualty numbers.

"Think about it Yule! What if all these huge wars we have had, these multi-nation conflicts and civil wars, what if they were all a way to try and power up the doorway whats-her-face made here to get away! What if she took her court to a fast paced world, who would get her the technology she needs *faster*, and then bring them back here to finish the job!"

Gremlin was holding onto Yule's arm as she spoke, and was

pointing at the dates on the Crazy Wall. To be fair, a lot of the dates were massacres, and a lot of the wars indeed did have major body counts... but would that even work?

Yule looked down at her, his face puzzled "Gremlin, if that was the case, how would she gather up all the blood to power her Gate?"

Despite his lack of support, Gremlin was undeterred. "Beats me! But this makes the most sense for the time being. Grab the board boys! We're taking this back to the Inn!"

Imra spoke up from her little snuggle spot in her chair, pressing her own Translation Amulet to her head. "Board has to stay here."

Gremlin went from pointing to the board, to pointing at the books. "Grab the books then boys!"

Imra leaned forward, the liquid inside the bottle sloshing, and she grinned at Gremlin. "Books have to stay as well."

"We shall take the notes then!" Gremlin roared with awkward bravado after being stonewalled twice, and pointed to the legion of sticky notes they had managed to stick around the place, as their thoughts were running wild with the previous hours of investigation.

"That'll do." Imra hummed, and offered her hand to Yule. "Help a pretty lady up, would you?

Yule grabbed her hand, and hefted her up and off the chair, while Gremlin and the other Veil Riders scrabbled at the many post-it notes in the library.

After all the notes were brought back to the Sparkling Unicorn, and Yule had escorted Imra back to her room in the Royal Quarter (In which he more or less handed her off to one of the maids on hand, as she kept drinking the entire way there, and demanded Yule watch her make his clothes disappear), Gremlin made her own personal Crazy Wall in her room and poured over it constantly. She kept this up for the days afterwards while Yule waited for the Brush Feathered. She was even doing it still, as Yule woke up and rubbed the sweat from his body with a nearby towel and got dressed. He rubbed at his face to work the blood back into his brain as he thumped down the hallway and knocked on Gremlin's door. It was unlocked, and he walked in to see both Gremlin and Britta standing in the middle of a spider web of yarn string that ran back and forth from the walls of her room.

On her desk, she had all of her laptops open with notes typed up on theml, which casted weird shadows about the place due to the lack of sun shine on this side of the Inn. Yule could see from the doorway that she was breaking down old fairy tales for clues, and some of the typing was in German.

"Any luck, crazies?" Yule groaned, rubbing at his temples to sooth the pounding in his head.

All he had to see was the grinning of their mouths to know he was in for more theories on the subject. Britta was being allowed more freedom in her movement when it came to the Inn; Yule had his Riders gearing up for battle and they wouldn't be able to watch her anyway. At this point, getting stabbed in the back by Britta would be a blessing, because it would mean his problems would get lumped onto someone else.

Before they could launch into the explanation that the Market Garden Invasion was orchestrated by a Unseelie Court Elf who took the place of Montgomery, and Hitler being a Changling because, clearly, he was vegetarian and liked animals over humans, Yule just softly closed the door. He made his way down the staircase to the dining area in the vain hope that a Brush Feathered was waiting for him downstairs.

While he was happy to see Airis and Yethis waiting for him, and heard Alavara humming in the kitchen, he would have traded them all in for a single one of his little feathered spies to be sitting there in the chair waiting for him to wake up. He greeted them all with a groggy 'Good morning', and Airis clicked over on the wood floor boards to give him a hug.

This was a new thing that she was doing. Yule noticed she would hug him once, for roughly three seconds, then trot back over and sit back at the table to continue eating. This all became a part of her ritual since he told her about his unfairly taken wife. Yethis also seemed to be in some kind competition with Alavara, and she sat there slowly wavering back and forth from her place on the bench seat.

Yule could see she was immensely tired, and had kept this up for days, struggling to wake up early and join the rest in the morning work load. She claimed it was to keep track on the blood needed for the Amulet, but the times he did need her, he would have to softly rock her awake. She would usually fall asleep next to her mug of tea a few minutes after Yule would greet her, and begin doing his morning paperwork and correspondence.

Yethis's eyelids fluttered up and down as she struggled to cling to consciousnesses for the fourth day in a row, and Yule found himself setting both his hands on her shoulders and leaning down to whisper in her long Elven ear.

"The chairs over there are very comfy, and I can wake you if I need you."

Yethis just nodded tiredly and plodded over to the larger of the chairs that was made for Goliaths, plopping down into it and falling instantly back to sleep.

Alavara gave a chuckle as she walked over with Yule's special tea and set it down next to him. Then she set down another mug next to Airis, who began to demand the same kind of tea Yule got, for some reason, despite the fact it tasted awful to her and made her sniff a lot.

"You can always tell who are not morning people." She said, walking over and throwing a blanket over Yethis.

"Don't chide her too much." Yule said, unraveling a scroll stamped with the signet of Fokhet and laying it out on the table. "She feels left out and wants to be included."

Airis nodded from beside yule, using her wing digits to spoon warm oatmeal burgoo into her mouth, having already eaten the sausage that was on top of it. Yule saw he had been given extra sausage on his own burgoo and picked up the additional protein, ladling it into Airis's bowl and receiving happy sounds from the Harpy next to him.

Alavara sat down next to Yule and began helping him unfold or open letters that Airis had brought in, and began pre-reading them with Yule to speed along his mornings. She would read the letters to him as he wrote down a response to others, forming a nice little chain of information,. Then the two would each start sealing up the letter for travel. Airis, wanting to also feel like she was helping, would hold the extra wax and plop a little bit here or there in the candle warmer when they would pour some out.

Yule reached over and plucked out the scroll that he knew was Kokos' report. As he unraveled it and read down the lines, the hair on his arms stood on end and a single bead of sweat began to form in the middle of his back. In the letter, Koko let him know that he had managed to capture some night vision goggles after a massive ambush against a blue helmet Platoon, and were using them to combat the daily night raids that were happening along the borders of Artry and Regenesson. 'We found a column moving along a tree line and we were watching them from the brush, but we found something odd about some of the troopers. When some of my lads would pan their night vision over them, some of their eyes would light up like cats and dogs do. We began the ambush and ran them off, but we couldn't find any bodies that had the same effect."

He looked up from the letter and began to truly wonder if what Gremlin said was true . . . have they been among us the entire time? Yule quickly rolled the letter back up and breathed in deep, his mind buzzing as thoughts sped past at lightning speed. Was all of this bullshit really true? He unfurled the letter from Fokhet back open and laid it out flat. Fokhet was already halfway through machining out the tools to mass produce what looked like blocky versions of the FAL and K2 rifles, and had mentioned in the letter that the Dwarves were gearing up to go on the offensive with them due to the sudden lurch in pressure from the Chosen Children in the South.

Yule knew the decision he had to make, and the right answer to it. He couldn't keep letting Koko's Company take all the pressure from the Veil, and had to start moving in to try and combat what was coming from home. In three days time, the entirety of Cosmoline Company would move out and set up a field head quarters in the forests of Sanrion, and push the enemy back as far as they could. Yule let anyone he knew would care know about his intentions and finished up his correspondence. After which, he then helped clean the wax off of Airis so she could head off and take the letters to who they were addressed. When she left, Yule turned to Alavara.

"We're gonna have to move out here soon and begin doing what we agreed to for you guys. They're creeping their way up here and if we just sit here and hang out, they're going to get their fingers on this city like they have the towns to the South."

Alavara stared at him, chewing on her cheek for a few moments before nodding a few times. "I understand. We'll try and get everything ready for you when the time comes."

When the rest of the Veil Riders came down, Yule made the announcement to everyone that they would be going on the offensive, and the Riders cheered with honest vigor at the prospect of actual battle after such a long stretch stuck in town. Word had gotten out to the city shortly after, and the streets were buzzing with the news. Information was flowing in from Artry to Imlnoris thanks to Pumpa-Rum, and almost everyone knew of the battles to the South East and what they were facing. They also knew of the constantly growing pressure from all of the straggling refugees that came in a steady stream.

On the last night, before the final day of preparation, Yule was writing a list of all the Veil Riders that were currently in the Company, sixty six names plus Airis, Chikily, and Yethis, who would be joining them on the journey out. He was in his room, having pried himself away from the partying down below to write this macabre list to give to Erlan, the Elf who owned the Inn. Yule had slipped him some gold to carve the names somewhere on the building, a place of his choice, in order to make sure the names of his Veil Riders wouldn't be forgotten, one way or another. If they truly failed, and the Inn was destroyed, then all was truly lost and they would slip from the memory of the living ... but Yule had made up his mind that this was simply not an option to even think over. Yule had just reached the 55th name when he heard the door open behind him, and turned in his creaky wooden chair to see Alavara standing in the doorway. Around the door, the sounds of cheering and song echoed up from the dining room, and Yule recognized the voice of that Bard from the first days of them being here. He also heard Chikily screeching for someone to put him down, and he hoped the Harpy wasn't being tossed around or something of that nature.

"What brings you up here, Alavara?" Yule said, placing his looted bic-pen down on the table.

Alavara closed the door behind her to keep out the noise, and she had a look in her eyes that Yule had not seen before. "Well, I didn't expect you to leave so soon, and I have been busy with preparing you and your Riders before now. I had something I wanted to say before you left."

She wrung her hands nervously, and seemed to be fighting with figuring out the correct words to say. "I ... Don't want you to leave out to the field before I got a chance to discuss something with you, something you may not like."

Yule drew his brows together and stood, arching his back to crack his spine. "What? Is something wrong?"

Alavara stepped over towards him, her mind hooks open and slithering around Yule to prick and pull at whatever thought that managed to poke out enough for her to grab.

"I don't want you to go out and ... run the risk of dying after all these years of being alone. Since you've gotten here, you have taken none to your bed, for three long years you have slept bereft of someone to warm you in the night, or hold you to keep away your nightmares."

She paused, and a few thoughts lept away from Yule, her hooks snatching them like a cat clawing at moths fluttering around a lantern. She felt his apprehension, his longing, his lust, and his fear. She tread forward slowly, and reached over to take Yule's hands into hers. She noticed that both her and his hands were rough from a hard life, and she felt solace in this knowledge.

"I don't ask for love, and I don't ask for commitment. If in the field the urge to take another comes to your fancy, I won't mind in the least. However, all I ask is that for one night, you let me hold you as you sleep, and keep the specters away. If not for you, let me into your bed so you can command your Riders better, with a clear mind and fresh eye."

Yule looked down at her hands, and he slowly curled his fingers around hers. He had an idea Alavara was interested in him. He may have been a downer, but he was not a fool, and knew the signs well enough. Usually by this point he would have turned back into his shell, and pushed the other person away ... but for some reason Alavara felt different. She was so nice to him, all the time, without asking for a thing in return.

"One night..." Yule murmured, and he felt his mouth go dry.

Alavara then saw it for the first time, the looming ghost of his grief rising up and trying to fold over onto him like a hood, and her hooks dug into it, pulling it away as if she were a monster yanking at prey that had fallen into her snare. She pulled hard, and felt the grief give way, and her hooks shredded it off of Yule like an old blanket.

"One night." She whispered, and leaned forward on her tippy toes to kiss Yule on the forehead.

Downstairs, the Veil Riders of Cosmoline Company made merry and drank as if it could be their last time to do so. Arm wrestling was had, Veil Riders took men or women to their rooms to have their own carefree fun, and others drank themselves to the point they could be medically classified as more beer than person.

Upstairs, in Yule's room, he felt pleasure for the first time in years and the warmth of a body against his own. For the first time since the death of his wife, he ran his fingers through the hair of a woman and felt her breath on his neck. For the first time, in a long time, Yule slept soundly without his mind being torn apart by the hauntings of his life on Terra. Alavara stood guard the entire night over him as his own essence mingled inside of her, her hooks grabbing and ripping at anything that came from his mind. Like a Gorgon of dreams, she wrapped him in her tendrils, and made sure nothing could disturb his rest.

As Yule slept, she studied his face with her crimson eyes, and bore him into her memory, along with the feelings he gave her. Her fingernails traced lines down his skin to make them ripple in goosebumps, and it made her smile. She hoped, deep down inside, that he would be back, and that Yethis could keep him alive long enough so he could return. She could, perhaps, be foolish enough to give it another try, the whole being a wife thing, but she had her doubts that Yule would ever treat her to such a measure. After a few hours had passed, she felt no other disturbances to his slumber, and she snuggled in close to him under the covers of the bed to find her own rest.

When morning came, Alavara woke when Yule did, and the two looked into each other's eyes as the early day sun glittered in through the window to bask them in the light.

"Mind helping me get ready?" Yule asked her in a hushed tone, and with his hand he brushed loose strands of her hair away from her face.

"Of course." She whispered with a smile, but she had something she wanted to do, first, and they did not end up putting on their clothes until some time after they had woken up.

When they had toweled the sweat off of their bodies, Alavara helped Yule get ready before she got dressed, letting Yule savor her naked form as she assisted him in putting on his battle vest, loading up all of his supplies into his rucksack, and double checking all of his gear. Every once in a while, when she was close enough, she would catch him smiling, and it in turn would cause her to crack a grin back.

Yule finished his list of Veil Riders for Erlan, watched Alavara slip on her clothes, which she teased him for, and escorted her back downstairs, leaving nothing in the room except the scent of them both from the night before and the coupling from the new morning.

As Yule reached the bottom of the stairs, he found that all of his Veil Riders were ready to go and loaded to the nines with all of their kit. Yule squinted in annoyance as they all, of course, noticed Alavara walking down with him, and a cheer went up from Domino.

"There ya go Yule!"

The rest of the Veil Riders cheered and whooped along with Domino, and Yule quietly wished they had chosen this morning to sleep in as they usually did.

CHAPTER 11

DOMINO SNIFFED AT Yule's neck, inhaling sharply and audibly. "You still smell like her, boss."

"God *damn it* get away from me!" Yule roared, and swung around to try and land a slap on the sniffing Rider.

Domino danced away with a laugh and dived over one of the many tall bushes that rippled the forest floor, escaping his judgment once again. Yule had been taking a lot of guff from his troopers for spending a night with Alavara, and they all seemed to revel in the fun that was to poke at him, or say that he 'was glowing'.

Cosmoline Company arrived in the thickly wooded area a few days after leaving Imlnoris, and made a small outpost in the deepest part of the trees. They were able to find a small clearing where they could get their vehicles in and out, and have a highly defensible position on the peak of a large hill. The slight elevation allowed them to have an eye on anything coming their direction, except for their rear, which faced Imlnoris. Hours were spent marking a driving route for the vehicles so they could travel in and out of the camp, then finding two more of them in case of an emergency. With a bit of digging and chopping, the deed was done with little sweat of the brow. The majority of this hilltop outpost was earth works, with the Company digging into rock and earth to form their pillboxes or trenches, then stacking some of the felled lumber here and there for cover.

Yethis commented that it looked like a giant beaver nest when she saw it finished, and the Company was surprised that they had beavers here in the first place. Down below on the rear of the hill, the Dragoons constructed a rough wooden corral to hold their horses, and had rotations where they would shepherd the herd out into the grassy areas so the horses could graze. The compliant nature of the breed made this an easier deal than it should have been, and the Dragoons breathed out a sigh of relief that the Valley Elves had bred some intelligence into the steeds.

Chikily was given the task of staking out in the tree tops and looking out for anything that may be coming or going in the distance, and could usually be seen skipping along the tree tops to and fro as he made his rounds. Airis stayed tight to Yule in case he had to send her off in a hurry to ask for help, while normal Pumpa-Rum runners brought letters and mail to Yule from the city. It took four more days before the Brush Feathered appeared, and they were not alone, either, as they had brought some friends with them.

Yule was using a woods exi, a broad bladed axe made by the Valley Elves, to hew at a piece of halved tree for a field table, when he saw Chikily running across the treetops and yelling Yules name. Yule almost cricked his neck from how hard he spun it to the yelling, and hefted the exi in his right hand while running down the hill, drawing out his M9 with his left as his boots pounded the ground. Airis stepped after him along with ten of his Riders, and Chikily flapped down from the trees to land in the grass before them with a whump of weight and air pressure. He pointed both his wings into the forest, his face alight with excitement.

"Chikily saw them, they've finally returned! And there are other Riders with them!"

Yule narrowed his eyes and looked off into the forest where Chikily was pointing. "Not Riders, Chik. Not Riders."

Yule looked down to Airis and pointed the exi towards the hill fort, of which barrels of multiple weapons began to swivel in rough wooden pillboxes and turn towards the forest. "Go fetch Britta, please."

Airis left the ground with a single strong beat, and Yule waited near the tree line with his other Riders for the Harpies to come out of the brush. With the rustle of leaves, they finally appeared, and they looked as if they were walking dead. Yule took one look at them before turning on his heel and bellowing at the outpost. "Gruesome! Yethis!"

Yule heard Gruesome before he saw him emerge from the fortifications, the Corpsman's boots thudding so hard on the ground that it was like the grass suddenly grew a heartbeat. Yethis sprang like a deer after him, but almost stumbled and tumbled down the hill, thankfully catching herself and rolling back into a run.

The Brush Feathered were covered in blood and gunshot wounds, many of which appeared to be shrapnel fragments or buckshot, and there were only two of them, not the five that had set out from Imlnoris. The only ones that stood before Yule now were the singular female and the smaller of the males, both of whom still wore the Ghillie Suits he had given the group before they had left. Behind the blood stained Harpies emerged a ragged Platoon of soldiers, and they looked as rough as the Brush Feathered did.

The entire rag-tag group looked as if they had been peppered with munitions for miles, some of them still hefting their rucksacks while others just had their weapon and battle rigging. A lot of them wore the Black, Crimson, and Gold of Germany, while others bore the Czech Blue, Red, and White, and a small sprinkle of them wore the White and Red of Poland. Yule flattened his hat to his head to make sure the Amulet made contact, and spoke aloud to the one in front, which wore a field cap and no helmet. "I appreciate you keeping my Harpies safe. I hope you come here as friends."

The grizzled man in front of him was a German, having a strong, proud jaw that clenched purely on reflex. His face had enough grooves in it that a blind man could read that he had seen a thing or two, and done even more.

"Your German is flawless for a redneck." He growled out, but it bore humor.

"I wish I could take the credit." Yule replied, and smiled with his eyes, but kept his mouth in a line.

"Neither can we for getting here. These brave little Vogelfolk won the day . . . and even then so little of us made it through."

"So little of you?" Yule asked, and leaned to the right to peer over the man's shoulder.

"We set out with a full company, this is all that is left." The man motioned back towards the battered group of soldiers behind him." The Vogelfolk were able to get into the base and leave the leaflets from Britta. It appears they had been hiding all around us, and gathering information from what we can guess, as we don't speak their twittery language. However, they were there at the meeting point when the day came, and we brought all of our men with us. Things have been fishy ever since we arrived, and nothing has been as agreed to."

Gruesome arrived and ripped open his medical bag before he came to a skidding stop. Inside were the usual Earthen implements used for field operations, but also bags of what looked like greasy sludge, bottles of many colored liquids, and a kind of bandage that looked like it was constantly wiggling. Gruesome pulled out his tweezers and began pulling shrapnel from the Brush Feathered, his mouth set in a grim but professional frown.

"40mm grenades." Gruesome murmured, and flicked a large shard of metal at Yule which had come out of the female Harpies leg. Yule caught it, surprised Gruesome had spoken, and held it in his hand, rolling the bloody metal fragment over in his digits. Yethis began to cut open her finger and speak the rituals of healing as she walked towards the Harpies, and the Brush Feathered closed their eyes, knowing that the worst of it was over. As Gruesome was pulling metal out of the female Brush Feathered, she began to tremble as the exhaustion and relief set in. The more metal Gruesome pulled out of her, the more it became apparent these troopers were running for their lives the entire way here. Slugs from rifles, shrapnel from explosives, wood fragments from trees . . . it was like they had been hunted the entire way to the outpost.

"What the hell happened?" Yule asked, but heard a noise and turned his head.

He looked over to see the female Harpy was starting to choke and sob, her feathers almost rattling from how hard she shook. Tears streamed down her dirty face and left trails as it cleansed away the filth. Gruesome set down his tools as she began to cry while looking down at her bloodied feet, and he cleaned away the blood on his hands. Gruesome, the scarred veteran of many tours in the desert, the last person many of his brother Marines saw as they passed in the field, the man whose job it was to patch together the broken . . . knelt down and wrapped his huge arms around the shuddering Harpy, and whispered to her in perfect Tunkah.

"It's okay. It's alright."

"I-I tried . . ." She sobbed back in the language, her shoulders heaving as she hiccuped, and snot began to drip from her nose.

"I know. I know. It's okay. You made it here." Gruesome pulled her in tight, then scooped up the other Harpy and pulled him into the hug as well. The male just leaned against Gruesome. He didn't cry, or weep, but just went limp against the huge Corpsman, exhausted. Yule and the German looked down at the little scene with set jaws, while Yethis quickly shuffled over and added her own arms to the hug as well while still healing the smaller male with her bloody finger.

The German looked over to Yule, then held out his hand. "Oberfeldwebel Peiper."

Yule clapped the hand in his own. "Yule."

Britta could be heard running her way there and came to a halt in front of Peiper, giving him a salute in which he returned. She then spoke out in German while reaching out to shake his hand as well.

"Peiper! You're alive!" Yule heard her say, and her eyes were filled with happiness.

"Just barely, we all thought you were dead as well, good to see that is not the case."

"They did their best." Britta said with a grin, and then looked behind him. "This is all that's left?"

Peiper nodded, and began their tale:

Since arriving on the other side of the Veil, their markers were taken, they were disarmed while inside the base, and plugged away into a corner of the base footprint along with everyone else who was not a part of this 'mysterious main clique' that ran the base.

"I am used to elitism among the ranks, but this was odd, even for me." Peiper said with a rueful glare, and watched Gruesome pick up both of the Harpies and carry them over towards the outpost, while Yethis picked up his medical bag and carried it behind them.

Peiper went on to tell Yule how men and women of the Company started going missing. Every dawn, Peiper would hold a formation and do a count, and they were always down a trooper every morning without fail, at the average rate of a soldier a day. When he would go to command to ask where his trooper was, he would then be told that they were out on a 'special assignment' . . . but the soldier would never return. Additionally, the Southern Elves were being quickly folded into the ranks of the main guard at the camp until they were the majority in number, and still further the Terrans were pushed into the corner of the base. There were even times when command and the Chosen Children would speak of the Terran soldiers with open disdain, and all requests for Veil transfers were always denied. More and more he observed personnel coming through the Veil, and they always wore the same face when they would look upon a Terran or Valley Elf: Open Disgust.

"I knew things were beyond strange when I caught one of the upper command off guard when I had burst into his quarters, after news of the ambush had happened. For a split second, his eyes . . . they were all black. I had but a moment to see this when his eyes sprang back to their normal brown I had known them to be, and he started watching me closely, every day since."

Peiper ran the pad of his index finger down the bridge of his nose as he took a moment to think. " I don't know how they were doing it, as they never told any of us when we asked, but they are growing the size of the Veil, expanding it and hewing out the rock. What was once a cave is now like a giant cavern, allowing them to bring in more things from the 'States. We were told that you folk slaughtered the entry team, and that you were terrorists trying to occupy the Veil and ransom the world for your own gains. We were given the assignment to come in and eradicate you . . . but all we did was get shoved into the corner of the base, get sent on suicide missions, or just disappear completely. When I finally caught them speaking Elvish in the open, right out of the Veil, greeting each other, that's when I knew something was definitely not right. After a while, we found the letters . . . and made our escape. They hounded us through the fields and grass, cutting us down when they could find us. The Harpies hid us as best as they could, and we fought back when we were able, but they somehow had the ability to find out where we were without actually seeing us, raining down mortar fire, or a Fennek would suddenly lurch out of the tree line and pin us down with its grenade launcher."

Peiper lit up a crumpled cigarette, and gave a harsh inhale, before blowing the smoke out of his nose and rubbing the thumb of his smoking hand across his forehead. "Yule . . . We set out with a Company of riflemen. This is all that's left. We were hunted down by our own countrymen . . . why? What is going on?"

Britta looked to Yule, and Yule stepped forward, motioning to the troopers who were waiting patiently in the background despite how tired they were.

"Head on up to the outpost, we have food and water there. Britta . . . if you want you can fill him in, you're not under my command." With that, he began his walk back towards the outpost. Britta started to fill in Peiper on her and Gremlins findings, and slowly the two pieced together all the things that seemed to be part of the same puzzle.

Yule had already come to the same conclusion on his walk back to the outpost, but one fact still dug a deep burrow in his skull: They were making the Veil gate *bigger*. To him, that meant they wanted to bring in the bigger weaponry. He knew what a Fennek was, it was around the same footprint as an M1117, but a bigger gate meant tanks, larger armored combat vehicles, and aerial vehicles. Yule mounted the top of a pillbox and thumped down the other end, landing solidly on the bottoms of his boots. He kinda regretted that, as now his heels were buzzing, but still he trudged on into the center of the outpost.

In the middle of the outpost was the main command bunker, nestled deep down into the hill where they had hit rock, and they made it as strong as they could with timbers and felled trees in case they came under attack by ranged supporting ordinance. Inside this main bunker, Gruesome was cleaning off the Harpies with a wet rag. Yethis was helping him, currently wiping away at the male Brush Feathered's cheeks and cleaning away the grime and powder burns.

"Chikily?" Yule asked to the room, and Chikily plodded over, looking worriedly at the other Harpies. "Chikily, hey. Don't worry about them, they'll be fine."

"There were five Brush Feathered when they left . . ." Chikily said softly, and he looked up at Yule, a worried expression across his face.

Yule's eyes stared down at the Harpy as his mouth formed an angry frown, and Chikily could see the hard regret that began to rim Yule's eyes. ". . . Yes, Chikily. I know. I know there was . . . Now there are two. I know. Look bud . . . I need you to run a message to Koko. Can you do that for me?"

Chikily puffed out his chest, and spoke with as solid a voice as he could muster. "No fear in these feathers. Chikily hears."

Yule nodded and quickly scribbled out a long note, handing it to Chikily. Chikily went to grab it, but found Yule still holding on to the rolled up note, and Chikily paused. "Chikily. If things get hairy, you punch out and come back. Y'hear?"

"Y'hear." Chikily asserted with a determined smile . . . and Yule released the scroll.

Chikily ran around, gathering up his equipment for the flight, while Airis stalked over and began to try and comfort the still crying female Harpy, who clung to Gruesome as he tried to clean all of the dried blood from her war-torn body.

Peiper and Britta were just mounting the edge of the outpost when Chikily soared over the top of their heads, almost taking off Peiper's field cap, and he flapped aggressively up to his cruising altitude. Peiper chuckled once, then turned around to watch him fly off into the high sky. When Chikily was but a smear on the big blue, Peiper turned to see his troopers had already passed out asleep, scattered amongst the many bunkers and fox holes where Veil Riders stood over them, taking the guard as they slept.

Britta had filled Peiper in on what happened to the column, and he knew full well these men had ripped those vehicles apart themselves... but it was already past time to be caring about that. The enemy had been playing them all against each other, and last he checked it wasn't these Americans who had hunted them down. From now on, every Terran had to be on the same side if they ever wished to make it back home.

Britta led Peiper into the bunker, both of them arriving in time to see Yule addressing his NCOs.

"... and they're trying to make it bigger. I've sent word to Zerg Company that we have to start moving in on this thing. If they bring in even one Apache we're all *fucked*, and they're going to hunt us down like they did the Europeans. Keep watch over them, make sure they are fed, and help them get back into fighting form. Dismissed."

The NCOs of Cosmoline Company turned and filed past Peiper, many of them clapping the German NCO on the shoulder before exiting out the mouth of the bunker.

Yule turned with the clink of tin mugs, and held two brimming cups of his precious retort coffee. He held one out to Peiper, who took the cup in both hands, leaning in to savor the smell.

"Pretty fucked up, I know... Played us like a fiddle." Yule said chidingly, taking a sip of his own tin cup. "They knew how we would react when we saw blue helmets pop out of the Veil. Then they twisted the narrative all the way around its head to their own needs. To think... all those tinfoil hats were speaken' the truth. 'Cept they got it wrong of course."

Peiper raised his eyebrows to Yule, taking off his cap and sipping heavily from the cup.

"They pinned it on lizards. If only they knew it was fairies the entire time."

Peiper gave a wet chuckle as he tried to swallow his coffee without choking on it, and they both shared a wry spout of laughter. Britta stood nearby, watching them both closely.

Peiper coughed once, then spoke up. "After what Britta hast told me, I think that maybe her convoy was sent as some kind of lure, to try and draw you out. Give them ammunition to use in order to bring in heavier vehicles."

"Highly possible." Yule agreed.

"I would have done the same if I had come across the convoy. Germans already have the tendency programmed, after all." Peiper said with a grin, and Yule laughed quietly, getting the reference of the ambushes the Germans had perfected in World War Two.

The two men looked over to Gruesome, who was now just holding the female Brush Feathered as she choked out in sobs, and the two cleared their throats awkwardly. Perhaps, this was not the time for gentle banter.

"Anyway, uh, Oberfeldwebel. You are welcome among my men. I'm afraid that if we wish to continue killing each other, it will have to wait until we have dealt with the Veil."

"I'm sure ve can set up a date later on for that if ve wish." Peiper added, and he heard Britta snort in the background. Old habits among soldiers die hard, it seemed, as there was no better time for humor than when in the company of the miserable.

"How many more regular Human troopers are left at the base?" Yule asked, putting a hand in his pocket as he supped.

"Not many. Maybe a few Platoons. I don't even know if they are even . . . human, after all. I know all my lads are, at least."

"Hm." Yule mused, pulling over a crate or two for them to sit on. "How many total combat elements?"

"Quite a few, actually. The Children of the Chosen, or whatever they are, have been getting drilled hard in the base and are more or less the bulk of the combat arms there. So . . . ve have been played by Elven Fae, have ve?"

"Seems that way."

Peiper grunted, and sat down heavily on one of the crates Yule had pulled over. "What a bunch of bullshit. So they're plan is to use our tech to invade this place, eh?"

Yule nodded, and Peiper just guffawed. "Gott im Himmel, that is playing the long game at its finest."

Yule filled in Peiper on their current strength, the resources they had, as well as what his co-commander Koko had been up to in the east. He also told the German of what the Dwarves were cooking up in the North, and the support they had from some of the races. When Peiper had all the holes filled in, Yule gave him his own personal bunk space to sleep, and headed out of the command bunker to get some fresh air. Fresh air, and to get away from the female Brush feathered, who had not stopped crying the entire time, and it was starting to weigh on Yule's conscience like stones would on a feather pillow.

The European troopers were still sleeping, and the Veil Riders were slowly trading out the watch to keep guard over them, detaching off to go eat, sleep themselves, or take care of the horses down below in the corrals. Yule found a rough wooden seat and plunked himself down on it. After a moment of staring down into the dirt, he slowly brought his head down and rested it in his hands, running his fingers through his hair. His mind was on the dead Brush Feathered, whose bodies were littering the path here with the rest of the slaughtered European soldiers. It was a gamble to do what he did, he knew that much when he had sent them off. But the gamble ended up being a net loss, with more than seventy people dead and rotting in the open without a proper burial. He felt something hush near him, and he looked up to see Airis looking down at him, her wings brought together in front of her.

Yule breathed in deep and leaned back. "Yeah kid, whats up?"

Airis didn't speak for a few moments, but just leaned onto Yule's shoulder and hugged him with both wings. She buried her face into his neck, and let out a sigh. "Is okay Yule."

Yule sat still for some seconds after she had spoken, but leaned his head over slightly to bump his head against hers. "It's not, Airis. But I know what you mean."

She sighed, and just held Yule. Her eyes looked up and saw that Yule had flicked something from his face, and saw a bit of water sparkle in the sunlight near the edge of his eye.

Inside the Command Bunker, Yethis stretched and cracked her back. She had given a lot of blood for the healing of the Harpies alone, and thanked the heavens that the other Humans were as easy to take care of. She looked down and smiled sadly at Gruesome, who was still holding the wounded Harpy in his arms. She was finally asleep, clinging still to the grizzled Corpsman, and Gruesome looked up at Yethis.

"Can you grab me a blanket, please?" He whispered in Tunkah, and Yethis bowed slightly, before running off to fetch him a blanket and a pillow as well. Yethis then left out into the approaching dusk and began to heal the sleeping European survivors who lay scattered around the outpost; A splotch of healing here, a yank of metal there, until finally she herself was spent, and needed to recoup with some rest of her own. Gruesome stayed with the Harpy the entire night, guarding her as she slept. He knew the nightmares would come . . . and he would be there to ease their onslaught.

* * *

The next morning came with little fanfare, but with a lot more curious accents. While the Company and their guest Platoon under Peiper breakfasted together, Yule took stock of the current personnel numbers under his umbrella of power: He had taken all of his Veil Riders with him, numbering sixty six in strength, along with four additional troopers if he included Britta, which he couldn't have left behind and had dragged her along just to reduce headache. Peiper, after he and his Platoon had rested, held a morning formation to do a count, and also say prayers for their fallen brothers and sisters in the field. To Peiper's delight, he found that he had miscounted through all the chaos of getting here, and was happy to tell Yule that he in fact had thirty nine soldiers alive and well, making them a larger sized Platoon element than he had previously thought.

Peiper was also happy to see his explosives expert had survived the trip in, and quickly rounded her up to introduce her to Yule. Tatiana Moskal was almost as slight as Gremlin was, except instead of black hair, she sported a ruddy red mane that was long on the top and shaved under on the sides. In her hair was also all a manner of wire tucked away in case she needed it, and she constantly smelled of explosives and ozone. When Yule shook her hand and looked into her sparkling green eyes, all he saw was the madness of someone who was touched by the raw power of the shockwave spirit, and knew full well this woman was dangerous beyond all comparison. Despite the air of danger around her, she still held the pleasant diamond shaped face that he knew a lot of Polish women sported, and her full lips were always held in a pleasant, if unnerving, smile.

"Nice to meet you, Corporal Moskal." Yule said, shaking her hand firmly. Corporal Moskal gripped his hand back.

"Do you mind if I go see what kind of ordinance you're trucking around?" Moskal said with another alarming grin, and Yule flicked his eyes to his left where the make-shift ammo depot was.

"Uh... Sure. Just dont use any of it."

Moskal rubbed her hands together with a gleeful giggle and trotted over to the area Yule pointed her to. Yule smelled his hand as he watched her leave, and found it to smell curiously of smoke. He then looked up to Peiper, who was watching him. "You know she's fucken' crazy, right?"

Peiper just laughed. "Oh yes, a few bats short of a belfry."

After meeting Moskal, Peiper then introduced Yule to his other soldiers, the majority of whom were country Germans looking for a bit of adventure. Then came the Czechs, who came purely for answers as to why their unit was disbanded after a mission in the desert during Enduring Freedom. The Polish all seemed to share the same outlook on why they came; They would be damned if they got left behind on this trip, and were keen to show the Germans how real soldiers operated. Yule couldn't help but chuckle at this and the heckling that followed soon after as the Germans and Polish shared rude gestures and good natured teasing.

Summed up, there were nineteen German Heer Troopers, one Luftwaffe Security Trooper who had apparently snuck his way into the Heer group, ten soldiers of the Polish Wojska Lądowe, and nine Czech paratroopers from the disbanded 601st, whom had long wondered just *why* they had been disbanded in the first place. This being after finding some relics while operating in Afghanistan in 2008. While the Veil Riders egged on the Polish and Germans, Yule worked his way through the boisterous crowd to where the Czechs were huddled around a small fire making tea, and saddled up to a log nearby to sit on.

The Czech 601st troopers nodded towards Yule, and he checked to make sure his Amulet had plenty of blood in it, before cramming it back into his patrol cap and back onto his head. "So. How many of you came through?"

A man bearing the double stars of a Sergeant First Class spoke up while looking down into the pot of tea, stirring it gently with a giant field spoon. "Only fifteen. All we could manage to slip in."

"And nine remain..." Yule murmured. "I'll cut to the chase: What did you find in Afghanistan."

The spoon scrapped to a stop in the pot, and the man's eyes slowly rose up to meet Yule's. All of the other 601st operators looked to each other, heads unmoving, before coming back to Yule.

"We found... a body." The Sergeant First Class murmured, and slowly spun the spoon in the pot, as well as the tale of their mission.

It was March in Afghanistan, and the moon was shining bright overhead, letting plenty of light filter in through their helmet mounted night vision to illuminate the cave system in front of them. They were out here on this god forsaken mountain under the belief that the head of the insurgency in the area was hiding within, using the herd paths around the mountain and the valley to launch mortar and rocket strikes into FOB Shank. To help alleviate this madness, the 601st sent out a small strike team to cut the head from the snake.

There was no resistance the entire way up, not that they expected any, as the drone hovering overhead didn't report anything in their way. With the flick of a toggle, their PEQ's shot out their lasers and lit the cave mouth up with light, and they moved into the inky black, snuffed out one by one from the gaze of the moon. Gravel and sand crunched under their feet like snow as they silently wound their way down the tunnel. Their first contact was a man asleep where he sat, his RPK resting across his lap as his head lulled on the back of his ramshackle steel chair.

One of the 601st slid out his knife, the metal hissing on the nylon scabbard, before bringing it down with both hands into the eye socket of the man and punching through the skull into the brain. The ruffle of fabric, a squelch of flesh, and the crunch of his spine breaking on the back of the metal chair were the only sounds to entertain the walls of the cave. The knife bearing operator ripped the knife out, and then buried it into the neck and armpit of the dead sentry for good measure, before wiping the blade clean on the dead man's shirt and slipping it back into the scabbard. The Sergeant First Class looked down at the lantern that had burned down to the wick and smiled; If the insurgent had been a little more disciplined, there would have been light in here, and he may have been able to see their faces before he died.

A pity.

The 601st strike team moved further into the cave system and found two more resting insurgents, this time actually sleeping in bed rolls instead of on guard, and dispatched them quickly by two of the strike team stomping down with their heels onto the throats of the sleeping men. Despite shattering their throats, they held their heels there until the gurgling stopped, while the rest of the strike team watched down the cave way for any movement. Once the sleeping men were laid to *eternal* rest, the strike team moved further into the cave, finally finding the main chamber. They had been making sure to snuff out any candle or lantern they came across, keeping the darkness for themselves, and letting their enemies not have the comfort of the light.

Peeking out from the dim, they observed the main chamber, and saw their target: the leader of this little school yard insurgency. Around him were about six fighters still armed; Some of them listening in on radios, watching movies off of VCRs, or reading through Vogue magazines. The strike team of the 601st pushed in like a tidal wave of lead, weapons flashing and barking like hounds of lightning released to the hunt. Insurgents fell to the cave floor or died where they sat, except for one.

For some reason, none of the bullets had struck the Insurgent leader, somehow being just enough off course to avoid striking their target. Which of course made no sense to the strike team leader, as his men were crack shots and they were only twenty yards away. While he dropped his magazine and grabbed another from his chest rig, he saw a flash of light and heard a scream. A fireball had whipped across the room and engulfed one of his troopers, who screamed and danced in the writhing flame. Shouts and curses echoed in the cavern as some of the strike team tried to put him out . . . but it was like the flame could not be snuffed. Another fireball roared across the cavern and slammed into the trooper trying to extinguish his brother in arms with a nearby blanket, and now he too wailed in anguish as the fire licked and ate at his flesh, burning it to blackened char. The Sergeant First Class couldn't see what the hell was shooting the fire, and could barely see their main target through the haze, but he had had enough of this shit. Pulling out his knife and a tomahawk gifted by an American Ranger, he began to sprint towards the figure who seemed to be . . . twirling in the heat haze, and laughing.

He had to duck as another fireball swirled through the air, singing his back and sucking at the air in his lungs as it soared overhead and impacted another of his team. As he sprinted forward, he spared a fleeting glance over his shoulder as time seemed to crawl. He saw them, clawing at their faces as flames moved along their skin, rolling on the ground to try and get the fire off of them, screaming as they desperately tried to pull off their gear and crackling clothes. The fire seemed to be alive, wrestling them and coiling around their bodies like a great wyrm of flame as they shrieked. He had no idea what kind of chemical could burn like that . . . but the secret would die here, and now.

Raw heat radiated off of his mission target, burning him like he was ducking his head into a blazing bonfire, but he still lurched forward, leaping with both of his feet to launch himself through the air. As he penetrated the haze, he saw the figure for the first time, what was truly burning his men alive.

"It had black eyes . . . and skin like charcoal. I had never seen anything like it in all my days. It cackled at me, even as I buried that tomahawk right into its skull. It took a good few whacks, but it died, and the flames along with it."

The Sergeant First Class paused for a moment, before pouring some tea into his field cup, and setting the small pot back onto the fire. "It had Elf ears, much like that one over there." He pointed towards Yethis, who was happily braiding a German man's long golden hair, "but it looked so . . . alien. So . . . evil. We killed it, though, and brought the body back, along with the bodies of my men. The Elf thing was quickly snatched up by some suits who were waiting for us after I reported what we were returning with. Even diverted the bird from Shank to McClain, which made no sense to me. They snatched up the body, ordered us not to speak of it . . . and that was it. Soon after, we were disbanded the following year with no reason behind it . . . but I have an inkling."

Yule stared at him hard for a long time, watching the memories play back in the man's eyes as he sipped his tea, along with the others who all seemed to bear the same loss and pain, not only of their fellow troopers, but an entire unit and brotherhood.

Yule broke the silence, holding out his hand. "Im Yule."

The Sergeant First Class eyed Yule's hand for a breath, before reaching out and taking it in his. "Prusík"

Yule nodded comfortingly, before reaching his hand out to another Czech. "Good to meet you guys, now what's your name?"

Later that night, Yule sat back in his little office area inside the command bunker and sighed, resting his head back onto his rucksack. After dinner, the Veil Riders decided to officially indoctrinate the Europeans into the Company, giving them the few precious extra patches they had in storage from their first trip in. Having made them official, Peiper took Britta back into his command and Yule made the Czechs autonomous, showing respect to their training and veterancy.

What this meant for Cosmoline Company was that now their total strength was at 109 or 110 depending on what native was doing what, and how many Harpies they had with them. This finally allowed for proper Platoon grouping, and he had spent most of dinner appointing Platoon Sergeants and other such bookkeeping so things ran smoothly.

The Brush Feathered had recovered as well, and the female was sticking to Gruesome like glue, learning and inhaling all the knowledge that the Corpsman would give her. The little Harpy had even learned how to wrap a bandage with her wings and how to use her claws to operate some of the finer details of a tourniquet in the field. The male was still willing to act as a scoutl, and wanted to be with the 601st troopers as their personal assistant. Yule was fine with that and paid them both their gold so the contract would at least be fulfilled, despite it being a hollow assurance to the loss of their fellow Harpies.

Britta being folded back in with her fellow Germans alleviated the baby sitting of her, and it appeared that many of the Europeans didn't harbor too many hard feelings about the ambush. This was the trickiest evolution of combat any of Cosmoline Company knew, and there was far more hate for the Fae than there was for each other at the current moment. Yule knew this couldn't last forever, and eventually that chicken would come home to roost... but for now there was a common enemy that they would work against, and keep things in line. Yule was tired, deep in his soul, and looked to his side where Alavara once lay. He had to admit he was getting *the feelings* about the whole ordeal and ached to have her next to him again as he slept, and the letters he would send to her would usually just aggravate the pain even more when a response came. He quietly pondered what his long past wife would have said about this... probably something akin to 'She can do better', which made him sadly chuckle. He stared into the dim light for a bit longer as his mind churned, before reaching over and twisting the lantern so the light died into pitch black.

Three more days passed as Fokhet was sending almost daily letters to Yule, keeping him abreast of the production line that was being set up in the Engineer hold. Additionally, the Humans of Cosmoline company were mingling happily, which eased some stress off of Yule. On the fourth day, a flight from Saveriss came into the Outpost, flying in from Imlnoris to bring ammunition and supplies. While the rest of the Company were able to get fresh bottles of wine and ammo, Yule couldn't help but break out into a nervous sweat.

Saveriss was in this flight, and she was holding a long package in her feet. He also saw she had a pistol strapped to a drop holster on one of her legs... it seemed Koko had completed the contract for him, despite hoping that the bird woman would simply forget. Chikily was in there as well, and landed down in the middle of the Veil Riders with multiple bags tied to him. With a roar of glee he pulled out two of the bottles, in which grain alcohol glittered. The roar was met in volume by the Veil Riders, who showered Chikily with praise while unpacking the bottles from him. The Harpy looked ragged from flying with the weight, but was in good spirits.

The rest of the Himalayan Harpies landed down, shaking themselves or stretching their long wings as other Veil Riders grabbed small crates of ammunition and took them to the depot. Then, with a whoosh of wings and air pressure, Saveriss landed before Yule, her merlot red eyes staring into his as a grin played across her fangs.

"Long time, no see." She purred, and grabbed the long package from her feet up with her wing digits, resting it against her breasts and shoulder.

"Saveriss... how good to see you again." Yule replied, trying to look anywhere but the Harpy.

"Liar." She said flatly, but was still smiling all the same. "Thought Saveriss would not be back, Hmm?"

"One could hope." Yule murmured, and Saveriss spread the smile to her dangerous eyes.

"Saveriss has package for you." The Harpy said and stroked the long thing in her wings, while tilting her head to Yule.

"But it come with price."

Here we fucking go... Thought Yule, and he sighed, resting his hands on his hips. "What, Saveriss."

"Saveriss hear from little birdy you finally took someone to your bed."

Yule glared at her, then both of them trailed their eyes to Chikily. Chikily was currently laughing and holding an open bottle of the grain alcohol he brought back, and then saw the two staring at him. His laugh quickly died in his throat and he choked a bit, seeing Yule glaring at him from under the bill of his hat, while Saveriss winked.

Chikily raised a foot and quickly goose stepped around the back end of the packed Veil Riders, getting himself out of view.

"Alright. So I did. What does that have to do with *you*." Yule growled, and took his hands from his hips and now crossed them on his chest.

Saveriss acted as if she was playing with the wrapping of the package, which Yule assumed was his rifle coming back from Fokhet, and played her face into a look of idle amusement.

"Saveriss have little birdies everywhere. Saveriss knows the she-Elf is not attached to you yet, nor you to her. Saveriss also knows that she gave you okay for . . . field interactions." The Harpy simpered at Yule. "Saveriss just want chance to meet the great and mighty Yule in the duel between the blankets . . ."

"Hot chance in hell, fairy feathers." Yule barked, and looked down at the slowly flustering Himalaya Harpy Queen.

Saveriss was now angry, and the feathers on her wings were slowly starting to rise, her hair poofed slightly. "T-That fine, Saveriss just keep this package as payment for her long trip!" She hissed, and her eyes flashed dangerously.

"That's fine, I got plenty of rifles. Don't want mine smelling like bird feet anyway." Yule stated flatly, and didn't uncross his arms. His own anger was starting to slowly eat away as his ingrained bird of prey fear. His back however was becoming slick with sweat, regardless.

"Chikily said this rifle was special to you, he heard short legged Prince say so!" Saveriss was now starting to really fluff up in rage, seeing her plan fall apart in front of her eyes.

"Dime a dozen." Yule said, and spat at his feet. This was a lie, of course, but she didn't know that.

Around the camp, everyone was staring, and the Himalayan Harpies were just trying to look anywhere but their Queen as they tried to hide their snorts of laughter.

The pitched yelling began to grow between the two as Peiper turned to Domino, who was watching the fight gleefully.

"Vhy are they fighting?" Peiper mused, as he heard Chikily swallow a gulp of alcohol while hiding among the taller troopers.

"Bird lady wants Yule in order to cement her power or something. Yule is afraid of danger birds." Domino replied, his voice thick with humor, and the two combatant's voices raised to a fever pitch.

Peiper just raised his eyebrows at this information and blinked a few times, before looking back over at the argument.

"Here! Take gross Yule rifle, probably full of beard hair and stupidity!" Saveriss tossed the rifle on the ground, her hair and feathers as puffed up as her temper. She was almost dark red in the face and sweating from how pissed off she was. "Anyone would kill to bed a Harpy Queen! I wouldn't want your children anyway, would probably fly upside down and eat rocks!"

"Aye sure, and they would get that from their *Mother*." Yule bit back, and stooped down to pick up the rifle still nestled in its travel wrappings.

Saveriss was so angry that tears were welling up in her eyes. She knew she was beautiful, as many had told her so, and stories were written about her in some chronicles from her prowess in combat. She was so frustrated at the Human that she was almost ready to cry from how rude and hard headed he was being, since it was a rare occurrence that she didn't get her way, and this meat head and done it to her twice.

There was a break in the combat, as Yule dusted off his package, watching her with rage in his eyes. Seconds passed as the two stared at each other, Saveriss grinding her teeth.

"S-Saveriss needs a few days to rest for trip back." She stammered, fighting back the indignant tears.

"Fine. Stay out of the command bunker." Yule ordered grimly, and spun on his heel to take the rifle back inside, ducking down into the headquarters building. Saveriss watched him go, shaking with fury, before letting out a scream of annoyance that only a royal could possess, and stomping away from the command bunker. Everyone watched her angrily wipe at her face with her wings, and a few of her Harpies ran after her.

Domino let out a whistle. "Man, he really does not like her."

Some of the Himalayan Harpies that were around them shrugged, and took off their flying rigging. Gruesome had to be called over to translate for them, but he confirmed that Saveriss wanted to try and use Yule to pull in more power to take over other Harpy clans.

A pretty female Harpy sat down on a log seat and stretched out her wings and her back, crackling her spine happily and whimpering in pleasure. "Saveriss thinks seducing Yule will also let her be able to use his men at arms for conquest. Eerie don't see why, she already control biggest Harpy clan as it is. Eerie think she just jealous of Chikily."

Peiper, after hearing Gruesome translate the words from the little darling of a Harpy, gave a wry 'hmmf'. "Rather shrewd of her to think it would be that easy. I've only known the man for a few days and even I can see the challenge of the task she has set herself."

Gruesome turned to Eerie and translated, in which Eerie just gave tinkling laughter while kicking her feet happily. Sitting on Gruesome shoulders was the Brush Feathered Harpy female, who was resting her head on Gruesome's and looking bored with the whole thing. "Salili thinks whole thing stupid."

Again Gruesome translated, and everyone laughed at the real truth of what she said. It all was a bit silly to the Humans, but it was just the way things seemed to be here in this world. Through the rest of the day, everyone mingled with the Himalayas and shared their meals with them, as well as relishing in the supplies they brought with them. They later learned in the evening that the Harpies were just the forward supply chain of a longer train of wagons coming in down the road, and indeed the next morning, several long covered wagons arrived bearing additional building supplies, more ammunition, some of the Dwarven mortar tubes that were fresh from the engineering hold, a few Dwarven engineers, and fresh food stuffs for the outpost to live off of. There were also a lot of volunteers that came up to help cook and take care of the place, and eventually Yule was worn down by them to let them stay.

Unfortunately for Yule, Saveriss also wormed her way into staying on the base, declaring that Yule had hurt her feelings, and that she was owed recompense by being able to stay and do proper scouting for Cosmoline Company. The first several times she tried, he said no. But by the fifth hour of her constantly screeching at Yule, he finally yelled back at her that he'll allow it, but that she herself was banned from ever entering the command bunker during her stay.

Feeling she had finally won one over Yule, she didn't stop acting smug for the entire week that the Outpost was expanded. Mortar tubes were dug in deep, and the Engineers showed the Veil Riders how the operate the Bloop Toobs', while the volunteers of Valley Elves, Brimtouched, Onii, and Dwarves helped carve out a more livable space on the Outpost, including building actual bunk houses and dining quarters from the lumber surrounding the place.

The Dwarves had outdone themselves with the mortar tubes: The entire length of the barrels were done up with runes, and the openings of the mortars were carved into the shapes of belching Trolls or roaring Dwarven gods. Even the sights were extremely squared away, perfect mimicries of the actual mortar sights used on Earth, except these were enchanted, and automatically adjusted for wind. They would even self adjust by the gunner shouting Dwarvish at them. The Veil Riders who would be manning them had to take crash courses on rough Dwarvish directions and numbers, phrases such as 'down two' or 'left twenty'.

With the outpost now looking like a proper forward operating base, or FOB, Yule began drafting his plans for operations and sorties to harass and tarry any enemies that were nearby, and sent out some of the Himalayans to scout from above. He warned them not to get too close, and to stay as high and hidden as possible. With their feathers and markings being mostly white, he didn't want them anywhere near the ground or the dark green forest. He also sent word back for any volunteers who wanted to fight; With the Dwarves here ready for war, and the Chosen Children drilling themselves into an army . . . he was going to need all the help he could get.

It was time for Yule to break his taboo, and give an Elf a rifle.

CHAPTER 12

Yule blinked away the rain drops that ran down the bill of his patrol cap and gave a soft snort of annoyance. It seemed that no matter when or where he was, it always wanted to rain when he was laying in wait during an ambush. He looked down the line of riflemen that were hiding along the same natural berm that he was hunkered down behind, and couldn't help but crack a wry grin. "What a buncha' lord of the rings bullshit this is . . ."

All along the berm were strewn Valley Elves, Dwarves, Brimtouched, Onii, and his own Veil Riders, a mish mash of gear, uniforms, weapons, and armor. Yule was direly behind schedule for his operations, and really wanted to get out into the field sooner, but even he knew he had a man power problem. When the call for volunteers went out over the mail network, able bodied men and women from the cities surrounding Imlnoris came in droves to be drilled into competent, if green, Veil Rider Infantry Auxiliaries. Yule was grateful for the confederation that these people had set up hundreds of years before, which allowed him to dip his hand into all of the cultures at once.

Not only was the outpost, now named Valhalla Hill due to the carvings and scroll works the Dwarves and Brimtouched put up about the place, a huge FOB of its own accord, but it stretched all the way down to the bottom of the hill, resembling some kind of weird post-modern fortification town. Except, where buildings and markets should have been, there were instead pillboxes, kill holes, and workshops where weapons were maintained or even created. Yule was quite taken aback by how many of the Veil Folk showed up to volunteer, and took to having them drilled in the arts of riferly and basic Platoon based tactics. He even took the training of the Auxiliary NCOs into his own hands, and held many a late night classroom sessions where he put the Amulet to good use. Yethis was also helping him get more of his Tunkah down pat, drilling him on basic phrases as he drilled the folk around him.

Yule looked over to Yethis, who was grumbling irritably as rain dripped in fat drops from her own patrol cap and hair braid. Yethis had been christened the Top Shirt of the Healer Corps, with Gruesome serving as the overall Command Sergeant Major and instructing them on basic combat casualty care, how to pack their medical kits, as well as headlining more advanced forms of combat medicines. Yethis herself preened for days after she was given the rank, and continuously made sure the other healers called her 'First Sergeant". Thankfully, the Onii were skilled weavers, and were able to crank out the majority of the U.S Army ranks that were required to sew onto uniforms for designations. The Onii were taking up a lot of the textile work load, along with the Valley Elves, and now there could be found professional looking uniforms on this side of the Veil, designed by the well loved Urmstronj. They were mirrored after the U.S Army Standard Battle Dress Uniform of the 1980s, but in a solid moss type color that was as close as they could get to olive drab green. In addition to these uniforms, there were also fresh unit patches being made for the Auxiliary, now sharing the same unit brotherhood of the Veil Riders. The only ones who did not partake in the unit patch were the 601st, but everyone was more than happy to let them make their own decisions.

The 601st themselves took a keen interest in some of the volunteers that came in from the surrounding countryside, and picked out a trooper here or there that showed promise in the more ungentlemanly aspects of combat. They themselves had re-creations of their own unit patch, and now consisted of a small platoon of troopers that operated on their own accord. Yule had no problems with this, and just asked Prusík to make sure to watch out for the Veil Folk. Prusík had no arguments with this request, and kept Yule up to date on their comings and goings from Valhalla Hill. The 601st Platoon was actually why they were all out hugging this berm, watching the opening from a forest while the rain pelted down from on high.

The 601st's recon outings allowed them to stumble upon a large company of infantry moving North from Sanrion, and spent some length of time harassing them during the night, even going as far as to take out an entire squad in their sleep and leaving the bleeding bodies in their bed rolls to be discovered the morning after. The 601st did not have the manpower to take out the entire Company, as they were traveling with two LGS Fenneks and an M1117 ASV. When the male Brush Feathered landed down near the command bunker and told Yule the news, he scrabbled together an ambush force and immediately set out, his aim to take the vehicles whole and undamaged so they could make use of them themselves.

It was those vehicles they waited on, soggy and laying in the grass as patiently as they could. The Dwarven machine gunners chuckled and drank from their flasks, manning a Veil Rider M240b, while the Brimtouched and Onii took the time to perfect the camo netting they had draped around their horns. The 1st Dragoons all lounged in the spitting rain, a few having dragged tarpaulins over themselves to try and stay as dry as they could manage. Yethis saddled up next to Yule, shaking the water from her rifle as she did, and grumped softly.

"Im cold." She murmured, and Yule felt her snuggle up next to him.

"Hi cold, im Yule." He said back with a grin, and she punched him in the shoulder with the wet 'splack' of rain sodden clothing. Yule looked down at her rifle as he rubbed his shoulder, and couldn't help but marvel at it. The Dwarves had done a remarkable job copying the Daewoo K2, but instead of plastic, it had stained hardwood furniture and runic embellishments all down the frame. They even had runes inscribed on the bolt and bolt release, something to do with making sure they never fail, or explode. The exploding bit made him curious, and pondered just what happened during the testing phase, but shook it from his head. From the wood work that went into the rifle, he was almost tempted to trade his Daewoo for one of theirs. There was something wholesome about the aesthetic they had accomplished with blending the dark Dwarven steel and almost red-blonde lumber they had used for the hand-guard and buttstock. It really harked back to a more classic time in Human history, when steel was steel and wood was wood, and those two things made up the body of a real rifle.

Down the line, he saw a lot of the same, with the dwarves of the ambush team instead going for the runic FALs, which also had the same runes inscribed on them and wooden furniture to boot. A few yards away was Domino and Chicks, who had somehow convinced the Onii To craft them some rustic version of a Boonie Hat, which currently poured rain water onto their rifles and shoulders. Their eyes were pressed hard to their scopes as they peered through the gloom and murk of the rain, watching the road with killer intent in their eyes. Chicks and Domino were both ever keen to be in on the ambushes, even getting into physical altercations with other Dragoons on who would get to go. It even got to the point that the two would threaten other Dragoons if they were too late to the meeting or sign up call, and one Dragoon had even found their rifle missing their bolt, having been taken hostage until their position was given up.

Hours passed as the rain continued to pour down, and by that time, the Dwarven machine gunners were on their fifth flask, both of them chuckling to each other in Dwarvish, while the other Dwarven riflemen were busily rubbing oil and lubricants into their rifles to make sure the rain was kept at bay. Yule craned his head up and saw a Brimtouched was making a small stick house with a Valley Elf, and rolled his eyes. If this was just an elaborate trap to get the 1st Dragoons and their Auxiliaries soaked in the rain, they should be happy with the results. Even Yule was beginning to get taxed, as he was chilled to the bone at this point, and Yethis had cuddled up so close to him that she was probably soaking up any warmth his body managed to produce.

"Lights." Domino and Chicks said at the same time, and Yule saw their barrels slowly tracking something in the distance. Shrugging off Yethis, he crawled up the berm a little and poked his eyes over the top of it. Way out into the forest trail, he could see something akin to faintly glowing orbs popping up and disappearing through the trunks of the trees. He shuffled back down and hissed down both sides of the ambush line.

"Quit fucken' about, time to do the war thing." He forgot the word for combat in Tunkah, and instead interjected what he knew. Yethis gave a snort of laughter and reminded Yule of the word for 'combat', in which he then spouted, "Combat time!", in a hushed but loud tone. The last thing he wanted was for his voice to carry, but the rain coming down was so loud, it was doubtful one could hear a Giant far from a foot away.

The Veil Riders and their Auxiliaries wiggle wormed their way up the berm and barrels now drew down on the road that exited out of the woods. From where they were set up, the column would have to exit out the forest and then turn right, which would stretch them out all along the main firing lane the ambush was going to make use of. This in turn only left the column a few decisions: They could hunker down and fight back in the open, run back into the woods and abandon the road, try and push through the ambush down the road, or try and back up their entire column. Yule expected them to flee through the forest, which only provided slight cover for the infantry, and they would have to leave their vehicles behind, the main mission objective for Yule.

With the majority of the column on foot, that meant they were mostly unarmored, unlike the first ambush in which they had plenty of trucks and disembarked to avoid getting killed in them. These Chosen Children troopers were probably extremely green, and what that meant to Yule was that these cats would drop and look for cover as soon as the first belt of machine gun fire was ripped through. This would leave his line plenty of time to cut them down and pick them apart as they worked through their avenues of retreat.

Yule got deja-vu from his first ambush when he heard the rumble of engines in the distance, and he quickly scrambled up and down the line to double check the orders he had given to the Auxilaries and Dragoons. In lead of the column was the ASV, the turret facing the front, while three whole Platoons just strolled behind it. Behind those Platoons was a Fennek, another three Platoons, the last Fennek which towed a wagon of some sorts, and two more Platoons behind that. All of the turrets were facing forwards, and they were moseying along at a crawl through the rain. The last Fennek didn't even bother to point its turret to the rear, and Yule snorted as he passed Domino.

"Fuckin' Amateurs."

Domino smiled brightly, his teeth shining despite the gloom of the evening. "Just makes you want to teach them somethin' new."

"I'll teach them how to die like the dumb knife ear cunts they are" Chicks sneered, and heard Yethis make a scoff noise, in which she took her eye from her scope and looked at her.

"Not your kind of ears Yethis, you have long cute ears, they have cunt ears."

Yethis knitted her eyebrows at Chics and stuck her tongue out at her, which Chics answered with her own tongue and then went back to her scope.

The column was now beginning to turn out from the forest and follow the road around the bend, and he heard troopers down the line double checking their weapons.

"On me." Yule hissed, and checked his own bolt to make sure there was brass peeking out to greet him in the receiver. He heard his order repeated down the line, and a lot of eyes were resting on him.

"Also, don't shoot the fucking tires, those damn things are gold." Yule reminded them, and he now wondered if this realm even had rubber trees to begin with.

"Ready girl?" Yule asked Yethis, and slapped her on the back to get her attention.

Yethis gave a shuddered 'Yes' in return, and flicked her rifle's safety around to fire.

Rain tinked on the barrels that protruded out from the berm, and Yule was getting frustrated. At this distance and with the weight of the rain, the column was hard to see, and even the keen eyed Elves were having trouble making out the figures through the pelting sheets. The longer they waited, the further the column would get down the road, and the entire ambush would be spoiled, requiring Yule to retreat all of his squads and push in parallel to try and catch them again down the road. Just as Yule was about to wave off the ambush and tell them to retreat, there was suddenly a deafening silence. He looked around from where he was laying, and now water only dripped down here and there from the trees, instead of pouring down from the sky. He crawled up and peeked over the berm to see the column was doing the same, and had actually halted just inside their ambush corridor. He could hear them laughing from where he was, and speaking in their Southern Dialect.

"Haha, hey look, it's like the rain just turned off!" One Chosen Child cried out, and he laughed along with his Platoon mates as they all shook their rifles clear of rain water. From the hatches of the vehicles, the driver's heads popped out, having risen their seats up so they could drive and able to get some fresh air. It was the first time Yule had seen their uniforms clearly, and they were wearing some kind of dark green digital camouflage that reminded him of tiger stripe a bit, and then heard the 'scritch' of a velcro pocket being undone.

Yule pointed at Domino and whispered. "Confirm targets!"

Domino panned left and right quickly, grimacing hard in focus before whispering back. "They're all Elves from what I can tell. They ain't none of ours, and they have UN markings. Oh look one actually says Unsee-"

Yule hadn't waited for him to finish, having high crawled all the way up to the top of the berm after Domino had said 'none of ours', pressed his free hand on top of his hand guard, and rotated his selector switch to its third setting. Fokhet had asked why Yule's K2 didn't have an Auto Sere like the other rifles, and said he was more than happy to put one in himself if Yule wanted one.

A crisp click of the trigger broke the air as Yule slammed the mechanism back, and his rifle spewed Dwarven 5.56 in full auto down at the Platoon that was behind the second Fennek. Brass sang through the air as the bullets cracked out of the barrel, slamming into the bodies of the Chosen Children troopers and showering mud everywhere as they impacted the road. Many of them were still looking up at the sky as steel shot ripped through their flesh and wrent apart their bodies. The magazine went quickly, and Yule dropped the empty vessel with the depression of his mag release, then clicking a fresh one into the magwell with smooth and professional precision. Domino and Chicks fired their first salvo right after Yule opened up, and Yule saw two of the drivers flop over in their seats, the rounds having spliced right through the sides of their heads and showered the hatch next to them in brain matter.

A split second after the two snipers, the Veil Riders opened up and rained hell down on the convoy. The Auxiliaries were caught off guard, but snapped back to reality and joined in on the gunfire. The Dwarves bellowed out war cries as they fired their weapons, the machine gunners laughing as their M240b's roared with the other rifles around it. Yethis was frozen, looking from Yule to the Elves dying in droves below.

Yule looked over at her, pressing the bolt release of his rifle, and it slammed home, startling water off of the rifle as it vibrated its frame.

"Yethis! Fire your weapon, Yethis!" He barked, and Yethis looked to him wide eyed. Yule reached over and hefted Yethis up towards him by her harness, making her squeak in shock as she was dragged a few feet up and over where Yule was.

From this vantage point, she could better see what was happening down below. Water and mud leaped and danced off the ground as rounds impacted, and Elves were falling all over the road. True to Yule's predictions, they had no idea how to react to the sudden ambush, and had dropped right onto the ground, firing wildly at the flashes in the distance. Dirt and mud spacked and thwacked here and there along the ambush line, but their fire never ceased onto the damned souls below.

"Your weapon Yethis! Use it! Fire your weapon! Just like I showed you!"

Yethis looked at Yule, then shrugged down behind her rifle, looking down the sights. Unlike Yule's eyes, Yethis had a heightened sense like most Elves did, allowing her to focus deeper and see farther to a more accurate degree. She trained her sights along the column, the black lead post swaying back and forth. Beside her, Yule resumed firing in bursts, and she could see his tracers trailing along the bodies. She watched the Elves below dive and shrink away from the rounds, as well as the ones who were too slow screech in shock as the rounds punched through them. She saw the Dwarves trail one Elf who was running, the 240b's stream of bullets whipping up water after the Elf, who was trying to sprint their way to the safety of a vehicle's rear hatch. The trail quickly caught up, and Yethis watched as her body was ripped apart by the heavy 7.62 ammunition.

The Elf screamed as the first few rounds tore through her leg and arm, but the scream was cut short as the follow up rounds turned her face and head to mush. Yethis could hear her blood thundering in her ears along with the subtle ringing of the gunfire, and she trailed her sights to a small group of Chosen who were trying to deploy a small field mortar. She had seen what the Dwarves could do with theirs after they launched a round at a goat, and wanted nothing like that coming her way. She squeezed the trigger in short bursts, and cut them all down before she was even half way through her magazine. The first Elf took one round to the throat and went down in the mud, rolling and kicking his boots frantically as his hands clutched at the waterfall of blood that poured out from his neck. The second Elf took all of hers in the chest, slumping forward and falling over the mortar tube, smashing it into the road. The third Elf turned to run . . . and Yethis shot him in the back twice, watching him land heavily onto the road, splashing in the water to move no more.

When she looked over to Yule, he was grinning at her, having watched her the entire time she was shooting. She swallowed hard, her ears twitching, before she grimaced and went back to her sights. Yule gave her a pat on the shoulder, yelling, "Keep it up Slayer!", before dropping his second mag to load in a fresh one. After locking it into place, he ran down the length of the ambush line, watching how all the troopers were operating. The Dwarves were all having a real time of it, roaring and shouting curses as they fired. The Onii and Valley Elves all had this kind of business face on, quiet and working away at the triggers of their rifles as if they were fussing with just another tool in the workshop. The Brimtouched . . . they all seemed to be grinning in a malicious way, and Yule watched them slowly pick off runners who tried to make a break through the forest.

That's rough, Yule thought, before checking on his Dragoons, who were all spending more time coaching the Auxiliaries around them than actually firing. He popped his head back up and made a painful face at what he saw down below; All of the vehicles were not moving, not even the turrets had spun their direction, and he saw that all the hatches were open, probably because the crews decided 'fuck this', and bailed. The road itself was littered with the dead and the dying, who wailed or clutched at their wounds. Yule ran his eyes up and down the road, and saw that anything that wasn't dying in the mud had made a break for survival, and no longer did they have incoming fire. He waved his hand back and forth to signal them all to cease firing.

"Cease fire! Cease fire! Give me a team on overwatch, everyone else, get down there and secure those vehicles. If there's anything left alive, keep it alive, we need prisoners for answers."

Casualties were light for the Veil Riders in this ambush, only suffering minor grazes and gun shot wounds due to their slight elevation and natural cover of the berm. One Veil Rider had a graze on the side of his head and was rattled pretty hard by the concussion of it, but seemed to be doing fine in the hands of the Healer Corps. The Dwarven machine gunners and the sharpshooters were set up high and hard on the berm while everyone else walked down towards the road, weapons held at the high ready as they approached. The scene below was just another slaughter, and Yule clicked his tongue distastefully. None of the green Chosen Children soldiers had even tried to defuse the ambush, and many had died where they laid or stood. He even saw that most of them had smoke grenades, and quietly pondered if they had been trained at all besides basic soldiering.

Yule spun around as he heard fresh gunfire bursting behind him, and brought up his rifle in time to empty a whole magazine into a Chosen trooper that had been playing possum on the road. Before Yule ended him right then and there, the trooper had rolled over and gunned down two Veil Riders and three Valley Elf Auxiliaries with his M4 Carbine. Only one of the Valley Elves was alive, and Yethis sprinted over towards them, her boots splashing on the ground. Everyone else on the approach went down to a knee and had their rifles up, scanning for targets just as Yule had taught them, and Yule ran over to the small huddle of bodies that lay around the now dead Chosen trooper.

The faces of his fellow terrans were frozen in surprise, the bullets from the burst fire rifle having killed them instantly purely by luck of the draw, impacting their spinal columns or punching right through their hearts. He had been with these Veil Riders since the beginning; Mark was a steel worker from Ohio, and Beth a coffee barista that was just tired of doing the same thing every day, both of them looking to get in on a grand adventure. Yule reached down and closed their wide, shocked eyes, then ripped the patches off of their uniforms, tucking them inside one of his pockets. Yethis coaxed the one wounded Elf back into the solidarity of this realm, and Yule turned to look at the road.

He saw that many bodies were squirming or laying very still while their chests still moved, and he frowned harshly. He had intended, after the cock up with Britta, to take as many prisoners as he could manage, and be the good guy for once. But now . . . now that idea flapped away from the window, tweeting out a bloodlusting tune. Yule turned to the Veil Riders behind him, who were trying their best not to look at their fallen comrades.

He held up five fingers, and spoke in a steely manner. "I want five alive, kill the rest."

Without a word more, the Veil Riders stood and began moving through the road, killing anything that was suspect and only taking what was alive and raising their hands when they approached. Yule kept count of every rifle burst as he stared down at his dead troopers, who were being made ready to be hauled back to Valhalla Hill for burial. *From 69 to 64 original Terrans . . .* Yule thought, as he kept counting the rifle reports, and looked over to see Yethis and another Auxiliary help the wounded Elf limp back towards the berm. The Elf had taken most of his rounds to the legs and stomach, and while healed, the pain would still render his limbs difficult to use. Yule heard no more gunshots, and murmured aloud.

"Eighteen possible prisoners . . . a pity. Truly a pity."

He turned and saw the Onii and Dwarves dragging along what looked like five mud-logged Elves, three of which bore the red crosses of medics. The Auxiliaries tossed the Elves towards Yule, and they splashed down hard onto the mud and water puddles of the road. Yule slowly squatted down on his heels, and used the barrel of his K2 to lift the chin of a female, who glared up at him with ivory white eyes. He then looked over to a male next to her, and saw that he instead had violet eyes, and heaved heavily while clutching his chest. Unlike their Valley Elf cousins, these Elves had higher, more proper pointed ears that reminded him of High Elves in fantasy games back home, and fine boned faces that harked back to Space Elves that were known in a popular sci-fi wargame on Earth. He looked back over at the female and saw that her hat had fallen off some time during the ambush, and her copper hair was full of blood and mud, which streaked down her face in ugly swaths. Their eyes did indeed share the same soft almond shape of the Valley Elves . . . but theirs were so much more sinister in their complexion, angled in a way that gave off constant aggression.

"Curious . . ." Yule murmured, then moved his barrel away from her chin with a ring of metal on skin. Her head bobbed and she exhaled sharply, having been expecting a bullet to fly out from the barrel and end her. "Bag their heads and toss them in the M1117, let's get our fallen out of this pit."

With the Southern Elf prisoners bagged like falcons and tossed into the engine stowage compartment of the M1117 ASV, the rest of the snatch and grab went with ease, since most of the German Veil Riders knew how to drive the Fenneks, and Yule was an old lover of the ASV himself. As he hauled out the dead driver and threw the body away from the wheels, he made a 'tsk' of disgust when he climbed into the seat and saw that half of the toggle switches were turned off in the TC's haste to get out of the vehicle. He popped his head up and saw that the TC must have slipped on his driver's brain matter, as there was a smear of red across the top deck of the ASV and a large mud splat down by the left front tire.

Yule heard the Fenneks fire back up behind him, driving off towards the ambush line, and he quickly toggled on the fuel pump and other critical functions on the switchboard in order to get the girl back up and running. Behind him, a Veil Rider was scrambling into the gunner basket and turning on the electrics.

"Whos in my fucken' truck?" Yule asked, reaching down to ignite the engine and then listening to the Cummins 6CTA8 rumble back to life behind him.

"McCormick!" He heard behind him, and then felt the electronic motors of the turret click on and swing the basket to the left.

The next thing he felt was the clap of air ten feet away from his truck, and Yule popped his head back up and out of the driver hatch when the metal stopped pinging off of the ASV's armor. A mortar round had fallen down and exploded almost on top of the deck plate, and that was a mighty big hole staring back at him from the mud. The dead driver was also, now all over the top of the armor deck. He heard another dull explosion behind him, and a great cascade of debris and mud was flung into the air. It was by luck that the majority of the ambush party had already moved away back towards the berm, and he saw that a lot of the Veil Riders had their heads down in the grass and looking around wildly.

He leaned over the side of his driver hatch and bellowed out to those laying in the grass. "Clear out of the open! Get back to the berm and fall back to the horses! Get the fuck out of here! You lot," Yule pointed to a small huddle of Veil Rider Auxiliaries that were using the ASV for cover, "Get in this fucken' truck or die!."

Yule pressed the transmission into automatic and made sure the four wheel drive selector was initiated. Seeing that it was in fact in two wheel drive, Yule slapped it to four wheel drive, eliciting a hiss from the rumbling engine. It was around the time that the Veil Rider Auxiliaries closed the open side hatch that another round impacted right next to where they were huddled, and the concussion of the impact rocked the armored vehicle from side to side.

With little ceremony, Yule cranked the wheel one handed towards the berm and punched the accelerator, lurching them into motion as he wrangled the blood covered headset around his face. As he wheeled around, he saw that all of the other Veil Riders had already hoofed it over the berm and into the brush to get to the horses. Mortar fire continued to rain down around them, and Yule grimaced, the Auxiliaries screaming in panic as the vehicle was rocked back and forth.

Yule toggled the headset with his free hand, rolling the wheel to straight and putting the ASV back down in a lower gear to mount the climb to the berm. "McCormik do you see anything in the woods to our rear?" He swerved to avoid a fresh mortar crater, which caused more Veil flavored screaming to erupt as they were thrown across the very tight passage corridor. The Elves shoved into the engine stowage were screaming as well, but it was blessedly muffled by the double door. The gunner basket whirred and spun to the rear of the ASV, and he heard McCormik yelling at the Auxiliaries to keep their hands away from the bottom of the basket.

"Negative Yule, I don't see any spotters."

"Then how the hell are they *spotting* us?" Yule grunted, the ASV's nose pitching upwards, and then down as they came off of the berm. He let off the throttle and switched the transmission back into automatic, and hit the gas hard to catch up to the rest of the Veil Riders. The mortars continued to rain down around them, throwing earth and torn plant matter into the air. There was a hollow bong as a round impacted on the angled plate of the turret, causing the vehicle to vibrate like a bell for a moment.

"All good!" McCormik called out, and swung the basket back around towards the front. A great gout of mud splashed over the window screens of the driver seat, and when Yule went to turn on the wipers, he found that the switch had been broken off by the panicked boot of the TC on his way out.

"Fuck fuck fuck fuck fuck..." Yule growled as he swung the driver hatch door back open and began to raise his seat, just enough to poke his eyes over the lip of the opening. The wind ripped his patrol cap off of his head and tossed it back into the hatch, causing his hair to whip around him wildly, and smack him in the eyes. That problem was soon fixed as a fresh deluge of wet earth slapped across the deck of the vehicle, and pinned his mud matted hair to his face, which he tossed his head back and forth to try and remove. Yule gritted his teeth, spitting out mud that had gotten inside, and swung the truck right to avoid another huge mortar hole. Ahead of him he saw the running lights of the Fenneks and the dozens of blurrs that were the horses, and pressed the pedal to the floor.

"Finite range... Finite range..." Yule chanted this to himself under the roar of the Cummins engine and the impacts of mortar rounds around the vehicle. He had no idea how the hell the mortar fire was this accurate even over the berm, and was furious they were able to even get rounds at him so soon after the ambush. What were they using, drones? They were bracketing him left right and center at full speed! Another round exploded on top of the ASV, this time hitting just above the left side hatch. The impact almost tore the door away and filled the vehicle with smoke.

"Impact! Door is all kinds of fucked up! No serious injuries!" McCormik yelled over the mic, and Yule could hear him yelling something in Tunkah.

The ASV was rocking hard now as the suspension struggled to keep up with the terrain, but the old birds were made to do this kind of stuff at full speed. Yule didn't breathe easy until the mortar fire became more staggered, and finally stopped entirely, leaving him free and clear of any more incoming indirect fire. The huge engine roared and spewed black smoke out from its exhaust as Yule heaved and whirled the wheel to bring the heavy vehicle in line with the tracks of the Fenneks. He spared a moment to duck his head inside and peer into the smokey dim of the inner compartment, and saw Auxiliaries sprawled across the deck plating, while his gunner had his face pressed hard to the optic mount. The Onii seemed to be having the worst time of it, the larger female was more or less curled into a ball and trying not to roll across the deck anymore than she already had. A fresh gash had split open on her forehead, and a Brimtouched seemed to have had one of his horns broken off half way. They were alive, however, despite that door hit from the mortar, and that was enough for Yule. As the terrain leveled out, he made sure the vehicle was in the correct format for it, used a bullet to crack the wipers on to clear away the mud, and brought the vehicle in formation with the Fenneks, the three vehicles in an offset pattern to keep from splattering the vehicle behind them with mud. The Dragoons galloped and whooped beside them as the vehicles roared onward, the low rumble of the mortar fire being left behind on the horizon.

The ride back to Valhalla hill took some time, but the freshly acquired vehicles rolled up the wagon path to the top of the hill with victorious applause. To save the horses, a lot of the Dragoons switched off their mounts and instead rode on top of the armored vehicles, waving and blowing kisses to the other Veil Riders as they laughed and cheered at the ambush unit. The horses themselves would show up in a few days and wait outside of the corral; They had been doing this for a few weeks, and it was a handy bit of training to have in case there was no time to remount, or the Dragoons had to scatter their horses due to artillery fire. Yule nodded to Peiper, who waved at him from the command bunker, and he rolled the ASV up with the hiss of hydraulics and guttering of the diesel engine. Soft clicking echoed out from the drivers hatch as Yule switched off the engine and the pumps, while the passengers inside unhinged both of the side hatches and piled out into the freedom of fresh air. After ticking down the after-check list and making sure the vehicle was squared away, Yule groaned and crawled his way up and out of the hatch. Forgetting that the thing was covered in still wet mud, blood, and Elf bits, his hand slipped as he tried to heave up and over, only getting the over and instead, and involuntarily heaved himself down the front of the windows, tumbling over the guide bars with the loud cacophony of curses and roars of pain.

Yule landed with a wet smack on the ground in front of the command bunker, and Peiper leaned into view, holding a mugroot cigar in his smiling teeth.

"Rough drive, Yule?"

"Shattap ya Kraut..." Yule said through gritted teeth, and groaned as he got up to a knee, mud still sticking his hair to his face. His legs were also sore from bouncing around inside the lower drive compartment, and the concussions rocking the chassis had caused him to bang his knees quite few times on the bolts that were designed to hurt the driver, as all Army vehicles are. Peiper laughed heartily, more at Yules expense than anything else, and helped him to his feet fully, brushing off his shoulders like a fussy nanny.

"Can't take you Americans anyvhere, alvays get so dirty." Peiper mused, and chucked his teeth disapprovingly.

"Oh *ha ha*," Yule retorted, slapping at Peipers hands as he laughed at him some more, and dusted off his own pants and shirt, dried mud coming way in flakes and chunks, "Got some Chosen locked away in the engine compartment, lets get them out of there and into the bunker."

Peiper raised his eyebrows, then tucked his fingers into his mouth and gave a sharp whistle. McCormik was making his way out of the gunner basket when five of the European Veil Riders trotted over and leveled their weapons at the hatch, while Peiper undid the latch locks. The top part of the hatch hissed up, while the bottom part slowly came down with the hydraulic dampeners, and a silence fell down around the rear team. Yule was prying his muddy hair away from his face when he heard Peiper call from the rear of the vehicle.

"Ah... how many vere supposed to be alive?"

Yule brought his eyebrows together, actually having to stop and remember before calling out. "Five, why?"

"Vell... there is only one."

"What? ..." Yule murmured, and stomped his way around to the back of the vehicle. When he poked his head all the way around to look inside of the engine stowage lane, he couldn't help but blink silently in astonishment. The inside of the compartment was covered in bright blood, as if a fight scene from a particularly good Tarantino movie had happened inside. The bodies of the other surviving Elves were ripped and torn into pieces, their throats rended open all the way to the meat and sinews that gleamed white in the open air. The only thing living inside of the vehicle was the female Elf from before, who sat on the small mound of bodies with a combat knife clutched in both of her hands. Yule turned his head and called out for Domino to bring him 'the hacky sack', before looking back inside of the corridor and walking more into sight. The thing that caught his eye the most was that some of the blood inside had little flecks of gold in it that shimmered in the light, and Yule stood now within full sight of the hatch, both of his hands poised at his sides.

"S-Stay back!" The Elven woman roared, and Yule squinted a bit as he tried to make out her name tag.

"Fadithas huh? Cool name ..." Yule remarked, and reached up to scratch his head. As he scratched his bare hair, realization slowly dawned on him, but he was able to keep his face in check, remaining cool.

"You speak English, do you?"

The Elf shrinked back further into the vehicle, but in her haste clipped the side of her forehead on a compartment door knob, giving her a short gash which began to bleed steadily. She hissed at the pain and brought her knife up, brandishing it with both hands. "Stay back! Stay back you fucking rustblood currs!"

Yule stared at her, eyes narrowed, watching the little trail of blood slowly ooze out from the wound and trail down her temple. Peiper gave a hard puff of his cigar, the dried mugroot inside crackling merrily, and the rest of the Veil Riders murmured to themselves.

Yule stepped forward, resting his right boot on the bottom door and leaned in, reaching a hand back behind his leg with open fingers.

"Mighty curious blood you got there, stranger. One may say you were born under a special moon."

"Don't you try and flatter me, rustblood! You step inside here, and I'll gut you like the rest of these useless fuc-"

The rest of the words didn't really have the air to formulate, after Domino handed something to Yule around the time she said "rustblood". In her efforts to be aggressive and keep her ground, Fadithas failed to see the short barreled pistol gripped shotgun get shoved into Yule's hands. Her words were cut short, and off, as Yule whipped the shotgun up and fired it once, blowing out her eardrums with the concussion in the small space. Of course, her ears hurt far less than the beanbag that caught her in the middle of the chest.

"Kuh!" She gasped, the beanbag bouncing off of her bones and patterning off the wall of the engine compartment. The knife flew from her hands as she was catapulted backwards off of the small mound of dead Elves, landing near the cooling beanbag. Her lungs spasmed and heaved as she tried to breathe; She had never felt a pain like this before in her very long life, long even for an Elf, and the pain was like nothing she had ever imagined. Her mouth was agape, and it seemed she could not get any air into her lungs no matter how hard she tried to force them to work. She gasped in panic, which caused her lungs to smart painfully, when something grabbed onto her combat boot, and yanked her hard out from her little hidey hole.

When she fell back, her boots stayed in view, and Yule was able to reach in and grab them. She felt herself get pulled out of the vehicle unceremoniously, her head bouncing harshly on the bottom half of the hatch door, as Yule just walked backwards while holding her boots. She finally came out onto the firm ground in a bodily thud, and she didn't even have the breath to curl into a ball. Fadithas's eyes rolled as she took in her surroundings; She saw the one who she knew was Yule, having seen his face in all the reports back on the Veil Base, and a Valley Elf she had never seen before standing next to him, wearing her hair in a long braid off of her shoulder.

"She has that gold flecked blood, 'cept hers is red and not pink." Yule said, pointing to Fadithas's forehead where she was bleeding.

The gift of tongues was able to give her the understanding of their language, as Yethis leaned in towards Yule and said, "She's a half breed."

"H-Half breed?!" Fadithas gasped out, her chest still heaving with pain, and she made to sit up. "Who are you calling, half breed, you Valley eared who-AUGH!"

The shotgun reported again, and another bea bag slammed into her chest, this time right and high above the breast. Fadithas was thrown back onto the ground hard, and she screamed silently in pain. The beanbag hung a bit in the air, then bounced off of the bottom hatch of the ASV, finally coming to a rest on the ground after doinking Fadithas on the face.

Fadithas lay there. writhing on the ground, as Yule turned and smiled at Domino, who was grinning down at the Elf while tapping the ends of his fingers together. "I really am glad you brought this stupid thing."

Domino looked at Yule while never taking the grin from his face. "Less than lethal entertainment at the highest order."

"Made getting her out of the vehicle easier, that's for sure. I don't feel like getting stabbed again." Yule handed him back his shotgun, then walked over towards the Southern Elf who was curling up on the ground. He then looked up inside of the hatch to the four heavily cut up bodies and pressed his lips together disapprovingly.

"Man... what on earth. Why would she just cut them all up like that?"

Yule tapped his booted foot a few times while walking around the Elf, watching her grimace, eyes closed, and holding her chest with her arms crossed over them. He pulled out a little iron nail from the HQ bunker, and kneeled down, touching it to her exposed hand. When nothing happened, he gave it a little harder rub, and after a few seconds saw that the flesh seemed to flush, but nothing else really came of it.

"Hm... thought you would start burning like a vampire or something." Yule hummed, before standing back up, and flicking the nail down at Fadithas. The nail bounced off of her ear, and she hissed angrily, eyes still closed and body curled up.

"Well, guess we get to try out the little jail they built. Drag her over there." Yule pointed to ten Veil Riders who had gathered nearby. "All of you. Keep her hands out of reach of your kit, check her for anything metal, and take her shoe laces. Make sure some of the other Elves are there with you, don't want you guys getting fae-tranced or somethin'."

Down below, Faditha's hissed a painful laugh. "You people really are as stupid as the dirt you came from."

The Veil Riders hauled the Southern Elf off to the small jail system inside the grain holding center, and Yule waved Yethis over after watching them go. He then fetched his patrol cap and placed it firmly on his head, feeling the small bump of the amulet.

"Half breeds, huh?"

Yethis nodded. "They are known, the coupling of Fae and Elf. They lose a lot of the natural power of their Fae parent, but still gain a lot of the minor powers they can possess, such as transfiguration, long life, the gift of tongues, so on. A few are even still living to this day in our borders, but they mostly stick to themselves as hermits."

Yule stroked his beard in thought. "But why would she cut up all these poor bastards?" He motioned towards the sliced up bodies that were being hauled from the back of the ASV, and grimaced at the sight of them.

"Perhaps they had knowledge she wanted to keep. Maybe she needed their blood, maybe they knew something she didn't want getting out. I know, however, that the male there." Yethis pointed at a male Elf whos head was almost sawed completely off, the holes of his airways and other inner workings born to the air. "Was a secret keeper, he bears the markings of one there on his sleeve."

Yule looked, and just as Yethis described, there were intricate tattoos going up from the wrist of his hand and into his torn sleeve.

Yethis continued. "The secret keepers know of the prophecies and the inner workings of the Fae, as well as their old plans. Knowing you, you could have probably cracked that Elf like an egg. But the Half-Fae ... she will prove to be a far more competent opponent."

Yule frowned, and looked up across the base to the horizon, watching the fading light with annoyance. As he stood there with Yethis, he saw small white dots appear along the tree line. The longer he waited, the larger the dots got, and after a while he saw that it was a small flight of Himalaya Harpies coming in from a scout run. He looked over at the road, and saw that even more Veil folk had shown up from the countryside and cities. At this point, he may have an entire Division under his command if he counted right. He heard the flap of wings beating on the air and turned back around to see the flight was heading right towards him.

They landed with a woosh of air and trotted up to Yule, giving him their report. Yule listened intently, before thanking them and sending them on their way to rest. He gave Yethis a short hug, thanked her for her help, and took off at a jog to find his NCOs. He was sweating by the time he found them in the chow hall, and when he burst in through the door, a Dwarf drinking by the door leapt to his feet from his tool.

"Attention to the front!"

Everyone sprung up to their feet as Yule panted, and he called out for his NCOs, who ran over, some still clutching their three pronged forks or spoons. Yule took off his hat to try and cool his head, and quietly wished the winter would come faster. He looked to his NCOs ... then stood back, and decided to address the room instead, fitting his patrol cap back onto his head.

"The Himalayas report that this forest crawls. They're digging in large artillery pieces near Sanrion, large enough that they will be able to shell anything within a twenty mile radius. Somehow ... some way, they've dragged triple 7's through the Veil, along with self propelled tracked artillery. We are going on the offensive in a few days, in a big way. If we do not go ... We all may die here on this hill when they shell us to death. My Veil Riders, I know you are steady to go and ready to kill, but to you Auxiliaries, I will give you a choice. If you wish to go, I will take you, but I will not make you. Tomorrow morning there will be a formation, anyone who is willing to toss in their rifle, show up there at 8am."

Yule turned to leave.

"As you were. I'll see you in the morning."

CHAPTER 13

WHEN YULE AWOKE the next dawn and stepped out onto the parade grounds with his cup of tea, he was startled to find it packed from top to bottom with Veil folk. So much in fact, that Yule had to turn some of the them away in order to keep Valhalla Hill staffed. He found no disparagement from the races, as the volunteers were a healthy mixture of Elves, Dwarves, Onii, and Brimtouched, all wearing their uniforms and holding their Dwarf-issued weapons. Standing behind the uniformed Auxiliaries were the fresh new boots from the surrounding areas, and they were sorely disappointed when Yule told them they had to be trained up first before they could enter the field. The amount of fresh recruits flowing into Valhalla Hill would require a lot of manpower to train, forcing Yule to pull away his entire 1st Dragoons and the majority of Cosmoline Company's Human fighters just to drill them. This left Yule with the majority of his fighters being locals, however these were at least trained to an acceptable standard proficiency, and the veterans of the ambush had tossed in their lot as well.

The days before his offensive push went past swiftly as everyone was loaded out with provisions for the field, and given last minute instructions on what was to happen if they were shelled. Yule was also leaving behind the vehicles to guard the base, as he assumed the majority of the fighting would be done stealthily, crawling up into the wire and getting in as close as possible to avoid getting pounded on the approach into any towns or cities they came across. Four Platoons were drawn up from the volunteer Auxiliaries, and put under command of three Veil Riders who would act as their Platoon Sergeants. While these Platoons would head out to skirmish and hopefully take care of the artillery, another small Company under the command of Domino would head out to see what they could do about Sanrion. Peiper in turn would take up administrative duties for Valhalla Hill, while the 601st would be out on their own doing their ghost duties in the wilds of the Valley Lands.

Members of Cosmoline Company had issues with sending out Yule on his own with so many green troopers, some of which only having a few weeks of training under their belt, but Yule was adamant on going out with as few Human Veil Riders as he could manage. Yule acknowledged that the largest wealth of tactical and modern warfare comprehension lay in the Humans that walked the Veil with him on that first day, and he needed to keep as many alive as possible training the Auxiliaries. He felt uneasy taking as many as he was out on this offensive, and had a mind to make them all stay while heading off on his own with his troopers. The Veil Riders who he had given command of the Platoons outright told him to go pound sand when he brought up having them stay behind as a caution, and he walked the idea back quickly in order to avoid a mutiny. A small Squad of Himalayas also volunteered to accompany Yule, which he took in stride and made them the main scouting element to his Platoons. Saveriss tried to weasel her way into Yule's Himalayan volunteers, but he instead pinned her with the job of watching over Valhalla Hill, the two finding themselves in multiple shouting matches through the days to him leaving.

Yethis demanded to go with Yule out into the field, but he told her he needed her to stay. He told her that she was needed here, to train more medical personnel with Gruesome, and to make sure nothing hokey happened with the locals while he was gone. She fought viciously against him, until he put both his hands on her shoulders and leaned in towards her face one night during dinner. "There's only a few people who I trust to watch over things here, and one of them is you. If you don't think you're able to manage things for me while I'm gone, I can find someone else if you so wish."

After that, there was no more push back to be found from Yethis. She did leave him multiple bottles of her blood, just in case he needed to refuel his Translation Amulet, and left little encouraging notes on the labels so Yule would have a morale boost out in the field. Yule didn't think they needed nearly as many doodles as they had on them, but he figured the blood would come in handy. His Tunkah still needed a lot of work, and his Midwestern accent really did butcher the pronunciations.

On the final day, Yule and his small Company set out from Valhalla Hill and dove hard to the West, working off of the reports from the Himalayans that they saw some weird looking things moving about a small city called Emalone. The first week of travel went by lively, and Yule came to enjoy the bickering that happened around him on the road. His second in command for this offensive was Mullen, a rather blase' man from South Dakota that was never easily excited. He was shorter than Yule, with mousy brown hair, brown eyes, and a dusting of brown freckles that ran down his nose. Those in the company called him Mousen, which he took with derisive eyerolls. Between Mullen and Yule, managing the march onwards was more like wrangling cats every day. One persistent issue was making sure the Platoons kept their spacing on the road, and to make sure the Dwarves and Onii didn't hurt themselves in their nightly arm wrestling contests. The Himalayans proved to be not what Yule had hoped, preferring to ride on the shoulders of the taller Veil Auxiliaries or lope alongside the formations as they walked. When Yule would task them to go and actually do their job of scouting, they would return back after a few minutes of flight to report they saw nothing, and return to playing around the Platoons or running off with small pieces of equipment. It wasn't until they came across their first enemy picket that everyone understood this was not a morning hike into the woods.

Most shocking to Yule was how many small patrols they *did* meet on their way to Emalone; Skirmishes were a daily occurrence in some cases, usually starting with Yule and his Platoons coming into contact with a Chosen Children patrol and pushing them back and away, or lying in wait for a Squad that the Himalayans had spotted during their rounds. Casualties were light during their movements, and those who had fallen in battle were given a small burial and the grave marked with large stones. In a ritual that was slowly becoming the norm, a lot of the fallen would have their patches ripped off and handed to Yule, which he kept in his breast pocket. After two weeks, that pocket was getting slowly fuller and fuller, weighing on his mind with each passing fire fight. Things weren't always so dreary though, as in their skirmishes they had come across a small vehicle or two, gaining them gradual access to a small fleet of battered Humvees and Gators. These small graces allowed them to carry greater weights of gear with them, and kept the 'Cosmoline Train' rolling until they were only a few days away from the city.

The stiffest resistance was met here, as Yule's Auxiliary Platoons now came face to face with an enemy Company. The offensive started at a small farming village called Meseriam, which Yule assumed was like a small suburb of Emalone. The skirmishes before they got to Meseriam had primed the Platoons to be on alert for anything, as an ambush by the Chosen Children had done a fair bit of damage to one Platoon in particular, shaking the greenness from them like a sapling in a hurricane. Yule knew what was happening a few heart beats after the buildings of the small village suddenly lit up with automatic rifle fire, and a small field of Elven wheat to their right began popping with the staccato rhythm of machine guns. His Company had been spread out and moving across open ground, their only cover consisting of tall grass and a few scattered bushes. When the gunfire erupted, they were caught out in the approach to the village, and the Chosen Children inside the village had waited until they were fully inside their firing lanes. Yule spun his head left and right, standing straight up while the rest of his men and women dove into the tall grass for cover. Bullets snapped and hissed by his head as he looked around, and he saw no obvious alleys of escape from where they were pinned, leaving him with the same choices as that second ambush long ago for the armored vehicles: Push through, stay and return fire, or flee. Yule didn't feel much like fleeing, as they would probably just be cut down as they all stood to run, or tried to crawl away in the grass. Crawling would keep the gunfire at bay, but then they could just lob grenades at them and shell them into oblivion. Trying to stay here and return fire had the same issues, as they would be in the open and ripe for the artillery to pour down on them. He bet that he would have to get in close and grab their belt buckles so they wouldn't be able to rip his Platoons apart with artillery fire, so he spun around to face his Auxiliaries laying in the grass.

"Mullen!" Yule shouted, and he knelt down near a small cluster of brush, pulling at looted smoke grenades that were hung loosely on his chest.

Mullen got up and barreled towards Yule at a low run, tracer rounds cracking around them both as they knelt down in a small huddle. Around their position, the Auxiliaries were returning fire as best as they could, popping off shots whenever they thought they could tell a flash in the windows of a building, or through the stalks of wheat. A Brimtouched MG3 team, having looted the machine gun from the fallen Chosen Children, began spraying rounds wildly back at the village, splattering wood and glass from windows, or tracing lines of holes down walls. The Brimtouched holding the MG3 on her shoulder, like Peiper had taught her, was grinning madly as they both traced the barrel back and forth.

"Whats up Yule?" Mullen asked calmly, and he pushed the bill of his patrol cap up. A bullet clipped the brim of his cap and sent it spinning off of his head to land on the ground beside them. Mullen made an annoyed sound and reached down to grab his now holed head cover, and plopped it back onto his head. To the rear, the vehicles were doing their best to open up with their gunners, the drivers trying to surge forward and put pressure on the village. After just a few seconds, the passengers began diving out of hurriedly flung open doors into cover, machine gun rounds pelting and pinging off the lightly armored Humvees, shattering glass and sending sparks of metal spinning into the air.

"We gotta' smoke our way out of here and push into that village." Yule said calmly, gesturing with a bladed hand at the buildings ahead of him as a pair of bullets ripped through his rucksack. "We'll get in close and take them at the boot tips so they can't shell us. Tell the lads to throw smoke at that field over there and follow my own smoke in."

Mullen nodded and scurried back off towards the rest of the troops down the field, who were doing their best to suppress whatever the hell was shooting at them and pinning them down. Yule pulled out his first smoke grenade and pulled the pin, tossing it straight down at his feet so he could stand up straight and advance. Purple smoke poured out around his feet and he grimaced. "Fucken' purple, really? . . ."

Now fully standing under the cover of the smoke, he pulled the pin on another grenade and threw it ten yards away, waiting for its smoke to furl up before running over to that spot and pulling another grenade's pin. He repeated this for five grenades, and created a lane of advance through the open field towards the buildings under the cover of white, purple, amber, red, and even orange smoke. Thankfully the wind was in their favor and dragging the smoke across the entire ambush lane, and would do the job of covering their advance. Yule was coughing hard when he emerged near the edge of the first building, and had to cover his mouth to deafen the noise when a home loomed ahead of him. He dove down near a small garden that lay around ten feet away from the house, and he peered out from the smokey haze. Before him was a window with shadows moving around inside, and he had just enough time to roll to the left and out of the way before the barrel of a M249 poked out. It began spitting leaden death at the figures crawling along in the grass, kicking up rooster tails of dirt, grass, and sometimes flesh. Yule fussed with his battle vest while the gunfire cracked above him, filling his ears with even more tinnitus than he really needed, until he found the fragmentation grenade that was tucked into its corresponding pocket. He pulled the pin on the little ball of death and chucked it into the room lazily, the spoon clinging off the sill and tumbling into the grass.

"Kobe." Yule muttered, and watched the window.

With their attention on firing through the smoke, the Elves inside never saw the grenade thunk down onto the ground beside them, and had only a few more seconds of life to enjoy before it detonated, throwing its payload around the room. Shrapnel churned through muscle, and a dust cloud swallowed the room, sending the small cluster of Elves splattering all over the walls and floor. The small cloud puffed out of the window wetly, mingling with the aerosolized blood and giving it a foamy red tint. To be fair, the ten Elves who had packed themselves into the small living space of the house never assumed that some crazy bastard would just run at them through smoke and lob a death ball into their midst . . . but that lack of planning was now why they were *mist* themselves. With the machine gun silenced, the Auxiliaries funneled into the village through the smoke and poured into the houses and roadways, engaging the Chosen Children in close quarter battle or extremely close range gun fights. Yule stood up and trailed behind his rushing troopers, coughing and hacking violently at the smoke that was in his lungs. He rounded the corner of the now meat strewn home and saw that in the center of the village was a small cluster of taller buildings, one of which sported multiple antennas that stabbed up into the sky. He brought up his Daewoo and began firing rounds randomly at the windows, shattering the glass and just making sure that if anyone *was* behind them, their heads would certainly be down and not shooting at his soldiers.

As he walked and dropped his empty magazine, he looked around. Near the center of the village, which was quickly filling with bodies, Dwarves had pulled out pistols and hand axes to start engaging a small squad of Chosen that were trying to pour out of what he assumed to be a travelers Inn. The Dwarves allowed them to exit the doorway, standing pressed against the outer wall, before falling upon them, their axes hewing at the legs and joints of their taller foes. When the Elves fell to their crippled knees, the Dwarves would then point their pistols at their heads and administer a coup de grace, spattering their brain matter over the stones of the road. The Brimtouched and Onii saw it more fitting to just use their rifles, beating down and bayoneting any Elf that was stupid enough to try and do the same to them. The Valley Elves took it to a more personal level, and Yule could spy multiple short sword and knife fights whirling across the battlespace, the Elves nothing but blurs of movement. Yule watched in fascination as a huge Onii man lifted a shrieking Chosen Elf above his head, then impaled him on his stout center horn. The Southern Elf screamed in agony as the horn split into his stomach, and bright red blood washed down the face of the Onii and his uniform. The Onii tossed the fatally wounded Elf to the ground, then looked at Yule, who was giving him an appreciative look and a thumbs up.

The Onii just chuckled, and ran off to find someone else to kill. The ambushers from the wheat field were now filtering into the village proper, engaging the now scattered Platoons in sporadic fighting. Mullen grabbed some elements and directed them to the right flank to deal with these new issues, and the fighting grew with further intensity. Grenades cooked off here and there as Yule slammed another magazine home, and he looked around for Mullen as a small group of Valley Elf Auxiliaries ran by with medical bags. Yule ran after them, firing over their shoulders at rifle barrels that were pointing out of the upper floors of the Inn building. Ahead of them, open fighting boiled in the streets as both forces mingled and danced with the devil, with both parties firing back and forth over the heads of the bloody melee. Veil Rider Auxiliaries took cover behind garden walls or sheds to fire at the shooters who leaned out of windows or scrambled along roofs, all the while those in between took to it with knuckles and blade.

Yule ducked as a rifle butt came swinging his way, causing him to jerk his rifle the wrong way to deal with the sudden threat. He deftly pulled out his M9 with a left handed cross draw, having to grab it and spin it around mid air to get it into his hand, before pulling the trigger and riddling the chest of a Southern Elf with bullet holes. A short sword bounced off of his right shoulder and Yule bellowed, swinging around to blast another Southern Elf in the face, his deltoid stinging and hot with wet blood. He spun around and saw that there was no longer a front line, let alone a zone of control, and the village was now a chaotic swirling melee with pockets of gunfire erupting everywhere he looked. While he had achieved the goal of getting in close... shit was getting down right medieval at this point.

"Son of a bitch!" Yule howled, and he slung his rifle over his wounded shoulder with a hiss. Bodies were blurring all around him as control spiraled out of order, and he saw one of his Valley Elves get thrown to the ground out of the corner of his eye, a Southern Elf raising his weapon to brain the Auxiliary on the ground, prepared to use it like a baseball bat. Yule rushed forward and shoulder checked the Elf in the chest, causing Yule to roar in pain as his sword wound screamed, more blood pulsing out and oozing down his sleeve. The Elf toppled over and Yule pumped him with his M9 until the slide locked back, only then reaching down to help the Valley Elf back up to her feet. 9mm brass tinkled down her chest and stomach as she shook herself, and she thanked Yule, before picking up her rifle and going to rush ahead.

"Ah! Hold it you!" Yule said, irritated, and grabbed the back of her uniform top with his bloody right hand, dragging her backwards and throwing her towards the gun line of troopers that were behind a low wall. "Get in order! I said *GET IN ORDER!*" Yule dropped his empty pistol magazine while getting another one out with difficulty, turning on his boot heels and shouting at the Auxiliaries running around him.

"Fall back and use your damn rifles! Quit duelin' in the middle of the A-O! Fall back damn yo- hey, you! C'mere!" Yule grabbed a Brimtouched trying to sneak by him with his short sword out and flashing in the sun, getting a grip on his horns and throwing him back towards the now slowly forming gun line. "Fall in, my little bastard children! Fall in!" Yule turned and rammed the magazine into his M9, the force causing the slide to slam forward on its own, and he fired rapidly into a group of charging Southern Elves. The ones who didn't fall to Yule were quickly gunned down by his Auxiliaries, who were now getting their senses back and forming into ranks, remembering their training.

"Where the fuck is Mullen? Mullen!" Yule yelled, and ducked behind what looked like the remains of a wagon.

Unfortunately for Yule, he didn't have much of a chance to really look around for Mullen. Yule looked up and blinked at a curious noise that was getting past the ringing in his ears, and saw a Himalayan Harpy flying overhead. At first, he was there, flapping his wings and dropping something down onto the roof of the antenna adorned building, and the next second, there was nothing but a spray of blood and feathers. A heartbeat after the Harpy poofed into a cloud of bloody feathers, he felt the ground rumble under his feet, and saw a huge plume of dirt cascade into the sky from the far side of the village. Yule heard the keening buzz of artillery shrapnel flying through the air, and he dropped his jaw in astonishment.

"They're walking it towards us!" Screamed Mullen from behind, and Yule looked over to see the man crouching near the backside of a cottage with a small group of Auxiliaries.

More artillery shells impacted on the other side of the village and crawled their way towards the Veil Riders, the huge fountains of dirt and stone rumbling like the footsteps of an angry monster. One building was hit directly by one of the artillery rounds, and the whole construction disintegrated into dust and shattered wood. Then the Inn caught two direct hits, and the whole thing blew apart as if the god of wind had sneezed on it. Yule got up and dove near a woodpile, covering his head as lumber and body parts rained down onto him from the explosion. When he went to stand and yell at Mullen, someone's leg brained him on the side of the head, and Yule went back down to the ground, dazed. The bone from the broken femur left a gash on his cheek, and he stumbled back to his feet while throwing his rifle back over his shoulder. As he looked around he saw that already half of his Company had been decimated, the bodies of broken Dwarves, Onii, Brimtouched, and Valley Elves lying scattered around in various states of dismemberment. Even more alarming was the amount of dead Southern Elves that lay on top of them, all of those below being viewed as the same target in the eyes of the artillery.

"Fall back!" Yule roared, and waved his arm to signal them all to retreat, despite the cut and pain. A small Squad of Dwarves and Onii sprinted past, and the Onii reached down to grab whatever fallen troopers they could carry, one female Onii already having two bleeding Valley Elves tucked under her arms. The Dwarves simply dragged anyone they could snatch, their thick legs pumping through the weight. Yule spied Mullen yelling at the remnants of a Platoon to beat feet, a large piece of metal fragmentation embedded in his chest and his leg bleeding profusely. Despite this, Mullen still seemed calm, and was giving orders to anyone frozen in place out of fear or shock.

"Mullen! Mullen you get them the fuck outta' here!" Yule bellowed, and pointed at him. Mullen looked back at Yule, and his eyes went wide, and began shouting something that Yule couldn't hear, pointing at something over Yule's shoulder. Yule turned around and realized what Mullen was saying; He was the only one standing where he was. All his Auxiliaries had followed his orders and run past him, and the only ones around him were the dead or the dying.

"Right, lets go, c'mon now." Yule said through gritted teeth as he reached down and grabbed a Valley Elf by his battle harness, shuffling his M9 to his bloodied right hand to holster the weapon. The Elf moaned painfully as Yule began to drag him, more artillery coming down behind them and churning earth their direction. Yule heard something keening and warbling awkwardly through the air towards him, and turned in time to see the blur of shrapnel that punched through the stomach of the Elf he was dragging, then embed harshly into his left calf muscle. Yule screamed in agony as he went down to his left knee, and the Elf gurgled hoarsely before falling over onto his side, blood foaming out of his mouth and nostrils. Yule stumbled once again to his feet, and began to hobble towards Mullen and a small group of his troopers that were running towards him.

That's when Yule felt it; the crawling of his spine, the innate sense of knowing when death himself was looking down at you. Time slowed down to an aching crawl as Yule knit his brows together and turned his head to look behind him. Dirt and chunks of earth were cascading down from the sky, buildings and homes were exploding out, being torn apart by the concussion of the artillery detonating within. The explosions were outpacing his men, traveling far faster than his soldiers ever could, and Yule pressed his lips together in aggravation. He turned back towards Mullen, and said one final phrase before the cottage next to him erupted into flames.

"Get them home, Mullen."

Yule felt his patrol cap lift away from his head, and his hair brush past his face. He felt the hot air roll around him as the shell detonated its payload and turned the cottage into stone fragments and splinters. Shrapnel tumbled past his field of vision as he watched Mullen and the Auxiliaries slowly open their mouths to yell.

Artillery, Yule thought, as his feet began to leave the ground, his body getting caught up in the blast wave from the house, *of all the ways to die, its to fucking artillery.*

Yule had another moment to spare, looking down at the fleeing troopers below. It seemed that around half of the force would be able to get away, the vehicles probably too fucked to drive, but not too many of his lads and ladies would have to die like this.

A shame really . . . I had thought we would have time to scatter before they started shelling us. Plan was to push straight past the village and get out of the zone of fire. I assumed that they would shell our approach and follow it out, not start at their fucking end, of all things . . .

Yule looked down at his feet and saw that one of his boots had been blown away, exposing the dirty sock underneath, the other's laces trailing in the wind.

Underestimated my enemies willingness to kill their own in order to get me I guess. Blood thirsty lot, those fae, literally started their artillery on their own lines and brought it towards us to ensure our deaths. Ah well. Shame I didn't get to see Alavara again . . .

Time slowly came back into speed, his ears filling with ringing and the roars of the concussion around him. Yule felt himself get shunted through the air and slam through the partially remaining wall of an already ruined home. Blackness took Yule as he tumbled through the blasted inner walls. His ears slowly dulled away the sounds of impacting artillery, and the screams of his Veil Riders.

Mullen watched Yule get thrown through the wall, wincing as his chest and leg wounds pained when he tried to rush forward, but he no longer had control of his own movements. The Auxiliaries around him grabbed hold of his battle vest and began dragging him away. When he fought, he was hefted over the shoulder of an Onii and they themselves ran Mullen out of there while the shells rained down around them. The artillery chased them out of the village and back down the field they came from, like hounds baying at the heels of foxes, and only stopped when the remnants of the Company had run past the broken vehicles. They didn't stop running until they were half a mile away from the ruined village, and only then did they stop to regroup and regain their breath. Thirty five percent of the Company was battle worthy, the wounded outnumbering the able bodied two to one. Mullen passed out as soon as they stopped, and the healers had to work hard to keep his soul from passing on to the other plane. With Mullen down, the

Auxiliaries realized quickly that he was the only Human left alive, the other four Human Platoon leaders having died either in the battle, or during the artillery strike trying to get their soldiers out. Leaderless, they came to the only conclusion they could think of, and made camp, waiting for Mullen to awaken.

* * *

Yule felt numb, as if he was wrapped in a giant wool blanket of blackness. If this was what dying was like, he's certainly had worse, and at least now he couldn't feel anymore pain. It was if he was suspended in a giant dish of black butter, but he didn't open his eyes, just keeping them closed and letting the sensation wash over him. Over all... he thought he did alright. He made the mistake of thinking the Fae, Unseelie, U.N, whatever they were, would fight like Humans. Instead they fought like Ant Queens, tossing their soldiers ahead into the meat grinder and caring not what happened to them. He was still shocked that they had shelled their own troopers like that. Shit didn't even make sense, as well as being horribly wasteful. He floated in the nothingness for what seemed like days, devoid of all senses except for the very faint thrum of his heart.

Sure is taking a long time... Yule thought angrily, and began to ponder if even dying had to be tedious.

"You're not dying." Said a voice from the void, and Yule rolled his closed eyes towards the sound. Sound was a relative term, more like rolled his eyes towards the corner of his brain that the uninvited thought came from.

Excuse me, I'm pretty sure my watch is over. Got blown up, thrown through a wall. Probably have a Fae teabagging my forehead right now.

"You're not going to die, Human." Came the voice again, and Yule was seriously starting to get angry at this point. The frustration became a glimmer of light that he gripped onto, and he felt his body a little more accurately than he had been previously. He could certainly feel something in his calf, anyway.

Pardon me, but my number came up. What, is some kind of Veil God goin' to drag me back to the fucking realm of the living?

"Something like that." It echoed out, and he heard the faint noise of tinkling laughter.

I swear to fuck, if you bring me back I will be talkin' to your manager. This is horrible customer service.

More laughter echoed out from the void, and Yule began to feel more and more of his aches and pains. His back hurt, his calf had something in it, his right arm felt like someone was digging in it with a small angry shovel, and his head rang like he had gotten a left hook from The Pigeon King himself. Dimly, light began to glow from his eyelids, and Yule gave an internal, spiritual sigh as he came to understand what was happening.

"Oh . . . this is so lame . . ." Yule groaned, and his eyelids shuttered weakly as he opened them, looking up into the bright glow of the moon. Of course, he knew where the moon *was*, but couldn't see it because someone was standing over him. He gave a pained sigh, and weakly pushed some masonry off of his plate carrier, looking up at the woman standing over him. "You better be here to finish me off woman, I'm not in the mood."

She laughed happily, and Yule recognized the laughter from just a few moments before. "Aw damn it . . . you're a God, aren't you? Get away from me, fucken' hell . . ."

Yule rolled over with noises of complaint and tried to wiggle his way up to a seated position, leaning against the pieces of the destroyed cottage roof to prop himself up. The woman slowly stepped out and around to face Yule, since he had turned his back to her, and her delicate bare feet stepped gingerly around the broken stone, shingle, and metal of the ruined home. Yule looked like hot ass; His shoulder was still bleeding, a broken rib was poking out of his ribcage, gleaming white in the moonlight, and his face was a bloody mess, framed by dozens of deep cuts and two blackened eyes. He gave a harsh cough and propped his good left arm on the piece of roof, gesturing at her with his hand.

"I will literally pay you to kill me and fuck off." Yule said, coughing a little more and spitting out a glob of blood onto the ground near his bootless foot.

The woman was wearing what looked like simple but elegant armor that reminded him of what the Valkyries were proposed to wear, what with the ornate leather and chainmail chest armor, a skirt of armored plates, and shoulder pads of more tooled leather and furs. The furs were dark red, and paired quite well with her pale flesh and white hair. She styled her mane in a Germanic way, some of her hair spun into a clean braid that wrapped around the top of her forehead, while the rest of her hair fell loosely down her shoulders and back. Yule didn't like the look of the skulls that were embossed everywhere on her armor, and was still lost as to why the woman wasn't wearing any shoes. He looked up into her brilliant white eyes, and weakly gestured with his left hand again.

"What's up with the no shoes thing? You run out of money for socks or somethin'..." He coughed again, and snorted.

Being sassy was taking a lot out of him, and he hurt too much to be as angry as he had been in the void. Right now, he just wanted to lay back down and go to sleep, or try to wiggle his way back into the void; It was nice there, and there wasn't some creepy woman staring down at him without any shoes on.

"I do not like shoes." She said softly, and she smiled at him, squatting down at the knee and sitting back slightly on her heels.

Yule rolled his eyes and spoke in a pained mumble. "Yeah and I don't like wearing pants, yet I do." He looked around the village and saw that they had continued shelling well after he had been thrown through the cottage wall, but was happy seeing far less bodies than he had expected to. That, or they had been shelled into more pieces than he could see, which made him chuckle grimly. He coughed a few more times, then looked back over to the woman, who seemed to be watching him intently.

"Who are you." Yule said flatly, and leaned his head against the roof piece. He had a splitting headache, and even the woman's eyes were bright enough to cause him discomfort.

She tilted her head prettily, and it reminded him a lot of Yethis. "Death."

Yule barked out wry laughter, his teeth red and black with dirt and blood. "Well what the fuck lady, you gonna do your job or what?"

While Yule knew he was being rude, he thought the hard slap to the top of his head was a bit much, and he howled harshly with searing pain as her hand bounced off of his filthy hair. The woman however was smiling still, her canines flashing. "Such rudeness. Far too rude to die. My husband says you still have work to do."

"Ow! What the hell lady!" Yule rubbed the top of his bloody, dusty head with his right hand, wincing at his shoulder. "Who's yer husband? Why's he callen' the shots over me?"

"He handles the deaths on your side of the plane that is linked to this one. Many gods of Death, but we handle this as a couple for these two places. Linked by the Veil, anchored by blood and fate." She pulled over a large stone with little effort and sat down on it, folding her legs neatly over one another.

Yule sat up a little more and sighed, reaching back onto his webbing to try and find a canteen. He found one, but it had been shot during the ambush and now lay empty. He tossed it over his shoulder and sighed again, more angrily, as it hollowly 'tinked' and 'tanged' off of broken stone. He hung his head while looking up at her slightly. "... Your husband is the Grim?"

She smiled sweetly at the Human nickname. "That is one name you have grown to call him. I call him my Elder Flower"

"Charming." Yule muttered, and wiggled his socked foot. "So what's the deal? You got some kind of magical errand you need me to run or something? Some kind of quest I was born to do, or whatever they say in the stories..."

The Death God laughed again, and flicked Yule hard in the middle of the forehead. Yule howled out a "What the fuck?!" as she continued to laugh.

"You listen to too many stories. When your work is done, you may die. Not till then."

She held out her hand to him, and Yule looked at it while rubbing at the mark on his forehead. In her hand she held a tight stack of Veil Rider patches, many of them blood stained or filthy with earth, but all tied neatly with some kind of string. Yule looked at the stack and brought his eyebrows together, reaching forward with his good left hand to take the stack.

"How many?" Yule said curtly, running his thumb over the top patch.

"Sixty Six." She stated, and patted Yule on the shoulder. "Many of your fellow Humans did not make it. One named Mullen passed briefly into the afterlife, but they brought him back. The others I took. They are well. Worry not."

She stood and dusted off her armored skirt as Yule looked down at the stack of patches in his hand, still rubbing his thumb back and forth along the blood riddled top patch. "They died honorably, and await you in the halls. Good deaths. Be proud, bearded Human."

Yule looked up sharply and locked eyes with the God. Unbeknownst to him, he had done what thousands of Veil Folk feared to do, and to lock eyes with the Death God more than once was something only known to the most foolhardy . . . or insane. ". . . Will you take care of my troopers? Tell them I'm sorry?"

The Death God beamed down at him, smiling all the way to her eyes. "Best of care, Human."

She said nothing else, then unfurled two huge white wings from her back. Yule hadn't seen any signs of her even having wings, but the sudden burst of movement made him jerk back, and her take off threw dust into the air as she ascended. Yule ducked his head as she lifted away and coughed a few times, hearing her wings thud the air before he was left in the aching silence. Yule blinked a few times before rubbing at his face, his flesh rasping harshly from the caked dirt and blood.

"This fucken' place . . ." Yule growled, and he slowly got to his feet, leaning heavily on his rifle like a cane. His Daewoo was shattered and broken, far beyond repair, and he mourned for it quietly as he looked around. A couple yards away he saw what looked like the remains of Healer Corps medic and their bag, and hobbled towards it. The buttstock of his rifle gave way after a few hobbled steps, and Yule yowled as he went down hard onto the shattered road.

He wheezed, and began to crawl towards the bag. He felt something poking into his lung from his ribcage, and quite frankly was fed up with the bullshit at this point. "Only breaks I'm gettin' around here are my own damn bones . . ."

The short journey felt like an eternity, having to use his good leg and performing an awkward slug crawl towards the bag, but he got the job done. The poor Elf that was in charge of the bag had caught a lot of artillery shrapnel to his back and spine, and Yule patted the dead Elf's shoulder sadly. "Sorry buddy."

The bag had caught a lot of the shrapnel too, shattering the majority of the healing potions and vials that were inside. Thankfully, or unthankfully, the wriggling, living bandages seemed to have soaked up a lot of the liquid, and were now bright red with the spilled potions. Yule grimaced and paused for a few seconds in contemplation, then grabbed harshly at the living bandage, spashing it into his lips. Amusingly, the bandage seemed to have a mind to fight him, and Yule had to bite onto it to make it behave and bleed, sucking hungrily at the moisture and potion that was inside of the bandage. It tasted like death, and Yule was pretty sure the Elf's blood had gotten onto the bandage as well, but he could feel the potion working as his rib slowly pulled out of his lung. As he drank the bandage dry, he reached in for the other one that was trying to crawl away, his other hand pulling the shrapnel piece from his calf. He bit down onto the now dead bandage and yelled muffledly into it as the metal came out wetly from his calf, then yanked the other bandage over to his mouth, biting down onto it and sucking at it greedily.

After this bandage was sucked dry, he looked for other medical bags around the area, now being able to hobble his way around on his feet. He also found his missing boot, and slipped it over his bare sock. After a few minutes of searching, he found a canteen of water and an intact healing potion, and sat down on a crumpled chimney to sip at both. The village was a ruin, and not a single building except for a dog house was left standing. It looked like a bombed out city in Europe during World War II, an entire area laid to waste just to snuff out the enemy. Yule couldn't find any working weapons either, only having his M9 and a boot knife left to his devices. When he had drained the canteen and the health potion, he stretched his back and popped whatever was left of his spine into place. His shoulder was slowly knitting back together, but he thought angrily that there was no hope for the large cut on his face, and it would probably scar up horribly. He looked up at the moon and stood, following its rise and seeing which way South was.

"Someone is going to eat my boot knife by the end of this..." He murmured, and began to make his way through the rubble and remains of his Company.

CHAPTER 14

If there ever was a hell on Earth, Yule doubted it could be any worse than how he felt right now. Usually, after the hero of the story was deus ex machina'd from certain death, they would be right as rain and able to easily take care of whatever needed taking care of. Yule was beginning to think that Nordic looking death-tart had forgotten to cure him of his wounds, or didn't do so just to spite him. For the next week after leaving the ruins of the village that once was, Yule was in constant, searing pain all over his body; His spine felt like it was made out of rocks and marbles, his knees clicked and cracked after he got up from sleeping, his face was a partially ruined mess, and he still had a slight wheeze when he breathed. The health potion, as much of it that there was in the living bandages he sucked dry, merely managed to stabilize him and keep him from dying. It however did nothing for his outward appearance, and after looking down into a shallow pond, Yule saw that he looked like a ghost stepping out from a Vietnam jungle.

It was by luck that he was even managing to feed and water himself, stumbling upon streams that held water he could drop salt tablets into, and fish that were just a tad too slow to avoid his hungry hands. He still lacked a lot of gear he needed for a comfortable outdoor stay, only able to scrounge up scraps of things from his dead troopers, and only a single vial of Yethis's precious blood survived his rucksack getting thrown through a wall with Yule attached to it. A lot of supplies in his own pack didn't survive the impromptu interior redesigning of the cottage, his cellphone smashed, various bottles of liquids broken, and his shelter half was more like shelter tatters at this point. All of his maps were on his phone, having left the physical copies at Valhalla Hill, which meant that Yule was dead reckoning himself in the general direction towards Emalone, using the rumble of artillery to fine tune. The one thing that kept Yule going was the ever simmering anger inside of him, along with the frustration of constantly being in pain and out of touch with his mangled Company. The artillery had destroyed any kind of radio or communication device, and not even the rare walkie talkies managed to survive the shelling.

Yule had to assume that Mullen was following his orders and taking the surviving Auxiliaries back to base, or the survivors themselves would understand the situation and head back themselves. This in turn meant that, to Yule, he was entirely on his own, and at this point he was fine with that. If these Veil Gods wanted to screw around with his well deserved mortality, then Yule was going to fuck around and find out just how much patience they really had. The going was, however, slow, as Yule was in no shape to just sprint to Emalone and start round house kicking anything with pointed ears that he came across. This far back behind enemy lines, there was a sharp decline in enemy patrols, allowing him to make his way along the tree line with more freedom than he had in the past weeks.

The silence that constantly whispered around him was uneasing; Not even the birds of this place felt like singing, or the bugs to churr and click. Every once and awhile, Yule would come across some lonely home, or group of houses tucked away near the forest in little clearings. They were always empty and devoid of any life, some looking like they were ruffled and rampaged by either someone leaving in a hurry, or someone looking for something valuable. To Yule's annoyance, this usually meant that the larders were picked clean and nothing of real use to him was available, but every once in a while he would get lucky and find some wool blankets, old jars of food, and even a knife or two if he was really rolling hot on the dice. The rain came in a consistent sneezing of showers, allowing the small creeks and rivers that ran around the place to be nice and full of moving water, which at least gave Yule some solace that hydration could be one less worry on his mind.

Mile by mile he drew closer and closer to Emalone, the rumble of artillery turning into audible reports the nearer he got, until one morning he popped out of the dense foliage to spy the distant tall buildings and homes that clustered around some kind of earth works.

Yule's battered body was smarting raucously at this point, and half of his boot falls felt like he was wearing sacks of glass and angry crabs around his feet. He found a nice shady tree and sat down heavily, staring out into the distant city. Normally he would be down in the grass and staying out of sight, but he was just too tired to care if the enemy saw him or not. He did not, funnily enough, have any desire to walk out to the city in broad daylight, and came to the conclusion he would wait until nightfall before he made his approach. As he sat against the tree, he pulled his dirty, shredded patrol cap low on his face to block out the low sun, and popped the top on a jar of some berry jam he had found in a house along the way here. He was thankful he had stumbled upon his old hat when he was foraging for gear, as he had worn it for years, and was an old anniversary present his passed wife had gotten for him long ago.

Thoughts of his deceased wife hit Yule like a sucker punch to the chest, and he felt his heart do a little squeeze as he pulled an old metal spoon from his ruck. Yule sat in the grass, rubbing his thumb idly up and down the jar while staring down into the tall strands of grass in-between his legs.

"Would have finally gotten' to say I'm sorry . . ." Yule murmured, his mouth giving a slight twitch, before he shook his head and poked his spoon into the jar of jam.

Another thought caressed its way into his mind, and he thought of Alavara back at Imlnoris. Even as the sweet and tart berry confection coursed over his tongue, he sighed and closed his eyes, leaning forward slightly off the tree.

Alavara, he thought, and his mind conjured back the images of her face, her eyes, her smile, the way her hands had felt on his skin, the way the sun had sparkled within the sweat on her soft flesh. Yule opened his eyes slightly and a small, sad smile played on his lips.

Well. Maybe not dyin' wasn't all that unfair . . .

He popped his spoon back into the jar and lifted out another mound of the stuff, plopping it into his mouth. Alavara was one of the few things that actually made him feel weightless and happy nowadays, and he wiggled his ripped boots back and forth as he thought more and more of her. He cared for his little Harpy friends, and felt some levels of affection for Yethis, but Alavara was just so *real* with him, and always seemed to know what he wanted or what he needed. He had never felt such a connection in a long time, and even now, the thoughts of her slowly drained the anger from his heart, and his feet seemed to hurt just a little less. The cheerful thoughts of Alavara's body and the shape of her slowly gave way to another nagging thought that he had been suppressing for the long walk here: The other Elves. There was that captured Half-Fae at Valhalla Hill, and he was about to dive into a stronghold of them here in just a few hours. The week before, he had thought of them as just another enemy he had to contend with in order to get to the Veil . . . but they had been shelled into pieces just like his Company.

He had been there after all, searching the ruins for anything useful, and had seen their bodies strewn about the ground and in the rubble of the destroyed buildings. They fought so eagerly and adamantly, but were they okay with being shelled like that? Not even their command building had been spared, the large radios and their operators scattered along the stones.

Yule's teeth clinked quietly as he tapped them on the spoon in thought, thinking back to the artillery strike. If he remembered right, they seemed as surprised as he was. He even remembered seeing some of the Chosen Children soldiers running away from the blasts, or screaming in terror as they were thrown through the air. If they were in on the extreme Broken Arrow type shelling, why would they have ran? Why would they seem afraid? There was no doubt they had some kind of intelligence agencies on their side at this point, spies running around and doing their spy things, they would *know* that Yule didn't have anything more than Dwarven mortars. While Yule would have preferred to think more about Alavara getting dressed, he knew he had to mull long and hard over what he was going to do once he got inside Emalone. He had little doubt that he could probably kill every last fucking Elf inside that city if he had a mind to, and he had slaughtered so many as it was . . . but did they deserve it at this point? Were they even aware of what was even going on outside of their own bubbles of communication?

Remembering what the Half-Fae had done to her fellow survivors, he had an inkling that there was more to the story of the Chosen Children than what he had assumed. After all, there had been so many twists and turns to the tale of the Veil, that Yule wasn't sure who was enemy and who was friend at this point. Shoot, he had beaten Britta black and blue at one time and now the two breakfasted together. He had ambushed a convoy of European soldiers, only to have a whole litter of them running around his Company after getting gunned down by their own would be Elven allies.

Yule groaned and dug his spoon back down into the jar, his shoulder blade clicking with the movement. "What a fucken' headache . . ."

The Fae were definitely playing a lot of games at once, and abusing their play pieces in order to get to their end goal. On the surface that goal seemed to be 'Take over the World', the signs all pretty much pointed to that, and it was obvious.

And therein lies the issue, Yule mused, as he rummaged around for a canteen. It was obvious, very obvious, but where had obvious things gotten him so far? How many times had he been proven wrong by following the obvious trains of thought, leaping to the obvious conclusions. With a sad thought, Yule unscrewed the top of his canteen and swigged a few mouthfuls of water, some of it trickling down the side of his mouth and twisting into his beard. His wife had been good at this kind of thinking, being able to play 4D chess with the best of them, and she would doubtlessly be screeching the answer to him from wherever she was resting as a spirit.

Alavara would probably know too. She always seems to know what others don't.

Yule chuckled a bit, another reason why he wished Alavara was here, and screwed the cap back onto his canteen. He rested his eyes on the far away buildings and pulled his legs close to him, wrapping his arms around his knees. The tree wasn't comfortable, but he leaned against it all the same, his muscles throbbing from the innumerable injuries they still bore. Yule sat and waited for the sun to go down, listening to the wind rustle through the tops of the trees, the distant sounds of the city, and the deep throaty rumble of the artillery. When night came, and everyone in Emalone began their complacent nightly rituals, they moved about unaware of the reckoning that was walking amongst them.

* * *

After listening to the two sentries talk for a few minutes, Yule had come to the conclusion that they were no future allies of his. He had low crawled all the way up to the small clearing in order to not glow in the partial moonlight, and achieved getting not only around them, but behind them. Yule did his level best to give them a fair shake, something he was trying to do more now since he had given it a long thought before he crawled down here, but they seemed to have no love for his lads and ladies at Valhalla Hill. One of the sentries was a taller female Chosen, while the other was a slightly shorter male. The two were in full battle rattle and stayed standing the entire time as they spoke, looking out into the clearing before them. They didn't move much either, preferring to just stand in their little knee deep hole. It was not going to be an easy kill, doubly so from the state of Yule's body, but he was going to have to do what he could in order to secure these mooks' weapons. They were also pretty isolated, almost as if they were a picket, and were the only real chance he had that didn't involve more Elves being aware of the attack.

Yule crawled up until he was only ten feet away from the female, and silently pulled the knife from his boot.

"I've seen some of the things they're pulling out of the Queen's Doorway, something named 'Bradley'." The female said, scuffing the heel of her boot on the ground.

The male fussed with the chin strap of his helmet, the lip of which getting thrown down over his eyes as he fingered the fasteners. "Oh yeah, the little angry boxes that look like they have a tiny ogre head on top. Alwin said they will allow us to dismantle whatever this Valhallia Hill is. With that barbarian leader of theirs supposedly dead, they could be relatively easy to push North."

He finished fussing with his chin strap and righted his helmet, looking over for the female Elf's reply. As his eyes came into focus, they widened as he took in what was lurking behind her back. The female Elf had barely opened her mouth when the dagger punched straight into her neck, Yule's momentum carrying it forward and shredding the entire length of flesh right to her collar bone. Blood sprayed into the air and droplets of crimson splashed across the male's face. She gurgled, both of her hands clamping down onto her neck as she fell down to her knees, but Yule didn't stop moving. Before the male Elf had time to register what was going on and fully lift his rifle, Yule's boot tip thumped muffledly into his groin, and all air left the Elf's lungs. The kick was so violent that both of the Elf's boot heels left the ground, and when he came back down, he came down hard onto his stomach, vomit splashing out onto the ground beside his face. Yule spared no time for either of them to suffer, dispatching both with two swift stabs to their armpits.

Yule flicked his fingers a few times to rid them of the rivulets of blood, then leaned down to brush his hands against the uniform of the male Elf, getting most of the blood off of his hands. The male Elf's eyes were locked onto his, and Yule stared back down at him, his vomit covered lips twitching as if trying to make words. Yule didn't see anger, or resentment in his eyes . . . just fear. The fear of death, the fear of dying, of knowing it is the end, and no one was going to be nearby to help. Yule frowned, and bent lower to the Elf, resting on a single aching knee.

". . . It's nothing personal, bud. Im . . . sorry." Yule whispered, and noticed how uncomfortable it was to kill with a conscience now. While the female Elf died quickly, the male seemed to cling on to life for as long as he could, clawing at the last precious seconds of dwindling consciousness. With monumental effort, the Elf dragged his hand up and held it up slightly at the wrist, palm exposed, the fingers shaking with the blood loss. Yule looked down at the hand, and knew what the Elf wanted, as he had seen the exact same gesture countless times over his life not only on Earth, but here on this side of the Veil as well. Yule reached down and took the hand in his, and he felt the feeble fingers of the dying Elf squeeze with as much strength as they could muster. Holding the trembling hand, Yule patiently waited until it no longer shook, the Elven eyes no longer focused on him, but staring silently into nothing.

Yule gave the hand a little wiggle and sighed, hanging his head with a slight shake then speaking in a hushed, pained tone. "Yeah, that was uncomfortable."

He placed the hand down near the dead Elf, tucking it in close to the body so it looked like he was just sleeping on his stomach with his legs curled, and turned around to look at the female. Unlike her male compatriot, she had died visibly outraged, and even her death mask bore a snarl of indignation. Yule didn't feel nearly as bad about killing her, but still arranged her in a less sprawled configuration. Being nice to them just felt weird to Yule, but he did it to at least try and humanize his thoughts about them before he entered the city. Thankfully they were out here in full kit, and Yule scooped up a blood covered M4, tucking the rest of the full magazines into his own empty holders. He didn't dare take much else, needing to stay as quiet as possible, and didn't want to rattle too much with a bunch of looted stuff he didn't need. The most important thing he found was that the female Elf had a set of head-strap night vision goggles tucked into her dump pouch, and Yule wasted no time strapping them onto his sore face.

As Yule moved through the tall grass by the side of the road leading into town, he was angry for a whole new reason. For the first time in a while, he felt bad about a kill. While Yule had done some rather regrettable things in the Army, he never really felt *bad* about it. Sometimes soldiers kill, sometimes soldiers die, but it's usually under a certain set of rules and understandings between combatants. There is a clear conviction between the two parties that made war... but the Fae had perverted the whole sacred process. Why did that male Elf die? Did he even know? Why did they shell their own people to pieces just to take out a small company of Veil Riders. Killing the Elves would have never even been a blip on his radar a few weeks ago, but everything was wrong now. He died in combat, yet here he was, another kink in the process, another fouling of the tradition. The Fae were perverting the rules of combat further by abusing the soldiers under their command more than any Human ever had. Even the most bloodthirsty of the Humans still held themselves to rules, commandments given down from the first steps of man by the Gods of War.

Yule rounded a small fence and saw light ahead, taking an alleyway that held no light within it. He could hear Elves walking and talking all around him, and he carefully laid every step to avoid detection. Whenever he could, he kept to the shadows and plowed on where the light did not touch, keeping his night vision on and only flipping them up to see where the Elves were walking. He knelt down near a pile of supply crates and poked the barest sliver of his face around the wood, watching the Elves that were hanging around outside of a tavern, some place called the Drooling Pony. As Yule watched them, his skin became hotter, and the coals of anger stoking themselves back to life. This whole thing... was a dumpster fire. The Elf should never have died because Yule shouldn't even be alive. These Southern Elves shouldn't have rifles or be caught up in this war, and only were because they were being spun like a top by these fucking Fae that seemed to be pulling all the strings. The Elf didn't die a hardened soldier with convictions, he died as a scared pawn of something bigger than the both of them. If Yule got his way, he was going to set every race free of their grasp on this plane, and die trying. Or die again trying, he wasn't sure of how dying worked here anymore, which was aggravating.

A bundle of Elves spilled out of the tavern, and the words coming from what looked like an officer were loud and heated. Yule pressed his patrol cap back down tightly onto his head, but nothing came to him from what he could hear.

Must be too far away. Yule thought, and he slid back into the shadows, walking across the rear gardens of multiple townhouses as he stalked the group. The Officer had what looked like a younger female Southern Elf by the scruff of her uniform top, while two other Elves walked beside him, rifles slung and held lazily by one hand across their chest. The little cluster was moving towards a darker and quieter part of the city, away from the artillery much to Yule's annoyance, but he kept shadowing them nonetheless. When some stray Elves that were smoking near a few homes inquired about what was going on, they were ignored, and the Officer dragged the female onward. It was quite dark here now, such to the point that the two elves walking with the Officer pulled out their flash lights to light the way, and Yule had a growing bad feeling about the whole thing.

As they closed in distance, Yule's amulet began to pick up some of the words being spoken, but nothing made sense to him. Despite the throbbing of his back and knees, Yule managed to keep pace with them, painfully having to hurdle low stone walls or duck down low to avoid being spotted out of someone's window. After another two hundred meters of winding and random turns in the road, Yule began to smell a pungent odor, and wrinkled his nose. They had dragged the Elf all the way to what looked like the trash heap of the city, and Yule could see a few Earth-borrowed Bobcats here and there. He guessed the machines were being used for piling or carrying away buckets of garbage and refuse. Yule then spied a single pole in the middle of it all with ropes around it, and he almost rolled his eyes from how cartoonishly evil the whole set up was.

They're going to kill her at a dump? Yule pondered, and began trying to work an angle on the flanks of the small group. It took some doing, and a small cat seemed to take a liking to him, chasing after the loose straps on his chest rig, but Yule managed to get a view on the whole scene, only ten meters away. They had strode forward and tied the Elf to the pole, who was now yelling at the Officer while the other two Elves worked the knots around her wrists.

"She was my sister, Erolith! I heard her over the radio, they never asked for artillery to be that close! I heard her call out the coordinates!"

She howled, and Yule could hear her choking with the rage that stung at her eyes.

The Officer, who Yule assumed to be Erolith, shook his head from side to side, but Yule couldn't see his face yet, only hearing his voice. "You just had to pull the cable and send the rounds, Fino. Your sister was killed by the Veil Rid-"

Erolith was cut short by Fino, who lurched forward against her bindings, roaring at him fiercely. "Yule? The giant hairy monkey?! No, Erolith, *we killed her,* and you've been lying to us all this entire time!"

Under the illumination of the night vision, Yule could see her snarling at this Erolith character as the two other Elves finished their rope tying.

"Everyone else is smart enough to know their place." Stated Erolith, turning to walk away from Fino. "And yours shall be here in this dump, all because you kept poking your nose where it shouldn't be."

Yule stiffened, and not because the small cat was biting his calf, mewling happily as it dug in its teeth. As Erolith turned, the night vision goggles brought the Elf's eyes into focus, and they glowed bright, just as Koko had said in his report so long ago.

"Fae." Yule whispered, the words gravely in his throat. He set the rifle on the ground, reaching down to pull out the boot knife from its sheath and a kitchen knife from his belt. The Elves walked a few paces away and turned back around to face Fino, whose face was now wet with angry tears. Yule stepped out and around from the corner of the house he was hiding near, his night vision humming on his forehead

Fino was staring straight ahead at Erolith and the other two Elves as the trio cocked back the bolts on their rifles.

"On the bright side, you'll see your sister again here soon. Call it a uh, oh what did the Humans call it, a uh . . . Pyrrhic victory." Erolith gave a short laugh as he brought up his rifle and placed the red dot of his optic on Fino's chest. Fino glared at him through the lens of the glass, but then her eyes darted to the left. Erolith watched as she raised her head and twitched her eyes slightly, squinting as if trying to see something. Then her eyes went wide as Yule stepped into the faint over glow of their flashlights, as if he were a many-eyed monster that materialized out of the shadow itself, holding the still bloody blade in his hand.

"Gods above . . ." She gasped, and shrunk back against the pole, her eyes following Yule as he came within feet of Erolith, his hands raised and posed for the strike.

If Erolith had something clever or snarky to say to Fino, he should have said it while he could. The boot knife came around and punched right up under his chin, spiking the blade deep into the bottom of his brain. It was instant lights out for the Officer, his legs going dead to the world as soon as his brain was punctured, and the body rag dolled to the ground in a clumsy heap. The Elf next to Erolith turned, startled, and brought the barrel of his M4 Carbine up. Yule simply helped it along, slapping the barrel up in time with his jerking arm and smashed the muzzle of it into his face. It was enough of an opening for Yule to sink one of the looted kitchen knives into the eye socket of the Elf and jerk the rifle out of his now curling hands. The last Elf was shocked cold-fingered, seeing both his commander and his comrade go from breathing to dead in such a short manner of time, and turned to run after a few moments of hesitation. Those wasted seconds cost him dearly, as Yule leapt forward and grabbed the Elf in a naked rear choke, dragging them both to the ground in the darkness. The beams of flashlights spun and caught the puffs of dust from the road, scrabbling feet kicking up small clouds from the ground as the two beings wrestled. Fino could only see flashes of movement, a boot here, a hand reaching out there, but the fight was fought in the darkness of the night.

Fino heard grunting and gurgling from the darkness, until she then heard nothing at all. Her chest heaved as she strained her eyes to pierce the gloom, trying desperately to see what was going on behind the glow of the flash lights. Her high Southern Elf ears heard something stand up, the crunch of gravel under boots, and the flash lights went out one by one, until there was nothing in front of her, the moon not strong enough to light her way. The boot falls came towards her, and she leaned back against the pole, staring at the looming shadow that came towards her. She could smell Yule, the stank of sweat, blood and old wounds, of old worn clothes and unwashed skin. Her heart pounded painfully in her chest as the thing stood before her, and she winced from both the smell of him and the fear of the knife that would soon be coming down onto her neck or skull. She had read the reports of how these Humans took out their prey in close combat, and she just hoped this one knew how to do it quickly.

Fino closed her eyes and waited, panting in and out of her nose harshly... but the blow never came, just the low measured breathing of the thing in front of her.

"They started the artillery from your end of the village."

Fino jerked her head up, her heart still thumping in her ears. "W... What?"

Somehow the Human knew Elfringil, and hearing it caught her off guard. She felt the Human lean past her, it's beard rubbing against her shoulder as it cut away her bindings.

"When we attacked, they started the artillery from deep within your end of the village, and walked it towards us. The entire Chosen Children Company was decimated along with my own."

Fino didn't know her blood could run any colder than it already was, but she was finding many things were possible tonight. She felt Yule's night vision push down around her head and come across her eyes, and she now stared into the eyes of the man she had seen in so many reports. The facial scar was new, but it was definitely him. It was definitely-

"Yule. You're Yule." She whispered in shock, and he smiled at her with a toothy grin, the blood of her Officer still speckled on his cheek.

"I am. And I am sorry for your sister... She fought fiercely, and died a warrior."

There was a small pause before Fino whispered. "Thank you."

Fino saw Yule nod before standing up and popping his wrists. He looked down at her, his eyes dark with thought, before he held out his hand to her.

"What are your feelins' on revenge, Miss Fino?"

CHAPTER 15

Fino's fingers shook with nervous energy as he spliced together two wires, completing the circuit for a massive daisy chain of explosives that wrapped around the munitions building's entire interior. Yule had cleared the way into the building in the manner that Humans were known for: With extreme prejudice. After being cut away from the execution pole, Fino was too full of fear and fury to say no to the prospect of revenge for his fallen sister, but it quickly became clear to him that the Human thought he was female, remarking that 'She would be happy to see her sister getting back at her murderers' after cutting her down, referring to his dead sister being happy to see her 'sister' getting revenge. Fino had read in reports that Humans, or at least Yule, were more lenient to female prisoners, and he was not going to risk popping his precious bubble of mercy. Now that they were both inside of the ammo depot, Fino wasn't sure just how long that secret was going to last. He really had to pee, and Yule almost scared it out of him every time the Human looked in his direction. Between the strain of remembering how the plastic explosives worked, watching Yule dismantle Elves, and trying to hold in his bladder, Fino was being stretched thin beyond belief. He poked his eyes over the top of the massive stack of MAC propellant bags and watched Yule, tying together the daisy chain.

From atop another stack of propellant bags, Yule was finishing off his fifth healing potion, swishing the reddish liquid in his mouth before swallowing and popping the cork back into the empty bottle. He rolled his shoulders and sighed, all of his muscles itching and burning as if a million fire ants were busily chewing his body back together. The bone repairing was the worst of it, and it reminded him of the time he was bitten by a Black Widow spider, except this time it was the bone expanding and growing instead of a toxin attacking his flesh. Using the pocket mirror taken off of a dead Elf, he inspected his face. From the top of his left eye and down around the middle of his right jaw, the huge scar was like a crack in a marble statue, running along his face in a thick line. He poked at the ugly thing and grimaced, noticing that while the raw flesh was healing, the scar itself wasn't going away, something that Yule hoped would happen. He looked at himself from a few angles while knitting his brows together, bared his teeth in a light snarl, then snapped the pocket mirror shut before angrily tossing it into the corner of the depot. Fino saw him wing the mirror across the building and ducked slightly, eyes flicking from Yule to where the mirror landed. When it became clear that no other mirrors would be tossed in his direction, he slowly brought his head back up.

He made sure to keep his tone as heavily femimine, which he noted with inner annoyance was not hard to do. "Uhm... I think it looks quite dashing, as far as scars go."

"A pretty lie for an ugly man." Yule growled, and scooted down off of the propellant sacks, stretching his muscles to make the ants stop biting him so much. "So, Miss Fino, are we ready to go?"

Fino did a small spin to check his wire work, and found it to be sufficient. Having been assigned to an artillery unit, he had to study all kinds of weird materials on the subject, including how to work with the strange clay explosives that were sent in from the other side of the Veil. The books had been a pretty engaging read, and Fino snapped up any literature on the subject that could get his hands on after working through the English language. His sister always told him he was better off reading about the radio magics, like she was, but he found the circuit board layouts to be a bore, and the English associated with it gave him headaches. When put in comparison to the concussive blast of a C4 snowman, radios just couldn't keep up.

After he finished checking over his work, he stood back up and straightened his uniform top. "This should be more than enough to take out this building and the other six buildings around it. The blast bubble alone should detonate anything within range."

Yule formed his mouth into a muggish smile, something that confused Fino, as he had never seen such an expression before, and watched as Yule pulled out a small hunk of chalk.

"Want to make it personal? Always more fun."

"More personal?" Fino asked, and blinked a few times.

"Watch and learn, Elfling." Yule said with a mirthful grin, and Fino had to guess he was feeling better after downing so many health potions. He watched as Yule scribbled in chalk on the wooden floor boards, mouthing the words as he saw them form.

"I . . . Cast . . . Explosion?" Fino murmured, while Yule gave a wry chuckle and finished the sentence with a quick sketch of a wizard's scholarly hat.

"Here, your turn."

Yule handed Fino the bit of chalk while dusting his other fingers off on his pants. Fino wracked his mind for something that was in the same category, some kind of signature that he could place next to Yule's. Obviously there was no need to write out his entire feelings or an epitaph, since this place would just be dust in a few minutes, but something funny did come to mind. He remembered one book on improvised explosives had some kind of phallic symbol written on random pages, and thought it to be some kind of joke that Humans of the same skill set used. Something called 'Marines' we're all about the weird shape, a kind of rallying icon like how the Veil Riders had that weird looking Unicorn. Fino stuck his tongue out a little and began to draw just below Yule's writings, and after a few minutes had finished it, tossing the piece of chalk triumphantly onto a random stack of propellant.

Yule was looking down at the symbol, arms crossed and brows raised, having watched the entire thing get drawn from start to finish. Even as Fino turned to look at the Human, Yule was still staring down at the giant phallic drawing on the floor boards.

". . . Not gonna lie Fino, not what I imagined you to put there." Yule said, pulling a hand from his crossed arms and holding it up, palm open. "But I dare say, you did an excellent job on the execution, spray splurts and all. Looks like something you'd see doodled on a 21 Palms bunker wall."

Fino beamed at Yule, and held out his hands towards the spurting symbol. "Yes! I saw this in a book that was marked all over by them and their sayings. It was everywhere, and I thought it must be some kind of brotherhood icon of those who work with explosives, yes?"

Yule blinked a few times, then looked down at Fino, who looked way too happy and proud of himself, and Yule couldn't find the heart to tell him. ". . . Yup, nail right on the head there, Fino. Mind you it's not a very lady-like symbol, and you should avoid drawing it on anything you own."

Fino squinted a bit at the lady-like comment, but quickly remembered to keep his ace still up his sleeve. "Ah right, I'll be sure to keep that in mind. Uh, what do you want to set the timer for?"

Yule watched him pick up some kind of electrical timer and he shook his head. "Nah, we're going to do this manually, grab those wires and their spools, we're headen' outside."

"Manually?" Fino questioned, but gathered the two wire spools that were connected to the dizzying number of blasting caps that were plugged into bricks of C-4 all over the room.

"Ooooh yeah..." Yule murmured, and poked his head out of the rear door of the building, looking out at a long firing line of M109A7 Paladins and a small cluster of Elves standing watch. Yule's grin expanded along his broken face, and the glimmer of blood lust crackled to life in his eyes once again.

* * *

Inside the Paladin, Yule drummed a finger on the loading ramp of the gun, the other finger scrolling along the screen of a tablet's song collection. The tablet had been left inside of the artillery vehicle, and Yule had a mighty need for some theme music. Thrilling heroics always need a catchy tune behind them to really bring the scene together, after all. Fino was looking a bit green around the gills, and Yule leaned his head back to look at the Elf. Fino was sitting beside a spare battery they had found, his legs dangling over the edge of the rear entry hatch.

"You doin ok ma'am?"

Fino looked out onto the dozen bodies laying around the Paladin, still holding the two spools of wire in his hands.

"I ... have to pee."

"Well make it quick, we gotta scoot."

Fino ducked and stood up from the rear access door of the M109A7, walking around the side out of view. It was the third time he almost pissed himself watching the Human work, and witnessing Yule choke the last remaining Elf to death almost made him trickle into his boots. Fino opened his fly and let loose his bladder onto the little bit of remaining grass, exhaling in relief, and his free hand began to shake. How easy could that Human kill him? Were Humans honestly that much stronger than Elves? The last Elf, a Sergeant, had shoulder checked Yule in the gut after he had broken the spine of a male Elf Private, ramming him face first into the ground, but the Human didn't even *budge*. Yule just scooped her up with . . . contempt, and the both of them whirled to the ground, Yule's arms swimming around her neck like a pair of thick snakes. Fino had been hiding behind a dividing sandbag wall and watched it all, the spools of wire rattling in his hands, and he couldn't help but watch in aw. The Sergeant's boots kicked and scrabbled in the loose sandy earth as she was able to rip an arm free and claw at Yule' face, but Yule just bit down on it and continued to apply his choke hold. Fino watched her face turn red, panic roll across her eyes, and the manic struggle as she tried to get free of his arms. She snorted and choked, trying to speak, trying to reason with the human, but Yule's face was set, looking down at the side of her profile, simply waiting. Her struggles became sluggish, her breath rasping, until soon she didn't struggle at all. Fino had watched Yule spit out the blood that had collected in his mouth, dust himself off, and walk off towards Paladin as if he had done nothing but move some furniture around a room.

    Fino gave his privates a few shakes before tucking it back behind his pants fly, re-buttoning it, then turning around to go back inside the Paladin. If he hadn't been dragged out and tied to the post . . . would he have fallen victim to Yule? Would Yule have run him down like he had the other Elves? Fino's mind began to whirl, thinking about what it would feel like, what it would look like as Yule hunted him, tackling him down and choking the life out of him just so he wouldn't make a sound . . .

    His knee wobbled weakly as he went to crawl back inside the gunnery compartment, and Yule was plugging an auxiliary cord from the tablet into a small stereo, at which a bizarre song began to play at full volume.

    "Cocker Cannons?!" Fino yelled over the full volume of the music, gathering the two ends of wire and poising them over the vehicle battery.

    Yule flashed him a wolfish grin. "They're a classic! Wait for a good moment to touch the battery, a catchy lyric or something!"

    Fino stared at Yule in horror as the Human ducked out of the firing compartment and sprinted to the driver hatch. The bass from the radio was deep, the volume at max, which caused it to echo painfully around Fino's ears.

He wouldn't kill me for setting it off at a bad lyric right? Fino thought, but then looked out onto the dozen dead and broken bodies laying around the rest area.

. . . Right. Wait for the gruesome bit in this song. Fino nodded and tossed out the spools while holding the active ends of the wires he needed to touch to the battery. With the roar of the Detroit Diesel engine, Yule wasted no time and slammed the Paladin forward, roaring up and over the small sand wall in front of the artillery vehicle. Fino screeched and almost fell out of the back of the rear door, starfishing himself to catch any edge he could, both of the wires clutched in his hands. Fino bounced up and down, slamming bodily on the gun deck as the Paladin rolled and roared ahead The music flared up around him, thumping his eardrums with the sound of their beat.

"*Gonna go and slam it home!*
Break them like the siege of Rome!
Raise the barrel and prime the coord!
The concussion is just her loving purr!
Ra-Ra-Ra-Ra!"

Fino shook his head and squeaked as he began to slide across the gun deck towards the ammo storage, Yule putting the Paladin into a hard sliding turn. Fino could hear Yule laughing above the music, and a trickle of blood was tickling down the side of his face. Fino scrambled towards the door and caught the battery before it, too, fell out of the gunnery compartment, and hugged it to his knees, sitting up as much as he could to watch the spools. They were full spools, but he couldn't see them anymore, and reckoned he had maybe a few more feet of wire before he ran the risk of lacking slack. Fino was unsure of just how tough this wire was, and quietly wondered if he should have double checked the blast caps to make sure he hadn't jerked them out by accident. He couldn't help it, but he smiled at the absurdity of it all as the song continued to play around him, the vehicle jittering and bouncing wildly. This plan was beyond stupid, insane even. Yule was trusting all of this on a battery they didn't even bother to test in the first place.

"*Your wings come from within our shells*
coming towards you with the sounds of hell!"

Fino shook his head and held up both the wires, holding them above the battery terminals.

> *"Feel the bite of our singing steel*
> *We'll break your bodies like Catharine's wheel!"*

"That will do." Fino said flatly, and touched the wires down onto the terminals.

For a split moment, Fino was afraid that something had gone wrong. There were two heart beats of time before he saw a flash in the windows of the ammo depot. As the battery bounced from under Fino and fell out onto the rushing ground below, he came down onto his chest and elbows, still watching out into the chaos he had wrought. He had only read about such explosions, the massive detonations fabled to level entire towns and be heard miles away, but to see one in the flesh was something to behold. The building seemed to disappear in a bright pulse, replaced by the roaring impact of a god's fist, the concussion shattering the sky. A great curling pillar of smoke reached up into the heavens, and the air itself was pushed away in a rippling white expansion, as if the explosion had blown a massive bubble. The bubble coursed through the town, and like a titan puffing out a breath, blew away the buildings and toppled them over, throwing wood and stone like they were but shreds of paper before a fan. From the pillar of smoke, flame coiled and rolled up into the sky like the burning heart of the explosion, boiling up higher and higher and feeding on whatever it could. That flame whirled and lit up Fino's eyes, as well as the white teeth of his smile. The moment was pierced by the arrival of the shockwave, and they were close enough that it lifted Fino up and shoved him back towards the gun breech of the vehicle. Fino slid to a stop and thumped against the wall, a smile still proudly on his face, and ears ringing with the tones of success.

"Awesome." Fino murmured, as the metal music continued to play in the background, and Yule whistled happily from the driver seat of the Paladin.

Overall, Yule was happy with their progress. His muscles felt better, he 'sploded the ammo dump and probably ruined that city, got revenge for his Company, and found a little informant that had a grudge against his enemy. The performance of the Paladin was pretty good too. Luckily, they kept the artillery vehicle stocked full of fuel and had a few fuel cans strapped to the side of it. After driving about fifty miles, he pulled the Paladin to a stop and left it idling, hopping out and checking in on Fino. Poking his head inside the gunnery area, he saw the Elf sitting in a small seat and drinking a canteen of water. Yule gave Fino a thumbs up, which Fino returned, and then returned to the driver seat and set back off at full speed. Fino was confused to feel the vehicle lurch back into motion, but just shrugged and took that moment to shut the rear hatch door and scramble back to his seat. For the next hour . . . not much happened or was said, both Fino and Yule caught up in their own thoughts as they traversed the road back towards Imlnoris. Fino was worried about the moment when Yule would find out he wasn't a girl. There were no records of male prisoners being taken, and if that was the case, Fino had to think up information that would make him valuable. As the chassis rocked back and forth, Fino scribbled down in a little notepad all the things he knew, and after twenty minutes, realized he didn't know much of anything besides how to operate the damned machine he was riding in.

"Ah . . . shit." Fino groaned, and he leaned back against the hull wall beside him. Despair was beginning to grip Fino, and he almost missed the buzzing, tinny sound coming from a small shelf. He saw it was a headset and pursed his lips, reaching out and grabbing it. The closer he brought it to his face, the more he recognized that someone was yelling over it. The Paladin also did a hard left turn and began to pick up speed, almost throwing Fino from his chair.

"What in Krinja's clothes drawer . . ." Fino swore, and quickly clamped the headset over his ears.

Yule's bellowing voice filled his ears as soon as the muffs came around his ears, and he winced from the noise. "-oad it, load that fucken' cannon Fino!."

"What!?" Fino yelled, and quickly pulled himself up to open the turret hatch. As he popped his head out, bullets sang and whizzed by, causing him to screech again and duck down behind the 240B mounted on top of the pintle. He poked his head back up and saw that ahead of him, a massive fire fight was erupting between two forces, one trying to hold the top of a tree lined hill, and the other trying to surge across an open valley and onto the hill to take it.

"Fino!" Yule bellowed again, and Fino jerked in surprise, ducking back down as a long stream of machine gun fire skittered across the machine gun and hatch lid.

"Im here! Im here!" Fino called out, and got back down into the gunnery deck, looking around in a panic as the deck rolled under his feet like a ship in a storm.

"Fino my men are on that hill! Load that cannon!"

"Yule a-a Paladin can't fire on the move! We have to unlock the gun, ask the digital gremlin for a firing vec-"

"Load the gun and I'll point it in the general direction, just do it!"

Fino almost asked 'or what?', before he remembered that Yule strangled Elves to death with his bare hands, then jumped up and began pressing buttons on the command pad. The shell ramp kept rattling violently as Fino struggled with a round from the ready rack, but managed to get the shell onto the skid without tripping and crushing himself with it. Fino was just glad the loading ramp and plunger were working while on the move after fiddling with it for a few minutes, and it rotated out of the way after he jumped over it and pressed the button on the control panel. His boots squeaked on the gun deck as the Paladin went over a bump, the propellant bundle twirling out of his hands and thunking down onto the gun deck. Fino scrambled after it, scooped it up, smashed the side of his head on a wheel handle, then tossed it into the breach. He pressed up on the breech release and it closed, then smashed the other side of his head against a toggle box. The Elf tasted blood in his mouth, but pulled a primer out of the bandoleer that swung wildly back and forth with the movements of the rumbling Paladin. The worst part of this entire process was getting the primer into its slot and in the correct position, the bouncing elements to the gun making it almost impossible until he just jammed his finger into the slot and man handled it into place, clicking the trigger over it. The hook for the firing land yard seemed to fight back as he tried to get the hook over it, but eventually he triumphed, trailing the lanyard as he went to pop his head back up and out of the hatch.

"I've got it! I got a 'heatch 'hee round loaded and I got the lanyard!" Fino shouted to Yule through the mic, and he looked back and forth between the two lines. From on top of the hill he saw nothing but the flashes of gun barrels and the inky smoke of burned powder, while down below Elves were rushing up the steep incline. Fino could see the flash and booms of grenades being chucked by the advancing Elves, and winced as one well tossed grenade cooked off in the trees and tossed a few bodies forward out of the brush line, their bodies ripped and ragged as they made the short trip into the air. At the same time, the hilltop defenders were firing down at the Paladin and the advancing Elves, their rounds whizzing off of the armor or splattering against hatch lids.

"Right, turn right." Fino said, and gripped the lanyard in his hand. Below he saw Yule's arms working the wheel from the open hatch, turning the Paladin, and Fino squinted. It wasn't the best trying to sight down the barrel from above it, but it would be folly to try and use the aiming reticles with how Yule was driving. It was around the time of thinking that when Yule hit a low spot in the ground and then a high spot right after it, rattling Fino around in the hatch opening as if he were a loose carriage bolt on a wagon. Fino heard a loud metallic pang and a shudder of metal, and after getting back to his vantage point, saw that the barrel clamp had come loose and slammed down onto the front plate of the paladin, allowing the barrel to swing freely. Fino went to throw his arms up into the air in celebration, as the barrel was now free of the clamp and free of damage, but regretted it almost within the same millisecond of thought; The report of the gun caused his teeth to rattle, and the jellies of his eyes to vibrate. The massive barrel recoiled and spat out its payload, which landed right at the base of the hill by pure luck. The round exploded in a cloud of dust and shrapnel, turning bodies to pulps of meat and shreds of clothing in an instant.

Working off of instinct, Fino then grabbed the 240b machine gun and began firing it, the weapon having survived rounds bouncing off of it, and chattered away randomly. Fino didn't have the arm strength to accurately control the machine gun, and more guided it towards its targets than aimed it. The coin dropped for the Elves, having believed it to be their own Paladin, and they began to route in earnest, throwing down their weapons and chest rigs in order to beat feet faster than with them on. Those in the woodline pushed forward, rifles and weapons still up and firing at those below, and within a few moments had retaken the top of the hill, as well as pushing forward over the crest into the slope below. Yule aimed the Paladin towards his platoons while Fino 'guided' the 240b over towards the Elves, the entire attacking force in full flight from the combat. Fino saw Yule's men jump into the artillery crater and pile the ruined bodies up like sandbags, even using them to rest their weapons on. Upon seeing this, Fino realized he was outclassed by multiple levels of soldiering, and quietly thanked the Gods that he was put into artillery. From below, Fino realized that the stereo had gotten turned back on, and up from below came the boosted bass of pop music, a rather lewd number named after the sound a rifle would make when fired twice.

Fino couldn't help but shake his head in bewilderment as the 240B machine fun clunked to a halt, the belt dry. From below, Fino could even hear Yule singing along, roaring out above the sound of the Paladin's engine. Fino was not sure what was more off-putting about the whole situation; Firing on his own race, the song selection on the tablet, or the fact that Yule knew the lyrics to this one by heart.

The Paladin roared up the hill towards the Veil Riders at the top, the stereo still blasting random choices on whatever playlist it fell upon, and Yule jacked up his seat so his head could pop out of the hatch, smiling down upon the remnants of his surviving Platoons. Staring back at him were the astonished faces of those who thought him dead, all of them cheering and yelling at those mopping up below. Fino kept his head low in the hatch ring, just the top of his head and the tips of his ears poking out as he looked out around him. The Paladin came to a halt, the broken barrel rest clanging loudly against the armor, and Yule killed the engine, ripping off his headset with a shake of his hair to replace it with his patrol cap.

"Well!" A voice shouted, and Yule looked over to see the limping form of Mullen coming out of the wood line, smiling brightly and using a rough piece of branch as a cane.

"Mullen!" Yule cried out happily, and hopped out of the driver hatch after setting the parking brake, sliding down the front of the armor to land flat on his boot heels. "Yeah you bunch'a fuckers too, get over here." Yule gestured to the rest of his troopers, and held out his arms.

Dwarf, Elf, Brimtouched, and Onii all embraced Yule, some of them trying to hide tears as they were not only saved in the nick of time, but by the Commander they thought to be dead. Yule rustled hair, pinched ears, or tugged on horns as he made his way to Mullen, who held out a hand that was missing part of its ring finger. Yule clasped Mullen's hand and pulled him in close for a hug as well, which he returned, patting Yule on the back a few times before pulling away.

"Kept us waiting, did you?"

Yule chuckled, and turned, pointing at where Fino was hiding. "Well, I would have been even more tardy if it wasn't for a little turncoat. Let me introduce you to the sister who brought down the shells that killed us."

CHAPTER 16

THE RIDE BACK to Valhalla hill was a stressful time for Fino; The number of Veil Riders in his bubble grew from just Yule, to now the vehicle being full of them as well as riding on top to avoid walking. To say that he was drenched in nervous sweat, by the time they reached the first checkpoint to the base, would be an understatement, and he kept having to keep his voice in check to sound as feminine as possible. Mullen and Yule chatted to each other the entire time Yule drove, and the man kept throwing his thumb back towards Fino, in which Mullen would look over his shoulder and give Fino suspicious looks. Or more accurately, gave Fino's ear tips and eyebrows looks, as he Southern Elf was not all that keen to lock eyes with the Human, and barely poked his head above the rim of the hatch. While Yule was known, Mullen was not, and the fact he walked away from that artillery strike meant he was probably just as tough . . . and mad.

The checkpoint, staffed by Valley Elves, saluted Yule smartly and pushed open the swing gate that had been constructed by the Dwarven Engineer Corps. One of the Harpy messenger runners was sent up to the main base to get the medical company rousted and ready to receive wounded, as healing potions were hard to come by in the field and a lot of the Auxiliaries had infected wounds that would need immediate tending to. Yule was whistling happily as he drove the captured Paladin up to the main parade of Valhalla Hill, noticing the entire way that buildings had seemed to triple since his foray into the field; Not only had they constructed long barracks buildings all set in tidy rows on the back side of the hill, but a proper stables had been built as well, along with any other building a base could possibly need. There was even a huge rough wooden Tavern, of which soldiers were piling out of, cheering and waving at the survivors of the artillery ambush. As the Paladin came to a stop in front of the now expanded command bunker, Yule could see Yethis wringing her hands in front of forty medical personnel, many of whom were bearing stretchers for those who could not walk.

Yule's boots had barely hit the ground before Yethis drove herself into him with a hug, standing back and running a finger down his facial scar. "What in the heavens did you do!?"

Yule shrugged, pressing the top of his patrol cap, and the Amulet with what little remaining blood it had, to his scalp. "Got blown through a building."

"What?!" Yethis yelled, and began aggressively inspecting Yule's ears for brain leakage, who fought back by leaning backwards.

"Whoa hey, calm down, I'm alive, relax. You can check me out later, go make sure no one else dies."

Yethis made to argue, but the look from Yule made her choose otherwise, moving off to start tending to the wounded being hauled out of the Paladin gun deck.

Chikily came running out of the command bunker and was next to slam into Yule, hugging him tightly as Peiper walked out behind him, giving a sly whistle to the artillery vehicle.

"The Dwarves vill like this one . . ."

"They better, cost me quite a few Joes to get it."

Peiper looked to the rear of the Paladin where wounded were being off loaded, and then to the tired looking foot troop that had walked behind the vehicle the entire way. "How many?"

"Well. I set out with a small Company if you remember." Yule shrugged off his chest rig and set it down on the ground, in which his breast pockets were finally exposed. He pulled out three thick stacks of Auxiliary patches tied with twine and held them in his hands, looking down at them solemnly. "I believe . . . I have maybe three Platoons left. Only Humans that made it out were Mullen and I. They brought their shells right onto their own troopers and dragged it across the town towards us. Obliterated the entire town and wiped us out."

Peiper twitched his eyebrows up in shock, but his face remained impassive as he reached out, taking a stack of the patches from Yule's hands. "Seems . . . ve Humans grow ever thinner as every day passes."

"Quite." Yule said dryly, and asked Peiper for what all had gone on. Peiper was candid, and told him that the Czechs were harassing Chosen Children units up and down their lines, while Domino and another NCO had taken the less green Auxiliaries out to harass Sanrion. The Dwarves had taken a small complement of mortars with them to shell the picket lines outside of the city.

"They are heavily dug in there, like ticks as you vould say, so Domino is making sure they do not get much sleep."

"Sounds like a job he would enjoy doing."

Peiper went on to explain that Domino had allowed the Dwarves to dig in along a tree line that was just within range of the city, and a small combat outpost had been set up, allowing them defensive abilities while pelting the city with mortar fire. The Dwarves had also figured out how to make a bazooka of sorts after a training incident in the Engineer Hold. A drunken Dwarf had had a 'hold my ale' moment, attempting to fire the mortar by holding it over his shoulder. It gave them a light bulb spark, and after a short round of tests, the Belcher had been born, named after the Dwarf who barely survived the encounter with the mortar.

"They have been quite good in testing it and refining it, Gremlin told them about the Panzerschreck and . . . vell."

Yule gave a small chuckle. "What's next, Panther tanks?"

Peiper didn't laugh with him, and Yule blinked a few times. "Peiper, you're not serious are you?"

"They vere quite smitten by the idea of the Hetzer as vell, I'm afraid."

"But they don't even know how to build them, they don't have the industry for making *tanks*."

Peiper pulled a hand rolled root cigarette from his pocket and tilted his head slightly as he spoke, rolling the patches around in his hand. "Gremlin has a lot of information on zose laptops of hers, she may have shared too much."

"Christ alive and knittin' . . ." Yule growled, and Peiper laughed. It was not the fact she gave out the information, but the fact she might have given it out for *free* that made Yule angry. Money made from selling technology was the linchpin in keeping his outfit going, and that was a lot of money that may have slipped from his fingers. Yule then remembered Chikily was still attached to him, and he patted the Harpy's back. "Keeping everyone in line Chik?"

"Always!" Chikily said with a laugh, and finally let him go. "Builders made bunker bigger, Chikily even has room inside. They made Yule's room bigger too."

Peiper puffed a bit of smoke out from his mouth, gesturing with his cigarette. "And they made your room bigger, that also happened. In fact ve all got rooms now, they even made barracks for the regular soldiers."

"Well, I'll look at that whenever I have time. Chikily could you grab the head engineer and bring him here?"

Chikily flapped off without delay, and soon a heavily armored Dwarf was rolling up the road in a Gator. Naturally he was ecstatic at the opportunity to buy and study the Paladin, under the conditions he didn't take the entire thing apart, and soon a small shipment of coinage would be hitting Yule's coffers. Additionally, Yule brought forward Fino, dragging him up from the vehicle to explain how the Paladin worked. Fino, while explaining what he could to the excited Dwarf, began to notice a lot of the Veil Riders were beginning to gather around, wondering just as to why a Chosen Child was in Valhalla Hill, and not in chains. Fino was able to talk at length for about ten minutes before a Brimtouched finally broke the ice, pointing at the much shorter Fino.

"Why is a Southern Elf here? He should be locked up with the other mad one that keeps trying to escape."

Yule turned his head slightly to look at the Brimtouched, who shrank slightly as Yule's eyes bore into his own. "This is Fino, her sister was killed when the Chosen Children Command shelled their own in order to get to us. She's as much as a victim as anyone else."

An Onii female Specialist began to slowly smile, looking back and forth from Fino to Yule. "Um . . . Commander, why are you calling him a 'she'?"

Fino began to almost vibrate as terror shot up and down his nerves, and he turned around from the Dwarf, who was writing down something in his journal, and looked up at Yule, who had now turned completely towards the Onii.

"Private Yuriko, what are you on about?"

Chikily also stepped forward, tapping his small claws together. "The Onii is right, this is male Chosen Child."

The Onii gestured towards Chikily, who gestured towards Fino, who was looking as if he was going to faint. The Southern Elf held out his hands while his voice shook. "W-wait, hold on n-now."

A Goliath stepped forward, his giant fingers twirling his mustache in thought. "Ears are longer and more pointed at the tips, high angle, he's a bit scrawny but that's definitely a male."

Specialist Yuriko stepped forward, crackling her knuckles. "If he ain't gonna confess, I know a sure fire way to solve this mystery..."

Fino stutter stepped backwards from her and bumped into Yule, causing him to spin around and look up at the Human. Fear was getting the better of Fino, and he had begun sweating so much, that his dirty, ragged uniform was sticking to his skin like a wet bed sheet.

Yule placed his hands on his hips and cocked his head at the Southern Elf, his scarred face one of confusion. "Fino, if you were a man why didn't you tell me? I've been calling you ma'am the entire time and you never corrected me."

Fino's ears drooped slightly from how strangely hurt Yule's voice sounded, and he brought his hands up together as if asking for forgiveness. "Mr. Yule... I'm so sorry. It was a strange night, I was about to be shot, and then the monster from the reports I've been reading suddenly lurched out of the darkness and snuffed out my accusers like a wraith. I had read you were more lenient with female prisoners... you already assumed I was female, so I just rolled with it in the hopes you'd be less likely to kill me in the end."

Yule moved his jaw from one side to the other, rolling it in thought, and the muscles popped faintly. He looked down at Fino as a bead of sweat dripped from the Elf's chin, and sighed. "That's the reputation that precedes me?"

"I mean..." Fino looked at the Veil Riders who stood around him, and rubbed his right shoulder awkwardly.

Yule looked up at the clouds, gave another sigh, then nudged Fino. "Look, your sister was killed in cold blood along with my Auxiliaries. You're a victim here, not an enemy."

He sucked in some air and began speaking louder, addressing the troopers that had amassed around him. "This Elf, Fino, is as much a victim as anyone, just as I had stated, and *his* sister was killed by *his* Command. Then, after digging as to why, they were going to shoot him the very night I arrived. Fino is not an enemy. Fino is a friend and my guest. Treat *him* as such." When Yule said the last 'him', he slapped Fino on the shoulder, and the Elf had to stifle a panicked screech.

Chikily bared his fangs at Fino in an aggressive smile. "Sissy Elf."

"Chikily come on now, what did I just say."

"If harness fits."

Yule scooped Chikily up in a headlock and gave him a playful noogie while dragging him away. "Why can't you play nice with the other kids? Fino, finish up with the Master Engineer and then meet me back at the command bunker."

Fino stood there, gaping at Yule as he walked away, and the rest of his soldiers followed suit, walking behind him while laughing sporadically at Fino.

"So about this giant gun..." Began the Dwarf, and Fino turned around, shaking himself mentally and wiping the sweat from his forehead with his dirty sleeve.

"Right, right, uh, works off of a two part charge. First you load the main shell..."

* * *

Yule spent a bit of time with Chikily, letting the Harpy tell him all the scuttlebutt and small rumblings that he had heard while around the base and out on aerial patrol. While Yule was away, it seemed that Saveriss had gotten impatient with Yule and had instead begun going after his NCOs. Much to her annoyance, only Domino seemed to be game for taking her on, and even the Harpy Queen found him almost too much to bear. Not that Yule was complaining, as he had no love to spare for the particular Harpy, and wished she would stay away from him for as many wing spans as he could put between them. With Domino heading out to the field, Saveriss and a small contingent had followed them out, now acting as runners and scouts for the COP that was created by the edge of the Sanrion woods. Besides that, the Terrans were drilling every new recruit they could get their hands on into a soldier, and some grasped the concept far faster than others. Goliaths had begun showing up in larger numbers, however they were slower at adapting to new ideas and technology.

The Dwarves and Elves were the exact opposite, digesting any information they could get their hands on and spinning it to their own devices. Supplies from the Engineering Holds were coming in on long wagon trains, keeping ammunition and weapons flowing in a steady stream. The Onii and Brimtouched were able to break ground on developing a rudimentary type of kevlar, except unlike Earth, they were able to weave in special fabrics and blessed materials into the materials, allowing it to be stronger and lighter than normal Human kevlar. Attached to the Auxiliary plate carriers, again made by the Onii and Brimtouched, were classic elements of steel armor, just in case things came to close combat. To Yule, as he watched a small troop of patrolling Auxiliaries walk by, the shoulder armor looked a lot like Lorica Segmentata, a classic Roman steel plate armor, except that the top plate was broader and came further down the shoulder. After watching them go by, he thought it didn't look too shabby, and the crazy lads had painted camouflage designs on the steel so it wouldn't shine in the sun. After giving Chikily his fill of hugs and stories, the Harpy ran off to collect his NCOs and whatever other leadership still remained in the base. When all were gathered, he relayed what he had learned and what had happened the days after the shelling, omitting some parts such as the Goddess coming down and ruining his perfectly good death.

"Bradleys?" Kole asked, now sporting a locally made patrol cap and having gotten a fresh haircut from somewhere on base. "What kind of Bradleys we talkin' 'bout here? Linebackers? M2A3's?"

Yule turned his hands, exposing his palms as he rested on an actual proper chair, cushioning and all. "I don't know. Fino didn't know much about it either. If things are still churnin' faster on that side of the Veil, they could be pushin' all kinds of things towards us. They're also expandin' the Veil opening somehow, which means they want to drag the real hardware through."

Chicks shrugged "I mean, those Dwarves made a bazooka on accident and then morphed it into a Panzerschreck, we could probably gank most of the armor that comes through the Veil."

"Not armor I'm worried about." Yule leaned back, taking a small sip of tea from a canteen that Chikily had brought him. "If they get airborne elements in here, we could be staring down the barrel of an M230 with thermals."

Chicks winced. "Ah right, there is that."

"What's that?" Chikily asked, who had walked in with a small cup of milk for Yule's tea.

Chicks filled him in on what an Apache was, and what it could do, but Chikily seemed unphased. "What about throwing magnet mine on it? Have Harpy just fly under and slap it on the big metal bird."

Yule looked from Chikily to Chicks.

Chicks gave a nervous chuckle. "Ah, well, Gremlin showed the Dwarves-"

"Go. Get. Me. Gremlin."

Yule was furious, and it showed in his voice as much as it did on his face. Chikily didn't like how Yule looked when he was angry, and volunteered without delay to go fetch the female Human. Yule could not believe just how much technology Gremlin had handed out for free, and the magnet mine, while not a perfect weapon, could have set up the Veil Riders for years alone. Yule dismissed his NCOs after asking them to write up reports on how many troops they had, supplies, and current movements in the field, then sat in front of the door in the now reeking leather chair. Yule had still not bathed since his arrival at Valhalla Hill, and the smell threatened to turn the leather different colors. Gremlin poked her head through the door some minutes later, and the only thing to greet her was the looming figure of Yule, holding the metal canteen in his hand, and the rest of the command bunker personnel who were keeping as far away from the splash zone as possible.

"Heeeeyyy Yule..." Gremlin coo'd nervously, stepping past the door and shutting it behind her. "I heard you were back!"

"Uh huh." Yule growled, and Gremlin could see his eyes were alight with rage. "So, Gremlin, I hear you are giving out free workshops on Terran Tech."

There was a small pause between the two, Gremlin shifting her feet nervously as she began to check where the closest window was. "W-well... I was talking with a few of the Engineers, they gave me some pretty good beer, I may have gotten drunk and dived into the files saved on one of my laptops..."

"Panther Tanks!? Magnetic Mines, Gremlin!" Yule's timber was full of vexation.

Gremlin held out her hand, the other pushing her black hair from her face. "I didn't show them the Salamander and Me262 schematics at least!"

Yule opened his eyes wide and shook his head in incredulity. "You have *what* on those laptops?"

"...Nothing."

Gremlin gave Yule a chipper smile, while Yule wanted to take her laptops and make her surf on them.

"Look. Stop giving away tech for free. We need those to make money an-... Gremlin. Hey, Gremlin, im angry at you, look over here." Yule snapped his fingers a few times in her sight line, but she was staring over the top of Yule's head at something behind him. Yule twisted around in the chair, trying to follow what she was looking at. When he saw it, he screwed his eyes shut as if he was suddenly struck by a head pain. "For fucks sakes . . ."

From the back of the command bunker's rear door, Fino had made his way in, having heard Yule shouting at someone and wanting to have nothing to do with it. However, instead of coming directly from the Engineer, Fino had stopped by the bath house and also the supply building, acquiring a collection of clothes to replace his soiled ones. Yule judged that Fino must have spent the majority of his time in the bath house, as he had taken the time to not only wash his long hair, but also braid it, dragging it over his shoulder much like Yethis did. Yule realized now that Fino's hair was white, despite thinking it was brown, and guessed it must have been from not being washed for a couple of days and rough wear. Where he had been keeping all the hair under his cap was a mystery. More Elven trickery if Yule had to reckon. With a bath and a wash, Fino looked more female than he had previously, and Yule still had no idea what the hell people were on about with the whole ear angle thing. If he had not been told, Yule still would have judged Fino to be a beautiful woman just from a glance.

"Who . . . is that a Southern Elf?"

Yule turned to look at Gremlin, whose hands were resting on her cheeks. Despair coursed through Yule, remembering who Gremlin was and what kind of boards on the internet she tended to frequent. "Gremlin, this is Fino, he's the Elf who helped us steal the Paladin."

"He?" Gremlin whispered, and a grin spread across her face.

"Gremlin, no."

"Gremlin yes" She purred, and went to step forward before she stopped, her hands moving from her cheeks to her head.

"I haven't done my hair." She mouthed, her voice not even audible, then turned and bolted out of the door she had come in from.

"Gremlin. Gremlin! We're not done here! Get your ass . . . oh forget it." Yule stomped his boot as the door slammed shut, and Fino padded up behind him, wearing a pair of simple fiber sandals. The troopers working inside the command area all began to snort with quiet laughter as Fino looked around in confusion.

"Who was that?"

"Another headache. She may also try and eat you."

Fino jumped, looking quickly from Yule to the door. "She what?!"

"Nothen'. Found some clothes did you?"

Fino gathered himself and looked down at his simple linen tunic and uniform pants. "Well, I shouldn't be walking around in my uniform I would imagine, and they wouldn't give me a full set. Said I didn't deserve to wear the colors and only gave me the pants to be polite."

Yule gave a snort and stood up from the chair, deciding he should hit the bath house as well before his ruined uniform began growing roots into his skin. "For your . . . safety, take a room in here, up near mine. Private, come here and show Fino to a free room would you?"

A Valley Elf female Private trotted over, giving Fino the stinkeye but bowing slightly to Yule. "Yes sir, this way . . . you."

Fino squinted at her as she refused to use his name, but didn't want to press his luck in regards to the more muscular Valley Elf punching him in the back of the head when making their way up the staircase to the living quarters. For now, he could deal with being called 'you' if it meant prolonging his safety, even going as far as to not tell the engineer everything he knew just to make sure he saw the morning light of the following day. Yule watched the pair step up the staircase, finished the canteen of tea, then made his own way to the bath house. If one were to make a judgment of his current hygiene status via smell, it would certainly be ranking somewhere in the neighborhood of 'dead animal or good cheese'.

The bathhouse was crafted with care from what Yule could tell, showing the hallmarks of seasoned builders and engineers. It was odd for him to see so much love and craft go into a place where people wash themselves, and found it to be very Roman in its way of thinking; If one thing has to be nice, let it be the bath house. Yule was happy to see it wasn't staffed by more than a few people on boiler duty, who walked back and forth checking on the towels and whatever else they were told to do in the place. Gremlin must have gotten her little crooked fingers in on this place too, as Yule told one of the Privates to show him around; Not only was water coming into the place via pipe systems, but there were also Dwarf crafted hot water heaters and boilers. These made it so the Bathhouse had hot water on demand, coming in from a spigot and going right into the personal tubs or the group bathing area. The group bathing area didn't really do the small swimming pool justice, and Yule just knew that somehow Gremlin must have had some old Roman paintings on one of her laptops. There were even mosaics of tanks, mortars, rifles, and infantry running around the walls. Yule slowly turned on the spot, and he realized that someone had taken the time to show the process of a normal citizen turning into a soldier by training and the fires of combat. The open bath house came to a crescendo on the far wall, where the Unicorn and M2 of the Veil Rider unit patch stood imposing above the tub, bristling with gold, silver, and precious gem accents.

Yule sniffed as the steam began to make his nose run, and eyed the huge mural while scratching at the scar on his face. "Seems a bit overboard, but I wasn't exactly here to stop them . . ."

"I think it's nice."

Yule turned to see a male Onii Private standing a few feet away, holding a towel that had a small bar of soap resting on it.. "Y'think so, Private Wakamiki?"

Private Wakamiki shrugged. "Well, a blank wall would be a little boring."

Yule tilted his head back a little and dropped his eye lids at the Private, who coughed and tried to look somewhere else other than Yule. "Very funny, smart ass."

He opted to not take part in the giant swimming pool of body-soup, and instead went for one of the private tubs in the rear of the bath house. Here one could bathe in comfort, with only four other tubs sharing the room. Three rooms with a total of twelve tubs just for those who wished to only sit in their own special flavor of body broth. Yule shoo'd Private Wakamiki away and hopped into a tub, just letting the hot water soak into his body and bones. He didn't think this through particularly well, because he was in fact so filthy, that the water had to be drained and refilled several times until he was able to eventually soap himself. Yule was also surprised to find that the bathhouse was co-ed, as around the third time his bath needed drained a female Brimtouched Specialist had barged in with a tub scrubber, and almost caused Yule to bash his face on the tiled floor when he tried to scrabble back into the tub.

What she saw, he had no idea, but she was smirking far too much for his own comfort. He stood grumpily in the corner, wrapped hastily in a towel as she emptied and scrubbed the sides of the tub. She only gave him a sly grin when she pulled down on the hot-water leaver to refill the tub, and made her exit. It was not that Yule was ashamed of his appearance, but some things were better left to the imagination of those who he didn't share a bed with. His nerves cooled as he got down to getting clean, scrubbing down with the soap and a small cloth to get any other dirt too stubborn to come out with the regular water. In his hair, he found down near the roots to be crusted with old dried blood, causing the water to pink slightly, but he was not in the mood for the Brimtouched to come back in and feast her eyes on more of his flesh. He had to admit, getting clean again was doing wonders for his mental exhaustion, but was also loosening up his forever-tight muscles. Soreness seeped into his soul, and sleep was beckoning him as sweetly as death could. Or Alavara, and he would take one or the other at this point. Private Wakamiki was standing outside with a fresh uniform of Yule's, assuming he had run off and gotten it from his room in the command bunker, and Yule slipped it on, wincing at the effort of having to move his achy and tired joints. When he had made his way back across the parade grounds, and saluting a few of the Auxiliaries who did it to him first, he found where his room was. His little cozy corner, consisting of a rough field table, his rucksack, and a wool blanket, had gotten upgraded to a full room; A proper bed with a rifle rack next to it was in the corner, a small wooden wardrobe, a sofachair, a couch, and a proper desk were all arranged within. Yule breathed in deep and smelled the scents of fresh carved wood, lacquer, cotton, and wool. He found them comforting, and they reminded him of home. Someone had taken it upon themselves to unpack his rucksack, and saw that almost all of his clothes were missing.

"The hell..." He murmured, and turned his rucksack upside down. From the large opening a note fell out, bearing writing that he recognized as Yethis's.

"These smelled like death, took to wash what could be, may burn the rest. Be back with food soon."

Yule blew a drawn out raspberry as he read, before tossing his ruck back into the little wardrobe. "Annoying little shit..."

He sat down heavily on the sofachair and breathed out, stretching out his feet and giving his toes a little wiggle. He was tired, dead tired, and he was curious how true that would hold. He had slept out in the woods before he had found Fino, but he was worried that a full night's rest would send him back to the spirit world. Then again, even if it did, he had no doubts that the Grim's little slice of pie would drag him back kicking and screaming. He chuckled a little at the thought, closing his eyes, and heard a faint knock at the door.

"Open." Yule grunted, and he could hear the door knob click open along with what he assumed to be the feet of a Harpy. When the door fully swung in, he saw Chikily standing in the portal way with a cup of tea in his other wing-claw, and Yule couldn't help but chuckle.

Yule cracked his eyes open a little more. "How many times did you spill that tea coming from the chow hall?"

Chikily stalked forward, carefully balancing the cup with both hands once he closed the door, and set it down on the small table near Yule. "Chikily has broken two cups so far."

Yule placed his hand over the mug, letting the warmth flow up into his palm. "Not bad."

Another voice rang out from the hallway, and Yule flicked his eyes fully open at Yethis's voice. "He is not keen on asking for help."

Yule turned his head a little more and saw the Valley Elf had managed to open the door silently after Chikily had closed it on her, and was bearing a small mess kit of bread, cheese, and sausage.

"I can get my own food, y'know."

"Im aware." Yethis chided in Tunkah, and set the mess kit down alongside Yule's tea.

Yule was not sure why the gestures hit him as hard as they did, but he supposed that the exhaustion and trials of the time since his refunded death were starting to get to him. Chikily looked at Yethis, worried as Yule's face flashed with the emotion. Chikily didn't have much time to ponder it, as he was quickly anaconda'd by Yule's arm, dragging the Harpy into him for a hug. He held out his other arm for Yethis, and found it quickly filled with the body of the Elf who hugged him back fiercely.

"Thanks fellas." Yule whispered, his voice cracking slightly as he fought to remain neutral voiced, but the two in his arms just murmured back their replies, burying their faces into his chest. Yule sat in the sofachair with both Chikily and Yethis curled up on him, their bodies pressed close to his, and he took their familiar smells into his nose. Chikily's wild and windswept scent, the smell of Yethis's hair, and the curious twang of the healing salves she messed with lulled him to sleep. He fell soul first into the yielding black, right then and there. No dream came for Yule, nor a nightmare, and he instead had what many soldiers called 'the long blink', where one moment you are asleep, and awake the next.

Sunlight was filtering in through the windows as his eyes creaked open, and he noticed that there were still two lumps attached to his body. Chikily had somehow snuggled down beside him in the sofachair, burying his head under Yule's arm as if he were a chick snuggling into a mother hen. Yethis had taken up the majority of his lap, her head resting just below his chin. Yule smiled, as it reminded him of his daughter back on Terra when they would fall asleep watching movies, and he reached over for the now cold cup of tea. As Chikily and Yethis continued to sleep, Yule took a moment to quench his thirst and get a little bit of food into his empty belly. When it became apparent the two were too far into the caressing arms of dream land, he moved them both to his bed, throwing the top cover over them and taking off Yethis's boots. He looked down at the both of them, breathing softly as the morning sun warmed their faces, and he felt a pang in his chest. A pang of his old role as Father, of Husband, and he wrinkled his nose a bit at the memory. Outside his window, he heard the early morning crow of soldiers doing PT, of formations coming together with cadence being called, and the thud of feet coming down as one on the march. Yule tucked his two sleepy chair mates into the sheet and put on a fresh uniform, figuring that if he was right, morning chow would be coming up soon.

And it would be quite fun to give the new boots a good spook.

* * *

The first unfortunates to fall under Yule's gaze were an entire Company doing PT out near the parade ground, all of the troopers in separated Platoon formations with their guidon bearers out front. Each Platoon's guidon had what looked like a personalized Platoon banner, and then a larger Company banner underneath. Thanks to some vials of blood that Yethis had left on his desk, he had a fully powered translation amulet, and he could make out the names of the Platoons and their Company. This one was 8th Company, 'Spittlejack's Reapers', and Yule assumed the grizzled looking Dwarf out front must be the one in charge of them. The Dwarf, the one likely known as Spittlejack, bore the triple chevrons and rocker of a Staff Sergeant, with two basic Sergeants behind him. One was a Valley Elf, and the other a large Onii female. Spittlejack had to be some kind of retired monster hunter, as the Dwarf was a mess of scars and wounds. He and his Company were in their PT clothes, a simple shirt emblazoned with the Veil Rider crest and a pair of drawstring shorts. Yule studied the Dwarf's exposed flesh as he strolled towards them, seeing that his entire body must be a wound-map of scars and close calls during his time as a hunter. The Valley Elf was clear of any wounds, had short brown hair, a single long ear had been studded with a small hoop of gold, and he had mastered the 'Sergeant Stare' with his pearly blues. The Onii female was a head taller than the Valley Elf, and her bulging muscles strained against every opening of her clothes. She was a blue skinned variety, whatever that meant, and her white hair was put up in a thick laurel braid that ran around her head. Her eyes were dark yellow, and didn't even glow in the morning sun, soaking in the light and devouring it. Yule could tell their eye colors because the two were staring at him as he made his way up the parade, his boots crunching on the ground as he headed towards the grassy patch they occupied. The Onii Sergeant froze, mouth agape cutely, while the Valley Elf Sergeant had to shake the morning cobwebs from his head, suddenly turning to the Company before him.

"Company! Atten-SHUN!" He barked, and all of the Auxiliary troopers snapped to attention from their at ease, the guidons' banners cracking in the breeze from the sudden snatch of the pole. Spittlejack looked up in alarm, spinning around at his NCOs.

"What in the devil are you shouting fo-, Oh, bugger me, Mr.Yule!"

Spittlejack held out his huge Dwarf hand, and Yule clasped it in his own "Just Yule will do. Going to do a little PT are we?"

"It is the time of day for it." Spittlejack said with a grin, and held out his arms to his Platoons. "If you like, you are more than welcome to take the reins."

"I assume you learned from my Veil Riders during your NCO training right?"

"Straight from the little book they brought."

"Excellent. Guidons, fallout and stack your banners behind the Company, then fall into your respective Platoons."

With a whirl, all of the guidon bearers took a step back and then ran to the rear of the formation, leaning their banners together like they were rifles in the field. Usually, they never carried guidons to PT when Yule was in the Army, but he suspected flags were a special icon to the Veil folk when it came to their identity and self pride. After all, they even made special flags for each Platoon. When the bearers had fallen into the rear of their formations, Yule took in a deep breath, and bellowed out.

"Ex-tend to the left, MARCH!"

All of the troopers began to yell as they all gained their arms wide space. With them a more spread out, Yule could see this was a well mixed platoon, and even a few Harpies were studded in among the ranks. As he called out to left face and extend once again, he had to admit, it felt good to be in a proper military presence again. A few of his more fastidious Veil Riders had brought a collection of manuals with them, and they had all been training Auxiliary NCOs quite literally by the book. When all the troopers were spaced, he called them to their right and then ordered them to count off. As he listened, the numbers definitely reflected a full Company, and he looked around while the troopers counted out. All around him he could hear the same commands, and had to wager he had at least a full Battalion now, if not a Brigade.

"Even numbers to the left, UNCOVER!"

Now almost all of them could see him, and he could almost see all of them. He smiled broadly, taking off his uniform top to his bare shirt underneath, and rubbed his hands together gleefully. "Ah well, we can stretch after this, it's been awhile. The PUSH UP!"

All of the troopers bellowed out the name of the exercise in return, and went to the ground when the command was given, some trying to beat Yule since he gave the command well after he began to drop himself. Many an Auxiliary experienced of the feeling of their chins thudding off the grass. To his amusement, Yule saw the Onii, Sergeant Akagi, frowning as she did her push ups, and surmised she must not have been a fan. The frown grew instantly when Yule called out the same exercise, and led them in another set of two counts. Staff Sergeant Spittlejack was as game as Yule, even doing them one armed while jeering at his own troopers. Afterwards, doing their proper stretches and not just doing pushups, Yule engaged in teaching them non-by-the-book exercises, such as buddy squats, buddy drags, wheelbarrows, and water-can strides. Sergeant Akagi couldn't help but burst out into laughter when Yule used her as his squat buddy, hefting her up in a fireman's carry and showing them the form. Then to add inflection, he continued to walk about with the Onii on his shoulders, who had to hold her hand over her face to muffle her snorting giggles.

"There may be a time where you will have to lift your battle brother or sister from the field of combat. Dragging is not always an option, and you may have to defend both of yourselves from the enemy. You accomplish this by mastering the fireman carry, and these exercises will- quit laughing damn it." Yule reached up with his free hand and slapped Sergeant Akagi on the buttcheek, which just caused further laughter from the Onii and from all of the troopers. Yule had to suppress his own laughter to continue. "Push ups and mountain climbers are good, but you will need to build up your chest, your leg, and your back muscles if you hope to get both of you to safety. I will show you how even that Harpy there will be able to haul one of you louts to safety. Now find a dancing partner, the real training begins."

The Onii was almost purple in the face from trying to hold in her laughter, and her white hair was coming out in strands over her cheeks. "S-Sir please, im gonna die up here."

Yule set her down and then shoved her off towards her troopers with a chuckle, the Onii giggling, while Staff Sergeant Spittlejack and Sergeant Kortin laughed at her, the Valley Elf currently laying over the Dwarf's shoulders. By the end of the hour, he had mingled with plenty of the Company, and must have hauled half of them over his shoulders. For the last exercise, right before the final few minutes of PT, Yule challenged the NCOs of the Company to a buddy-race, even calling out the Corporals out for this one. When they all lined up, ready to heft their partner and run to the point Yule pointed to, Yule himself scooped up a random male Harpy Private and took off at a dead sprint, catching all of them off guard. The Harpy screeched in panic as Yule picked him up, and was praying loudly to his Gods in the hope Yule didn't fall over. Despite his obvious cheat, Yule was overtaken by a pair of quicker thinking Brimtouched, and they took the victory in stride. Laughter was shared, as well as many an Auxiliary calling Yule a cheat, but it was all in good humor. Yule bid the Company farewell, told them to remember his work outs, and then put on his uniform top after getting cooled down by a few spell slingers in the 2nd Platoon.

Checking the time on a spare cell phone he had in his packs, he saw it was near breakfast time, and he knew the perfect game to play with whoever was on headcount duty. Headcount as something of both a blessing and a curse, as while getting picked for it meant you got to skip PT, you had to literally count how many people came into the DFAC, or the 'Dining Facility', as well as take money for those who were not enlisted. The most nerve wracking of the duties was to call the building to attention when a high rank stepped in to have breakfast, and it was here that most fuck-fuck games commenced. The line into the DFAC was quite long when Yule arrived in front of the huge building, and he judged from the smells coming from inside that actual cooks were toiling away, not some Joe who barely knew how to boil eggs correctly. In fact, it smelled damned good, and Yule was curious to see just how well his troopers were eating. He slotted into the line, stepping in behind a Brimtouched that was chatting up a relatively cute looking Valley Elf.

Yule leaned in towards the two from behind and spoke in Tunkah. "What are they scooping up today?"

"Beats me friend, yesterday they were serving something called a 'hash brown surprise' that a Human came up with."

"I hear those Humans do love themselves some tubers."

The Brimtouched turned around with a smile, ready to reply, but wilted when he saw Yule had leaned down and was eye to eye with him. Yule was easily six inches taller than this particular Brimtouched, and the Valley Elf turned when he made a strangled noise at seeing Yule, the sun casting shadows over his face from behind. While the Brimtouched looked horrified, the Valley Elf appeared to have no idea who Yule was from how darkened his face was in the early rising sun. Yule saw she was a Specialist, bearing the black shield and golden eagle on her shoulder, and she tilted her head as she observed his uniform. The Brimtouched gawked in horror as she looked at Yule, her hands on her hips.

"Hey mister, where's your rank and name tape?"

Yule stage gasped and looked down at his shoulder, rustling the fabric with his finger tips. "Goodness, I think a Harpy must have stolen it!"

The Elven Specialist actually took Yule by the elbow and began to turn him, pointing in the general direction of the larger supply building on the other side of the base. "Well you better go get your uniform in order before a Human sees you! Imagine Commander Yule's face if he saw ... you ...". With Yule now turned around into the sun, his face lit up by the rays, the Elven Specialist now saw just who she was admonishing for their uniform. The Brimtouched was almost hyperventilating in panic, while the other Auxiliaries around them were having to hide their faces behind their patrol caps, chuckling and laughing into the fabric. The Elven Specialist swallowed hard, her eyes almost tearing up in distress and embarrassment, and she very slowly took her hand away from Yule's elbow. In the shadows from Yule's patrol cap, she had thought that he had been one of the Half-Goliaths that were running around nowadays, and truly had just wanted him to be squared away.

"Ah . . . Good morning, Commander."

Yule Placed an arm around her shoulder, then the Brimtouched, and pulled them both to his sides. He gave them both a shake, while smiling brightly. "Good mornen' breakfast buddies."

If either of the troopers had been looking for a relaxing breakfast, they were not going to find it while the Human had them gripped to his sides. Yule chatted to both of the sweating troopers, asking them what they had learned, what kind of training they were doing and the like, while the line slowly churned forward into the building. The Troopers around the little trio gave them a wide berth, and whispers were circulating around Yule as they all wondered why he was down here in the first place. After all, they expected him to dine in the command building, there was even a kitchen there just for Yule, Peiper, and the Seconds to Yule. The Elven Specialist relaxed with Yule, but was still sweating just from nerves of having him so close to her, while the Brimtouched Private First Class was about to melt out of his uniform. Eventually they were in front of the doors, and Yule leaned in close to the two, hooking his arms around their heads and pulling them in towards his.

"Why don't you two let them know I'll be comen', would only be fair."

Both of them nodded vigorously, and he patted them both on the backs, sending them forward. While the Elven Specialist maintained an even stride, the Brimtouched skedaddled inside like a started meerkat, and Yule could hear them telling the troopers on head count what was awaiting them outside. Yule waited, looked behind him at the troopers waiting in line, and looked at the non-existent watch on his wrist. Everyone in view chuckled, as watches had caught on fast thanks to the Humans, and now almost everyone that could afford them had one attached to their wrist from here to the high country. After waiting far longer than he should have, Yule stepped forward to the door, and peeked inside. He had his boots just barely against the threshold of the door, and could see two very nervous looking Valley Elves staring back at him from behind a small desk. They both looked poised to stand up, their hands and elbows cocked on the desk to bolt upright, and their eyes locked on his boots. Their eyes flicked for a moment to Yule's face, and they both brought their shoulders up higher when they saw the wolfish grin on his lips.

Yule lifted his boot quickly and held it over the entryway, scant inches above the ground, and one of the Valley Elf Privates let out a yelp, going to call the building to 'At Ease', but then strangling the remark in his throat when he saw Yule hadn't actually taken a step inside the building. Yule had made it known he wanted nothing to do with the Officer ranks, and his group of NCOs had built their entire training program around the NCO Corps, only using 'Attention' for Company formations, and only if a very high ranking NCO walked into their midst, like Yule had on Spittlejacks Company. Yule saw from the small entry door to the dining room that a Human was having breakfast, saw what Yule was doing, and sprinted off for some reason. Within moments, he returned with a few of Yule's Seconds, all of them bearing Master Sergeant rockers and little golden stars glittering from the space within. Yule made a note to make fun of them later for even wearing the damn things, but he knew what they were getting ready to do. Blood was in the water, and the sharks were beginning to circle. Behind Yule, everyone was crowding around, trying to get a peek inside, and Yule lifted his boot away, the Private breathing out a puff of air and sitting back down. Yule watched Kole round the entryway, his bowl of burgoo still in hand, and called out to the Privates, who lept from their chairs to At Ease, facing Kole.

It was at that moment Yule stepped into the building, crossing the space between the door and the desk. "Oh, so someone in this place outranks me then eh?! I can't wait to meet them!"

Both of the Privates whirled around in horror, ears as high as they could go, and then the flank attack was launched by Yule's Seconds, a small storm of blustering false rage that swept the two Valley Elves up in its gusts. "Oh is that what we do now, not call the building At Ease for the Company Commander?!"

The noise was deafening as Yule stepped back and admired the little trick, the swarm of NCOs boiling around the two jammed up Privates. Knife hands were inches from elegant Elven noses as they bellowed, roared, barked, and growled. Yule could have sworn he heard Donnahue command one of the Privates to stand on his head, the Private hesitating, unknowing if he really meant the command or not. He let it go on for a few more seconds before he himself issued an order to the group as a whole.

"That's enough, I don't think they have potions for heart attacks."

The NCOs went from false red rage to laughing and joshing in an instant, shaking the now nervously smiling Privates by the shoulders and telling them they were not in trouble. Those behind Yule were laughing all the way down the line, and Yule heard, halting his own laugh and spinning around, ripping his patrol cap from his head.

"Something you find funny, boots?!" He roared, and barged out of the DFAC entryway, his NCOs instantly taking up the warcry and exiting out with him. The two Privates now got to enjoy the sudden turning of tables, and took much pleasure in the schadenfreude. Outside, Yule howled.

"Half right, Face! Front leaning rest position, MOVE! Half way down!"

As he belted out the orders, his flock of hawks circled and barked out nonsensical orders, commanding Privates to sing Human songs they knew not the lyrics of, or to calculate the flight speed of a laden swallow. One Harpy in particular became panicked because she in fact was a Swallow Harpy, and had no idea what the hell a coconut was. The surprise attack was brief, and by the end, everyone was laughing . . . or pretending to laugh to try and hide the stricken tears in their eyes, believing for a moment that they were actually in trouble. Yule stepped back into the building, of which At Ease was called properly, and then commanded his NCOs to finish 'their damn breakfast'. The dining room was rife with chatter which echoed out into the dish line. Behind the glass sneeze catchers, village cooks worked and toiled away at large stoves and pots, and Yule surmised that they must be getting paid to work up here. All of them looked like mothers and grandmothers, working away while their children or grandchildren helped chop vegetables or dress meat. Every race was here as well, working together to feed the Auxiliary troops. Yule bid them good morning, and they chided him for picking on the poor troopers.

One older Valley Elf waved a spoon at him, and he was curious just how old she was to have such little winkles. Even at her age, she would still be able to hold her own with younger Human women. "Why do you have to pick on those poor soldiers? They have enough to worry about as it is."

"Build's character." Yule answered back, holding out his tray to a little Brimtouched boy who slapped a few pancakes onto his plate. Yule inwardly hoped that he was washing his hands often.

She squinted an eye at him, then tucked a loose strand of dark brown hair behind her ear, it having fallen out from her head wrap. "Mhm, and I bet no bacon will help you build character too."

A little Valley Elf girl, who Yule assumed to be her daughter from the same dark brown hair and head wrap cloth, called out "No bacon!", and snatched them off his plate as soon as she had dropped them onto it, reacting to her mother's whims.

Yule placed his free hand on his hip, looking down at the little girl who stared back defiantly. "Wha, hey! I'm the Commander of this place you know."

"Mommy commands the kitchen! No bacon for Mr. Yule!"

Yule did his best to make her blink, but the little spitfire didn't even bat a lash. He looked from her, to her grinning mother, while in the background the rest of the cook staff were chuckling.

"Future NCO in this one. Fine, no bacon, I bet you put Elf cooties on them anyway."

Yule stuck his tongue out at the little Elven child, who stuck hers out right back, the both of them giggling. After losing his bacon privileges, he got a bowl of meat burgoo from a Dwarven woman working a massive cauldron of the stuff, some scrambled eggs, and then a steak of some random smoked fish. It looked a lot like salmon, but was purple and smelled like pork when he leaned down to sniff at it. With his laden tray, he walked out and picked his next victims. The dining area was a collection of long tables, lengthy enough that you could seat half a Company at one if they all got friendly in the process. He saw that there was a space for him at a particularly packed table, and he swept into it, nudging his elbow into a Dwarf's shoulder.

"Hey hand me the water pitcher wouldja'?"

The Dwarf almost choked on his toast, but caught himself just in time, reaching over to grab the pitcher as well as a cup for Yule.

"Ah thanks bud. Is there any hot sauce around here?" Yule arranged his food in a logical order, and decided to start with the pancakes and eggs so the burgoo could cool.

"Devil sauce over here." Someone called, and a glass bottle was handed down towards Yule, who took it from his other seat mate, a male Brush Feathered Private who for some reason smelled like lavender. Yule popped the metallic stopper off and poured it over his eggs, at which everyone around him recoiled. To Yule, it smelled like a standard pepper sauce, and when he popped a spoonful of eggs into his mouth, found it to be quite mild. Judging from the looks others were giving him, it may as well have been molten lead he was tossing down his throat.

"What?" Yule asked, chewing his eggs as he poured himself a glass of lemon water.

"Commander, how do you Humans just eat that stuff like it's nothing? An Elf needed to get dragged to the medico's after he mistook it for tomato sauce once, and stopped breathing."

Yule shrugged, and cut into his pancakes. "On Earth, Army food is usually almost edible, and the hot sauce helps not only flavor it, but kill bacteria on it." He poured a smidge on his burgoo as well, and gave it a little stir before tasting it.

A female Brimtouched stared at Yule, confused, her spoon scraping up the last of her own burgoo. "... you use it to sanitize your food?"

"More or less."

"What do you even eat over there, then?"

Yule looked up, thinking back to the ingredients of the MREs he had eaten, whatever had come out of the kitchens on the bases he had been stationed on, as well as having to run down and kill a rabbit with his boot just to have something with actual meat for a meal while stuck in Africa. "... Everything, really."

"Jeeze.." She muttered, before spooning the last of her breakfast into her mouth.

Yule continued his line of questioning here as well, feeling out how things were going on base. Despite trying to find fault, everything was positive all the way around, except that Chikily was playing pranks on people, and Kole was collecting small animals in his NCOs cottage, some of which tended to hoot loudly at night. Besides that, every Veil Folk he talked to were excited for all the new changes, telling Yule that this was the escape from their basic lives of farming, or crafting. The possibility of going into battle alongside Yule and the Terrans, fighting against the Fae, and taking back lands from the Chosen Children were a key point in all of them, and Yule did his best to keep his face upbeat. Afterall, the volunteer Platoons he took to the field thought the same, and barely any of them had made it back to Valhalla Hill. It was good that their morale was up, and he let them tell him about where they came from, about their old jobs, and what they thought about the crazy stuff that Gremlin kept telling them about. All of them were excited to see such things as the television, or hold one of the prized communication devices that were favored by the Humans themselves. To the Veil folk, the Humans were the key to unlocking the ability to jump forward hundreds of years technologically, and they were thirsty for the independence that the tech brought with it.

Yule was skeptical. He knew what the internet could do to people, and he was pretty sure the people of this realm weren't ready for that kind of mental and spiritual warfare. Then again, he noticed that there were daily comic and joke drawings near the front of the DFAC, a rudimentary 'message board' if one would. Perhaps, maybe, he could discuss the idea with Gremlin, as he himself had no idea how the internet actually worked, let alone circuit boards for computers. When it came to that wheelhouse of knowledge, Yule knew he would barely be qualified to shovel coal into the boilers. Thankfully, plenty of his Veil Riders knew the science behind it, and just maybe they could bring this realm sprinting into modern communications like a runner being chased by a grizzly bear. Due to all the talking, his meal had gotten a touch cold, and he finished up quickly in true Army fashion. When Yule went to deposit his dishes and tray at the wash station, there were curious creatures bustling around the place, and he couldn't help but lean in to look at them.

". . . Who in the hell are you lot?"

Dozens of faces whirled around to stare at Yule, and he really had to take a moment to take them in. They reminded Yule of Elves, but as if they had been crossed with some kind of fish, or amphibian. Their skin was ever so slightly blue and green, and looked wet from how shiney it was. Their eyes were wide, the iris of which were slits, but slanted in towards their nose. Their ears reminded him of a Gremlin, but after they had gotten wet and went around town setting things on fire and fighting bikers. Despite the comparison, they were still awfully *cute*, and were around the same height as a standard Sparrow Harpy. Their hair was almost all white, with only a few manifesting into the gray range, and the color kept to their eyebrows as well. Their fingers, curiously, were webbed, and were thickly muscled as if they were used to dig deep into the mud, or for swimming.

The one standing in front of him tapped his fingers on the edge of a bin. "Mistah' Yool'. Yoo 'playss 'playte in bin."

Yule looked down at him and slowly placed his dishes in the bin, looking the creature up and down. "Seriously, what are you guys."

"We are the Yamatu!" A voice piped up from the rear, and from how the pitch was, it must have been a female.

"The Yamatu? Are you guys . . . water types or somethin'?"

The whole dish crew shared a small spout of chittering laughter, before the male in front of Yule began handing off his dishes to the Yamatu standing next to him. "Yamatu are 'waytur Elves, we 'tayke care of rivurs, and'tha bays. Build our homes in'tha banks and 'clyffs. We need moisture, we 'hayndle wet 'wurk on 'Vaylhalla 'Hyll."

"Good to have you here . . ." Yule said, unsure, and kept staring at the Yamatu's teeth, as they were throwing him off his game. The majority of the Veil folk had long canines, or at least normal teeth like Humans, but the Yamatu had very flat, fine teeth, as if they were used for crushing things instead of biting through flesh. "Kinda curious, what do you folk eat?"

"Shellfesh, mustly. Red meat hurts tummies."

"Hm . . . Noted."

Yule turned away from the Yamatu dish crew and began to walk away, but kept having to look over his shoulder. When he did, they would all wave, and he would wave back. It was something about their ears that really made him uneasy, despite how adorable they may look on the outside. Years of childhood training had taught any Human that something with those kinds of ears should never be in water, and the damn things lived in it. Judging from how the females were built, they seemed to reproduce naturally, so at least he didn't have to worry about them popping out of each other's backs or something of that regard and swarming his base. With the sleeper cell of Yamatu behind him, and breakfast happily rumbling around in his belly, Yule decided to pay a visit to the prisoner he had left behind the few weeks before. If his hunch was right, they were using some kind of weird tracing spell on him or his units in some way, and any chance of breaking her compatriots was done in by her slitting all their throats. Yule remembered that someone had mentioned she kept trying to escape, and was curious to see how she was being held to keep that from happening.

As he walked down the paths that squirreled around Valhalla Hill, he began to get hard Vietnam vibes from the buildings around him, as well as the troopers who walked around in their olive drab green uniforms. If he were to start blasting some door gunner tunes, have a few Hueys fly over his head, and scattered some beer cans around, he was sure the scene would fall perfectly into an old war movie from his youth. The only thing that broke the illusion were the fantasy races running around, and the twang of magic being casted for jump starting a fire or cooling down hot machinery. Much like the barracks, the command building, and the bath house, the detention center was crafted by whatever had come through to build them all. Difference was, this building had a lot more metal in it, and all the windows had bars. Like any detention center, it held a skeleton guard, a few troopers who just had to make sure the prisoners wouldn't die of of thirst or dig out of their cells like demented prairie dogs.

One of the guards leapt to his feet, knocking over his chair. "AT EA-"

"As you were, where's the Elf woman?"

The guard blew out his air filled lungs, no longer needing it for the command, and his buddy pointed to the first cell, just behind them both. "She's in that cell, Commander."

Yule nodded, and walked past them, both of the troopers forming up on either side of his flanks. When he came before the cell, the woman inside was much different than the one he had left behind. The cell itself was quaint; There was a wash basin with only one inlet, more than likely just cold water, a flushing toilet, and a rough wooden bed, at which a single straw filled mattress sat. In the middle of the wooden floor Fadithas sat, her long high angled ears glowing with reddened runes. More than just her ears, her entire body was covered in the runic lettering, and Yule could tell more from smell than sight that it was blood. When the red runes flared, blue runes on the bars of her cell door and window would buzz up as if they were bug zappers, giving off a soft 'krack' as they caught whatever was sent off from her. While her runes were Elvish, the ones on the bars were Dwarvish. Yule smiled smugly, and squatted down.

"Shame your alphabet is shit in comparison to the Dwarves, hm?"

Fadithas's brows came together, and her eyelids slowly opened. Her seething, rage filled eyes met his own, and they stared into each other. She *detested* Yule, not for what he stood for, but purely for what he was. A Human. He *hated* her not for what she stood for, but for what she was. A Fae. Her hands did not move from her knees, contorted in a montric pose, held in place from her trying to cast her failed spell. Before she spoke, her left ear gave a twitch, and her left eyebrow ticked.

"Still alive. A shame, since you were prettier before you left."

Yule ran a finger down his scar, his face contorting. "Yes, even at your best, y'all can only marr my flesh and ruin my sleep. More the shame for that town, and all your people I killed within it."

"What town, Meseriam? That should have been your grave, along with the filth that followed you into battle."

Yule leaned forward, going down on a knee and resting his arms on his thigh. His hunch had been correct; this little half-Fae bitch had been broadcasting magically to her fellows until the Dwarves put up those bars. That could only mean those greasy pricks knew where Valhalla Hill was, and he had another hunch that those Bradleys would more than likely be beelining here, which meant they would hit Domino first.

"Emalone. We survived Meseriam."

Fadithas squinted an eye, before grinning widely and baring her fangs at Yule. "*Bollocks*. There's no way you could have survived the artillery. You wouldn't even be able to sneak into Ema-"

"Erolith's skull crunched like an egg when I stabbed into it. I was surprised to see that Fae shit themselves when they died."

The grin on her lips slid away into a snarl, her nose wrinkling and her eyebrows coming down on her eyes. He could see the anger boiling the magic behind her irises. "You lie. You're no match for Erolith."

Yule slid the knife out of his pocket, still covered in the gore from his killings, and her nostrils flared, scenting the magical blood on the blade. "I plunged this into him, right up through his mouth and into his brain. He died like the stupid little turd that he was, and I left him to rot in the sun."

Her eyes flashed, and Yule saw her knuckles go white, clenching in their pose. The muscles running along her arms flexed as she strained to not react to Yule, trying to not give him the fury that he wanted. Yule continued, turning the blade over in the light, and even the troopers next to him had to look away from it. "I plan on adding more of your *disgusting* Fae blood to this knife. By the time I'm finished with your petulant race, this blade will be *shining* gold."

This was enough. Fadithas launched herself from her sitting position and slammed into the bars, the frame rattling from the impact, and blue sparks arced and danced into the air from her hands. Those same motes of light reflected and sparkled in her eyes as she stared across at Yule from her knees, pressing her face against the space between the bars as if trying to push her own skull through them just to get to Yule.

"You fucking Rust-Blood! We controlled your squaling race for hundreds of generations and twisted you to our own desires! How dare you kill your betters!" She was almost foaming at the mouth, reaching through the bars and trying to grab at Yule's face.

Yule, without even an ounce of emotion, whirled his knife through the air and stabbed it through her hand, pinning it to the wooden floor. She screeched in anguish as the thick blade went through her palm, the pressure agony against her hand bones. The fury, the wrath, however, did not leave her face, and she sucked air in and out through her bared teeth, eyes still locked on Yules. Yule leaned in, his face inches from hers, and he began to slowly twist the knife. As she let out a silent scream, breathing out hoarsely from the roaring pain in her hand, he reached through the bars and grabbed the side of her face, bringing her hard against the bars by the ear.

"You slaughtered my troopers and those Southern Elves like they were nothing to you, as if they were but toys to your machinations. Not only did you dishonor my Auxiliaries, you dishonored their enemy, and this I cannot abide."

Yule wrenched the blade the other direction and began to drag it across the wooden floor, and Fadithas broke, mewling, her mouth open in silent torture.

"You Fae, are abhorrent. Even you little half-breeds are repugnant. When I get done with your people, you will be nothing but a horrible stain on the histories of two worlds."

Fadithas puffed out her cheeks, and squinted her eyes open, staring up into Yule's. She had one last jab, one last low blow to make sure Yule didn't walk away from their duel completely in victory. She grinned horribly, despite the pain, and steadied her voice. "Just, as you, are history, to your wife and daughter."

To punctuate her insult, she pursed her lips, and blew Yule a kiss.

In response, Yule shot his other hand forward, and began to strangle her.

Fadithas had to admit, she didn't see that coming, and thought her insult perhaps better sent when she wasn't already in his clutches. Yule had her hard around the throat with both hands, and she coughed hard, her free hand scratching and clutching at his fingers. Both of the troopers had lept into action, pulling back hard on Yule, one of them even wrapping his arms around Yule's neck and pushing against the bars with his boots, but Yule's grip was fueled by old, bitter pain. Fadithas was beginning to make frightened gurgling noises as she fought for air, trying to force it into her lungs past Yule's iron grip, her face slowly turning darker shades of red.

Both of the troopers were straining against Yule's arms, and the one not wrapped around him ran to the front, trying to work his fingers into Yule's to try and loosen his grip. "Yule! Yule let her go! You're better than this sir!"

Yule watched Fadithas's eyes begin to empty of her anger, and instead fill with fear. The same look he had seen so many other times. The same look that Southern Elf outside Emalone had when Yule held his hand as he died. The fear of knowing death would soon be drawing down upon them, and their last few seconds of reality would soon be impressed by the void. He felt the anger draw from his heart as he remembered that dead Southern Elf boy, and he loosened his grip a hair, Fadithas ceasing to shake in his strain.

The trooper that had wrapped around him spoke hushedly into his ear, and Yule could hear the near panic warbling in his voice. "Sir, she's our prisoner. Please, stop, you don't have to do this. It's not right. I don't know what she said, but you don't have to do this."

Yule could do it. A few more seconds of gold-flecked blood not going to her brain, and she would be dead, a sack of flesh to be discarded. Horribly, the slight loosening of his grip allowed some air to get into her lungs, and she gasped harshly before speaking, her voice strained.

"Please ... Don't ..."

Yule's face contorted, his breath short and rapid, before he finally threw her away, her form bouncing off the wood floor. Her hand was still pinned to the ground, but in terms of pain, that was a far memory. Her lungs heaved, and Fadithas choked down gulps of air in between sobs. She had never come that close to dying before, and she was not a big fan of the experience. Yule's face was still warped in seething hatred, but his troopers finally exhaled, breathing sighs of relief.

"Good sir, good. Let that ... stuff just settle."

Yule stared down at Fadithas's form, her back heaving as she forced air into her lungs, and he growled, ripping the knife out of the ground and out of her hand. She drew her wounded hand back and clutched it to her chest, and began to openly weep, curling into a ball.

Yule stood, spat down at his feet, and turned to leave the building, stepping slowly.

"Send a healer for her hand. Give her wine. Give her hot water. And Fadithas."

He heard the Elf twist her head around on the wooden floor boards, and he paused in his step.

"Fuck you."

He heard nothing in return, and he did not desire an answer, walking out of the detention center and back out into the sunlight.

CHAPTER 17

WORD SPREAD QUICKLY as the Auxiliaries in the detention center made calls to request a healer, and healers do tend to be a talkative bunch. By the time Yule had made it back to the command building, everyone was giving him a wide berth. Some of them bore false smiles of sadness, as they knew why Yule had broken. What Yule had done to Britta was known, as well as his attempts to take prisoners being thwarted by a Chosen Child playing possum and then gunning down a few of his Human survivors and Auxiliaries. Everyone knew that Yule was trying to be better about not killing everything he came across, and from the exaggerations of the telephone game being played about him, it was also known to everyone that Yule had almost killed Fadithas over mentioning his long past wife on the other side of theVeil. Before Yule could open the door, Chikily bundled out in a flurry of movement. He was carrying a message in his rig, and as he turned around to see Yule, he pressed himself up against the door, smiling awkwardly.

"H-hey Yule!"

Yule raised an eyebrow, but reached out to rustle Chikily's hair. "Hey bud, where you off to? Peiper sending you somewhere?"

Chikily didn't speak for a few heartbeats, then held up a wing claw. "Yes, sure, Peiper gave Chikily important message."

Yule leaned in to read the cover address of the letter, and saw barely any of it before Chikily covered it with his wing. Yule grinned a little and tilted his head a few degrees. "Chikily, why won't you let me read that?"

"Double double top secret." Chikily whispered, and a nervous sweat was beginning to break out on his forehead.

Yule leaned back, and looked down at the Harpy, slowly folding his arms. "Chikily, let me see the message."

Chikily had to make a quick decision here, as Yethis had told him not to let Yule see the message, as well as telling him *who* it was going to, and to not tell Yule even if he threatened to rip off his wings. Chikily took a deep breath, exhaled out his nose, and looked up to Yule, stiffening his resolve and bolstering his bravery.

"Yule..."

"Yes?..."

He took in another deep breath... and turned on his heel, lurching into a sprint. The movement caught Yule off guard and a surprised look lept onto his face "Chikily, hey!"

Chikily did not stop in his sprint, and once he had enough room to where he could use his wings without Yule grabbing him, he began to beat them and climb into the air. Yule only ran a few steps after him before the Harpy was rocketing into the sky, and he held out his hands in a gesture of silent confusion. When he understood that Chikily was not coming back, he turned and walked back towards the door, opening it and shutting it behind him quietly. It was around 1300 when he began to go through paperwork and read reports, and Peiper showed up with a few letters from Koko's Zerg Company, now named Zerg Brigade from what he could tell by the headers of the letters. Before Peiper could walk away, Yule called out to him.

"Hey Peiper, what did you send Chikily off t'deliver?"

Peiper rubbed his chin idly before he replied. "I haven't sent him off for anything, at least not today. Vhy?"

Yule squinted at him silently, rubbing the corner of a report between his thumb and forefinger as he mulled over his words. "No reason, thanks for grabbing the mail Peiper."

Peiper gave him two finger-gun gestures as an affirmation, then stepped out of the building to go run an errand with Britta. Yule opened up Koko's parcels and flattened them out on the large central table in the main meeting room of the building. He preferred this room, as it was large and only had one way in, surrounding him with comforting walls and the knowledge he wasn't going to be snuck up on. As he read, it seemed Koko was doing the same thing he was, recruiting the locals and drilling them into usable soldiers. He had been doing this before Yule in general, giving weapons to the folk who wanted to fight and using them as rudimentary guerilla fighters. Bellmoral had fallen to occupation, and the Chosen Children expanded out quickly, swallowing up land between Artry, Dreadfall, Olyfanor, and Orenbelle. Koko was frustrated at the loss of ground, but he was also getting more substantial troops like Yule was. The Regnesson Elves had finally convinced Koko to give them the formulas to explosives, and were now pumping out magical claymores that could tell friend and foe from small inscription spells that could be placed on the boots and pant legs of Auxiliary and Human soldiers. He included the inscription in the letter, and Yule called over an aid, having her write it down and run it up to the spell caster NCOs so they could have a look at it. Thanks to these claymores, they were able to stem the tide of Chosen Children, as well as cause massive casualties to anything not in a vehicle. The Elves of Regnesson were also developing an anti-vehicle mine they called Steel Renders, which would more or less turn a vehicle inside out from a magically infused shaped charge. Last but not least, Koko confirmed that his scouts had seen the production chassis for Bradleys and Abrams Tanks being shipped down to a city called Moongate, where they could be fitted properly and safe from their attacks. The last line to Yule from Koko was at the bottom, and he read it aloud to himself;

"We can halt them and take back Bellmoral, but I need you to attack the Veil. We cant let them bring in more vehicles."

Yule tapped his finger on that line, running it along the pen marks in the paper as he thought. "No . . . No we certainly cannot . . ."

He pulled out a slip of paper and began writing a letter to Fokhet. When he was done, he had at least ten pages of script, diagrams, requests, and a choice of favors he would owe the Dwarf.

"Call me a messenger." Yule yelled out, his voice carrying out past the door as he filled the letter holders and put them into a messenger package. Airis trotted up and filled the frame of the door, giving her hair a shake and finishing the process of clicking her harness together.

"Airis hears, as always."

Yule hadn't seen the Harpy in some time, and he stood up, smiling happily for the first time since his talk with Peiper. "Well hey there stranger, get over here and give me a hug! Thought you were off being a lump with Koko still."

Airis snorted, but clicked over to meet Yule halfway around the table, throwing her wings around him in a tight hug. "Nah, Airis been hiding and slacking off here instead."

"Well it's good to see you again. Got a letter to Koko and Fokhet."

Airis growled, looking up at Yule from his chest. "The Dwarf? He smells and so does Dwarf city. Always of coal and hot metal, no cool places to roost and rest . . ."

"Well then drop it off and fly back as soon as you can then. I don't expect him to write me back."

The Harpy bobbed her head from side to side, but nodded. "Good, quick drop off and fly back here in time for Taco day."

Yule broke their embrace and held her at arms length, looking down at her bare stomach. The Harpies had retro-fitted their uniform tops to end right below the ribs for males and females, something about how their wings moved made it uncomfortable for anything longer than that while in flight, but still gave them pockets as well as short sleeves for their rank and unit patches.

"You know, if you keep slacking off and eating, you'll be too fat to fly."

Airis formed her lips into a line and gave Yule a 'Really?' look, before plucking the letter bundle from his hands. As she clicked away past the door, Yule called out "Maybe you should take the long way home to burn off some extra pounds!", at which Airis poked her wing back around the door frame and gave him the finger with her middle wing claw. Judging from the waves of laughter coming from outside the room, Airis was definitely telling them what he had said. With his letters to Koko and Fokhet away, Yule finished up checking training schedules, ammunition shipments, and signing off on pay for the Auxiliaries. Once all the paper work was done and his fingers aching from all the writing, Yule judged his work done for the day and stood, walking back out into the light of the fading afternoon, the sun turning to the evening. He had enough time to light up his pipe before Yethis came walking up the parade with a Human, one he hadn't seen before. Now, Yule knew all the faces and names of his remaining Humans, but this blacked haired female was not one he recognized, and he puffed from his stem as he began walking towards them. Yethis saw him and began to jog over, her face flushed with giddy excitement. After she gave him a hug and took both of his hands into hers, which Yule found not really appropriate for working hours but let it slide, she gestured towards the strange Terran now a few feet away from them.

"This is my best work yet, you wont believe it."

Yule looked at her, confused, and took out his pipe, blowing the greenish smoke up and away from the corner of his mouth. When he looked back over at the Human, Yule's mouth opened a little, agape, and he breathed out in shock. "... Gremlin?"

Gremlin stood before them both, and Yethis was happily wiggling back and forth with her hands on her face. "Doesn't she look fantastic! She looks like an actual girl now!"

Gremlin glowered at the Elf. "Oh come on Yethis, that's not funny..."

Yule had to agree with Yethis, as Yule had never seen Gremlin this *feminine* before. Yethis had gone the whole nine yards, not only giving Gremlin a deep bathing, but also cleaning up her hair with a pair of scissors, brushing it, braiding it neatly into two thick twin braids, and doing a bit of make-up work around her eyes and lips. Yule bent down, hands on his knees, as he began to laugh, the cherry of his pipe falling out and scattering on the ground. "Wha- what on Earth!? Gremlin! You're like a solid nine now, what the fuck!"

Gremlin blushed, furious, while Yethis scooped her up in her arms, swinging her around as both of their braids swung in the air. "Look at her! Shes such a pretty woman nooooww!"

Gremlin had had enough of this, and wrenched herself from Yethis's happy arms, brushing her uniform to get the wrinkles under control as Yule wiped a tear from his eye. "Why would you let Yeth- Oh! Oh...." Yule stood up, squinting his eyes and pointing at her with his now empty pipe.

"Oooooh... you're doing this to seduce *Fino,* aren't you."

"Yes!" Yethis squealed, and bounced up and down on her feet in glee. "She told me she wants to be pretty and steal his heart away. Oh isn't it just the cutest?"

As Gremlin blushed further and held her left arm with her right hand in embarrassment, Yule stroked his beard as he thought. "Yes..."

He saw a pair of Specialists walking by, a Brimtouched and a Dwarf, and pointed them out, barking at them. "You two! Go grab Fino and bring him here, make sure he's fully dressed. GO."

They both jerked in alarm, their boots scattering gravel from the road, before they saluted and took off at a dead sprint for the command building. Gremlin was alarmed, looking from them to Yule. Before she could say anything, he held up a hand, motioning for silence. He then took that hand and put it on top of Yethis's head, stopping her from her near constant bouncing beside him. After a few minutes, there was a string of curses and yelling from the living quarters floor of the command building a few yards behind them, and the Dwarf bursted out of the front door, Fino hefted over his shoulder as he ran. The Brimtouched staggered out after them, holding a bloody nose and cursing under his breath. The Dwarf ran up to Yule and saluted.

"I have acquired the Elf, Commander."

"Just Yule will do, set him down please, and thank you, you are dismissed. Also get that nose looked at, but don't say who gave it to you." The Brimtouched rolled his eyes but gave Yule a thumbs up, and the two trotted away, leaving the four alone. Fino was livid, but quieted down once he saw it was Yule in front of him, and held out his hands.

"Why didn't you just come get me yourself!?"

"Mr.Fino, you are to be interrogated."

Fino's face dropped, and a fear began to swim in his eyes. He knew how Yule interrogated, and he had heard of what he did to the half-fae in the jail, and Britta loved bringing up that she survived a Yule interrogation with Fino. "W... wait, Yule, you can trust me, you said I was your guest!"

"I'm sorry, Fino, but I'm afraid I will have to assign our deadliest asset to interrogate you on your personal life, what you may know, your family, rituals and lives of the Southern Elves, as well as the type of training you went through. You may or may not come out of this the same as you went in, but I do hope you don't hold it against me. Desperate times, desperate measures and all that."

Without missing a beat, Yethis cracked her knuckles and flexed her arms while grinning toothily at the Southern Elf, at which Fino visibly recoiled and took a step back. Gremlin had her head in her hand, shaking it back and forth, as she knew exactly what Yule was going to say next. Yule waved at a pair of Auxiliary MPs that were standing near the command building, and they trotted over, having run around to the front of the building from their post after hearing Fino get yanked out of his room. Yule pulled them to him, whispered something in their ears, then spun them around to face Fino.

"Master Technical Sergeant Gremlin will be interrogating you in the command mess." Yule gestured towards Gremlin, who snapped her hands away from her face, resetting her appearance and posture, and put a pleasant smile on her lips while she idly played with the end of her left braid. Fino squinted his eyes, looking quickly from

Yule, to Gremlin, her hands waving a little when he looked over in her direction.

"I . . . what?"

He squeaked when both MPs scooped him up by the arms after Yule gestured at them, looking around at Yule when they turned him back towards the building he had been stolen from. "Again, my apologies Fino, may the Gods have mercy on your soul."

"What?!" Fino cried out, but he was already being hauled towards the building. Gremlin was starting to walk behind them, passing Yule and looking up into his laughter filled eyes.

"You're a real bastard, you know that?"

Yule just winked, and clasped his hands behind his back as she walked past him. Yethis had her hands balled up by her chest as she watched them walk off, then started giggling when Fino began calling out for Yule to 'grant him mercy'. His cries were cut short when the door shut behind Gremlin, and Yule relaxed his hands, bringing one up for a polite cough.

"Yethis. There is a window into the dining room where I told the MPs to take him."

Yethis launched into a run as if someone had poked her in the ass with an electric prod, and she quickly left Yule in the dust of her combat boots, sprinting towards the rear section where the kitchens and staff dining room were. Yule laughed for a few moments, dusting off the fronts of his pants, before he sighed, resting his hands on his hips and looking down at the ground. Setting up Fino and Gremlin on a date would probably not make up for him almost choking Fadithas to death, and the easement in his chest gave way to the tight feeling of shame once again. He lost control, he knew he did, all because the little half-breed had brought up his daughter and wife. Yule figured the fact she even knew about them had caught him off balance, causing him to snap and want to kill her simply for bringing them up in front of him. That thought gave way to another, and he began to slowly walk down the parade, a scowl growing on his face.

They knew about his daughter, and if they knew about her, they more than likely knew where she was. Had they talked to her? Disguised themselves as Feds and shown up to ask her questions about her 'radical terrorist father'? It dawned on Yule that he knew so little about what was going on over there, on the other side of the Veil, and he remembered something Britta had said a long time ago, when Yule was watching his troopers work her over in the back of the Sparkling Unicorn.

Yule stopped, and looked up from the ground, gazing out across the numerous barracks buildings and down at the thriving tavern below. He murmured out, watching his troopers carouse below after a day of training. "Your Midwest was almost in rebellion . . ."

He mulled the words over in his brain, reaching down and picking up a smooth looking stone from the walking path. Were the Midwestern States still in this rebellion? Were they trying to shut down the Veil? Just how much did they know as to what was going on with the Fae, and their plans? Yule sighed, and rubbed his cheek with his hand. He could really use more Humans over on this side of the Veil, more people with other expertise and knowledge that he could lean on. As it was, they were already such a small fraction of people, and he thought back to Kokos report. Zerg Brigade was losing Humans to small arms fire and artillery as much as he was. If his math was right, they had a small amount of casualties at the Veil when the supposed U.N forces had come through, then split with sixty six troopers for the both of them. Now, there were only 103 of them left, and it weighed heavily on both Koko and Yule. He looked down below at the Tavern, and saw that some of the Humans were there now, having gotten sets of cornhole boards made and were now playing against the Auxiliaries. Yule smiled warmly while he watched, and listened to the cheers and roars created from a game that only involved a couple of bean filled sacks, and a wooden plank with a hole in it. He stood there watching for an entire match before a noise caught his attention from the Medical Corps Headquarters, and saw Gruesome had stepped out for a smoke. Yule waved at him and began to walk over, and Gruesome waved back, scooting over on a wooden bench to make room for him

Yule groaned as he lowered down on the bench, and nudged Gruesome with his elbow. "You come up with that rank?"

Gruesome just smiled and shook his head, tossing his thumb over his shoulder and through the window behind him. Yule turned, and saw that Salili was inside tinkering with a few bottles of reddish liquid.

"Ah, your little doting hen made it up for you eh?"

Gruesome rolled his eyes, and blew some greenish smoke out of his nose. "She's creative, likes to make me feel important."

Yule chuckled and repacked his pipe, having lost most of his root tobacco when he saw Gremlin, and borrowed the Dwarven highland lighter from Gruesome to get his cherry going. While he puffed on the stem of his pipe, he looked down at Gruesome's arm patch, a Master Sergeant rank with a red cross planted in the middle, the edges of which were ringed in gold. It looked quite nice, and wondered if the rest of the medical and healer corps had the cross on their ranks as well.

The two veterans sat side by side in silence, both quietly puffing away on their root tobacco before Yule broke the quiet, stretching his legs as he did. "How is Salili doing, anywho?"

"Bed hog. Demands to help me shave every morning. Helps keep the nightmares away." Gruesome murmured, scuffing his boot on the ground in an almost bashful way. Yule watched him for a beat before leaning back against the wall behind them.

Yule kept his tone light, but with enough inflection to show that he knew exactly what Gruesome meant, thinking back to Alavara and their night at the Sparkling Unicorn. "Always nice, when the darkness is staved away."

Gruesome said nothing, just nodding and staring off into the distance. Silence took the two once again, both puffing out streams of green tinged smoke, and mulling over the memories that tended to haunt them when the sun came low on the horizon. A tinkling of jars rang out from inside the front entryway, and Salili opened the front door, her talons ticking softly as she stepped out and turned to shut the door. Salili saw Yule and smiled, bowing slightly to him. On her shoulder was a Staff Sergeant rank, with the same red cross in the middle, this time ringed in silver, not gold.

"Good to see, Salili hasn't seen Yule in fair amount of suns."

Yule smiled and bowed his head back to her. "Good to see you too, killer. I see you've been taking care of my medic."

Salili smiled brightly and nodded happily, stepping around Yule to Gruesome. Gruesome eyed Yule with a 'I'll fucking kill you if you tell anybody about this' stare, and he leaned forward, allowing Salili to rub her nose against his in a soft Kunik Kiss. A smile curled Yule's lips as he saw Gruesome melt in the heat of her affection, and she brushed her cheek past his scar covered one, whispering something in his ear. Gruesome went to smile, caught himself because Yule was clearly watching, and instead nodded, kissing Salili on the chin. She giggled, kissed him back on the forehead, and stepped back, bowing slightly to Yule again and then going on her way, walking down the parade. Gruesome watched her go, his eyes full of the smile he dared not show, then looked back over to Yule. Yule was leaning forward and resting his head on his hand, the elbow propped on his knees, and grinning smugly at the Corpsman, who frowned and growled at his Commander.

"That stays here, Yule."

"What? Your fraternization with the lower ranks?' Yule leaned up, clearing his throat and putting on an overly professional face, waggling his pipe up and down cheerfully. "I wouldn't dream of letting people know you love Eskimo kissing your little darling Harpy medic."

Gruesome, even though he was annoyed, blushed slightly and smiled angrily at yule, biting down on his own cigar. "Oh laugh now Army man, wait till you have a hole in you and I suddenly forget how to plug it."

Yule, mid pull from his pipe, laughed and began having a coughing fit, having inhaled harshly from the comment. The pair chuckled to themselves and finished their smoke, Gruesome grinding his stub on the ground and Yule tapping his pipe on the edge of the wooden bench to knock the ash out. The sun had fallen by that time into late dusk, and Yule stood, stretching and rolling his shoulders. In terms of getting things done, he did nothing more than scare his troopers, make a half-fae almost piss herself in terror, and do paperwork. Not the worst day, but also not the best. Yule bid Gruesome good night and walked off towards the bath house, washing himself of the day and letting one of the hired barbers trim his beard and hair after he had clicked his tongue at Yule disapprovingly. A few inches shorter all the way around his head, Yule put on his worn clothes and trudged back up towards the command bunker, walking in to find it deserted. He traced the murmuring of voices all the way to the rear near the kitchens and Command NCO dining area, where a huge huddle of personnel were stationed around the windows of the door. Yule bent down, looking past their heads, and saw that inside, Gremlin was still 'interrogating' Fino. It certainly didn't look like an interrogation, since Fino seemed about half drunk and Gremlin was pouring more wine into his glass even as Yule watched on. The two looked like they were having a pretty good time, laughing happily while gesturing at each other. Fino's face was flushed, and Gremlin kept fiddling with her braids when he spoke. Yule judged it to be just what he wanted it to be, and left them to it, heading up the stairs to his own room. As he took off his old clothes and pulled on a t-shirt and a pair of boxer briefs for bed, he frowned; There was no one here to soften the blow of his dreams, and he wasn't looking forward to dealing with that particular vice of the night.

He figured that he couldn't have everything he wanted, and crawled into his bed, sighing and setting the alarm on his phone. The generators that ran on an alcohol fuel mixture gave a lot of the base its power, and someone had been kind enough to provide his room with a single outlet, allowing him the ability to charge his phone and other electronics. To help not suck up too much power, his room still had oil and candle lamps, and he leaned over, blowing out the one on his side table next to the bed. His room was cast into shadow, and he laid back on the pillow, waiting for sleep to come for him again, this time alone. Sleep did not come easy, nor did the dreams come with good intentions, and through the night, Yule was treated to the memories of his deeds, the dead of the battlefield, and the eyes of a Southern Elf who died for nothing. As Yule dreamed, he thought the same four words over and over, as if he were practicing a montra in his sleep, or declaring the same oath over and over in his head.

I. Must. Do. Better.

* * *

Sunlight came in from the window, the first rays of the rising sun over the tops of the trees that surrounded Valhalla Hill, and Yule's eyes snapped open, giving a jerk of his arms as he did. His brain was mulling over how his daughter was doing, as the words of Fadithas had really dug into him for some reason, and he blinked tiredly, rubbing at his face with his palms. He slept, but no rest came to him, and he felt as tired as he had when he crawled under the sheets. His hands rasped over the skin of his face, and he coughed, looking around at his sunlit room. Yethis had been by, as there were vials of fresh blood on his desk, and he was not surprised he didn't hear her come in. She was spooky quiet at her worst, and if she knew he was asleep, she could ghost step like a wandering spirit better than the top special forces on Earth. With a groan, he rolled out of bed, his heels coming down on the floor with a thump and the creak of the bed frame. He yawned as he pulled on a shirt, his uniform, and grumbled as he put on his boots. His back hurt, his ribs seemed to be still knitting themselves together since being dragged back into the realm of the living, and he thought desperately that it could all be solved with an actual night of rest and not a night of thrashing. The door creaked open and he stepped out into the hallway, making his way down the dark corridor to the next few doors over, where he knew Fino was berthed. He knocked, heard nothing, then opened the door a crack, poking his head inside.

Yule snorted, and opened the door open wide, stepping into it and closing it behind him. In Fino's small bed was both he and Gremlin, the two curled around each other in a sleeping embrace. Amusingly, Fino's head was on Gremlins chest, and she had her face buried in his messy, partially braided hair, the two naked as jaybirds and Fino's neck covered in so many bite marks that it was like he had been attacked by leeches. Yule clasped his hands behind his back and strode over, rolling heel to toe to make as little noise as possible until he was beside Fino's bed. He cleared his throat softly, and Gremlin cracked open a hungover eye, blinking weakly in the sunlight filtering in through Fino's window.

"Interrogation went well, I see." Yule murmured, raising is eyebrows.

Gremlin didn't answer, but just pulled the blanket up around her and Fino. Fino responded in his sleep, snuggling in deeper to Gremlin and exhaling onto her collarbones. She brought a hand up and made a 'shoo shoo' motion with it, as if telling Yule he was ruining the moment that she had clearly worked so hard to create. He chuckled and opened the curtains fully, which caused Gremlin to growl in response.

"Go away . . ."

"I need to talk to you later today, after you've unwound yourself from the enemy."

Gremlin again made the 'shoo shoo' motion with her hand, and Yule turned, stepping over the piles of clothes and multiple wine bottles he had avoided the first time, and opened the door into the hallway once again. Downstairs, Chicks was waiting, drinking a hot cup of tea and writing up reports for Yule to read. She looked up and smiled brightly, her trusty rifle still slung over her shoulder. Now that he thought about it, Yule had never seen her without the damn thing, and had even seen her bathing with it to make sure no one else scooped it off of her. He looked to her shoulder and rolled his eyes, seeing that she too wore a Sergeant Major Rank, the golden star winking from within the space of the triple chevrons and rockers.

"Why are you guys wearing those things? Sergeant Majors? How tacky."

Chicks shrugged, her toothy canine smile radiating on her face. "Hey, we all agreed it would best fit our moods and mindsets. Command respect of the lower ranks and all that jazz."

"What's next, going to tell Privates to stay off the grass?" Yule said, sitting down next to her and pulling the report from her hands to read. She had been writing up the current strength of her Battalion, and he raised a brow to the numbers.

"Do each of you have a full Battalion?"

Chicks nodded. "We do. We have enough recruits that all of us have a healthy amount of Companies under us, so we all took a Battalion between us, giving out leadership ranks and drilling them by the book."

"I saw Donahue, Kole, and a few of the others were wearing Sergeant Major Ranks, who all took on the mantle of a Battalion Commander?"

Chicks leaned back in her chair, using her long rifle as a steady pole. "Well, me, obviously, I hand picked all the pretty boys for my Companies."

Yule stared at her, eyelids lowered and bringing his mouth into a line.

"... which i'm joking, of course. Anywhooo, Domino didn't take a full Battalion with him, but he wears the star. Kole, Donahue, Gruesome took the medical wing, Kentucky and Peiper also took up the star, bless 'em. Wulf volunteered, but has been busy working with the munitions and supply companies to whip them into shape."

Yule whistled, slapping his patrol cap on his thigh. "Eight Battalions? That's more or less a Division if you push the numbers around."

Chicks sipped her tea, setting down the metal mess cup with a small thud on the table. "All the Humans have taken up NCO ranks, all of us are teaching and commanding to the best of our ability. The veterans like you are thankfully full of military wisdom nuggets, and that's helped greatly. The Veil folk were chock full of their own veterans, and they were quickly promoted to help command, usually Guard Captains and Field Sergeants that trickled in."

She sighed, rolling her shooting shoulder to work out a few kinks from practicing the day before. "I'd call all of our drilled recruits green, but able."

Yule drummed his fingers on the table, chewing over a few thoughts that were doing doughnuts in his brain. "Do you think they are up to field operations?"

Chicks shrugged again, and picked her cup back up. "They'll have to be, won't they?"

"Yeah. I suppose they will. The Chosen have taken Bellmoral and pushed North. We have to start putting pressure on them and the Veil if we ever wish to get a grip on this situation."

She swirled the tea in her cup, watching Yule closely. "They are all very keen to get into the fight. The people you brought back from the push to Emalone have been filling them with stories, they want glory."

He chuckled in his throat, and put his patrol cap on his head, making sure the brim was flat and straight. "Those who want glory will only find death, Chicks."

She said nothing, but watched him stand, her dusky blue eyes watching him silently. Yule had gotten to the door and grabbed the handle when she spoke up, not looking back at him as she raised the cup to her lips, pausing before she drank to speak. "Every trooper on this base believes in us, in you, Yule. They see us as their salvation, for whatever reason. I can speak for most of us when I say we would happily die for them."

Yule paused himself, looking down at the door handle where his hand rested. He exhaled out his nose softly, before looking up and pulling open the door. "We already have, Chicks, and many more of us will find our resting place in this foreign soil."

Chicks smiled into her cup. "Ain't that the American way of it?"

A morose expression formed on Yule's face as he stared out into the morning light, shaking his head. "No, that's how it is for any soldier, I suppose."

Chicks raised the cup to her lips, and Yule closed the door behind him, walking out into the sounds of birds waking from their nests, and Companies of Auxiliary Troopers waking from their bunks to meet the day.

* * *

The next few days proceeded in a flurry of paperwork and crunch training for any and all Auxiliary Companies that volunteered for the push out to Sanrion. As one could expect, every Company wanted to go, so in the end, there was a base wide raffle to see who was going. Spittlejacks Reapers were one of the first ones pulled from the draw, and they happily added another streamer to their battle standard with the phrase 'First Picked' stitched onto it. Yule was unsure how long Fokhet was going to take with his request; While the Dwarves seemed to be full of magical handicaft, it was a tall order that Yule had requested, and he began making plans around it just in case it fell through. To deal with the armor coming through the Veil, Yule had enough Belchers ready with their rune-shaped charges, but he was not confident that they could pen through the composite plating that most modern vehicles sported for their frontal armor. He only had one vehicle to really test it on, after all, and the Paladin was a precious commodity that could not be wasted so frivolously. It was one night in the bath that Yule had the idea of seeing if they could be fired by horseback, and testing was done the next morning. To help the steed, they engineered a kind of plug for the horse's ears, so that way the horse wasn't in the business of losing their ability to hear after one shot. Recoil tests were then done, the engineers took the test Belcher and made a few modifications, and eventually the recoil was reduced to a dull body punch than the ripping rocket blast that it normally was. The Belcher mirrored the German Panzerschreck in every way except for the opening of the rocket tube having a face on it with its mouth open, usually a Dwarven face, or a Troll, and they were even working on putting more of the other species heads on the tubes as well. The Screeching Harpy faces would have a device inside that made it emit a high pitched screech when fired, which scared the ever living shit out of anything within fifty yards of it.

The Belcher could be used on horseback as long as the back blast was clear, a lesson the Veil species learned very early on after the Humans put a watermelon behind the tube and did a test fire to prove a point. Yule gave the horse he was on top of many, many treats after the test fires through the day, as while smart for a horse, the Elven horses liked explosions as much as any other equine, no matter the dimension. This knowledge in hand, and date night with the Fae troops looming ever closer, Yule called the drawn Company leaders into the command bunker, which many were just calling Headquarters now that it no longer resembled a bunker and more a proper building. With the Terran and Veil mid level NCOs present, Yule let them in on his plan; He was needing volunteers to fill out his 1st Dragoons, as well as a 2nd and 3rd Dragoons for the first push. The Dragoon units would be the tip of the spear, driving up through the line of advance to

Domino's dugout and then straight into Sanrion if they could manage. They lacked vehicles and a good line of fuel, so their best lay of course was to use horses to their biggest advantage. They were quieter, could operate stealthily at night, and could move through densely wooded areas where a vehicle could not. Behind the Dragoon columns would be everyone else moving up on foot to reinforce Sanrion if they managed to take it, or bolster the woodline dugout if they failed. A Brimtouched Staff Sergeant raised his hand, his name tape reading Rojik. This Brimtouched had an eye of extreme alley-intelligence about him, and was one of the few Brimtouched who trimmed down his horns for combat operations. Yule was taking more classes in Tunkah, and was trying to do this without his amulet for once.

"Sir, what about the Bradleys?"

Yule tossed his pencil down onto the table and put his hands on his hips. The command table had a huge map of the area on it and Yule had been drawing over it with pencil. After a Valley Elf Private made it known he could magic away markings, Yule had gone full bore on the pencil directions. "Well Staff Sergeant Rojik, that's where the Dragoons come into play. If Bradleys are present, you will spread out, like this."

Yule took out a sleeve of parchment and drew a single long square, then a column of smaller squares. "Bradleys are armored personnel carriers, these will more than likely be carrying troopers in the rear of them. If they are able to pin us and deploy, we're cooked. So, what we are going to do is ride up full steam with Belchers ready. The most important thing is to not waste the shot on the turret, or the front. What you do is, you spread out, spurr on as fast as possible, then try and outrun the gun that may be tracking you."

He saw a few of the Humans grimace.

"Yes, I know, its a shit game, but we're playing with outdated hardware fellas. We have to get in as close as possible, as quickly as possible, and get into the sides and rear of these vehicles. If, heavens forbid, an Abrahms is there, treat it the same, get in close, find the sides or the rear. If you're able to pen through the rear door, chances are you are going to shred the troopers within. Don't overthink it. Remember, they are your enemy, and they want to kill you just as badly. When you have fired your Belcher, do your best to reload it by yourself, or have another rider assist you. Each rider is going to carry three spare rockets to facilitate this."

Yule pulled out another piece of parchment and began drawing the top down layout of a Bradley, pointing to its hatches. "If by chance you are dehorsed and alive after the experience, you have two options: Sprint back to the safety of the trench line, or try and force your way into these things. Normally they will have the turrets locked so you can't do this, but stranger things have happened. This is where the driver sits, and here are the gunner and commander locations. If you find one unlocked, or able to somehow get one open, put your weapon inside and shoot anything that breathes. If you cannot get inside, you can still partially blind the vehicle by smashing the optics panels and destroying the periscopes."

Yule gestured to all of these components and the rough places they would be on the Bradley, even doodling a few, and more of the Terran NCOs chipped in their own knowledge. "Now, if there is a TANK, there, such as the Abrams . . . you kill it. Don't try to take it, don't be a hero, you pump rockets into it until the turret pops off and the thing is on fire."

Yule leaned down onto the table and looked over the wood lines and the large expanse of space between where Domino was and Sanrion. He hoped that the Bradleys would be nowhere near the area, and even if they were in the city, he could have Domino pump smoke out of the mortars and screen their way in. Yule frowned, and looked up into the faces of the soldiers in front of him. "Make it clear, after giving your orders and retelling what I've said here, that the Dragoons are going to experience heavy casualties. People are going to die purely because of the fact we have horses versus fighting vehicles. I'm expecting over half of us to not make it back here. Make it known, make it understood."

Everyone in the room saluted in response, and Yule leaned back up, saluting them crisply back. When the meeting was over, everyone shuffled out, and Yule turned to Yethis, who had been hanging back in the background, listening. Yule had confided to her what he *actually* thought the death numbers would look like, and the time for that conversation had come.

"Yethis, have you made preparations with the detail platoons?"

Yethis bowed slightly before she spoke, her face a mixed mask of resolution and sadness. "Yes, they will be ready to bury the fallen and collect names and patches. Are you still expecting over 80% casualties?"

Yule's shoulders sagged, and he felt tired. He looked down at the map, and quietly cursed in his mind as he thought about what had to be done. 'Yes, and I will be leading them into it. I can't let my troopers go at this alone while im in the rear safe and sound."

She stepped forward, placing a hand on his forearm. Her voice was soft, and almost pleading. "You dont have to lead the charge, there are other people that can do that. If we lose you, morale will plummet."

"If it gets as bad as I think its going to get Yethis, they are going to need something to rally around and keep fighting for. It would be irresponsible of me to send them out to their deaths and not be with them. The Dragoons have to pave the way for the rest of the troops coming in behind them, and if they must die, I will die with them."

Yule pulled Yethis in to a side hug, patting her shoulder with his hand as he stared down at the maps. It was reckless, and desperate, but they had to button up the Veil. Getting into Sanrion would allow for massive mortar emplacements to get set up and would let them shell the Veil day and night. If he waited any longer, or tried to push up more troopers on foot, they would be shelled, and there would also be the risk of vehicles ripping them apart as they moved in. Even with artillery support, the Bradleys had better optics and would clap them even as they charged in through the smoke on foot. It would be up to tactical horse movements to seize the city and outflank the vehicles, paving the way for the ground troops. The city of Imlnoris and Imra Ira Olora were doing their best to provide as many horses as possible that were war qualified, as well as driving any and all magic users to aid Yule, but there was so much more that a chaingun could do that a spell could not. Yule patted Yethis once more, and tossed his pencil onto the map with a wooden clatter.

This was not going to be pleasant, as if it ever was.

* * *

Domino's ears were ringing, and he held his palm to his eye, blinking blearly through the hazey, warbling view. That missile had caught him half footed, and he had barely enough time to duck his head down to avoid the majority of the blast. A few pieces of rock had skidded off of his skull though, and now his forehead was bleeding profusely. He heard people yelling around him, a dull and muffled sound, and looked over his shoulder in time to see Saveriss crash into him, bearing a med kit. She was screaming something at him, but he couldn't make it out, so he screamed something back that was cheerful and peppy.

"Hey pretty feathers!"

Saveriss shook her head, eyebrows furrowed, and started ripping open the medical bag by force when the zipper got caught on its teeth. After rending the bag open, she slapped a living bandage to the large cut on Domino's head, and he kissed her on the cheek with a cheeky grin. Saveriss, naturally, thumped him on the other side of his forehead, and Domino saw her mouth the words 'Not the time, stupid!' in Tunkah.

Domino blinked the blood out of his eye, his smile never faltering. "What? Combat is always a good time for mild firting!"

Saveriss couldn't help but smile, and she shook her head again in a more soft way. The moment was ruined when a string of 25mm rounds impacted along the front of the trench and they both ducked, avoiding the small fragments of metal that flew around them. Domino popped his head back over the top of the trench slightly to peer out at the huge open field in front of them, spying the little blocks that were coming at full speed and churning clouds behind them. There were constant flashes of light in front of them and then the impacts of whatever they were spitting out at the trench line. When it came to mornings, Domino had had better over the last few weeks, and this was not rating very high on the docket. They had completed a heavy mortar barrage into Sanrion only a few hours before the gun fire had begun, their heaviest yet, and they had been expecting maybe a probe or two to come by and try to shut them up with a little harassment. A TOW missile blowing apart a piece of his trench line was not a part of those expectations, nor was almost having his eye ripped out of his skull. This wasn't the first push by the Chosen Children, and all of his platoons were whirling into action, manning the machine gun emplacements and the hollow 'toonk' of Belchers being loaded were echoing out all along the winding trench.

The one kink in the battle plan was that there were no targets for the majority of his weapon teams, but he could at least maybe damage some optics on whatever was coming at them. He hoped they were only ASV's coming up, or maybe a Lynx or two . . . but he had an inkling that these may be those Bradleys that Yule was telling him about. Saveriss was having her boys and girls flying messages and ammo back and forth from the main base, their life line to keeping their mortar fire going, and it was only a shame they couldn't carry troopers back with them.

"Machine guns, I want ten round bursts, fire for effect on target, space 'em out! Belchers hold fire, we don't have much ammunition for them!" Domino was running up and down the trench yelling at the crowding Auxiliaries that were pressing to the trench front, taking pop shots with their rifles simply to tell their enemy, 'Im here, fuck you, come and get some'. Domino's mindset on battle was infectious, and after so many weeks together, it was almost as if there were platoons of Dominos running around with mad grins on their faces. His leadership skills while under constant counter barrage, assault, and probing by the enemy had kept morale soaring the entire time, even as casualties mounted on. Those who could fight, did, even firing their weapons as their wounds reopened and soaked through their bandages. Those who couldn't fight in the trench still did what they could, manning the mortars or running ammo to the best of their ability. Saveriss's talons were kicking up mud as she sprinted down the trench line, shoulder checking a Brimtouched out of the way as she ran down Domino.

"Domino, we can't fly, saw two try and go up and get gunned down, we're grounded."

He nodded at her. "Get your wings in cover, don't let them go up, we need them alive."

"What are we going to do then?! We are Harpies, we fly!" Saveriss was frustrated, and it showed on her face and eyes. They were not made and born for ground combat, they were born and made for aerial combat and acrobatics.

"Get your people a weapon that can use and stand by for boarders, Pretty Feathers."

Saveriss glowered at Domino. She hated it when he called her that, she really did, but he was showing remarkable leadership skills and a resolute contempt for fear when it came to combat, which was really growing on her. He also wasn't scared of her in the least, and seemed to always find a way to stonewall her, even now in the trenches among the explosions. A Valley Elf's head detonated like a pumpkin nearby, a 25mm round skipping on the dirt on the top of the trench and tumbling through his skull, showering the two and anyone else within a foot of him in brain matter and bone. Saveriss sniffed and flicked at a piece of skull cap on her cheek, while Domino brushed a bit of brain off of his rolled sleeves absentmindedly.

"Hm, seems they are getting kinda close. Better have the mortars try and fire for effect. Also, you've got red on you." Domino pointed at a large splash of cranial fluid on Saveriss's wing, and she tsk'd, forming her face into a mask of annoyance. Domino didn't stick around to hear her retort, jogging along the trenches and the lines of firing guns to the rear dug outs where the mortars sat. Here the wounded were stacked, laying against the walls of the large dugouts either unconscious or barely clinging to the din of the world around them. The more able wounded were lounging near the mortar tubes, already uncasing the rune-etched high explosive rounds.

"Oof, you guys look like shit." Domino said, jogging to a halt in front of the main echelon leader, another Brimtouched who was missing one of his low angled horns. He was missing the top portion of his ear as well, and his own eye was covered in thick bandages which wept blood from moving around too much.

"Aye, look who's talking Sergeant Major."

Domino and anyone awake had a good chuckle at the retort, and Domino ripped the full bandage from his head, tossing the blood filled little creature over the side of the dug out. "Alright, so we got vehicles coming at us in a scattered formation. We're not gonna be able to walk it with them, so I want you guys to start dropping rounds 50 yards away from us and push them back to 60, then bring them back to 50. Just have a saturated area of fire that they have to drive through. But first drop smoke 25 yards from the trench line, give us some cover. Okie dokie?"

Everyone gave Domino a thumbs up and echo'd his 'Okie Dokie' with their own. The smoke rounds left the tubes before Domino had even jogged a couple of paces, and he took the small window of time to hop up on the side of the trench path and look out at whatever was coming at him. His heart sank, as even from 200 yards away he could tell these were Bradleys coming at him, and both their coaxials and chain guns sang their song of death and demise towards the trench line. Casualties were light and a bit of maiming for the most part, but once they got close and were able to straddle a trench line, a single Bradley could just angle their gun down the line and decimate anything that sat within. He had to assume they were carrying troops as well, and would just walk the vehicles forward while the infantry mopped up whatever wasn't misted by the chain guns. The incoming fire was growing more intense by the second, and most of his troopers were starting to hunker down instead of taking pot-shots at the boxes of doom coming at them. Domino strolled ahead and stood next to Saveriss and a pair of her Harpy royal guards, all of whom were getting Betty ready with the last of the Dwarven armor piercing rounds that had come in that morning. The smoke rounds began to hit the ground when Domino picked up his belcher, loading a rocket into the rear of it and cocking the front lever that would generate the current to fire it. The white smoke was beginning to billow, but a few appeared to have hit something hard in the ground which fouled their purpose, instead throwing up a little bit of white smoke, and then dying in the ground.

This did however leave Domino a target in front of him, a Bradley that was charging gamely across the field towards the trench. He brought the rocket up and laid it on his shoulder, and when he turned to check the back blast, he saw Saveriss rack the charging handle on Betty and let out a screech of rage, snarling her nose and pressing down on the butterfly. Betty chugged out her AP rounds at the charging Bradley, and the rounds bounced and whizzed off into the distance, her fire tracing along the line of them coming towards the trenches. Domino looked back at his target, squinted his eye, and fired, the tube rocking him harshly as the warhead was launched and sent hissing after its target. Domino shook his head and watched the Bradley, as the rocket had a few seconds of flight time, and frowned when he saw the impact. It was a solid strike, cracking into the front of the armor plate, but from the lack of fucks given by the driver, must have struck the reactive plating. At the same time, Betty chunked to a stop beside him, and Saveriss looked to the Harpy on her left.

"More ammo Avise! Go get more ammo!"

Avise nodded and turned to run, but Domino halted her by catching her around the waste. "Belay that. No use for it. They're gonna push past the mortar curtain and they'll be on us shortly. COMPANY!"

Domino roared, turning and facing the bulk of his trench line. Heads came up and Platoon Sergeants began calling out in an echo to get the attention of their squads.

"AFFIX. *BAYONETS!*"

Everyone paused in shock for a heartbeat before the Platoon Sergeants echoed the order, and the rasp of hundreds of bayonets leaving their scabbards hissed down the trench line. Saveriss turned and screeched out to her Harpies who had bunkered down in cover, and a sudden flood of white feathered Himalayas poured into the trench line as well, flexing their claws and baring their long fanged teeth. Domino unslung his Dwarven FAL and clicked the rune-etched bayonet into place, then held out his elbow to Saveriss.

"M'lady, the enemy will soon be upon us, would you like to join me for a luncheon charge to the death?"

Saveriss was still gripping Betty's handles, and she looked up into the twinkling green eyes of Domino with both confusion and slight admiration. "You're going to charge them?"

Domino shrugged, his elbow still held out. "Eh, maybe we'll get lucky. Sure does beat dying in this trench. Feel the grass for the last time, not die like a cornered animal."

Saveriss leaned back while holding onto Betty's handles and laughed dryly. She knew what Domino meant. These things would be on them in moments, and even now she saw them rushing towards the wall of mortar fire churning up dirt and ground into the sky, as the smoke had died away. Belcher fire barked and thumped down the trench as the last of the ammunition was being used up, and only a few slowed down to a halt when their tracks were hit and rattled out from the drive wheels. Domino wanted to go out in glory, a final charge to the enemy, and was kind enough to invite her personally to the battle. Saveriss could not run; She was Himalayan Harpy Royalty, and they have always flown to the combat, not run from it. It had been that way for hundreds of generations . . . and it was not going to change, not with her. After she had her laugh, she released Betty, who tipped forward with the weight of her barrel.

"I agree. This trench would make for poor final resting place. Let us go touch the grass for final time." The Himlayas watched as Saveriss placed her claw into the crook of Domino's arm, and Domino placed a whistle into his mouth. The Harpies up and down the line began to chant an ancient Harpy battle song, and each species followed suit, all of them taking up a chorus of songs in their mother tongues and from their own cultures. Domino's Companies were going out loud, and in style.

"On the whistle!" Domino called out, and he pulled the whistle from his lips slightly, leaning down towards Saveriss as his order was echoed. She looked up at him, her face a grim but determined smile.

"You know, I've always found you quite fetching, Pretty Feathers."

Saveriss's smile grew into a toothy grin, and her grip on his elbow grew with more of her wing. "Who wouldn't. I am Saveriss, Queen of Himalayas."

Domino nodded in a sagely tone. "And you have very pretty feathers."

She couldn't help but giggle at the human, and then set her face back into her determined last stand look. "Yes. That too."

Domino could feel the treads of the tanks vibrating the ground now as they closed the distance, and they sped past the mortar curtain with very little damage over all to their vehicles. It was worth a shot, he wasn't mad about it. Dirt was falling from the walls of the trench as the vibrations grew, and Domino knew it was time. They had a better chance of charging than staying in the trenches and dying. If they tried to run, they would get gunned down by either the Bradleys or their infantry disembarking and hunting them down. All his riflemen had stopped singing, and were beating their rifle butts on the ground, thumping in rhythm with their bayonets glittering in the afternoon sun. The Bradleys were little more than 30 yards away now, and he brought the whistle up.

"Ready, Pretty Feathers?"

Saveriss nodded, and breathed in deep. "Let us hope the Gods smile down to us."

Domino nodded his head to the side. "Quite."

Domino put the whistle in his lips, and turned to look down the line of his trench before he blew. Now what he was expecting to do was take one last look at his troopers and cement them in his memory, just in case he somehow lived through this. What he was not expecting, was seeing Yule flying across the top of his trench on horseback and holding a Belcher in his hands. After Yule, dozens more horses followed, until it was nothing but a sea of legs and bodies leaping over the top of the trenches and roaring down towards the Bradleys. Saveriss's head was whipping back and forth, shock plain on her face, and they both watched as in a matter of seconds, almost an entire Dragoon unit had leapt over the trench network. After them another Dragoon unit passed over, their riders bellowing out their war cries, their unit banners flapping in the wind, and belchers held close to their sides while others fired rifles or smoke canisters. Domino saw the third Dragoon unit coming and blew his whistle shrilly.

"Up and over boys!" He roared, and pulled Saveriss with him, mounting the trench wall and sprinting down the slope of the fortification. Saveriss was giggling madly as she looked around and ran with Domino, while behind them, entire Companies cried out in unison and thundered down the trench slope, their bayonets flashing and shining in the sunlight as the last Dragoon unit swept to the right to go around the charge, and Himalayas took to the air with the cry of their Queen in their throats.

* * *

Yule landed hard on the other side of the trench and almost fell away from the saddle, clenching hard with his thighs. He coughed and righted himself, leaning down to keep a low profile as he looked around. They were running behind on time, and he had marched his Dragoons through the night to get here, and they had only managed to barely get here in time. A few more yards and the infantry fighting vehicles would have been right on top of the trenches, which would have been a horrible fate for Domino and his troopers. He swung his horse right to avoid a barrel swinging his way, and the chain gun churned up rooster tails of dirt and earth behind his mount's hooves, only barely getting away by rounding around the front of a slowing Bradley. As he swung around the other side, he took aim with his Dragoon Belcher and point-fired at the side of another Bradley a few feet away. The detonation of something inside exploded with enough force to rip the rear door off and away from the hinges, the heavy steel ramp rolling across the field like a danger plate. The passengers inside the troop compartment were blown out as well, mostly in pieces, and Yule grimaced; It was not normal for a Bradley to concuss that hard, and the only thing he could think of was that there had been something stored inside of the vehicle that cooked off with the heat round pierced the armor. The turret hatches blew open as well after a few more seconds of cook off, and flames poured out from the escape hatches. No one came out of them, and he assumed the entire crew to be cooked. He leaned right again and pulled out a spare rocket, fumbling with it and his Belcher as the horse took them in a wide arc. He was having trouble getting the rocket in when he saw another Bradley ahead was trying to offload its troopers, and in a split decision, whirled his rocket around like a mace and mashed in the face of a Southern Elf that had leapt down the ramp. The only noise Yule heard was the hollow crunch of the warhead denting facial bones and the gargle of the Elf, but was quickly off and away before his compatriots had known what happened. He pulled out another rocket and looked around, and found it to be a chaotic circus. Dragoons were dashing back and forth around tanks and pumping Belcher rounds into them at near point blank ranges, and also saw that Domino had charged down from the trenches, apparently having affixed bayonets and decided to not wait around for him to do all the work.

It was not all fun and games for the Dragoons, and the initial shock of their charge had worn off and now the turrets were spinning back and forth, chainguns pumping out high explosive rounds into horses with horrifying effectiveness. The screams of dying mounts and the sounds of gunfire was a noise Yule had never experienced, and he was not exactly super excited to indulge in it live and in color. He slammed his rocket home and knee steered his mount to the left, looking for a target, and saw a Bradley pull a hard right, charging down the main assault line it had been following with its fellow vehicles. He brought up the Belcher and fired, catching the Bradley's side armor at an angle when it lurched to the right, and while the warhead dug deep and spat its payload into the interior, the turret still turned and tracked Yule.

"Ah, fuck." Yule said matter of factly, and had enough time to pull his feet from the stirrups as six 25mm rounds impacted the side of his horse. Yule hoped the death was instant as the rounds tore through the chest and belly of his mount, and Yule leapt from the saddle as the body came down hard onto the ground. He tucked and rolled, but nothing could help the impact at the speed he was coming down at. Other Dragoons flew past him and he rolled back and forth, dodging out of the way of the hooves as the riders swarmed and pumped the assaulting Bradley with Belcher fire. The Bradley rolled to a stop as its hatches flew open, the driver and gunners trying to wiggle out and the back ramp coming down, and Yule pulled out his M9. Heaving for air, he came up to a kneeling position and pointed his pistol at the driver, spraying 9mm rounds in his direction until two struck him in the chest and neck. The Elven driver slumped to the side and slowly slipped back into his seat, and Yule took aim at the riflemen now swarming out of the passenger compartment. A rifle round split through his left thigh and Yule roared, rapid firing his M9 at a pair of Elves until the slide locked to the rear. One of the Elves went down, but another female was able to stay standing, clutching her stomach and firing her rifle one handed. Dirt impacts erupted around Yule as the Elf began charging him, firing wildly with her rifle, and he stood, roaring in challenge and pulling out another magazine. He slammed it home in his M9 and fired twice, the bullets finding their mark in the chest of the Southern Elf, and she fell hard to the ground, screeching in pain and dropping her rifle.

"Yule! Take mine!"

Yule spun around to the call and saw that Spittlejack was running his horse towards him, as well as holding out his Dwarven FAL for him to grab. Yule snatched the rifle and Spittlejack whirled, leaping from his horse with Dwarven War-axe in hand and taking a Southern Elf to the ground. Spittlejack had two gunshot wounds already, one in his arm and another in his hip, but it didn't slow him as he hacked the Elf on the ground to death, backhanding the rifle barrel away from him as if it were an annoying fly. Yule covered him and gunned down the rest of the passengers as they came around the rear of the Bradley, barely getting five steps into the battle as Dwarven 7.62x51 tore fist sized holes through their bodies. Yule clutched his chest, feeling a broken rib, and turned around as Spittlejack sidled up beside him, pulling out his side arm. Dominos forces had made it into the battle, and were either engaging the disembarked troops in melee combat or seizing entire vehicles. Himalaya Harpies screeched and pounced on Southern Elf troopers from above, biting deep into their flesh with claw, talon, and fang, or pinning them down with their strong legs as Auxiliaries bayoneted them on the ground. There were still more than enough Dragoons running around, and maybe he had only lost 10% of his initial forces, which was exceptional news. A Valley Elf private trotted up to them, saluting Yule.

"Yule, what do we do now?"

Yule pointed towards the approach of the Bradleys with his pistol. "Run down that way and see if anything else is waiting over there, then come back here."

"Yessir!"

The Elf spurred on his mount, Yule and Spittlejack watching as his horse kicked out small clods of dirt from the speed. Spittlejack went to say something to Yule, but the scream of a horse caught both of their attentions, and they looked back towards the Elf that had just departed. He had gotten maybe thirty feet away when he had ... hit something. The horse was toast, having rammed its skull into whatever it was it had hit, but the Elf had been thrown onto something ... and was *floating*.

Yule and Spittlejack stared on in apprehension as the Elf rolled onto his stomach, looking up and around in confusion and pain, before a head popped up next to him out of thin air. A Southern Elf looked at the Valley Elf, then shrugged up his shoulder, pistol in hand.

Yule turned and began to bellow out an order, Spittlejack turned and dove for cover behind the knocked out Bradley, and the Valley Elf rolled through the air towards the ground, a neat hole decorating his forehead. One by one, dozens of LAV-25 scout vehicles materialized into the view of the Dragoons and Domino's Companies, their barrels pointed forward and rear doors already coming open to disembark their passengers. The Dragoons whirled about, heard Yule, and spurred on, flying towards an enemy that only lay a few yards away. They roared in defiance of the odds, they held their banners aloft proudly as the wind caught them, and the only noise that could meet them was the boom of the 25mm Bushmasters, and the bark of the 240b secondary guns.

Ordinance wrought ruin on flesh, warheads spat their payloads through the thin frontal armor of the LAV-25s to snuff out those inside, and the screams of the dying echoed up into the sky.

The Fae had changed the rules yet again.

CHAPTER 18

THE CALL ECHOED out across the battlefield, following a multitude of screams and the bellow of fire. "Sprite! Fire Sprite! Get the fuck away from it!"

Yule slid another magazine into his Beretta, the weary metal rasping in the well of the pistol, while looking up and around, trying to find out who was yelling. He squinted, and across from the burning LAV-25 he was using as cover, he could see Auxiliaries and a few Human NCOs running at a full sprint away from a small cluster of the same vehicles, most of which were smoking and surrounded by their unloaded infantry. When the LAV-25s had appeared right in front of their battle lines, they had been only yards away, and began opening fire as soon as his Dragoons and Domino's Companies turned to engage. Their casualties had been light, despite the charge down the trench network and into the midst of the advancing Bradleys. However, being in the open, with a line of more Bushmasters staring them down, spelled doom for more Dragoons than Yule could bear. Closing the distance of less than twenty yards into withering cannon fire had skyrocketed casualties from 10% to almost 40% in a short manner of seconds, and the dead quickly piled up upon themselves in the charge. The Grim's Abacus calculations were swelled further by the spray of machine gun fire from coaxials, but his Auxiliaries had covered the distance and began fighting among the LAV-25s and their offloaded passengers. Yule had rounded up a small platoon of Domino's troopers and his own dehorsed Dragoons, leading them into a dive charge with Spittlejack rushing in beside him. They had caught two squads of Chosen Children as they were exiting out the doors of their vehicles, trying to push in on the blob flank of the main

Veil Rider force and roll them up towards the middle. Yule initiated close quarters combat with a spare fixed blade knife and his Beretta, cutting down Southern Elves left and right as another Veil Rider NCO brained Elves with a trench shovel beside him. Yule could recognize Master Sergeant 'Cheeki Breeki' Dolstov by just his usual outfit, as he had not been seen without his mask or his sharpened spade since they had come through the Veil in the first place. Master Sergeant Cheeki Breeki, while odd, was potent in close quarter battle, and helped keep both Yule and Spittlejack clear on their flanks as they pushed towards the LAV-25s to take them.

To no one's surprise, Cheeki Breeki knew the ins and outs of the vehicle and clambered inside into the driver seat once the crews' bodies were hastily removed. Cheeki Breeki turned the LAV-25 back on, clambered into the turret, pounded its partner vehicle with cannon fire until it bursted into flames, then shot out every smoke grenade that it had in its tubes. I was a messy affair, but Yule judged it to be a suitable application of the Bushmaster and the smoke munitions. Yule told Cheeki Breeki to rush the vehicle back to the trenches for safe keeping, then moved up to its freshly burning cousin to reload.

The warning call of the Fire Sprite and the sudden gush of a flame squirting out from the cluster of LAV-25s quickly grabbed Yule's attention when he got to the next LAV-25, and he formed the survivors of his ragtag squads around him.

"Spittlejack, we're going to creep in behind those trucks and wipe them out. Stay spread out, and keep your eyes open. Try to avoid bunchin' up and making easy targets for the Elves. If you see them pokin' their heads out of the mortar holes, pin them down and chuck a few grenades at them. If you see the Sprite, shoot him in the face."

Spittlejack barked out a laugh. "Well, not a very fancy plan but it will work."

"Fancy isn't really in my wheelhouse." Yule murmured, and hit the slide release on his Beretta, which rang slightly with the Dwarven ammunition going into battery. His Platoons moved in a large wing, Yule motioning for them to push out, and they crept forward slowly, cutting down any Southern Elves that ran out into their path and hauling away any wounded Dragoons that were alive on the ground. The battlefield was a mess of vehicles hammering away with their turreted guns, the screams and thundering of horses, and the near constant clash of weapons coming together in melee. A few squads of the smarter Southern Elves were packing in together and using their vehicles for cover, others running back and diving into mortar holes from barrages past, which either quickly filled with more Southern Elves, or screaming Auxiliaries jumping into them with bloodied bayonets gleaming. Yule shoved a female Dwarf down to the ground and opened fire with his pistol as a Southern Elf rounded the corner, racking a pistol grip shotgun and sending a load of buckshot whizzing over both of their heads. He heard someone cry out behind him, but didnt have time to look, putting three rounds into the Elf's chest in quick succession. Hot brass bounced off his face and then rolled down the back of the uniform top of Dwarf below, who hissed as the scorching metal kissed her skin. The Elf cried out, fired his shotgun wildly into the air, then toppled backwards onto the ground with a thump and jangle of gear.

"Eyes open, door-stop." Yule growled to the Dwarf, and she blushed in embarrassment, as she had been fussing with her weapon and never having seen the Elf round the corner. Yule tilted his head as he heard a Southern Elf talking loudly in their eloquent dialect, and pressed the Amulet to his head through his patrol cap. As he heard the words morph into English, he stalked forward, poking his head around the end of the LAV-25 and peeking into the passenger compartment.

". . . buying you time! They are all fucking around us and no one ran like we thought they would, they just charged into the vehicles! We're going to be swamped within minutes! . . . What do you mean you're only halfway done?! You told us it would be completed in- OH GODS HE'S HERE!"

Yule lurched forward into the passenger compartment and snatched up the lone radio operator by his uniform top and shook him, knocking the rifle from his shoulder and kicking it across the seats he was using as a table for the radio. He roared down into the Elf's face, and pointed his Beretta at his nose. "Done with what?! Halfway done with what!?"

The Elf squawked in terror and ripped his pistol from his holster, rushing to bring it up to his temple and kill himself before Yule could. Yule had his hands full with uniform and pistol, and instead of letting go of either, pitched forward and grabbed the Elf's wrist with his teeth. Yule bit down hard, and felt the crackle of bones breaking under the pressure of his canines, hearing them snap like twigs in his skull. The Southern Elf howled in pain and the pistol thudded down to the deck, tumbling towards the door and then sliding down the ramp into the eager hands of an Auxiliary. Yule spat flesh and blood from his mouth and brought the Elf back up into his face, bellowing as bright blood trickled down his chin.

"What is halfway done? Tell me! Tell me or I will rip your goddamn throat out!"

The Elf withered in Yule's grasp, and began to cry openly as panic gripped him, sobbing in the grasps of the boogy man himself. "The . . . the Queen's Gateway. It's being moved . . ."

Yule froze, and stared down at the Elf, who closed his eyes and waited for the final blow. The Elf screwed up his face, tears rippling down from the corners of his eyes, awaiting the final attack that would end his life. But no blow came, nor the click of a hammer and sudden blackness of death. His legs gave way and he crashed to the ground, Yule having released the iron grip from his uniform top. The Southern Elf wailed out in alarm and spluttered as he hit the ground, looking around in shock as he sprang back up from his back to a sitting position. Yule was standing still, his face impassive and hard to read as he looked at the radio, the glowing faces giving a flicker every few seconds.

"It was a ruse . . . This was all just a delayin' action to keep me from getting to the Gate." Yule said hollowly, and he looked over his shoulder at the Auxiliaries standing behind him near the rear of the entry hatch.

"What do you mean sir?" A Brimtouched asked, walking up and grabbing the foot of the Southern Elf. He dragged the Elf backwards and away from his thrown rifle, bringing him towards the Auxiliaries with a swift jerk. The Elf gave a short scream but silenced himself as the rest of Yule's troopers glared down at him.

Yule turned and walked out of the inner area of the LAV-25, sitting down roughly on the nearest edge seat with a rattle of shoulder armor and his battle vest. In the distance, he heard the roar of a flame and the screams of the burned, as well as the gleeful cackle of a Fae. "If I had left Domino and gone straight to the Gate, I could have dragged all three Dragoon wings into it. Instead, they knew I wouldn't let Domino die and would try to assist him, making a logical sweep up through Sanrion. These Bradleys and LAV-25s are a delaying action, nothing but a way to stall for time."

Everyone watched on silently, and even the Southern Elf was looking, mouth agape, as Yule tossed his patrol cap on the deck of the

LAV-25 and slid his Beretta into his holster. He ran the fingers of his rough hands through his sweaty hair and sighed. "They've won the first leg of this war. They're going to move the Veil as far back as they can and set up in a more strategic location, ain't they, kid?"

Yule was looking down at the Elf, who swallowed and slightly nodded. Yule shook his head a little and gave a short snort of bemusement. "You lot are heartless bastards, I'll give you that. That Fire Sprite some sort of commander?"

The Southern Elf nodded again, looking around at the glaring faces of Yule's Auxiliaries before he spoke out in English. "He is Almer Tornelis, Colonel."

"Does he like challenges?"

The Southern Elf squinted in confusion, but nodded once.

"Good." Yule said in a low tone, and put his patrol cap back onto his head, sliding his fixed blade into a separate sheath. He stood and strode over the Southern Elf, who recoiled and shrunk away from Yule, but then looked confused again when Yule stepped out onto the grass of the battlefield and strode away, Spittlejack jumping down and striding in Yule's wake. As the two walked towards the high cackling laughter in the distance, the Southern Elf swallowed thickly and placed his hands in his lap, looking up at his captors.

"Are you going to kill me?"

The Brimtouched from before barked out a laugh. "Fuck no, we're going to go watch! Here, come with us, this isn't going to be one to miss."

The Southern Elf was dragged up to his feet, checked for weapons, then brought along with the group as they walked well behind Yule and Spittlejack.

* * *

"Almer Tornelis!" Yule bellowed, and three platoons of Southern Elves whirled around in shock. Yule and Spittlejack had simply walked up into the middle of them, moving past those tending to the wounded or shouting into radios for checks on other squads. All of their attention was focused to the front of their ramshackle position, and had no mind to place a rear guard, which allowed Yule to just amble right up into their midst. Other Elves saw them on the way in, and seemed confused to see Yule just strolling along towards their commander, and actually waved back slightly when Yule held out a hand in greeting, as if to say 'Relax, we're not here to kill you". These Elves had formed a kind of wagon circle with a number of LAV-25s, and a fair number of dead Dragoons and Auxiliaries were littered around their last stand position, mixed in with their own dead. They had even begun dragging shattered horses up to fill the holes where the hulls of the LAV-25s couldn't fully cover those inside, and many Elves were huddled behind the carcasses, rapidly reloading loose shells into stanag magazines. Dozens of gun barrels whipped around to aim at Yule's chest, but neither he nor Spittlejack even blinked, waiting patiently for the Fire Sprite to step down from the top of the farthest vehicle. The Fire Sprite had his wings fully unfurled and beating on the air, heat radiating from them as if they were made from the coals of a forge fire, eating away at the oxygen around them. They swirled and twirled with the colors of fire; the roaring reds, the flickering yellows, the umber oranges, and at the very tips of the multi-part wings were the glowing blurr of blues and greens. To Yule, they reminded him of a DragonFly wing, but with six separate blades instead of the usual four. They buzzed as well, like some kind of demented bumble bee, and he found the noise to be irritating, akin to the sound of a grasshopper thudding across your path.

When he heard his name called out, the Fire Sprite turned from fleeing Dragoons sprinting away to look down at Yule, who had crossed his arms, even with dozens of rifle barrels trained on him. The Fire Sprite's voice was flat American, as if he was something out of an old black and white movie. "Oh! Oh ho! I never would have thought you would have come directly to me!"

The Fire Sprite was average for his height, most sprites lucky to push past five foot three, and shared the normal aspects of his Fae Race: Tidy long hair that was collected into multiple ponytails that ran down his back, the color of which matched his wings, large almond shaped eyes with red colorings all throughout around the slightly tapered pupil, and of course the huge wings that bore them aloft.

Colonel Tornelis touched down to the ground with a loud, locust like buzz of wings and held out his hands in greeting. "Well well! Mr.Yule, a pleasure! Im Colonel Almer Tornelis, Elder Sprite of the Ashul'Tee." He bowed, low, and to Yule it felt a bit mocking. Yule looked over the tips of his wings and saw that he had burned alive at least thirty of his troopers on his own, and he could smell the cooking flesh even from here.

"I hope your troopers can remember the name for me." Yule replied dryly, and Spittlejack gave a short chuckle.

Colonel Tornelis's face gave a twitch and he stood back up, bringing his hands together in front of him, fingertips pointing towards the ground. "Well. Anyway, its awfully brave of you to just walk up here. Even more shocking you weren't shot on sight. Oh, there are more of your lads now."

Yule turned to look over his shoulder, and saw that the platoons he had mustered were standing some feet away with their prisoner out front, and a few of his medics ushered forward, offering a few spare bandages to the Southern Elf Medics. Yule saw that the old saying of combat medics still rang true, as the Southern Elf Medics took them with a nod and began applying them to their own wounded; Any medical supplies are good medical supplies. Gunfire was still echoing and chattering around them, as well as the thump of belchers from the Auxiliaries, and Yule turned back around to the Fire Sprite.

"I caught wind of your plan, and you've won. I'll never get to the Veil in time." At the words, Colonel Tornelis smiled, and gave another short bow. "However."

Colonel Tornelis's head shot up at the 'however', and his face seemed suddenly unsure. Yule continued. "My lads and I will happily fight you to the death here, and those Himalayas will feast on the flesh of your lads and ladies tonight. You'll never make it out of here alive, and I do assume that was your plan; Delay to the death and fight for the seconds."

"Yes, that was indeed the plan we hoped to fulfill. And it appears to have worked."

"Right. Difference is, I'm tired of people dyin', always seems like wherever I go I'm havin' to either kill some poor bastard or watch my own men die. I have dead troopers all over this field for nothin'. It has all been for naught and I won't gain a single fuckin' thing from it. You've completed your objective and secured the victory conditions for your mission. As far as I see it, there is little reason to keep fightin', and the annihilation of your forces will be nothin' but bitter ash in my mouth."

Yule drew out one of his crossed arms and pointed at a very harried radio operator, her hair frayed from her headset and the stress of battle. "Order her to call for a cease fire."

Colonel Tornelis cocked his head to the side, a bemused grin on his teeth, but he turned to the operator and nodded to her.

She blinked and keyed up her radio, yelling into it just a tad too loudly. "C-Cease fire! Guidon, Guidon, Ember Actual, all units cease fire!" When she was done she looked up and around to the other confused Southern Elf soldiers sitting near her, back up to the eyes of Colonel Tornelis . . . and then to the eyes of Yule. Around the last stand position, the gunfire rumbled slowly away as if it were a thunderstorm rolling over them, and the two commanders didn't speak until the last clatter of gunfire chattered to nothing. The Elven operator went back to her radio and began talking normally into it, relaying to anyone listening what had gone on to that point, and Yule could hear the thump and rustle of hundreds of boots coming their way. Even now, Surviving Himalayan Harpies came down around them, clicking down onto the top of vehicles or dead horses, their claws covered in gore and soaked in blood up to their knees.

"So, Fae Colonel. I wish to issue a challenge."

Colonel Tornelis's eyes flared up with excitement at the words, his wings giving a flutter at the thought. "A *challenge?*"

"You're a dead Fae walking." Yule turned and looked around at the Southern Elves around him, both the wounded ones and the living. "You're all dead soldiers walking. You won't hold out much longer, we're in amongst you and will take you to close quarter battle until none of you are left to draw breath. Then the Harpies will make a meal of you."

At being mentioned, the Harpies ringing around the Southern Elves all grinned with their wickedly pointed teeth, some of them even licking at blood that already stained their lips. Colonel Tornelis leaned his head back, eyes hooded, and he played with the cuff of his left sleeve, the fabric smoking slightly at his touch.

"Ah, I see. Why suffer the deaths of a few hundred when you can only suffer the death of one."

"You win, you and your troopers head on home unmolested, mine will do the same and they will meet you on the field once again in the future. Plus I'll be dead, and none of this shit will be my problem anymore. If I win, I take your troopers as prisoners and keep them away from the lot of *you* bastards."

Colonel Tornelis closed his eyes and made a contemptuous movement with his lips, holding his hands palms up. "Why can't I take *your* soldiers prisoner?"

"I don't think they will allow that, Fae Colonel."

Colonel Tornelis snorted then laughed. "Probably a fair assessment. This 'Domino' wouldn't even budge off the hill, and even dug down into it to make his point. Very well Mr.Yule, name your terms."

Yule didn't move, nor did he hesitate after the Fire Sprite had finished. "To the Death."

"That's it?"

"That's it."

Colonel Tornelis looked quite surprised at the absolute lack of terms Yule had laid out, and looked around to the troopers that surrounded him. "Well . . . guess we'll be going home early then. Very well, Mr.Yule. Let's make a space for ourselves."

"Move away from here, leave the wounded to their dying, I'll meet you out in the middle. Staff Sergeant, clear all wounded out of the main combat area. Go find Domino and Saveriss, let them know what's up. Also, would you mind lending me a weapon?"

Spittlejack flipped his axe up, letting it turn a few times, before grabbing it by the back of the head and handing the handle towards Yule. "I'd be honored, Commander."

Yule drew out the golden flecked blade of gore from its fouled sheath, holding it with his off hand in an icepick grip while taking the Dwarven War Az in his main hand. Yule could use his Beretta in his off hand, but wasn't really in the mood. As he walked out of the last stand position and out onto the casualty strewn field, he was actually in a right *foul* mood; He had lost the battle for the Veil, and the enemy was clear and free to move it wherever they wanted, having taking advantage of his care for his own troopers. His mood was so foul in fact, that he reckoned that the only way to staunch it was to spill some Fae blood on this field and haul the body back as a trophy to Valhalla Hill. While he thought about it, he figured the wings would make as good a trophy as any. Southern Elf and Rider Auxiliary alike swarmed like worker ants to move wounded, the dead, or drag away dead horses to clear a dueling ring for the two commanders to perform in. Colonel Tornelis took the time to take off his uniform top and fold it, as if he intended to put it back on later, while Yule took off his patrol cap and tossed it to a nearby male Himalayan. The Himalayan plopped it onto his own head, figuring he could keep it warm for his Commander until he was done with his duel. Yule then took out a bit of twine from his pocket and tied back his hair, bringing it back into a single strand at the back of his head. He needed his eyes clear, and did not want this Fae to burn his last patrol cap away.

As the two prepared themselves, the ring of the circle filled with a mingling of races, all shoulder to shoulder, either sitting on the ground, standing around, or laying down on their stomachs, resting heads on rucksacks. Domino, supported partially by a bloodied Saveriss, trudged up to the ring as well. Saveriss had taken a few hard slashes across the chest and stomach, barely held in check by healing drafts, while Domino was missing a piece of one ear, his left eye was a bit of a mess, and spat out one of his own teeth as Saveriss took a canteen from a nearby Auxiliary.

"What's fucken' going on?" Domino murmured, taking the canteen after Saveriss took several gulps and held it out to him.

A solitary female combat medic Yammatu looked up, having pulled a spare healing potion out of her satchel for a wounded male Oni. "Commander Yule challenged Fire Fae to duel."

Domino squinted, water dribbling down his chin as he swallowed a mouthful of the canteen's contents. "Well.. thats pretty fucken' stupid."

Saveriss reached up and wiped away at his chin with a blood covered wing claw, and Domino knew it was probably the blood of the Elf she gored to death not even a few minutes prior. "Domino darling, you are leaking your water. Hey, Private Medic, do you have any bone draft? He has teeth to grow back."

The crowd surrounding the two commanders continued to murmur and chatter like this for a few minutes until the two combatants in the middle settled, staring at each other. No one was interested in causing an issue for their Commanders and distracting them from the duel, which caused most to give each other their space, or at least keep things amicable. There was a wide berth around the middle, as the Fire Sprites fire magic could fly quite a ways, and Colonel Tornelis looked quite comfortable from where he stood, roughly ten yards away from Yule. Yule looked as angry as he ever was when looking at a Fae, and the wind pulled at his beard slightly as it came across the battle scape. The two stared each other down, the crackling sounds of burning vehicles, the groans and moans of the wounded and dying, and the light hush of the wind whirling around them being the only sounds they could register. Yule tilted his head slightly, seeing the Fae wiggling his fingers a little as if he were a duelist in a Western, readying themselves for the draw.

... Hes going to throw fucking fire at me, why didnt I keep my pistol out? Yule thought, and slammed his knife back into his sheath around the same time Colonel Tornelis whipped up his palm. It was an awkward draw, but Yule managed to get his Beretta out around the same time a ball of fire roared past his shoulder, the heat so intense that he felt his skin blister just from it being within a foot of the exposed skin of his neck. Yule hefted the Az and brought up the pistol, firing at the Fire Sprite in a steady pace as he sprinted towards him. Colonel Tornelis brought up his other hand and Yule watched as the bullets impacted an invisible barrier, turning to molten metal and dripping down from the impact site as if they were warm honey hitting a hot pan.

Cheater. Yule thought, and began to rapid fire, peppering the Fae with copper jackets as he closed the distance. Colonel Tornelis threw out his non-shield hand and let loose what looked to Yule like a horizontal tornado of flames, the sound a terrifying mix of a forest fire roar and the low tone of a tornado. It spiraled towards Yule and he saw no other option than to chuck the pistol at the Fae and dive under the funnel of fire, rolling along the underside to pop out on the other side of it. The feeling made Yule wonder if it was what a pizza had to feel when running through a conveyor oven, and rolled onto his feet as he completed the dive. As Yule ducked and rolled, he was followed by a cloud of steam that rose up into the air behind him, the sweat and moisture from his body and clothes being flashed cooked away into mist. Colonel Tornelis was grinning as he held out the funnel of fire, burning and blackening the grass where Yule had been standing, but his smile disappeared from his face as quickly as the water had from Yule's body.

"Wha!" The Fire Sprite squawked, and brought his hands together, a thunderclap rippling through the air and booming towards Yule. Yule winced as the sound wave thundered over him, but kept his eyes open despite the protests of his instincts to close them. He was glad he didn't, as while this shockwave was noise at first, another wave of flame was whirling in the wake behind the concussion of air. It was slower than the fireballs, and he reckoned that it was to mop up whatever was dazed by the first strike. As it came towards him, Yule ducked low and shuffle ran towards Colonel Tornelis, who was sweating with the concentration of channeling two different spells at once. As he spotted Yule, wreathed in the steam of his quickly drying body and ducking under the fire wave, the Fire Sprite cursed and began to beat his wings deeply, the bass of the sound thudding the air and pushing away at the charred grass below his feet. Yule brought up the War Az from Spittlejack and drew out the gore-knife on the run, flipping it around in his hand and bringing it back into its ice pick configuration. Colonel Tornelis squinted his eyes at the blade, then flared them open with realization of just what Yule was planning to do.

"Oh no, not me! Not this one! I'm not going on that blade!" Colonel Tornelis roared, and brought up both hands, one forming into a small buckler shield of magical flame and the other into a long sword composed of pure magical radiant heat. Yule didn't even halt his advance, and slammed his shoulder into the Fae's chest. Colonel Tornelis expected a slash or a weapon attack, and had brought his weapons up accordingly, but was caught half footed by the sudden impact of Yule's armored shoulder into his sternum. Colonel Tornelis had lived all through the middle ages as a duelist, taking pleasure in dispatching humans folly enough to try and match blades. Centuries of leading the easy life and living mostly for the indulgences it had to offer had left him a bit rusty in his reactionary reflexes. The lack of keeping up his martial practice now blessed him with a broken clavicle from Yule's shoulder, and he wheezed, his wings beating rapidly to keep him balanced.

Yule was unrelenting, and brought the War Az up and then down towards the head of the Fire Sprite, who caught the blow on the dead center of the fire buckler. The edge of the bite became instantly cherry red with the heat of the contact, and the shield rang out with a magical twang as it fought back the thrice forged clan steel. A Dwarven edge, of course, could not be dulled by such trivial things as heat, and Yule ripped it away from the shield, trailing rivelts of flame that erupted into small hungry motes of fire on the ground. Despite the buckler, Colonel Tornelis had felt that blow, and beat his wings harder, wishing to get a height advantage above the tall Human. As he rose into the air, Yule sniffed and whirled both his weapons once in his hands, then came down into a high ready stance with them both. Colonel Tornelis roared and flew at Yule, slashing with his radiant longsword, and sent a long whip of the very essence of heat at Yule.

Yule decided to risk it, and let the whip of heat bounce off of his standard issue shoulder armor, so that he could perhaps have the chance of grabbing the Fae by the foot. As he watched the metal heat and then *melt*, he thought that maybe he had chosen the wrong course of action. As the cooling molten metal began to burn through the lower elements of the armor and scorch his skin, Yule threw the War Az at Colonel Tornelis, who's mouth opened in both surprise and his own horror. Standard issue armor for the Veil Riders was not Dwarven clan steel, but normal steel made via the ways of the Valley Elves and Brimtouched, and Colonel Tornelis had seen his own flames melt the steel down to slag just minutes before Yule had walked up into the last stand defensive area. He had judged that Yule would try to dodge it to conserve the Human's armor, giving himself the advantage of both height and having a free slash or two at Yule. Instead, the Human took the magical slash right on the shoulder armor and embraced the molten metal dripping down onto his uniform, and now Colonel Tornelis was on a collision path with a Human that could more than likely fold him into a pretzel. Colonel Tornelis put the brakes on with his wings, beating backwards as fast and as hard as he could to arrest his downwards ascent, but it was far too late to back out now, as he had to duck slightly to avoid the War Az. With a shout of indignation and surprise, the Fae was grabbed by the polished black boot by Yule, and whipped down onto the ground, the charred grass and dirt embracing him as softly as a rock would a clay pot.

Colonel Tornelis felt two of his wings crumple and crack as he rolled, the light bones that made up their construction being wrent apart as he was unable to tuck them in fast enough before the impact. He came up to his feet, wings askew, and coughed, a small trickle of blood pushing past his lips. He had bitten down hard onto his cheek when he met the earth, and now his mouth was beginning to fill with trickles of gold flecked crimson. Yule sniffed and tossed the gore-knife to his main hand, bringing it low into a hammer fist hold and his other hand into a high guard. Colonel Tornelis stiffened, as he remembered this kind of stance back when he used to fight against German Knights during the Teutonic Orders Wars. The Teutonic Orders had figured out they were being played, figured out who was doing it, and began to try and assassinate Fae after discovering a rudimentary way to tell who were Fae and who were not. Their toll of death on the Fae Kind was still felt all the way to the modern day, and it was only by bribery, infiltration, and political subterfuge that they were able to turn the Teutons away. Plus the Mongols really took them to the cleaners when it came to hiring fees . . .

But the stance of Yule, the wild long hair tucked back into a single curly ponytail, the look of pure hatred in his eyes . . . it harkened Colonel Tornelis all the way back to the days in the German and Polish countryside, fighting against the formidable early Teutonic Knights before they were watered down by Fae trickery. They had found power from something, something else that had come through the Queen's Gateway, and drew from it defiantly on their own crusade through Europe. They were men wreathed not only in steel plate, mail, and blade, but a conviction matched by none. That same conviction, that same . . . power, radiated from the Human in front of him, and he didn't like it . . . He didn't like it one bit. Colonel Tornelis lashed out again with the radiant long sword and then threw his flaming buckler at Yule as he charged, his feet thudding rapidly on the ground as he sprinted. Yule decided the lash would be as fun as the last one and ducked it, the crackling whip of heat whirling away into the crowd of onlookers who had to dive out of the flight path. The flaming buckler bounced off of his front armor plate and washed his mag pouches in licking fire, but Yule brushed them aside and strode forward towards the charging Fae. Flames were not nearly as scary as that whip of pure heat, and the scorch marks on his armor were superficial if anything.

Yule launched off his left foot into a two step sprint before slamming into Colonel Tornelis, who this time was ready for the bodily slam and rolled with it, swimming under Yule's arm and avoiding the upward punch of the gore-blade that was aimed for his chin. Yule felt the swim and spun on his heels, almost catching the Fae with his back swipe. The fight here was close, and when Colonel Tornelis moved his free hand up to use magic, Yule would slip forward under the hand and slug the Fae on the chin, or simply slap away the hand and bring up his knife to force the Fae to attack with his sword. It was a bit comical attacking a sword wielding opponent with more or less a pommeled boot dagger, but Yule could tell that this Fae was rusty, and feeling a bit dizzy after the third punch to the cheek. Colonel Tornelis was beginning to panic as his vision began to swim, and it was becoming harder and harder to keep the Human in front of him. Colonel Tornelis landed two good swipes onto Yule, but the Human would just hiss and riposte with his knife, the wound smoking and hissing as it boiled the exposed blood and cooked the flesh it touched. Deja vu began to strike him as he remembered this same thing happening in Poland, and only being spared death by mace to the nose when his Footmen had managed to stab the Teuton to death with spears. This time, however, there were no footmen, no spears, and only a very angry Human with a small dagger, that was slowly beginning to win. Colonel Tornelis had one last ace up his sleeve, and swallowed in a gulp of air after parrying a slash from Yule. The air in his lungs combusted, and Colonel Tornelis's eyes watered as he held it in, waiting for the right moment to breath it out, and went to spew it forth when Yule was recovering from the heavier parry. What Colonel Tornelis saw in his head was a gush of fire, the Human breathes it in, perhaps singes his eyeballs, hair catches on fire as a distraction, any of which would lead to an easy win after he dispatched Yule with his sword. What he didn't see happening was Yule shoving his entire hand into his mouth to block the flames, and the Fae's heart paused for a few beats as he felt the human's filthy knuckles pass his rear molars.

This was a thing that never happened, or at least was never discussed or seen: Fire Sprites were well fire resistant on the outside, normally able to plunge an entire hand into a coal fire and come out with nary a mark, but what happened when the fire from their lungs was blocked? It was not a pleasant process igniting the fuel in their lungs and breathing it out, and it was seen as a last resort kind of trick since it did cause a bit of irritation, and could lead to voice loss, but it was never known for anything to ever *block* the exit for the flames. Colonel Tornelis felt panic, and his flight response coursed down his nerves as the flames retreated back down into his chest, and sat there, burning inside of his lungs. His heart began to cook, the flesh of his esophagus began to blacken, and the pain was like nothing he had ever felt before. Yule, of course, thought the Fae was going to explode, which would have been spectacular by his reckoning, but instead of this, he felt his knuckles begin to blister and saw that smoke was starting to pour out around his fist and out of the ears of the Fae in front of him.

Hah . . . it appears we are not fireproof after all. He's going to cook me from the inside out . . . Good show. Colonel Tornelis thought, and his organs began to blaze.

Fire took to his heart, his lungs, his stomach, eating all the way down his tracts and charring him from the inside out. This fire, this magical fire, did not want to feed off of just air, but magic. With no more air to have, it instead attacked the only fuel source it had left; The blood and organs of the magical thing that had ignited it. Colonel Tornelis choked out around Yule's fist, dropping the radiant blade and clutching Yule's forearm with his hands, but Yule was unyielding, looking down at the Fae with furrowed brows as he was burned from the inside out. Only when Colonel Tornelis's eyes started to blister and blacken, his hands going slack, and bubbling fluids beginning to hiss out from his ears, did Yule decide it was enough and brought the blade across and through the side of his temple, dispatching the Fae with steel to his cooking brain. While Yule hated Fae ... the Colonel dueled him to end the fighting. He could make this one suffer a little less, even if he did not truly deserve it. Unknown to Yule, Colonel Tornelis was grateful for the mercy, having heard the hiss of the blade coming for the side of his head as his ear drums began to boil from the heat building up inside his body. The magical heat had been feeding off of the very magic in his blood, and he would have had a lot longer to die if Yule hadn't dispatched him as soon as he did. The metal rang as it punched through Colonel Tornelis's skull, and when Yule pulled it out, the metal was smoking from the heat, baking the gold flecks into the broad face of the blade. Yule ripped his hand from the Fae's mouth, his skin blistered and burned to the third degree, but the feeling was dulled by the nerves being cooked away down in the Fae's throat.

Colonel Tornelis's body ragged dolled to the ground, curling up on itself as the fire ate away at the interior of what was left of it, and smoke began to pour out of any place it could escape, whether it was from the nose, or a fresh new hole in the flesh. Those around Yule were silent, but when he turned around to hail a Medic, he saw that while his half of the viewers were looking on in a positive way, all the Southern Elves were stricken. No Auxiliary moved to disarm them, no one racked a weapon and began cutting them down, they all just stared on at their iron Commander. Two medical Sergeants rushed out from the crowd and began pulling out healing salves, at which Yule held out his heavily blistered hand and did his best to straighten out his fingers. As the Medics slapped on gobs of what looked like glowing beeswax and began wrapping it in fresh linen, Yule looked up, and addressed those around him.

"Who is your highest ranking officer, Chosen Children?"

Southern Elves looked around and began talking to each other, their voices hushed and hands clutched to their rifles. After a few minutes a female Southern Elf walked out from the larger throng of Southern Elves, down from where Colonel Tornelis had started the duel. Yule grinned with his canines out and turned as far as the Medics would let them, hearing her walk out from behind him. Despite her Southern Elf heritage, she looked less fine boned than her brethren, and her ears, while not as high angled, were far longer than any others he had seen before. She had bright copper hair that shimmered in the light of the sun, and her eyes were almost pearl white, flecked with little sparks of orange as if a chef had zested a citrus fruit onto a pair of white plates. Her face reminded him of someone back home, and he slid his gore-knife away into its sheath before placing the hand on his hip.

"I have to say, you look mighty familiar. You got a sister?"

"Had, a sister." The Elf said, and her voice was rugged in comparison to Fadithas's high arrogant tones.

"Your last name Fadithas like her?"

The Elf's mouth parted slightly, and she walked forward quickly a few more paces, her face losing its put upon stern look and gaining one of hope. "Have you seen her?"

"Yeah, she's alive. We're not friends. What's your rank?"

The Southern Elf smiled for a beat before wiping it from her face, standing tall and defiantly in front of the human. She may be only five foot nine, but she was going to make every inch count, even if she had to raise up her heels. "I am a Captain of the Queen's 13th."

From Yule's side, an Onii whistled in a mocking tone, in which all the Himalayan Harpies nearby whistled in return before they all broke down into cackling laughter. The Southern Elf Captain's face flushed red with indignation and she bristled visibly. Southern Elves were not the biggest fans of Harpies, as unlike they're Valley Elf Cousins, they were far easier to fly away with due to their lighter body builds, and it was not unknown in the histories for Harpies to freely hunt on Southern Elves during times of strife, migration, or lack of wartime activities to keep them preoccupied. Yule cleared his throat while looking pointedly at the Harpies, and they all coughed into their wings, keeping their mouths hidden as they continued to smile toothily.

"Captain Fadithas. I lied, when I said I was going to take you prisoner."

Captain Fadithas stepped back, her boot crunching on the blackened grass, and a ripple of panic erupted around the gathering of bodies. Southern Elf soldiers were looking back and forth, some even bringing up their weapons at a low ready, prepared to fight to their last if it came to it. Yule saw . . . and Yule approved.

"Im not going to take you prisoners, or even kill you. What do you have left, maybe half a Company? A few battle worthy Platoons? You were sent here to delay me, to die to the man." Yule turned slightly to look at his troops. "I am these trooper's Commander, and I am here, on the field. Where are *your* Commanders? Those who would send you out to your deaths with nary a second thought, and only spare a single of their kind? I knew I was sending my lads out here in the thick of it, in the risk of it, and I knew I had to come with them. What did yours think?"

Captain Fadithas set her jaw, her eyes dagger-like as they stared at Yule. "We had to keep you from getting there. That is what we were told."

"And then what."

"And then what?" She said, and seemed taken aback. "What do you mean?"

"Were they going to send help?"

Captain Fadithas turned to look at the radio operator from before, who shrugged, and then to a 1st Lieutenant who shook his head from side to side, no answer to give. She turned back to Yule, whos Medical Sergeants were finishing up with his hand. Yule gave his fingers a little wiggle to see how fast the salve was working, and raised his eyebrows in surprise. The pain was coming back in hot throbs, but that meant it was somehow healing his nerves back to full working order. While he flexed his hand, he walked towards Captain Fadithas slowly, looking around at the torn up ground of the battle field. His Auxilaries and Human NCOs moved up with him, striding proudly behind as Southern Elves ducked and ran towards their own on the other side of the dueling ring. Colonel Tornelis was nothing but ash now, and had long since blown away in the wind that washed across the open field. Yule gave all the Southern Elves time to gather, seeing they were some shy of a full Company, and far less than they had arrived with. Yule had to imagine, as he counted all the burning vehicles and the hundreds of dead littering the outside of the ring, they came into the battle a ways short of what Yule brought, and were now whittled down to just these combat abled.

"Were they going to send help, to get you out once the Veil was moved, Captain Fadithas?" Yule kept his face neutral, but was now standing right in front of her a few feet away, and slowly crossed his arms.

She looked away, just past Yule's hip, and pursed her lips together, mulling over what she wanted to say until she looked back up into Yule's eyes. "No. I suppose they weren't. We were told to hold for every second we could spare."

"A tactic that won them their victory, but at what cost, Captain Fadithas? I rode out of my way to bail out one of my subordinates-"

"Best friend actually!" Domino called out, and Yule heard Saveriss giggle.

"-and best friend, and his troopers. It may have cost me this victory, but they will all mostly be going home, always would have been, while you would have been cooling off in a mass heap in one of those mortar holes." Yule nodded towards a larger crater, and while she did not look away, a good portion of the Southern Elves looked over towards where Yule had nodded, and saw many give a shudder.

"They also shelled their own troops, just to try and kill me. I have a friend of mine back at my base that can attest to such. My quarrel is not with you, Southern Elf. I realized that when I killed a young lad and saw the fear in his eyes. You folk are as much a victim as my troopers, the elves that died in the artillery strike, and even that poor kid that was told to guard a picket on the wrong night. My quarrel is with the Fae, and I want to offer you a choice."

Southern Elves brought down their rifles, some even placing the buttstock on the ground and gripping the barrel as they stared on. The female radio operator looked around hurriedly as everyone brought down their arms, and she took off her headset, her hair fraying out around her long pointed ears.

"You can go back on your own, and we won't chase. We have things to prepare, and a good friend of mine is working on something special. Something you won't enjoy."

Southern Elves looked at each other, confused, while Captain Fadithas raised her chin slightly, eyes hooded. "And the other?"

"Simple, follow me home."

Yule smiled, uncrossed his arms, shrugged while holding his hands wide, and turned his back on Captain Fadithas. "Any vehicles that are driveable, get them running and back up to the trench network. Gather all the horses that are still walking and bring them back too. Gather the wounded into the trucks and haul them back, then gather all our dead.

We're burying them at the hill. Jesus christ Domino what happened to your face?"

"I tripped on this dummy thick Harpy."

"Don't be so rude Domino! I told you I was sorry, I had to take care of an Elf that was rushing you from behind . . ."

Captain Faditha's was bewildered, and only had a moment to stammer out a choked sound before Yule was swallowed up by his NCOs and other chains of command. The enemy turned and busied themselves with their orders, some lowering down dead drivers to idle Southern Elves so they could try and get their LAV-25s restarted. Captain Fadithas spun around to look at the survivors of the Queens 13th and they were as lost as she was, some of them barely functioning walking wounded and others gasping out their last breaths from where they lay on the ground further in the distance. She turned back around, trying to see Yule, but was instead greeted by a small staff of Medical personnel who dropped off spare satchels of supplies. Captain Fadithas tucked a few loose strands of hair that had escaped her hair bun back behind her ears and pursed her lips again, staring down at the bags of healing drafts and fresh salves. She stood there for a few moments, before turning around and addressing her surviving troops.

"Destroy that radio, and grab these bags. Lets get our wounded able to move."

* * *

There were quite a few vehicles still in working order, some of them blessedly being a pack of less-than-fair Bradleys and the majority being LAV-25s, with most of their crews being mulched by Belchers or having piled out to run. The Southern Elf survivors had retreated into the woodline to discuss what they were going to do, and left the forces of Yule to their work. The dead outnumbered the living by a margin that made Yule sick to his stomach, and the patches pulled from their uniforms filled multiple empty medical satchels, but he didn't feel good leaving them here or burying them in the trench network. These fallen, he was taking home to rest, as they had at least earned that respect, even the Southern Elves didn't deserve to lay in the holes here. Surviving Dragoon horses were hitched to wagons brought in by Domino that were stored far into the woods to avoid getting damaged by artillery or attacks, and the bodies were stacked upon these for transport. Harpies were flown to Valhalla Hill with news of their defeat and to ready the details Yethis had drummed up, while other Harpies were sent on straight to the main cities and holds of their allies. Everyone would have to know the Veil was moving, and to prepare for the worst. When all the bodies were loaded and everything was ready to go, Yule began sending vehicles and wagons in a long trail back home. He was sitting on top of the LAV-25 that Master Sergeant Cheeki Breeki had snatched up with Domino and Saveriss, the three of them chewing on field rations, sucking down health drafts, and discussing their wounds. Saveriss was boasting about her new scars and saying they were 'great marks of pride', while Domino was grumping about his eye. While his teeth were grown back bright, pearly, and white, and some of his missing ear had returned, his eye failed to recover, and was now covered with a spare wrapping of linen. Yule flexed his off hand, the skin a bit tough still, and remarked on how it looked.

"Looks as if I kept it out in the sun too long, gonna be red like this till I die I reckon."

Domino chuffed. "Well, at least you won't be looking like a cyclops."

Saveriss leaned on him and kissed his filthy, blood stained shoulder. "Don't worry, I have seen far uglier cyclops."

Domino tried to look angry, but his smile betrayed him. Yule made a disgusted sound and scooted away from Saveriss a few inches, who made a soft playful hiss at him. His skin crawled regardless, and he grimaced at her openly. Auxiliaries filed past below in formation, most of them talking about the day or their time in the trenches, and appeared to be in good spirits despite the defeat dealt to them by the Fae. As the companies filed past, a fresh face came up over the lip of the trench, and the copper hair of Captain Fadithas was like a beacon. Yule waved at her while Master Sergeant Cheeki Breeki glared from the driver seat, giving the engine a little rev.

Yule leaned down and tapped the Human on the top of his stylized Stahlhelm. "Lets not flatten our guest, Cheeki Breeki."

He leaned back up and slid down the front of the vehicle till his feet were able to dangle down, and Captain Fadithas stepped forward, stumbling over a bit of loose trench before regaining her footing.

"Mr.Yule, ah, where are our dead?"

Yule popped a dried blueberry into his mouth. "I'm taking them to be buried, you don't need to worry about them."

Captain Faditha's eyed him, but nodded, scuffing her boot on the dirt and sending a few harder pieces skittering across whatever grass was left. "I've made a decision."

"Oh?" Yule said, chewing and tossing another blueberry into his mouth. "What would that be?"

Captain Fadithas turned and stared back down towards the battlefield where vehicles still burned, or smoked, and then turned back to Yule. "I want to see my sister. I'm bringing the survivors of the 13th as an honor guard."

Yule chuckled, tossing a few more blueberries into his mouth before bowing slightly and holding out his arms wide. "By all means, I welcome you as guests. Feel free to travel with me in this truck and have your people fold into mine."

She seemed unsure, but whistled out over the hidden slope of the forward trench. In a tidy column, a formation of Southern Elves marched forward, flying their colors proudly and all their rifles at shoulder arms. Yule's troopers slowed to let them weave into the long file on the road, and their banners snapped and waved with the rest of the companies that walked along, the wind playing along the battered and blackened fabrics. Yule watched Fadithas as her eyes trailed her Company, and when she looked up to him, Yule was smiling softly, and holding out the bag of dried blueberries to her.

"So, tell me about the sister *you* know."

CHAPTER 19

"Fifteen minutes out, Yule."

"Thanks. Follow it down the line and let everyone know."

"Can do. Skinwalker 1 out."

Yule leaned his head back slightly as he gave the inner vehicle radio receiver back to Master Sergeant Cheeki Breeki, having to reach through the small space between the turret seat and the driver seat. He knew they were going to start naming the damn things, but they were already getting too creative in their process. The Bradleys were all named Skinwalker and then a numeral, while the LAV-25s were being named after whatever meme happened to pop into the heads of the Veil Riders in them. Behind Cheeki's vehicle, still unnamed, was Big Barreled Goth Girlfriend, and behind it, the Hotel Moscow. They had barely gone half the distance towards Valhalla Hill and they were already penciling in the names on data sheets. Yule was afraid to find out what the rest were named.

Unlike her sister, Captain Fadithas had been relatively good company; She trusted the Human as far as she could heft him, but he had spared her life and the lives of her Company for whatever reason. While she told him about her sister's youth and being blessed with a touch of the Fae, she began to go back over the reports she had read of Yule, as well as the warnings. Yule was supposed to be barbaric, incredibly violent, did not take prisoners unless they were female, and had been pinned as a bloodthirsty terrorist. There were even rumblings and rumors that the only reason he took females as prisoners was because he was trying to build a 'fantasy' harem to despoil at his every whim. But as she watched him listen to her intently while fussing with reports from his soldiers, he seemed more of an overworked dad trying to herd a bunch of children. There was of course a bit of truth to the report, as the man was as vicious as a cornered bear and took down an Elder Fae in a duel, but she didn't see the monster that he was played out to be. He held up a finger and took the receiver from Cheeki again, and a look of frustration came over his face as he began yelling at another vehicle over their name.

"No, *no*, I forbid you from naming it Femboy Hooters... No, damn it, Milf Dennys is just as stupid, what is wrong with you?"

Captain Fadithas had no idea what he was going on about, and shifted in her seat, looking around at the little cluster of Human Veil Riders that had come with Yule. The one named Domino was snoring lazily in his seat, while the others seemed to be reading little cartoon books or playing on handheld devices. Captain Fadithas had been introduced to smartphones via them getting brought in through the Veil, but had never had an opportunity to hold one; They were seen as items of status and power, with only Fae and high ranking Chosen Children being allowed to use them. The one thing that struck her as odd was... all of the Humans still wore the flag of their home kingdom, a flag with red and white stripes, and a field of blue in the corner with little motes of white that looked like pentagrams. She eye'd them as Yule continued badgering the person over the radio receiver, and Captain Fadithas looked up to the Humans sitting beside her.

"If you're terrorists... why do you still wear your kingdom's flag? The United Sovereigns. We were told you defected to try and take the Veil for yourself... yet you still bear your colors." Fadithas asked, loudly enough so that the entire compartment could hear.

Domino's closed eye snapped open, already looking at her, while the other Humans leaned back, rolling their tongues in their mouths with annoyance as they closed their books, or clicked off their smartphones. Even Yule stopped yelling for a moment into the receiver, his eyes slowly narrowing. Kole shuffled through the many pages of his comic book while sighing, then slapped it onto his hand before looking over at Captain Fadithas.

"Terrorists, is it? That what they said?"

Captain Fadithas nodded, and beads of sweat began to form along her hair line. She expected the one named Domino to answer, not to have all of them looking at her with daggers under their lashes. "Yes, they said you attacked a relief party and tried to take the realm as your own."

The humans all looked to each other, while Domino snorted. Captain Fadithas continued. "You were declared rogue, a terrorist group. They said you attacked friendly Human soldiers, were amassing guerilla fighters, and were planning on creating your own kingdom."

Kole smiled. "That sounds like a lot of work, nor is it entirely false. What did they tell you about the relief group?"

"It is said that they were United Sover-"

Kole interjected politely, holding up his hand. "States, United States."

Unlike Yule, Kole and the other NCOs were drilling themselves in the native language of Tunkah with fervor, as it seemed to be a shared language among the many folk of the Veil and was a language they could count on them knowing, besides the mother tongue of their nations.

Captain Fadithas leaned forward slightly. ". . . States, relief group to rotate you back into the Rust Blood Realm. It is said you refused to go back and killed the entire relief group, then fled away from the Veil in order to start recruiting soldiers for your own doing."

Yule and his Human NCOs were all looking heavily at Captain Fadithas, who swallowed and looked around to Yule, his eyes locking onto hers. What she saw inside them, whirling down below in the depths, almost made her double back on thinking he may not be as bloodthirsty as the reports had said.

Yule spoke up this time, setting the receiver on his thigh and pressing the Amulet down onto his scalp. He was catching words he did not like, but could not easily understand the rest. "What else is said."

"Well . . . I've just had reports to read, you understand, and have caught chatter from the Tavern and Dining Halls. It is said that you attacked the Human convoy and killed them, to the man, when they refused to join your side. Then you sent spies into the base that rings the Veil to turn others to your side, and they were pinned traitors and hunted down. There have been a few others, but they were either never found, or destroyed. Right now both sides of the Veil are working together to make sure you don't destroy and enslave this side. The nations of yours are working together to keep . . . us safe from . . . you."

Silence filled the interior of the combat vehicle as all the Humans stared at Fadithas, who was now looking confused down at her boots as she slowly rubbed her thumb along her knuckles. It stayed this way for some time before Yule spoke up.

"Do you believe this? This narrative that you are being presented."

Captain Fadithas looked over to Yule, her eyebrows drawn together and causing a slight wrinkle between them. "I . . . I don't know. I'm not sure. Judging from the reports, you never would have spared all of my riflemen, and would have taken me for a trophy. Yet here I am, still clothed, my riflemen marching along, alive, and the Rust Blood Beast looking at me with a radio in his hand."

Yule clenched his jaw as he eye'd Captain Fadithas, while in the background, he saw Kole mouth 'The Rust Blood Beast, *wow*' to the NCO beside him, who shook his head, eyes closed, and was fighting to keep a smile from his face. The receiver key'd up, and Yule held it next to his face, never taking his eyes from Fadithas.

"Five minutes out."

"Roger, Skinwalker 1."

"Skinwalker 1 out."

Yule held the receiver back to Cheeki Breeki, who took it and tossed it to his TC to put back on its cradle. Yule sighed out through his nose, broke his eyes from Captain Fadithas, and looked over to Domino.

"I'm going up and out, watch the Captain."

Domino nodded, then gave his eyebrow a wiggle. Yule already knew what he was on about as he went to stand up from within the turret, grabbing onto the turret latch. "And yes, do be sure the Captains clothes continue to stay on. Would hate for our reputations to proceed us."

The humans began to cackle with laughter, while Captain Fadithas looked embarrassed, doing her best to look normal while her face flushed so hard, it looked as if she had gotten an instant sunburn. Yule shook his head, creaked open the hatch, and made his way down the vehicle's top as it continued to rumble down the road, going back to his perch right near the driver's hatch. Cheeki Breeki opened the hatch when he realized Yule was there and raised his seat, his helmet and mask popping up over the rim of the armored lip. Yule looked down at him, then back up to the forested road, humming the same tune that he could hear Cheeki Breeki muffedly singing from under his mask;

"Wo alle Straßen enden, hört unser Weg nicht auf . . ."

* * *

The air was fresh and crisp from the front of the LAV-25, and the ride all the way to the first checkpoint outside of Valhalla Hill went smoothly. The convoy was waved on, the Harpy runner was sent on their way to the headquarters building, and Yule continued up the road towards the top of the base. The last checkpoint, or last gate, into the main section of the base was manned by Cockram, an Australian Veil Rider that spent most of his days tinkering on engines, and hoping one day that he would get to create a magical mech to operate in battle. Beside Cockram was another Veil Rider, one of the few that could instantly put a sour look on Yule's face, and he rolled his eyes as soon as the LAV-25 came to a halt in front of the gate. Cockram looked up from his wooden chair, tipped back his patrol cap, and gave a wave.

"Hey there Yule."

Yule clenched his jaw again while fixing Cockram with a flat stare, his lips drawing back into a displeased line. "Hello, Cockram."

Cockram had even gotten on the nerves of the Dwarven engineers with his lust for battle walkers and robots, and he also knew just how to vex Yule with barely any effort. Even now, Yule was making a concerted effort to not look beside Cockram, and the Australian wrapped an arm around the back of the other Veil Rider, holding out a hand and gesturing while he spoke.

"Commander Yule, why won't you address the other soldier on duty? That's mighty rude of ya', with all the work she puts in."

Master Sergeant Cheeki Breeki's shoulders were bucking from his laughter, muffled by the mask he wore. Yule knocked his knuckles on the back of Cheeki Breeki's helmet with a metallic thud, but did not remove his eyes from Cockram's.

"I have no doubt . . ." Yule flicked his eyes slightly to the Veil Rider beside Cockram, and his eye twitched. ". . . *Corporal* Megumin has done much for the moral of Cosmoline Company, but there is no need to address the body pillow directly."

Cockram gave a stage gasp and pulled the Megumin dakimakura closer to him, acting as if he were clamping his hands on either side of her head. "Commander Yule! How could you?! You know how she takes it when people call her a *body pillow*."

Anyone nearby the gate had caught onto what was going on, and were now chuckling and watching the exchange. To the Veil Folk, they found the weird mascot something of an oddity when it came to the Humans, and they all wondered just how they would react if they ever found a wizardess or sorceress that matched the strange cartoon's appearance. Cockram began to try and console the dakimakura while Cheeki Breeki was dropping his military bearings and skidding on them.

"Cockram! Open the fuckin' gate before I turn that body pillow into *cheese cloth*." Yule growled, but the Australian was not one to be cowed.

Cockram pulled the dakimakura around and placed it in front of him, holding its face in line with his own. "Say please."

'Please' was not needed, as when Cockram heard Yule cock the hammer on his Beretta, the Australian cackled and ran for the main gate retention latch, still holding the dakimakura in one arm. Yule decocked his Beretta and placed it back into his holster, mildly glad he had retrieved it from the duel site. Cockram opened the gate and stood by it, holding Megumin in his left arm while saluting with his right. As Yule passed, he just gave Cockram the finger while grinning, the Australian breaking down into fits of giggles along with the Auxiliaries around him. This was, unfortunately, the only bit of mirth Yule was going to be allowed, as when the lead LAV-25 had reached the headquarters building, Yethis was waiting there for him, along with the entire burial detail he had requested.

When all the vehicles were parked, their hatches were opened to reveal the stacked bodies stowed in them, the only vehicle with a completely living crew being Yule's. One by one, they were retrieved and placed side by side; Southern Elf beside Oni, Harpy beside Valley Elf, Brimtouched beside Dwarf, and here and there was a slain human, their eyes staring up into a foreign sky that was not of their homeland. Himlayan, Brush Feathered, and every Harpy inbetween came down to watch, many of them bloodied from the very battle that had happened before. There was a particularly strange looking Harpy that looked to be some kind of Raven, and none of the other Harpies were too keen to be near it, let alone look at it. Yule talked to Yethis and pointed all down the long parade, and she nodded, speaking up to the detail around her.

"Line the parade, one body per two feet. We will dig them into the ground afterwards." Yethis turned to look at Yule, and he crossed his arms, nodding once. "This is to remind us all of the cost of command, and the value of sacrifice."

She swallowed hard, turned, but stopped, seeing Captain Fadithas coming around the rear of Yule's LAV-25, the Southern Elf's eyes casting here and there as she looked around. Yethis's face twisted, and she went for her side arm almost immediately, but Yule cleared his throat, and pointed a free finger at a few Southern Elves already laying in line with the Cosmoline dead. Yethis set her jaw, glared at Captain Fadithas, but moved on with her duty, directing those in her funeral detail in their instructions. Captain Fadithas brought her hands together behind her back and looked down at the gravel and dirt of the parade, her eyes flicking around at the Auxiliaries around her and then to Yule. Pairs of Auxiliaries trudged past, one holding a pair of legs and the other gripping under armpits as they moved the bodies, while others carried slain Harpies along in their arms, cradling them before laying them down in their spot. Yule stood, arms crossed, and watched. His Human NCO's, those who lived through the battle, watched, and Saveriss flew down to stand beside Domino, who wrapped an arm around her shoulders.

The vehicles were more than half way empty when the wagons pulled up into the parade as well, the dead stacked high on them, and more funeral personnel walked over towards the wagons, pulling down bodies and hefting them to where they needed to be. The sun began to swing over towards late evening when Yule began to walk, arms still crossed and combat armor laid down on the parade, and he looked down into the faces of those down on the ground. Behind him, his NCOs followed, while Captain Faditha's brought up the rear. Yule remembered the faces of the Humans; a Californian here, a Texan there, a Montanian with his velcro patches stained in the blood from his throat. He stopped before the Montainian, his hands still locked in the death grip on his weapon, a Zastava M70. Yule grimaced, but stepped up to the body, removing the magazines from their holders and putting them in his own pockets.

"Im sorry, brother." Yule murmured quietly, slowly pulling the weapon away from his hands and placing the now empty palms down onto the front of his plate carrier. "I'm sorry this wasn't the adventure we had thought it would be."

Yule knew burying the Human with his rifle was the right thing to do, but he had a better idea in mind for the weapon, so that in a way, this Montanian would live on far longer than his bones and gravestone ever would. Yule watched as his NCOs did the same with every fallen human, collecting the arms of them to be preserved, to be placed in the histories along with their names. Yule handed the M70 and the magazines to a Dwarven Corporal nearby, giving him orders to take it to the Engineer Quarter and put it in for blue print harvesting and longevity treatments. The Dwarf bowed, and took the weapon, holding it with reverence, almost as if it itself were a part of the slain Human on the ground. Several Dwarves were sent off in this way, until every Veil Rider Human's armament was collected. The last of the carts were unloaded when the foot troops began their march up, and there were quiet, angry stares when the Queen's 13th arrived with them.

Each Company stood before the work being done on the parade, not sure what to do when they were put at parade rest. As they watched on, the 13th were shocked when they saw their Captain walking along with Yule, the Human gesturing down to other Humans laying on the ground. She was nodding every now and then as they walked along, while Veil Auxiliaries began arranging bodies so they could all fit within the length of the parade grounds. No one was sure what was more tragic when it came to the work being done; The fact there was so little parade to go around, or that even with the long expanse of space, there were far too many bodies to fit. Yethis jogged over to Yule and Captain Fadithas, and Yule bowed his head so she could speak into his ear. He nodded, and Yethis jogged away, spreading new orders. In order to get it to where all the bodies could be laid to rest along the parade . . .

. . . they would have to be arranged in multiple rows.

The holes took time to dig, and the Queen's 13th were in for their next shock as they stood at parade rest with the other Companies. As the bodies were being lowered into their earthen resting places, Yule took off his uniform top, and began to help. His NCOs moved to do the same, but a single look from Yule made them halt and reconsider their decisions. Domino stood behind Saveriss near the area where the Companies stood, his hands on her shoulders as she stoically tried to look like the warrior Queen she was, even when her bottom lip gave a wobble now that she saw just how many Harpies had died in battle.

Silently, Yule, Yethis, and the funeral detail lowered down the bodies in their holes, and everyone could see the hard look etched across Yule's face as he helped. Yethis seemed to always be on the verge of a breakdown, but held herself in check so she did not look weak in front of Yule. The rest of the detail were doing their own level best to look as professional as they could, but some sniffed heavily when they saw someone they recognized. Bodies were not tossed, but laid down gently, then arranged in a way that the slain looked as if they had merely laid down for a long rest. When a Harpy was arranged, the living Harpies would take turns plucking a feather from their wings, then laying it down under the hands of the body. The other bodies were left with other trinkets befitting their culture; The Oniiplaced a small empty bottle of wine in the hands of their own dead, The Brimtouched bound the hands and wrists of their slain brethren in bright white ribbon, wrapping it from the tips of their fingers to the tops of their shoulders. The Valley Elves placed sprigs of flowers and wheat along the chest of their dead, and baskets of the offerings were constantly being passed around from grave to grave. Dwarves placed down runed etchings on stone, placed directly onto the forehead and bound there with a single small mote of gold, dripped hot and directly onto the dead flesh so it bound the stone to the bone. The gold was of a magical variety, being poured from metal pots carried about by other Dwarves, and was cool to the touch until it touched something other than metal, where it cooled rapidly and stuck in place. The large detail toiled back and forth as they prepared the dead, while the rest of the base watched on silently.

The Companies watching on stood as they were told, but again, when the sight of someone they knew caught their eye, one could see a knee or two buckle as they fought for control. When all the bodies had been moved and prepared, the digging of churned earth began as they were covered with it, and Yule took to the task angrily. Sweat ran down his arms and soaked into his shirt as he dug, stabbing the spade into the mounds of soil, and others dug around him. He burned through five graves until he came before one of a younger female Southern Elf, her arms crossed over her slight chest. She had been hit with fragmentation from a Belcher, her body rippled with metal fragments that stuck out of her in harsh angles. She had bled to death, he could see, as the crimson trails still stained her chest, mouth, chin, and nose. He stabbed his spade into the ground and leaned onto it, looking down at her as he panted and wiped at his forehead with his hand.

"Who were you, I wonder . . ." He panted, looking down at her face, her eyelids closed and sparing him from their supernatural color. "A baker? An artist? What would you have been if I had never shown up, never come across the Veil."

"School teacher."

Yule closed his eyes, sighing out heavily as he looked at his patrol cap sitting some feet away. "Know English do you, Captain?"

"I do. She taught me. She was plucked from the scholarly to teach us and be an interpreter if it ever came to it."

Yule heard the Southern Elf walk up beside him, also hearing a spade tinkling on the ground as she dragged it. He opened an eye and looked to her as the sun began to set, causing the orange flecks in her eyes to burn. "What business does a school teacher have on the battlefield?"

Captain Fadithas looked down at the dead Elf's face, shrugging as her mouth gave a twitch. "I don't know. She was part of the 13th, we were all told to go."

She had been digging, as she had taken off her uniform top and her under shirt was speckled with sweat and soil. Her uniform top did a lot of good at hiding her figure it seemed, and Yule wagered she got all the curves while her sister got all the crazy instead. He shook his head and gave a short, harsh chuckle before standing up straight, pulling his spade up from the ground. The Brimtouched making notes for her headstone was finishing up with his annotations, and after he stuck a rod into the ground with the tag, he nodded to Yule.

"Well." Yule sighed again, and stabbed his spade into the dirt, looking over at Captain Fadithas as he put his boot on the spade's lug.

"Well." She sighed back, and she brought her spade up and around to her hands. As the ground began to hide the body down below, piling up around her form, Captain Fadithas paused as Yule continued to shift soil down into the hole.

"Does it get easier?"

Yule scooped up a load of dirt and paused, looking over to Captain Fadithas. A single tear was rolling down her cheek, and she was leaning hard on her shovel, her eyes bearing down on the slain Elf's face. The soil had not quite built up to cover her cheeks, and it was the last part of the Elf's body visible besides a small portion of her uniform and her hands, which were resting on her chest.

"Does what get easier, Captain?"

Captain Fadithas sniffed and looked up at Yule, still leaning on the shovel. "Burying your friends."

Yule stared at her with a hard, set face, then down at the slain Elf below, the clumps of dirt and soil mounded around her head. "No, Captain. It never gets easier. And their faces will haunt you till you yourself either die on the battlefield, or get lowered down into your own grave. That is the cost of command. This, is the weight of sacrifice. What matters, Captain . . ."

Captain Fadithas blinked the water from her eyes, and she could see the pain he held in his own as he spoke. ". . . Is how, and why they die. We are soldiers. We are born, created, and trained to die. We give ourselves to be used in great struggles, and we give ourselves *willingly*. The most egregious crime that any commander can commit, the greatest sin we can never atone for . . . is to waste, a soldier. To toss a soldier away readily, with no regret, and with abandon."

Yule looked down at the body below, free from her soldier hood and free from the strifes that come with it. Captain Fadithas gazed on in disbelief as small strands of tears began to run down Yule's cheeks, soaking down and hidden in his mustache and beard. "Only when death comes to take you, only when your boots are stacked at attention above your grave with your helmet resting upon your weapon, *only then* are we allowed to cease our charge. Only then are soldiers allowed to rest. Only then, will our duty be done."

Yule tipped the load of dirt down onto the face of the slain Elf, obscuring her from view. Captain Fadithas looked down at where the face used to be, and her mouth was parted slightly, more of her own angry tears falling down her cheeks.

"No Captain. It never gets easier. It never should."

* * *

All of the bodies were covered and laid to rest before the sun departed. Yule had personally dug more than his fair share of the graves, but with the amount of personnel Yethis had gathered for the detail, the job went by quickly and before the sun was chased away by the moon. Orders for stone were already sent out and would be there before the week was out, allowing those interred to have a proper head stone before their temporary ones were blown away or destroyed. After it was said and done, all Companies were dismissed back to their barracks. The Queens 13th were found berthing as well near the headquarters building, keeping out any chance of inter-racial scuffles and attempts at revenge. The captured vehicles were rolled down to the motorpool and sent in for repairs, as almost all of them bore scars from the battle where the Queens 13th had delayed them, and won the day for the Fae and their allies.

Yule now lay in the bath house, sitting in a tub of scorching hot water by himself, as no one else dared venture in and disturb him. Hundreds of soldiers now plagued his mind as they all lay in the still earth of his parade grounds, right outside of his headquarters building. If they had all died in victory, that would be one thing. Instead, they all died in a defeat that bittered Yule's very being. Hatred for both his enemy and himself curled and growled in his chest and head, circling him like a pair of wolves, one bearing flecks of gold and the blackness of his enemies soul, the other dripping with the blood of those whom he commanded. Water dripped from his arm as he brought it up and wiped his hand across his forehead, sighing out harshly as he felt the wolves beginning to circle closer. That was, until he heard a voice from behind him. He smelled cinnamon on the thick, hot air of the bathtub area, the smell of ale, of warm food, fresh baked bread, and skin he had tasted before so long ago.

"A little birdie tells me that you may have had it rough these last couple of days."

Yule closed his eyes, feeling a finger trail down the back of his shoulders, and the two wolves that were encircling him backed away, ducking their heads from something greater around them.

"Is that where Chikily got off to?" Yule asked, as great invisible snakes poised and threatened the wolves within him.

Alavara laughed softly, her mental tendrils wrapping around Yule like a great writhing blanket that he could not see, gripping and ripping away at the strifes and torments that his soul was producing. "Poor lad, I was off seeing family at a village some days away, by the time he found me, he was a bit panicked, and had another Harpy with him, one of the big white ones."

Yule felt the two wolves shrink away, baring their teeth at something he knew not of, but accepted the reprieve with a happy sigh. He leaned his head back and looked up into the crimson eyes of Alavara, bringing his hands up and resting one on her bare stomach, and the other on her naked hip.

"I'm glad you're here."

She leaned down and kissed the top of his head as her mental tendrils pulled away the last specter that was whirling around Yule, tossing it away as if it were nothing but thin paper. "So am I. Plus, I haven't had a bath in a while since I rushed here."

"Gross." Yule murmured, but scooted back, making room for her to sit in front of him and lay against his chest. She giggled and slapped at his shoulder at the comment, but sunk down into the hot water, laying against his chest as her hair played out on the slightly soapy surface, as if trying to mimic the tendrils she could command where no one else could see. Yule wrapped his arms around her, his hands cupping her breasts lightly and giving them a jiggle. He mulled over his Tunkah lessons and then spoke out the words, sighing as he did.

"Today sucked."

"Hm? What did it suck?" Alavara asked, turning her head and giving him a weird look.

Yule snorted. "Today was a bad day."

She nodded, running her hand down his leg. "I know. I heard. I saw you all come in from your room's window and didn't want to interrupt."

He patted her on the ribs "Thanks. Rough day. Lost a fight, not sure what to do."

She turned around and faced him, laying on his chest as her red eyes stared into his. "You can't always win all the battles. Sometimes, my Yule, you have to lose in order to win."

Yule's face saddened, but he still ran his hands down along her hips and rested them on her buttocks, lightly running his finger nails up and down her skin. "I do not like to lose, Alavara. More people die when you lose."

She saw this one lurch out of him, and her tendril shot out, grabbing it and ripping it away from him as quickly as it came. "I know. I know. That's why I'm here. I'm here to help, and make the losses a little less painful, and the victories all the more pleasurable. That way, Chikily doesn't have to act like your stuffed animal for bed."

Yule's eyes narrowed. "It was one time. He's not saying weird things is he?"

Alavara snickered. "It is Chikily."

"Right." He growled, but continued running his fingers up and down her back. She sighed happily, leaning against him fully now. They sat in the long tub like this for some time, Yule savoring the feel of her on his fingers until the water began to turn lukewarm.

"Want to help me finish this bath?"

Alavara smiled, and she rose slightly from the water, placing a hand on Yule's chest. "Took you long enough, I was afraid the water was going to need to be reheated. Would have spoiled the warm and tender moment."

She used a bit of complex Tunka Yule didn't know, but he understood rather quickly once Alavara got into the swing of things. By the time they were finished, the bath ended up needing reheated anyway and the sweat bathed away from their skin. The Onii who had to bring in the water kept blushing furiously and trying to look away from the two in the tub, but Alavara made it as awkward as possible with small talk, to the point he fled from the bathing room, bucket sight blocking the entire way. When they were re-bathed, freshly clothed with what Alavara had brought from Yule's room, and a bit of food stolen away to his room, the two enjoyed a night together, alone, with no one else to interrupt. Alavara poured him wine, taught him more words as they ate, and once their stomachs were full of warm food, bed called to Yule far more fiercely than it did Alavara. The Valley Elf stood guard again, just as she had before Yule left, and waited for the nightmares. She pretended to sleep, cradling his head in her naked chest, but her tendrils alerted her to her targets.

As she attacked and grappled with her mental tendrils, she caught glimpses of what they were, and truly understood what Yule was feeling. She saw his past, his losses beyond his late wife, to his other brothers in arms, and his own battles against the shadows that came from them. She saw and heard the roar of metal birds, the rumbles of metallic treads, and the clatter of gunfire crackling around her. The more she defended and attacked, the more she saw of the inner turmoil and anguish that Yule possessed, and the face of his daughter beyond the Veil. Then came the newest troubles, and she was with him as he moved across the fields towards a city, how he killed a young Elf boy and held his hand as he died, his run with another Elf as he saved them from being shot and escaping with them. The attack on the pursuers of his remnant platoons, finding those poor other Humans who had been hunted by the Fae, and then the great battle where he had suffered his first resolute loss. She was elated to see that Yule had taken no other woman since her, even despite Yethis's best efforts. She did see that he had a few lecherous thoughts about someone named Fadithas, but didn't feel too sore about it, as he had been busy digging a grave from what it seemed.

But something bugged her, something about the walk to the city. Her tendrils were more tender now, more caressing as they perused through his memories. There was... a blank space, here, when he was attacked by the Elven artillery. It was as if a bright piece of string had a blackened section, a section she could not see, just before he woke up and just after he had been blown through the building. Her tendrils wrapped around it, plying it, pulling it, attempting to wiggle and stretch out the memory so she could see it, understand it. But the more she tried, the harder it fought back, and the more it seemed like this was not a memory... but some*thing*.

Who are you, who dares rest in the mind of whom I claim? Alavara challenged, gripping the blank and blackened space with the full might of her tendrils. As she did... she felt the vines of winter crawl up her mental vines, she felt the burn of the moon on her mind, and she saw a woman loom up from the blackened memory, the claimed part of Yule that was not his, but hers. She wore her hair in a braid that ringed around her head, and the white hair was almost blinding compared to the deep red furs that ringed her neck. She bore armor etched with skulls and dancing skeletons, and her flesh was so pale, that it must have been created from the very light of the moon itself. What really struck her heart, what really rocked her cold, were the pale eyes that bore down into her. Her tendrils retreated away from the darkened space of Yule's mind, and instead wrapped around to defend everything else, and Alavara actually clutched Yules body tighter as she squeezed her eyelids tight.

She knew who this was. She knew of what this person could only be, the one God that could be wreathed in such cold, such hunger and attachment, the only God that would have a desire to be found in Yule.

...Krinja. What are you... Why are you... Alavara gasped mentally, still trying to instinctively shield Yule as much as she could, wrapping her tendrils around him tighter as the cold ebbed around her.

But Krinja spoke no words, made no moves to attack, only smiling at Alavara before withdrawing back into the darkened place, the blackened space within Yule. Like the snap of a bullet, Krinja retreated, the cold faded, and Alavara wrenched opened her eyes with a shuddering breath. Her skin was soaked in frigid sweat, and her lungs were painfully cold, so cold that her breath came out in clouds until they warmed once again from the heat of Yule and the blankets. She looked down at the top of Yule's head, and clutched him to her again, her eyes welling with tears as she understood what had just happened, and why there was a time she could not see.

Death had come to Yule, but instead of taking him, had marked him for greater things; As an icon of her rage and anger, a conduit to which she could channel her fury for whom she despised.

And the thought terrified Alavara, as in the end, there was nothing more greedy, more longing for revenge . . .

Than Death.

AFTER ACTION REPORT

Fokhet Alewench stepped down the stone steps into the bowels of the mountain, his bare feet slapping down on the surface with a muffled clap of flesh. He wore no clothes except for a simple groin covering of linen, and every inch of his skin was covered in blue or black runic letters, applied minutes before by Rune Priests. Fokhet was counting under his breath, keeping track of the number of steps purely out of curiosity. Time dragged on as she stepped down within the darkness; The steps were Dwarven craft, each one the same angle, the same length, and the same height. A drunken, blind Elf could have walked down them with no trouble, and to Fokhet, the lack of light was trivial. Kirbadir was special, more than just the fact it was an ancient Engineering Hold, but for what lived down in the heart of the mountain it resided in. Not many Dwarven gods chose to remain on the material plane, even fewer choosing to visit regularly, but Ordynn did things his own way. He was also known to be harshly traditional, which was one of the only reasons why Fokhet was walking around in his underwear with a large roll of scrolls in it. Ordynn had been with the Dwarves during their first creation in the Great Birthing, and knew them in their natural state, when they had asked for their first blessing in order to defeat the Fae.

Fokhet had counted over three thousand steps when he came before a great stone door, marked with the two double runes of Ordynn's fame. A single torch guttered near the door, casting it in muted light, and Fokhet made the signs of a prayer to his ancestors, holding his three center fingers to his forehead while touching his thumb to the first crease of his pinky finger. When he felt it was right, he pushed open the door and stepped into the great vaulted room, then closed the door behind him. The humming started as soon as the door thoomed shut, echoing around him from unknown throats. The sound was deep, throaty, and trembled inside his very bones, the sensation almost causing his vision to swim. Fokhet had never seen the room before, and was astounded by how rudimentary it was; The floor was smooth, perfectly leveled stone, flat and without decoration. The walls climbed up to a central point high above him, and as he followed the walls, he saw twinkling above, as if he was looking up into a night sky. If he had to gamble, he reckoned the twinkling colors above him were gigantic precious stones, arranged in runic constellations that he had never seen before, one looking like a giant cup with a long handle, out of which many more motes of light were being poured.

Fokhet looked away from the ceiling, having been walking the entire time, and realized he was standing before a simple stone throne, bereft of decoration, just like the walls and the floor. The entire room felt... cold, and lonely, which to Fokhet was odd, as he was sure Ordynn would have had a more grandeur space down in the mountain. This was... humble, an extreme level of humble, to the point it was lowly in nature.

"I have not seen one of your kind for some time." A voice said, and Fokhet turned around, having heard it come from behind him. When he spun around, he saw a Dwarf standing there some feet away, hands holding a simple walking axe and a pair of ravens perched on either shoulder. His armor was as simple as the room, unpolished steel and rough spun wool clothing with studs of metal here and there randomly. Ordynn's eyes were a cheerful green, a color you would find in spring when the world was coming back to life from winter, and did not match the room surrounding the two. His hair was grey and long in a single braid, of which his beard followed the same. His face looked like rough hewn stone, with long laugh lines coming out from the corners of his eyes. Fokhet bowed his head, but jerked it back up when he heard Ordynn begin to laugh.

"Don't bow your head, I know why you are here. You are here for the same reason your ancestor was here during the great war with the Fae. You may think just because i'm down here in the Mountain I don't see much, but all of the gods have felt what the Orgul Vilkingni had brought."

Ordynn walked past Fokhet and sat down on the edge of his stone throne, thudding the butt of his walking axe once onto the ground. The sound thundered and boomed around Fokhet, rolling all the way up into the ceiling until the motes of light flared to life, moving and whirling as they began to spin. Fokhet set his jaw, and clenched his fist.

"Yes, honored Ordynn, I have come to trade for the gift of knowledge."

Ordynn exhaled out through his nose, looking down at Fokhet as he tapped his fingers on the haft of his walking axe. Fokhet's face slackened when Ordynn spoke, and he wasn't sure how to react to the words.

"Why is it no one comes to visit? I hear your prayers and accept your offerings, deep down in the mountain, but it does get *lonely* you know."

Fokhet coughed in his fist as he grasped for the words. "W-well, honored Ordynn, it was divined that only the worthy and of Tonguril line could come and ask for the blessings of you and your might."

"Well yes, but that doesn't mean you can't come down and tell me the news, share a glass of mead or something of the sort."

Fokhet thought back to the priests telling him of what and who Ordynn was, and how it had been passed down all through the years to never trespass or disturb the God as he rested down below.

"Honored Ordynn, it was said that you wanted to be left undisturbed so you could rest."

Ordynn chuffed. "Yes, but that was maybe for a month or two after the first gift of steel and edge. After that, none of you ever came back down!"

"... my, uh, apologies, honored Ordynn, I will make sure to send word and visitors from now on."

Ordynn nodded. "Good. Maybe send them with a rug as well. Stone gets cold down here." The Dwarven God wiggled his fingers and toes, then leaned forward. "So. You have come for knowledge, but I see your Orgul Vilkingni has sent you with a few ideas of their own."

Fokhet looked down at his waistband where Ordynn was pointing, and pulled out the scrolls, walking towards the God and unfurling them. "Yes, Yule and one named Gremlin have given me schematics."

"Gremlin? What an odd name, must be the black haired female one." Ordynn took the scrolls, set the walking axe against the armrest of his throne, and began to happily shuffle through them, his eyes glittering with delight. Fokhet stood there awkwardly, hands clasped at his waist and tapping his thumbs together. From the stories, he expected a more intense experience when it came to the God, but to Fokhet, he looked no different than a Long Beard going over the homework from a Scruffling apprentice.

"I can't allow these, I'm afraid." Ordynn said, showing more than three quarters of the stack to Fokhet, who took them back and rolled them back up. " They are far, far too advanced, and I simply cannot allow them, it would be too far of a jump. But these . . . these I can work with. They are complex enough to keep it intriguing, but simple enough that even this Hold should have no problem getting them out and battle ready. This Orgul Vilkingni probably would prefer the others, but I do have my limits, you understand. However, with these, I'm sure you will advance naturally, just as you did when I gifted you with the knowledge of working iron. I must admit, these are outdoing me by a fair margin, but it is nice to not have to think too much about what to give you. With the Fae dragging in things that are not theirs, you will need something as close as possible anyway. Something that can combat them and keep them from their gains."

"Yes, honored Ordynn."

A raven from the shoulder of Ordynn fluffed, then took off in flight, arcing up into the ceiling with such speed, it caused Fokhet to jump in surprise.

"Don't mind her." Ordynn said, and thwacked the few sheafs of paper on his knee. "So. I will allow you access to these schematics, give you the secrets of producing them, and even give you a little head start on the machinery. However, there is a price, as i'm sure you are aware of."

Fokhet nodded, and drew out a dagger he had hidden behind his back, pulling it from its leather sheath. Before he could drag the edge across his flesh, Ordynn interrupted.

"Wait, before you do that, I have a request in mind, instead."

Fokhet paused, and looked up in surprise. "But . . . blood is was what was given last time, honored Ordynn."

"Yes yes I know, but would it be too much of an ask for you to run up and grab a few barrels of ale first? We can at least make it a little more fun for the two of us, then you can maybe share a few tales before we get down to the whole cutting bit."

Fokhet looked up into the glittering green eyes of Ordynn, before nodding once slowly. "Ah . . . Would you like a blonde ale? A red?"

Ordynn leaned back and smiled widely, crackling his knuckles before picking up Gremlin's schematics. "Oh, surprise me, and be quick about it, this is going to take a while. Also don't be afraid to wear clothes down here, It can get awfully cold."

Fokhet bowed, turned on his heel, and sucked in a breath, remembering the number of steps he took to get all the way down here. His calves ached at the thought, but he pulled the door open, and began his slow march back up to the center of the Hold.

"One . . . two . . . three . . . four . . . this seemed a lot easier in the books . . . five . . ."

www.ingramcontent.com/pod-product-compliance
Lightning Source LLC
LaVergne TN
LVHW041621060526
838200LV00040B/1379